DANGEROUS NOTES

DANGEROUS NOTES

Gillian Bradshaw

Fiction

Bradshaw, Gillian, 1956–

Dangerous notes

This first world edition published in Great Britain 2001 by
SEVERN HOUSE PUBLISHERS LTD of
9–15 High Street, Sutton, Surrey SM1 1DF.
This first world edition published in the USA 2001 by
SEVERN HOUSE PUBLISHERS INC of
595 Madison Avenue, New York, N.Y. 10022.

British Library Cataloguing in Publication Data

Bradshaw, Gillian, 1956–
    Dangerous notes
    I. Title
    813.5'4 [F]

    ISBN 0-7278-5757-6

Typeset by Hewer Text Ltd.,
Edinburgh, Scotland.
Printed and bound in Great Britain by
MPG Books Ltd., Bodmin, Cornwall.

One

They arrested me on the train to France.

They said I was fleeing the country, which is stupid, because what would be the point of fleeing from one part of the EU to another? To be honest, I hadn't even appreciated that I was supposed to stay in Britain. All I was trying to do was to get away for a few days because I felt I'd go bits if I stayed where I was.

This was in June of '32, three months after the Torrington murders and a month after all recipients of CICNPC treatment went on the sectionable list. The public no longer knew or cared what CICNPC had actually involved; most of them couldn't even remember what the acronym stood for. (Cerebral Implantation of Cloned Neural Progenitor Cells, if you're interested.) Instead they talked about 'sicknip-C' as though it were the third and worst variant of some terrible disease. The media had been in a frenzy over 'cloned-brain psychotics' for weeks. When the hysteria first started I'd complained loudly and angrily to all my friends – but by June I was keeping very quiet. 'You mean *you* had this treatment?' my friends had asked – and afterwards many of them avoided me. A young man who'd been pursuing me (and nearly caught me, too) suddenly lost all interest. Even the friends who didn't drop me kept advising me to go to a clinic, 'Just to have it checked.' My parents and the Student Health Service phoned to do the same. When I told them I'd go after I'd finished my Year Two exams, they shook their heads unhappily. My tutor called me in and gave me a Serious Talk about Public Concern and Responsible Health Practice. People whispered about me behind my back, and gave me funny looks.

1

My friend Alicia would probably have revelled in the notoriety, but I'm not made that way. I *hate* it when people stare at me. Oh, I don't mind doing solos at concerts – that's different, that's *music*. Having people stare at me for anything else makes me feel degraded. I suppose a lot of it goes all the way back to when I was in primary school. I was the tall, shy girl, all elbows, big hands and big clumsy feet, who sits at the back of the class – and, even worse, I was always having to go in for check-ups because of the accident I'd had as a baby, and everybody knew it. Even after I grew up and turned out quite pretty, I still felt uncomfortable if people stared at me. Having people look at me and wonder about my brain made me feel like I was eight years old again, back in the playground with Rebecca Timson taunting me for being 'mental'. I stopped going out anywhere – the college bar, the common room, even the cafeteria and the shops. I dropped out of the music society and the orchestra. I stayed in my room, studying, playing the guitar, eating cold cereal and doing my laundry in the middle of the night. I hated it and myself.

Then, the day I finished the exams, I got a formal letter from the Department of Health – recorded delivery, no less – telling me I was required to report to the nearest neurological clinic for 'risk assessment', and that 'failure to comply' would result in 'immediate legal action'. I decided I'd had enough. With hindsight, I suppose I was naive to think 'legal action' only meant they'd stop my student loan, but it never even occurred to me that it meant I'd be arrested. The worst crime I'd ever committed was to busk without a permit, and the idea that I somehow represented a threat to society seemed too ludicrous for anyone to take seriously.

I stuffed some clothes in a backpack and tied a sleeping bag underneath, then switched on my computer and checked the 'Last-Minute Bargains' section on RailNet. I wanted to get right away, off to somewhere where no one knew me and nobody would stare, but my bank balance was at its end-of-term low ebb and I couldn't afford to go very far. There was a good deal on Paris, so I booked it.

That, of course, must have been what triggered the arrest: the

Department of Health still considers France to be foreign. The rail computer undoubtedly checked its little list of who isn't supposed to leave the country, found me on it, and notified the police computer. At the time, though, all I worried about was that even the bargain fare finished off my bank balance. I wondered if I could ask my parents for money, then decided against it: I knew they'd tell me to go for the risk assessment check-up, and I simply couldn't face it. I told myself I could earn some money busking, and if I didn't earn enough to pay for both food and lodging – well, it was warm weather, and I could find somewhere to sleep out. I'd been told that Paris is a pretty safe place to do it, if you have to: there are usually plenty of other students around. I picked up my guitar and set off.

I was in Devon at the time – I'd been studying music at Dartington – so I had to take the bus into Torquay, the train to London Paddington and then the tube to Waterloo to catch the service to the Continent. I arrived at Waterloo Station at twenty to five in the evening of a clear, mild June day. The train to Paris didn't leave until 17:35, and I was short of cash, so I decided to do some busking.

I don't normally like to busk on my own – to be honest, I don't think I'd ever have busked at all if my friend Alicia hadn't talked me into it. The first time she'd done that, though, had been when we were both fourteen, and she'd been repeating the performance ever since. Busking is a very good way to earn beer money, if you happen to be a pair of music students with, respectively, a good voice and a lot of talent on the guitar, and by that summer I was so used to the expeditions that I didn't mind trying it on my own. Alicia had always done all the talking and singing for us, and I didn't expect to do as well without her, but I was sure I could manage something. Waterloo Station was full of departing commuters who didn't look in the mood for music, but I thought the South Bank would probably be receptive to a classical repertoire, so I took the short hike from the station down to the Thames.

The riverside did indeed have a more leisured feeling. Crowds eddied around the open-air bookstalls, there was a queue for the London Eye, and the ice-cream vendors were doing a

3

roaring trade. I strolled down to the quayside to admire the view. 'Earth hath not anything to show more fair' – looking up the Thames to Westminster Bridge and the Gothic elegance of Parliament, and downriver at the green Embankment and the domes and towers of the City, the old poem really seemed true. I stretched, feeling a weight of anger and anxiety drop away. It had been a thoroughly horrible couple of months, but things were bound to get better. The media were finally starting to lose interest in CICNPC – and my exams were over. The whole summer lay sweet and green before me – starting with a few days in Paris. Beautiful Paris, city of light! Croissants and dark roast coffee for breakfast; ice-cream from Berthillons; wandering through the Left Bank and Ile de la Cité, touring the museums, maybe taking in a concert or two . . . it would be the perfect break! Feeling more cheerful than I had for weeks, I took off my backpack, then arranged my guitar case in front of my feet and got out my guitar.

I serenaded the tourists and commuters with some Bach lute pieces, and by ten past five I'd managed to earn E15.50 – not much, perhaps, but enough to buy myself something to eat on the train. I returned to the station, found the right platform, and took my seat on the 17:35. I thought how I might have stayed in Devon moping, and felt very pleased with myself for having had the initiative to get away.

However, 17:35 came and went, and the train stayed where it was. The other passengers and I looked impatiently out the windows and checked our watches. We were just reaching the point where reserve breaks down and it becomes acceptable to comment on the delay when two police officers, a man and a woman, came through the train. They moved with a steady, implacable smoothness, studying the passengers intently and occasionally stopping to ask someone for ID. I hadn't even taken in the fact that all the people they'd asked were young women when they reached me and stopped. I noticed that they were both looking at me, and felt the first chill: one or the other of them had dealt with the other IDs on their own.

'May I see your ID?' said the man.

I obediently dug my wallet out of my jacket pocket and handed over my ID card.

The policeman studied it a moment, showed it to his colleague. Both faces were expressionless. Then the man handed the ID back. 'I'm afraid I must ask you to come with me, Miss Thornham,' he said grimly.

I gaped at him. I told myself that it *couldn't* be because of the CICNPC – and then felt even worse, because what else would the police want with me, except to tell me that someone in my family was dying? 'What?' I asked faintly. 'Why?'

'We have a warrant for your arrest under the Mental Health Act,' said the woman.

Dear God, it *was* the CICNPC. A cold sickness began in my gut and crawled upward. 'I don't . . .' I began.

'You were sent a notice, Miss Thornham, informing you that you were required to report for assessment as to whether your condition poses a threat to the community. Given that you are attempting to evade that assessment, we have no choice but to arrest you.'

Everyone in the carriage was staring at me. 'This is *crashed*!' I exclaimed, and noted, from some remote distance, that my voice was shrill. 'For God's sake! One lunatic who happens to have had Cicnip-C goes berserk, and suddenly four or five hundred perfectly innocent people are being treated like unexploded bombs! It's *degraded*!' I couldn't help noticing, though, that the moment I mentioned CICNPC all my fellow passengers shrank back in alarm.

'That's enough,' replied the policeman, suddenly very sharp. 'Are you going to come quietly?'

I pushed myself back into the corner of my seat. 'You can't do this! I haven't *done* anything!'

The policeman exchanged a glance with the policewoman. 'Miss Thornham,' the WPC said firmly, 'don't make things worse for yourself. We're permitted to use force if you resist arrest. We'd prefer not to.' She leaned over the armrest and took hold of my arm. 'Come on. Get up.'

I stared at her. She was in her mid-thirties, dark-haired and stout with cold eyes. I could hear the blood pounding in my ears.

'Come on,' she ordered again, and gave my arm a shake.

I got up. My legs were unsteady. The policewoman stepped back, and I edged my way out into the aisle.

'Turn around and put both hands against the seat,' ordered the policewoman.

'What?'

'I've got to search you. Come on.'

'You don't need . . . I haven't got . . .'

She took my shoulder and pushed me around to face the window. I put my hands against the back of the seat I'd just vacated. I had to bend over. I felt faint, and I was shaking. The policewoman ran her hands down me, checked my pockets, harvested my wallet, my train ticket, a used tissue, and a guitar pick. She confiscated the train ticket and returned the rest to me. 'OK,' she said. 'You can turn around now.'

When I turned back I saw that the policeman had taken out a pair of handcuffs.

I stared at them in disbelief. 'You don't need—' I began again – but he leaned forward and clipped one around my left wrist.

I couldn't believe it – couldn't get my mind around the fact that I, Valeria Thornham, a nice middle-class music student, was going to be dragged off a train in handcuffs like some dope dealer. I simply stood there shaking while the policeman adjusted the cuff and clipped its mate around the police-woman's wrist.

'Come on!' she ordered, and tugged.

'My backpack,' I muttered – then, louder, with anguish, 'My guitar!' It was sitting there next to my seat: I always keep it with me when I travel.

There was a moment of hesitation, and then the policeman leaned over the seat and picked up the guitar case. He banged it down on the courtesy table, opened it, lifted the instrument out by the neck and shook it to see if there was anything inside.

'You turgid *snail*!' I screamed, stunned incredulity abruptly giving way to rage. 'That's a *Segovia*! It cost five thousand euros *second hand*!'

The policeman stared a moment, but did not let go of the guitar. He inspected the sheet music at the bottom of the case, then put the instrument away and closed the case again – though I was relieved to see that this time he was careful about it. 'Any other luggage?' he asked.

'My backpack,' I said, and wiped my nose with the back of my free hand. It was only then that I realised I'd started crying.

We marched off the train: the policewoman; me; the policeman, carrying my backpack and guitar. The policewoman spoke briefly into her mobile, and the train doors closed behind us. The engine hummed, and the 17:35 pulled off, heading for Paris – twenty minutes late. The passengers all stared at me from the windows as they passed. Everyone on the platform was staring at me, too. I dug out my tatty tissue and wiped my face again. The tissue disintegrated. I gave up and was marched off with the tears streaming down my face.

They had a car at the main entrance to the station. The policeman put the backpack and the guitar in the boot, then got into the driver's seat. The policewoman and I got into the back. The policeman clicked on his collar mike and began speaking to the despatcher in some unintelligible code. I only really noticed what he was saying when he asked, 'Where do you want her, then?'

The reply came to his earphone, of course, and I couldn't hear it, but he glanced back at me, nodded, and started the engine. The car pulled out, logged on to London Traffic Control, and rounded the traffic circle, heading back past the station on Waterloo Road.

'Shouldn't you read me my rights or something?' I asked the policewoman.

'That's only if you're arrested on charges,' she replied, eyeing me warily. She was sitting as far from me as the handcuffs allowed. 'This comes under public safety measures.'

'You mean I don't have any rights?'

She snorted. 'Under the Mental Health Act any person classified as suffering from a mental illness that renders them a danger to the public can be forcibly detained for treatment. Apart from that, you have all your normal civil rights.'

'I'm not mentally ill,' I told her, wiping my nose on the back of my hand.

7

'You had the Cicnip treatment. That means you're section-able. I'm quite certain you know that.'

Sectionable. It sounded like it meant I could be cut to bits. I closed my eyes. 'Look, I'm not mentally ill,' I insisted. 'Cicnip-C was an experimental treatment for brain damage, not a disease! I had it after a car crash when I was just a baby. Other people may have had trouble because of it, but with me it worked *perfectly*. I had loads of tests when I was growing up. When I was twelve my local health authority said I didn't need to bother to come back for any more. My brain is *normal*.'

'So why did you try to leave the country?' asked the police-man, glancing over his shoulder.

'I was going on a fucking *holiday*!' I snarled, opening my eyes again. 'I'd just finished my exams!' The car turned right at a roundabout. 'Where are you taking me?'

'Back to the police station,' said the policeman. 'Somebody will pick you up from there.'

'Somebody? Who? I haven't—'

'The Department of Health has been notified,' the police-woman said primly, as we turned left. 'A specialist psychiatric hospital in Sussex is sending someone to collect you.' The car turned left again, on to a ramp that led under an unobtrusive twentieth-century building, and stopped in a small under-ground car park.

Collect me. Like a parcel. I swallowed a rising sense of panic. 'What if I don't want to go to a specialist mental hospital?'

The policewoman gave me a look of disgust. 'If you wanted to choose where to be assessed, you should've gone in volun-tarily.'

'I don't *believe* this! I haven't done *anything*!'

The policewoman gave a sudden sharp jerk on the handcuff and leaned towards me. 'Cut the crap.'

I stared at her, shocked.

'You know perfectly well that it wasn't just *one* guy with Cicnip who went berserk. Half the people who had that treat-ment have been involved in some episode or other, but every-body ignored it until Torrington used a gun. The doctors knew it was causing problems – that's why they abandoned it, isn't it?

– but they just turned all their brain-damaged weirdos loose in the community, kept quiet, and hoped. If you were really perfectly normal, you'd be worried. You'd've been asking for a check-up as soon as the story hit the news. Instead you refused to seek treatment until you got a letter requiring you to go in, and then you made a run for it. As far as I'm concerned, you represent a real danger to the public, and I have absolutely no doubt we're right to bring you in.'

She was perfectly sincere: she honestly believed I was a potential psychopath. What could I say to that? That the past few months had been the worst of my life, and I just wanted to get away? That I'd put off going for a check-up for the same reasons people put off going to the dentist or filling out their tax return? I couldn't argue with her angry contempt: everything I thought of to say sounded stupid.

Besides, deep down I knew that I'd been avoiding that check-up because I was afraid of what it might find. I suspected that there was indeed something strange inside my head – and someone might want to take it out.

Oh, God, they might. They might go in there with knives. Oh God.

I sat there shaking, unable to reply, unable even to think straight. At the edge of awareness, I heard music, guitar and strings in D major, *allegro con fuoco*. It wasn't a hallucination – I knew it sounded only in my mind – but it was so vivid I could feel the chords in the tendons of my wrists. What if they went in there with knives and cut out *that*?

Suddenly, stupidly and desperately, I wanted my mother. I wanted her to put her arms around me and make it all better, even though I knew she could do no such thing.

'I want to phone my parents,' I managed at last.

The policewoman let out her breath slowly in disgust. 'Don't you have a phone?'

I'd left it in Devon. I'd wanted to be unreachable. 'I forgot it.'

'You can use the phone in the station,' conceded the policewoman. 'Reverse the charges.'

The phone call was not a success. My mother cried. My father lost his temper. They both told me what a fool I was to

9

take off for France instead of making an appointment to have the check-up. I started crying again. At that my father offered to drive down and collect me, but the policewoman – still handcuffed to me, and listening – instantly grabbed the phone and informed him that I was being taken to a specialist hospital, and that he'd have to see me there. She didn't know its name, however, and the policeman, who did, had disappeared. She told my father to phone back later. My father promised to drive to the hospital as soon as he knew where it was. The police-woman looked impatiently at her watch and ended the call, leaving me even more upset and less coherent than I'd been before.

They put me in a holding cell to wait for the medics. It was a small bare cubicle with benches down three sides. I felt better at first because they took off the handcuffs – then I noticed the other two occupants of the cell, and cancelled the relief. In one corner, muttering to herself, slumped a tattered bag lady; in the other a skinny wildgirl with black and crimson dreadlocks sat smoking.

I folded up on the bench between the two and hiccuped as I tried to stop crying.

The wildgirl eyed me speculatively. She was wearing red lace shorts over a tiger-patterned leotard, and she had a leopard tattooed on her upper arm. She looked to be about sixteen, but she was wearing so much make-up it was hard to tell. Her eyes were feverishly bright, the pupils unnaturally dilated. 'Y'got any pot?' she asked.

I was surprised that she was asking me that inside a police holding cell – sure, pot is legal, but she didn't look old enough to buy any. I suppose she was too lit to care.

The bag lady stopped muttering and gave her a filthy look.

'No,' I replied, and swallowed.

'Anything to drink?'

The bag lady gave her another evil look and started mutter-ing again. I shook my head.

'Fuck!' said the wildgirl. She stubbed out her cigarette end and tugged at a dreadlock. 'I'm lit. I need something to damp it, y'know?' She looked me up and down, taking in the jeans, the green T-shirt and unexciting black cotton jacket. 'You're a middler, aren't you?'

Absolutely. Nice middle-class university student from a nice middle-class professional family, and feeling as out of place in a police holding cell as an octopus in a space capsule. I shrugged.

'Got any money, middler?'

I shook my head again.

'Not much fucking good, are you? What you in for, begging?'

I pulled my knees up and wrapped my arms around them. I told myself I did *not* need to feel intimidated by a skinny little sixteen-year-old.

'I'm up for GBH.' She announced it proudly. 'Middler bitch stuck her nose up at me, so I broke it. They can't do me for it, 'cause I'm under age, and I'm in an institution already. The mamas'll just come fetch me and tell me what a bad girl I am.' She laughed. 'When they can be bothered, that is. Don't hold your breath.'

The bag lady abruptly shrieked, 'Filthy slag!' then subsided again. I rested my forehead against my knees. In the back of my mind I heard music again – guitar alone, this time, in E minor, playing slowly.

'What you in for, then, middler bitch?' asked the wildgirl.

'I had Cicnip-C,' I told her, hoping it would convince her to shut up and leave me alone.

It certainly had an effect. She sat up and looked at me admiringly. 'Shit! Vero?' She moved over on to my bench, peering at me. 'You don't look crashed – but people who have it don't, most of the time, right? They have *episodes*.' She pronounced the term with relish. 'Like Torrington didn't know he'd done a thing, till he got home and saw the blood on his coat, and then he couldn't remember how it got there, right? What'd you do? Or don't you remember?'

'I didn't do anything,' I told her bitterly.

'You *think*,' she said, and laughed again.

The bag lady jumped up and rushed screaming to the door.

'Crashed bitch,' said the wildgirl contemptuously, raising her voice to be heard over the shrieks and the wild pounding. '*She's* in for being a sectionable loony. She's waitin' for somebody from a hospital, but they're in no hurry to fetch her.' She tapped out a rhythm on the bench and sang tunelessly, '*No*body loves us, *every*body hates us, guess we'll go eat worms!'

A policeman came to the door and looked wearily through the polycarbonate upper panel. The old woman hit the plastic in front of his face and he stepped back. 'What's the matter now?' he asked, bending to project his voice through the speaking slots.

'Murderers!' shrieked the bag lady. 'You locked me in with murderers!'

The policeman glared at me and the wildgirl. 'What've you two been saying to her?'

'I haven't said a fucking thing!' replied the wildgirl. 'The middler bitch said she has Cicnip-C. That veritable?'

The policeman turned the glare on me.

'I wasn't trying to threaten anybody,' I told him wretchedly. 'I just answered the question.'

'Yeah, well, keep quiet!' he growled. 'Somebody'll be along to collect you before too long – I hope.' He added the last under his breath.

'Could you bring me my guitar?' I asked desperately.

He looked puzzled.

'I have a guitar. That is, I had it when I was arrested. It's probably at your front desk or wherever by now. I'd really like to have it. Please? I could play something soothing, calm everyone down.' The person I really wanted to calm down was myself: in another minute or two I was going to start screaming as loudly as the old woman.

Perhaps the policeman saw that, or perhaps he only thought it would shut up the bag lady. At any rate, he went off and came back with my guitar. He unlocked the door, barred the old woman's exit with one arm, and extended the case to me. The bag lady recoiled when I got up to claim it. The policeman went off, locking the door again.

I sat down, opened the case with shaking hands and pulled the instrument up on to my lap. The curve it made against my thigh and the smoothness of the polished wood under my hands were indescribably comforting. My fingers began to steady as they checked the tuning. The bag lady, still standing by the door, stopped screaming and watched me warily.

'You know "Rainy Day, Sweaty Night"?' asked the wildgirl hopefully.

I shook my head, picked out a scale. 'Not my sort of music.'

'Yeah,' she agreed with contempt. 'Guess not. That thing's not even electric, is it?'

Of course not: it was a twelve-string Segovia concert guitar with a sound that worked magic in the blood, and the only reason I'd even been offered the chance to buy it was because I showed exceptional promise. I looked up at the wildgirl and tried to smile: I didn't want her to start shrieking as well. 'You said you needed something to damp down. OK if I play something quiet?'

She scrunched back into her corner. 'Why not? Better'n listening to the old bitch screaming.'

I didn't want to reach for the music in my head. Sometimes it won't come out, and when it does – well, it might attract too much attention. Instead I played the Largo from the Vivaldi D major lute concerto, which is probably the most soothing piece of music ever written. You can play it as a solo, since the strings don't say anything important, and I'd played it so often while busking that I hardly needed to think about it. It calmed me, anyway, and when I looked up I saw with relief that the bag lady had settled in her place again and had stopped muttering.

'That was pretty,' said the wildgirl, crossing her legs and twisting a dreadlock around her finger. 'Normally I think that kinda music's *boring* – but that was pretty. Play something else.'

I played some more slow pieces – a Bach sarabande, a variation on a theme by Mozart. The wildgirl sat twisting her dreadlocks, and the bag lady grinned inanely and waved a knotted finger in time with the beat. I was stretching my hands in an appreciative silence when the policeman came back.

'Thornham!' he commanded, unlocking the door.

'Shit!' said the wildgirl in disgust. 'Anything good always gets stopped.' She gave me a resigned look, almost wistful. 'They're in a hurry to collect *you*, aren't they?'

For a horrible moment I saw it all: the dysfunctional family,

13

the uncaring children's home, the rebellion into sex, drugs and violence which never satisfied the hollowness inside. She would graduate from her young offenders' institution to a prison, have a string of worthless boyfriends and abortions, lose any children she bore into care and end up – if she lived so long – like the bag lady. I tried to push the abominable vision away. I had troubles of my own . . .

I suddenly doubted whether any trouble I could have would ever be as bad. As for the bag lady's life – it was beyond my imagining.

I put the guitar back in its case and picked it up. 'Bye,' I told the wildgirl – and, moved by futile hope, added, 'Good luck.'

I suppose I'd passed the police station front desk when I'd come in, but I'd been in no state to pay attention to it. The drab waiting room looked familiar, however, when I was led back in. The policewoman who'd arrested me was now standing behind the counter. A man standing in front of it looked up eagerly as I came in, and I stared back at him, uncertain. I'd expected a white coat, but this was a young man in a plain blue shirt and dark trousers. He was good-looking in a pink, scrubbed sort of way, with fine fair hair, a teensy little blond moustache and an air of anxiety.

'Valeria Thornham?' he asked, coming over and offering his hand.

'Yeah,' I admitted. I shook the hand: I didn't know what else to do.

He beamed. 'I'm Dr Charles Spencer of the Laurel Hall Centre for Cognitive Research. We offered to assess anyone sectioned as a CICNPC recipient' – he spelled out the acronym – 'and the Department of Health contacted us about you this afternoon.' He replaced the smile with a serious look. 'I'd guess from the fact you tried to run away that you're frightened by the prospect of assessment. There's no need to be. It won't hurt, and it's very likely that even if you do have a problem it will be trivial to treat.' He resumed the smile, this time with an expectant look, like a man who's just thrown a ball and is waiting for his retriever to fetch.

I just stared, completely off balance.

'We've got a car outside,' said Dr Spencer, when I didn't

14

reply. 'We, uh, couldn't find a place to park, so my colleague's waiting with it. We'd better get going.'

'It would be safer if she were tagged,' said the policewoman disapprovingly.

Spencer grimaced. 'It's not required, is it?'

The policewoman shrugged in a way that made it clear that it wasn't required, but she thought it was advisable.

To my relief, Spencer shook his head. 'No, I really don't think we need to do that.'

The policewoman shrugged again. 'Then you just need to sign her out,' she said disapprovingly, and extended a ledger.

Spencer took it and fumbled in his pocket for a pen.

'Cognitive research?' I asked. 'I was told I was going to be sent to a mental hospital.'

He looked up frowning. His eyes were very blue. He had the sort of face that goes with pale weak-looking eyes, but his were an electric blue, very noticeable. 'Oh, no. I mean, you're not mentally ill, are you? A standard mental hospital couldn't even do the assessment.'

'I don't see why a cognitive research institute is even involved.'

He looked embarrassed. 'We have the right sort of brain-scanning equipment. It's expensive, and the NHS is short of it.' He signed the ledger.

I was silent a moment. Then I thought, quite clearly, No, that's wrong. It was barely an hour since my arrest. To get into central London from Sussex through the rush-hour traffic he must have set off before I reached the police station, possibly even before the arrest. What was more, he must have set off right at the end of a normal working day. I could believe that a research institute in possession of scarce and valuable brain-scanning equipment might offer to help out the health service in a crisis and so prove its worth to the government; I could not believe that it would send a doctor and a car hot-footing it into London after hours to pick up a patient it was only taking out of charity. The local health authority would surely have delivered me to them in the morning. It would have made more sense for them to wait.

15

I took a step back, clutching the handle of my guitar case hard. 'That doesn't add up,' I said loudly. 'Look, I think I'd prefer to let the NHS do the job.'

Spencer looked mortified. The policewoman, however, snapped angrily, 'I told you before, Miss Thornham: if you wanted to choose, you should've gone in voluntarily.'

'You don't—' began Spencer faintly, but the policewoman, glaring, went on, 'You can walk yourself out to the doctor's car, or you can be carried out to it in handcuffs: that's the only choice you're getting.'

'Please, that's not necessary,' said Spencer unhappily.

The policewoman paid no attention. 'This station has enough to do without babysitting lunatics and Social Services misfits. You're leaving *now*, Miss Thornham.'

Once again I was helpless before her cold-eyed disgust. 'I need my backpack,' I managed at last, unsteadily.

She pointed to it where it sat beside the counter. I picked it up. Spencer came over and belatedly tried to take it, then tried to take my guitar instead, but I held on to both. The policeman who'd brought me from the cell escorted us the rest of the way out.

Spencer's car was waiting just outside the station. It was a seven-seater Ford, blue, with 'Laurel Hall Centre for Cognitive Research' and a logo that was probably meant to be a bay tree stencilled on the front doors in gold. The 'colleague', a middle-aged man in a semi-formal blue cotton shirt and khaki trousers, sat at the wheel. I decided he was probably a driver, and not another doctor.

Spencer opened the rear door for me and tried to help while I stowed my luggage. I ignored his attempt, climbed in after the luggage, and slammed the door. He started round to the other side of the car, looking pained.

I thought, briefly, of opening the door again and running for it. Stupid thought: the escorting policeman was still watching, and anyway, what would I do if I succeeded in getting away? I didn't want to live in London as a homeless busker: I wanted to go back to my own life, to my degree and my ambitions for the future. I needed to have this check-up and get a clean bill of health. Maybe that would be hard to get – but there was no real reason to think this Laurel Hall would be a harder place to get it than anywhere else. They were eager, certainly, but perhaps that was only because CICNPC provided information useful for their own research.

Actually, it was not merely possible but extremely probable that they were interested in CICNPC regeneration because of the light it could throw on brain function. I probably had nothing to worry about.

Spencer climbed into the back of the car with me, shifting my backpack into the middle to make room for his legs. The driver started the engine and the central locking came on with a clunk. I clutched my guitar hard, feeling a fresh bubble of panic forming in my throat. The car logged on to London Traffic Control and pulled out.

'I'm sorry,' said Dr Spencer, into the silence. 'You must feel dismal.'

The sympathetic tone started my eyes running again. 'Do you have a tissue?' I choked, trying once again to wipe my nose without getting snot on my jacket.

The doctor scrabbled at his pockets, then leaned forward and asked the driver, 'Do you have any Kleenex, Mr Mickleson?'

Mickleson's eyes were flicking steadily from the road to the screen of the traffic computer, which was tracing routes to the south, but at once he fumbled open the glove box, extracted a small travel pack of Kleenex and held it up over his shoulder, all without looking. Spencer took the packet and handed it to me. I blew my nose.

'I'm sorry,' said Spencer again, vaguely.

'Why were you so eager to get hold of me?' I demanded bluntly.

He looked startled. 'I don't—'

'You came rushing down here the minute I was arrested. It must have been after hours even when you set off, but here you are, official car, official driver. If you'd waited till tomorrow, London Health would probably have delivered me.'

Surprise was replaced by embarrassment and a trace of guilt. 'Oh.'

'Oh, come on! If you hadn't thought of that, somebody must've.'

He shrugged. 'We normally provide transport for our volunteers.'

'I'm not a volunteer!'

He grimaced. 'Yes, I know . . . I mean, we normally provide transport for the people who take part in our research programmes. Most of them *are* volunteers, so I—'

'Research programmes?' I asked sharply.

He blinked. 'It's what the Hall is for. You probably know the sort of thing: we get a group of volunteers, give them some kind of cognitive test, and scan their brains while they're doing it. Then we see what happens if they play computer games for an hour, or drink four cups of coffee or three pints of lager or whatever. Most of our volunteers are students from one or another of the London University colleges. We can't afford to pay very well, and if we didn't provide their transport they probably wouldn't come.'

'What's this got to do with assessing whether Cicnip-C has turned somebody into a psychopath?'

'Cicnip-C doesn't turn people into psychopaths!' he declared, with sudden vehemence. 'It can't. Torrington was a naturally aggressive man: he regularly fantasised about shooting people who annoyed him. He probably wouldn't have *actually* shot anyone if the Cicnip treatment hadn't disturbed his consciousness, but the violent impulses were nothing to do with the treatment. Most Cicnip recipients, even the ones who've had episodes of lapsed consciousness, are not violent. You get guys who take their clothes off at the office and proposition the secretary, or girls who go skinny-dipping in the duck pond at the park. It's embarrassing, sure, but it's hardly a danger to the public. The media hysteria about the whole business has been completely over the top!'

He spoke with real and unmistakable anger, and I suddenly felt very much better. 'OK,' I said. 'I agree with you; I couldn't agree more. But you still haven't said why your Laurel Hall Centre is involved.'

He recollected himself. 'Sorry. Well, from the Department of

Health's point of view we have all the right equipment for determining whether somebody's brain is malfunctioning and, if it is, for pinpointing exactly what needs to be done to put it right.'

'And from your point of view,' I said cynically, 'Cicnip represents a great research resource, am I right? A random selection of brains which were damaged in one way or another, and which were induced to regenerate, but which didn't re-generate *exactly* the way brains normally grow – it's a natural experiment in brain function, yeah?'

He blushed, hesitating, then admitted sheepishly, 'Yes. You're right: that is why we offered to help with assessments. But—' he looked at me earnestly – 'the people we assess have a much better time of it than the people who get done by the NHS. I mean, we're *not* a "mental hospital". We're geared to working with paid volunteers, not psychiatric cases who may have been committed against their will. If we shoved our participants on to grubby wards stuffed with senile dementia patients and staffed with a few overworked nurses, they'd walk out. We have to provide a pleasant ambience – private rooms in a beautiful old house, pretty countryside, good food. Most of our volunteers come back repeatedly. We have all the latest equipment, too, and we'll be able to map your brain with far greater precision than you could get anywhere on the NHS. That means that if you do have to have treatment, it will be kept to the essential minimum.'

I gazed at him a moment, unimpressed. 'You want to do more than just a simple assessment, don't you?'

He blushed again, confounded. I told myself sternly that how nice his eyes looked was totally irrelevant.

'If all you were going to do was a simple assessment, you could have come to fetch me in the morning,' I pointed out. 'But you want to do some more detailed brain research as well, and for that you need my consent and cooperation. So you're being all friendly, plucking me out of a police cell and whisking me back to this beautiful old country house in the hope that I'll be so grateful I'll say, sure, when we've finished the assessment I'll stay on for a week and do cognitive tests for you.' I leaned back in the seat and crossed my arms. 'It won't work. I *hate* brain scans. You can do the assessment, and that's *it*.'

Spencer looked hurt, and I stepped hard on the impulse to feel sorry for him. Mickleson, the driver, laughed. 'You're no snail, are you?' he asked, glancing back at me.

'I hope not,' I replied.

'You're being a bit overly cynical, though,' he went on, his voice gentle. 'We've assessed a lot of Cicnip recipients already, and we've got some idea what you must have been going through. We came up to London in a hurry because we didn't *like* the idea of leaving you in a police cell overnight. What's your subject?'

'Music,' I said, now feeling a little ashamed of my cynicism.

'Music! I don't think we've had a musician before. You sing?'

'No,' I told him. I *can* sing, but mostly I don't, because my voice doesn't meet my own exacting standards. Besides, I'm an alto, and sopranos get all the best tunes. 'I play classical guitar. And viola, sometimes.' Viola gets you into orchestras, but doesn't oblige you to do anything too fancy.

'Really!' said Mickleson appreciatively. 'Makes a nice change to get a musician. Most of our volunteers are medics, psychologists, and sociologists, and they're a damned sight less entertaining than a guitarist.'

By this point we were well out of central London, driving south on the A23 through the endless twisting ring roads circling Streatham and Croydon, almost at the belt of business parks and DIY centres. The rush hour was long over, and the traffic was light. 'How far is it to Laurel Hall?' I asked.

'About fifty klicks,' Mickleson replied at once. 'It's southwest of Crawley, on the edge of the South Downs. We'll go faster once we reach the motorway.'

I nodded and sat back in my seat. The arrest was beginning to seem like some Kafkaesque nightmare, and I felt as though I were returning to the real world. Mickleson's attitude made me realise how long it had been since somebody who knew I'd had CICNPC had treated me naturally. I'd managed to defeat Spencer, too – he was now just sitting silent and looking worried. I *did* still have rights. Probably I'd worried about nothing, and nobody would care that I occasionally heard music inside my head. It wasn't any sort of danger to the public, after all.

'Could I borrow a phone?' I asked. 'I phoned my parents from the police station, but I couldn't tell them where I was going to be, and they must be worried.' I had no confidence that the police would tell my father anything when he phoned back.

Dr Spencer at once dug his phone out of his pocket and offered it. I thanked him and keyed in the number.

My father answered, and *was* very worried. I reassured him and got Laurel Hall's address from the doctor, but told him that he didn't need to rush down there. I'd be fine, I said. The place sounded perfectly civilised. 'They have student volunteers in all the time for their research programmes, so apparently they have lots of decent accommodation.'

'Will they charge you for it?' asked my father anxiously.

I relayed the question to Dr Spencer, who said no, of course not.

'When should I collect you?' Dad wanted to know.

I looked at Spencer again. He gestured, and I handed him the phone.

'Mr Thornham? I'm Dr Spencer, of Laurel Hall. First just let me assure you that your daughter's fine—'

My father made some inaudible comment, and Spencer said hotly, 'I'm not surprised! The police were incredibly heavy-handed. But she should be OK now.'

He listened for another moment. His eyes flicked to me again, with a look of doubt, and the back of my neck prickled: something my father had said bothered him. All he said, however, was, 'I'm sure of that.'

Another silence, and then he said, 'It depends on when we can get at the equipment. We have a research programme running at the minute, and some of the machines will be fully booked. We have to be very thorough with Cicnip-C assessments to satisfy the government . . . yes, lots of them. About thirty, I think . . . I don't know, maybe three days?'

'Three *days*?' I interrupted. 'That's not how long it's going to take you to assess whether I'm *dangerous*, is it?'

21

Dr Spencer gave me a look of mild reproach. 'We have to run a lot of tests,' he told me. 'Proving a negative is always difficult.'

'Three *days'* worth difficult?'

'We're going to have to fit you in around a study we're already running. Besides, if you went to the NHS, they might complete the most urgent tests in a day – but they'd be certain to call you back for more tests every few weeks for the next six months.'

That was undoubtedly true, but I wasn't convinced: it seemed to me very likely that Laurel Hall's list of tests for CICNPC recipients included some for cognitive function which the government couldn't care less about.

Spencer was talking to my father again. 'No, of course there's no charge. We *like* Cicnip-C, I'm afraid: it tells us all sorts of things about the brain which we couldn't learn otherwise. Your daughter worked *that* out in two seconds flat . . . I noticed . . . You're welcome to come down and check on her, if you're anxious, but really you don't need to worry . . . Certainly. We'll make sure she has access to a phone, too . . . I don't know – here, ask her!'

'What did you do with your own phone?' asked my father, as I took the phone again.

'I forgot it – it's in Devon,' I told him defensively.

He snorted derisively, but said only, 'Do you want me to fetch your things from Dartington?'

I considered that. 'No,' I said at last. 'I don't have to clear the room until the end of the month. When I've finished here, I'll go back and pack up. I've got all the clothes and things I was going to take to Paris, so I should be OK.'

'OK,' he said, sounding relieved. 'You're all right?'

I cast another uncertain look at Spencer; he responded with an encouraging smile, but his eyes were still doubtful. 'I'm all right,' I promised my father, and hoped that I wasn't lying.

Two

We turned off the motorway south of Crawley, tracked westward along a series of B roads skirting the Downs, and eventually came to a pair of white posts and a small blue and gold sign proclaiming that this was the 'Laurel Hall Centre for Cognitive Research'. The car turned left into a narrow drive flanked on both sides by a dark thicket of rhododendron. The shrubs were just at the end of their season, and the road was littered with pink-violet flowers. We passed through them to a wide sweep of lawn, and there was the hall. Red-gold Georgian brick glowed in the evening sun, and little diamond-paned windows shone like jewels. Ornate chimney pots and dormer windows poked from the high slate roof. There was a rose garden and oak trees, and behind the Hall, high and green, the sun-drenched rise of the Downs. It was an image of tranquil order, of a civilisation more leisurely and spacious than the twenty-first century's frenetic appetites allow.

The garage was a converted stable block, to the right of the house itself. Mickleson parked, switched off the engine and unlocked the doors. I took a deep breath, then got out, hauled out my backpack and slung it over my shoulder, and picked up my guitar.

'I can take that,' offered Spencer, but I shook my head. It seemed important to take myself into the place under my own control, the way I hoped to come out again.

We trudged out of the garage and up to the varnished oak door, Mickleson leading. The door buzzed just before he reached it, and I wondered if the lock were triggered by a keycard or a wire. Mickleson opened it, and we went through.

The entrance hall was an odd combination. It had its original high Georgian ceilings and ornamental plasterwork, a chandelier and a carved oak umbrella stand – but it also possessed no fewer than three computer screens and attendant terminals. The middle one was showing security camera views – at this angle I couldn't distinguish the images, but the flicker as the view changed every fifteen seconds was unmistakable.

Mickleson went to the nearest screen and punched a code. The screen lit up and showed the image of a middle-aged Asian woman turning towards it from her seat on a sofa.

'Oh, you're back!' she said, sounding pleased about it. 'Success?'

'Mission accomplished,' agreed Mickleson, with satisfaction. 'The poor kid was pretty shaken up, though. I think she needs to get up to her room and have a rest.'

'Be right there!' trilled the woman, and the screen went dark again.

'My wife, Amrita,' Mickleson explained. 'She'll check you in. She handles the house; I handle the grounds and the driving.'

I looked across at Spencer, who was hovering ineffectually. 'What do you do?'

'He's research staff,' Mickleson replied, before the doctor could. 'Technically they're only here during the day – but when we've got a programme running we're supposed to have a qualified doctor on hand at all times, and Dr Spencer is it.' He grinned. 'One of the penalties he pays for being single. His room is downstairs, in the lab.'

The door at the other side of the hall opened, and Amrita Mickleson came through, a small plump woman in loose cotton trousers and a blue semi-formal top much like her husband's. She had a kind face, and smiled at me warmly. 'You're . . . Valeria Thornham, isn't it?' she asked, shaking hands. 'I'm Amrita Mickleson. I hope Dr Spencer has been able to set your mind at rest about the Cicnip assessment.' She turned to the third computer, which sat on a desk in a little alcove, without waiting for me to respond. 'You don't need to worry: I'm sure that even if you do have some kind of problem with episodes, we can sort it out.' She hooked a stool out from under the desk, perched on it, and beckoned me over. I came, cautiously.

The screen was displaying a menu for the household computer. Mrs Mickleson selected 'Security' and then 'Keys', followed by 'Create new keycard'. A form flashed up. I saw, with misgivings, that my name and date of birth had already been filled in.

'We have an integrated security system,' Mrs Mickleson explained. 'Everyone who's allowed in the house – programme participants and staff – gets a keycard which gives them access to the rooms they're entitled to use.' She glanced up to see if I was attending. 'All the participants have a card for the house, their own room and the common areas; the staff have a card for the house, their offices and the common areas, and so on. Most of the doors work on a short-range scan, incidentally, so you shouldn't actually need to put your card through any of the lock swipes, though sometimes you have to when the weather's humid.'

Mr Mickleson snorted and rolled his eyes. His wife smiled at him. 'George is always having to call people in to fix the scanners! Oh, and I should tell you: sometimes the alarms go off because a scanner hasn't been able to read your card properly. If that happens you should just put your card through the lock and wait. Whoever's in charge should call you on the videophone right away, and cancel the alarm. Is that address right, by the way?'

My parents' address was listed in the form's 'Home Address' section. I thought of providing my college address, then decided that there was no point, so close to the end of term. I nodded, and Mrs Mickleson scrolled on down. The next box was labelled 'Programme', and she typed in 'Special', the current date and – disquietingly – a mere dash.

'I'm going to put you in Room 28,' she informed me, typing that number under 'Room'. 'I'm afraid it's fairly small, but it has a lovely view.' She frowned at the next section, then looked up again. 'I'm sorry, but technically you're supposed to be in custody until we've completed the assessment. I'm going to have to put restrictions on your card. I hope we can take some of them off later.' She zoomed down the form, ticking boxes so quickly I had no time to see what they were about. 'What I'm

25

going to do is restrict your key's function to your own room, for the present, and put that on a timer. It won't work between eight in the evening and eight in the morning, but during the day you'll be able to go in and out as you please. The lounge, dining room, and games room aren't usually locked, so you'll be able to use them as well. If you want to leave the house, though, you'll need to ask a member of staff. If you try to walk through any unauthorised door without a valid key it will set off the alarms, even if you're only going out to play tennis.'

'What if there's a fire?' I asked irritably.

She smiled. 'If there's a fire everything's supposed to unlock automatically. The complete fire procedures are printed up on the door in your room, but I won't bother you with them right now.' Her fingers flew over the computer keyboard, whisking the form to its end. 'Can you put your hand here on the screen? Lovely. Now, sign here.' She offered me a photopen.

I checked: the screen showed only a standard disclaimer saying that I would abide by the regulations of the Hall during my stay, and that I would be responsible for any damage to the room. I signed.

'Lovely,' said Mrs Mickleson again. She opened a drawer beneath the computer, drew out a blank keycard, and slipped it into a slot on the computer, then hit Return. The computer whirred. 'Have you had any supper?'

'No,' I admitted, aware as I did so that I was very hungry.

'Then I'll bring you some sandwiches as soon as I've shown you the room. You like cheese, hummus, corned beef salad – ?'

'Hummus and salad would be nice,' I told her. *Very* nice, I thought, salivating, after so many weeks of cold cereal.

'Fine,' smiled Mrs Mickleson. The computer chimed and spat out my new keycard. Mrs Mickleson took it, handed it to me, and jumped to her feet. 'This way, then!' she ordered cheerfully.

There was a staircase just beyond the entrance hall. From some room nearby came the sound of voices – a young man speaking excitedly, and a girl laughing. A door to the left bore a panel saying 'Caution! Sensitive Equipment May Be In Use! No Unsupervised Access Beyond This Point!', but one to the right had only a label, 'Lounge'. Mr Mickleson touched his wife's arm, nodded, and left us for the lounge. Mrs Mickleson started up the stairs. I followed, aware of Dr Spencer bringing up the rear – blocking my line of escape, I thought, then dismissed the idea as unduly melodramatic.

The first floor was another mix of country hotel and 'No Unsupervised Access', but the second floor seemed to be all bedrooms, each numbered. Room 28 was at the end of the corridor. The door buzzed as soon as Mrs Mickleson reached it: I guessed that she carried a master key. She flung it wide and ushered me in.

She was right: it had a beautiful view. I looked out over the oak woodland and across the Sussex hills, a patchwork of field and farm. It was after nine now, but the light was only just beginning to fade, and the scene had the orderly radiance of a painting by Constable.

The rest of the room was OK. Small, but comfortable-looking, with all the necessities: bed, desk, computer. The bed was made up with clean linen and a floral print bedspread that matched the curtains. A sliding door gave access to a small washroom, with a toilet, washbasin, shower cubicle, and big fluffy towels. I became aware that I was as grubby as I was hungry.

'The rooms are cleaned on Fridays between ten and four,' Mrs Mickleson informed me, 'but we ask participants to try to keep them tidy. One of the house rules is quiet upstairs after eleven – no loud music or noisy conversations. You can always go downstairs for those – or, no, I suppose *you* can't, at the moment, but perhaps later. Anyway, if you want to listen to music or watch a programme late, use earphones – there's a set there, with the computer. The computer is programmed to switch off its speaker at ten.

'There's a laundry room on the ground floor if you need to do any washing, and there's a bathroom on the first floor if you want a proper bath. The Hall also has a games room, with darts, a pool table, and a virtuo system for up to four players, and there's a lounge where you can get coffee and watch television. Meals are served downstairs in the dining room:

27

the times are eight to eight thirty for breakfast, twelve thirty to one thirty for lunch, and seven to eight for supper. Don't worry if you don't remember all that: it's on the desktop under "Laurel Hall".' She waved vaguely at the computer. 'Your computer also has access to the house system. We get a good news and entertainment package off the net, which you can use as you please. There's also a tie-in to the house videophone system. If you need anything, you can contact me or my husband or Dr Spencer at any time. The numbers are here.' She picked up a sheet of laminated paper from the desk, then set it down again.

I nodded, set my guitar down slowly, and eased off my backpack. 'What about phone calls and e-mails?'

'Don't you have a phone?'

I shook my head. 'I forgot and left it in Devon. Dr Spencer said he would try to arrange something.'

Dr Spencer shrugged, looking tired and embarrassed. '*Access* to a phone,' he muttered. 'I did say *access*. I can clear you to call your parents on the house phone.'

'Perhaps you could get a friend to post you your own phone from Devon,' suggested Mrs Mickleson. 'But you're welcome to use the phone downstairs. You'll just have to get clearance first. We used to let people use the house phone from their rooms, but . . . well, there were problems.' She smiled. 'Huge bills from porn rooms – and then there was the girl who phoned her mother in Shanghai every day for a week at our expense! Getting clearance isn't complicated: it's mostly just a matter of registering who you are and who you're calling, and paying any bills before you go. Do you want to phone someone now?'

I shook my head.

'Then I'll go get you your sandwich,' Mrs Mickleson told me. 'Would you like a hot drink as well? Coffee?'

I acquiesced and she bustled off. Spencer remained a moment, hanging on to the door handle and staring at me with an unhappy expression. I scowled back suspiciously.

'If you'd like a sleeping tablet—' he began.

'I wouldn't.'

'Oh. Right.' He swallowed. 'Goodnight, then.'

He went out, closing the door behind him. I went over to see if it would open again, but of course it wouldn't, even when I swiped my card through the slot in the lock. It was past eight o'clock, and I had been sent to bed.

I sat down on the bed and rested my chin in my hands. The back of my mind was playing music again – solo cello, for once, *andante cantabile* in G. I'd expected to be in Paris by this time – wandering through the scent of coffee and kebabs in the crowds on the Left Bank; listening to fellow buskers; perhaps earning enough myself to pay for a couscous and a half-litre of harsh red wine. Instead . . .

I told myself that it was better than being in the police cell with the bag lady and the wildgirl. This place was beautiful, it was equipped like a good family hotel, the people seemed friendly and well-intentioned.

Yes, but they also seemed competent. A hard-pressed NHS brain injuries clinic might miss the music in my head: a lavishly endowed 'centre for cognitive research' was far less likely to do so.

Perhaps there was nothing abnormal about hearing music. I'd never been entirely sure how unusual it was: most people complain of tunes they 'can't get out of their heads'. I *thought* that what I experienced was something different, however, because I too often got a bit of melody stuck in my mind, and that was always quite distinct from the other kind of music I heard. Stuck melodies were tunes I knew, and they were less vivid than the other sort – more like memories and less like perception. But maybe hearing music in your mind was just unusual, and not abnormal. Maybe it was something all really *serious* musicians experienced. Maybe I had nothing to worry about.

I bit my lip, feeling another bubble of panic rising. Like hell. On the occasions when I succeeded in drawing out the music in my mind, I was aware of nothing until I'd finished playing it. My friends had told me they too sometimes went into a sort of trance when they were playing, so I'd never worried about it – until the coverage of the Torrington murders made me realise that what happened to me fitted the description of an 'episode of lapsed consciousness' rather better than that of a 'trance'.

Even if they found an abnormality in my brain, did that necessarily mean they'd *excise* it? Dr Spencer had indignantly condemned the idea that all CICNPC recipients were potential killers, and he seemed to accept completely that even those who suffered episodes were not necessarily dangerous.

I knew even as I thought it that in the present climate Laurel Hall couldn't possibly diagnose a CICNPC recipient as having a brain abnormality leading to episodes of lapsed consciousness and then just *release* her. 'Under the Mental Health Act any person classified as suffering from a mental illness that renders them a danger to the public can be forcibly detained for treatment,' the policewoman had said. They would intervene, oh God, and, under the Mental Health Act, I was not entitled to resist anything they chose to do to me.

From their point of view, they could cure me. 'I'm sure that even if you do have some kind of problem with episodes,' Mrs Mickleson had said, 'we can sort it out.' CICNPC had never been a very effective way of repairing brain damage. It involved injecting neural progenitor cells – the cells which produce brain cells proper in a developing embryo – into a damaged brain and hoping that new brain cells grew in the right directions. In adults they mostly didn't; children under the age of two, who still have some of the embryonic machinery to guide neural growth, fared rather better – but the treatment was rarely as effective as it had been for me. The SGNS treatment which supplanted it is much more reliable. (SGNS, if you've forgotten, stands for Stimulated Growth of Neural Systems.) If they cut the music out of my mind, they could regenerate my brain so that it worked just like the brain of everybody else. A health authority would undoubtedly see nothing wrong with that. But I would lose . . . I would lose . . .

I couldn't sit still. I jumped up and went over to lean on the window sill. The window was genuinely old-fashioned: the only bit that opened was a little pane on one side. If I wanted to throw myself out, I would have to smash the glass.

That thought shocked me. I was twenty, healthy, talented, reasonably attractive. There was a world out there waiting for me. I wanted to fall in love, visit South America, become an internationally famous concert guitarist. In silent music-drunk moments of ambition I was even sure I could become a Great Female Composer. Of course I didn't want to throw myself out of a second-storey window!

The thought of living on, though, after being mutilated in my soul – that was too horrible to contemplate.

There was a knock at the door and a buzz from the lock at the same time. Amrita Mickleson came into the room with a tray. 'Here are your sandwiches,' she said; then, setting the tray down with a frown, 'What's the matter?'

I almost shouted, 'If you try to cut out the part of my brain that does music, I'll kill myself!' But when I opened my mouth, I remembered that they didn't know that part existed. They might not find it, in which case I would be crashed to tell them about it. Even if they did find it, it might be something they wouldn't bother about if I didn't tell them about the episodes.

'I was thinking about how I was arrested,' I said instead. 'It was horrible. They took me off the train in handcuffs, with everyone watching. When they locked me up there was an old bag lady in the cell who was completely bits, but she started screaming because she'd been locked up with *me!*'

Mrs Mickleson exclaimed sympathetically and came over to pat me on the shoulder. 'The way Cicnip-C has been covered is a disgrace!' she said warmly. 'We've done about thirty Cicnip assessments here since the publicity started, and they've all been perfectly reasonable people broken up by the way everyone's suddenly started treating them. Don't worry, I'm *sure* we'll be able to help. Here, I've brought you the coffee you asked for. Sit down and drink it while it's hot. Then you can have a shower and watch something from the entertainment site, and you'll feel better.'

'Thank you,' I said, and felt guilty about lying to her.

I took the hot shower, but I didn't download anything. Instead I took out my guitar and played all the most soothing pieces I could remember, until I felt calm enough to try to sleep. I stopped at eleven prompt, so that nobody would have cause to complain that I'd broken the 'Quiet Upstairs at Night' rule.

Rather to my surprise, I did manage to fall asleep without too much trouble. I suppose I was sufficiently drained by the events of the day, and of the weeks before, that exhaustion got the better of anxiety. When I woke, however, the watch I'd set on the bedside table told me it was still not quite five a.m.

This being June, it was already light. I lay in bed for a while watching the day brighten on the wall, then admitted to myself that there was no way I could go back to sleep, and got up.

The house was very quiet. When I opened the little panel on the window, I could hear the singing of birds and the sound of the wind on the slates. The lawn lay like a pool of sun-drenched emerald; the oak woodland was a darker green, speckled with a moving lacework of shadow and golden light. The air smelled of flowers and sunlight and cut grass. I leaned against the window sill and drew in great breaths of it. In the back of my mind, a trumpet played a fanfare.

Despite waking so early, I felt much better than I had the night before. The idea that the people in charge of such a beautiful place would mutilate me seemed absurd. It *was* a beautiful place, too, and God knew I could use a bit of comfort after the last few months. I ought to make up my mind now that I was going to *enjoy* it!

To start off, I ought to find out more about it. I went over to the computer, switched it on, and clicked on the folder titled 'Laurel Hall'.

The file contained one surprise straight off. I'd blithely assumed that Laurel Hall was a government research institute, funded by either the Science or the Medical Research Council. Not a bit of it.

'Laurel Hall Centre for Cognitive Research is an independent research body,' said the file, 'fully funded by the Apollo Foundation as part of its ongoing quest to understand and improve our modern society.'

I stared at the screen's lavish graphics as I mulled that one over. Like most people, I knew about the Apollo Foundation. I'd heard the story: how seven of the richest men in Europe, attending a conference in Rome, had spent a dinner together lamenting the ignorance and superstition of their associates (particularly their wives and mistresses, went the rumour); how

32

by the end of the evening they'd agreed to found an institution to promote knowledge and reason, and had each donated ten million euros to start it off; how further donations and intelligent stewardship had allowed that initial fund to swell faster than its expenditure, so that the Apollo Foundation was now one of the richest non-governmental bodies on the continent. It was humanist without being atheist, conservative on economics but liberal on social policy, and everyone agreed that it did a lot of good work. I was aware that it funded educational programmes for deprived children and struggling single mothers; I was familiar with the Foundation's think tank, the Centre for Rational Policy, whose research and recommendations were respected by governments across Europe; I'd occasionally noticed the gold Greek mask logo at the end of a television documentary or top of an information website. Like most people I considered it worthy, but a bit boring. I hadn't been aware that it was into cognitive research, but I supposed it was natural that it should be: after all, rationalism begins in the brain. I wasn't sure how I felt about being in a research facility operated by a private foundation – actually, yes, I was: I didn't like it. It wasn't that I trusted the British government and didn't trust a charitable foundation: it was just that I felt governments are scrutinised more closely, and are more quickly called to account. There was, however, nothing to be done about it: the policewoman had shown me that. Here I was, and here I would stay until the assessment was finished.

'The house was originally built in 1743,' the document continued – the graphics showed it going up – 'by Sir William Fitzhubert, a wealthy merchant and landowner who made his fortune in the tobacco trade.' An eighteenth century portrait came to life and smoked a cigar. 'It was sold by his son, Roderick, to pay off debts incurred after the loss of the family's American properties in the War of Independence.' The unfortunate Roderick was run off a tobacco field by a pitchfork-wielding Yankee Doodle Dandy, and then turned out his empty pockets before frowning partners at a card game. 'It then passed through several hands' – a succession of hands in various costumes was shown – 'before being bought by the Foundation in 2028.' The god Apollo, looking as a Greek god ought, smilingly handed over a large sack with the euro sign.

It seemed that the Hall had several interesting architectural features (pictured), which I'm afraid weren't interesting to me; and that the adjacent downland, reached by a public footpath, was both a Site of Special Scientific Interest – cue rare butterflies and wildflowers – and an Area of Outstanding Natural Beauty – cue outstandingly beautiful views.

The Apollo Foundation had provided this demi-paradise with all the most advanced brain-scanning equipment – four functional magnetic resonance imagers (pictures), a new-generation magnetoencephalograph (more pictures), a differential cerebral angiograph (even the picture didn't give away what *that* might be), and – this was apparently something *really* special – a neuropharmacological sampler, which possessed a horde of needles so fine they could be inserted through a volunteer's skull without damaging the bone or harming the living cells beneath, and which could then detect minute variances in the amount of different neurotransmitters in the upper levels of the cerebral cortex. The picture for that was of a patient lying on a table, covered with a green surgical cloth, with his head in what seemed to be some kind of helmet bristling with shiny little hairlike wires. For all the smiling white-coated confidence of the doctors around him, it frightened me. I've always hated needles.

To manage this second, scientific demi-paradise, a dedicated staff of the finest neurologists had been recruited from the very best universities. (About a dozen of them, all pictured, each with a brief potted biography.) The head of the institution appeared to be a suave grey-haired Frenchman by the name of Professor Michel Bernet, who'd previously held some Very Important Post on a French research council, and who was also a member of the Apollo Foundation board. (Dr Spencer, I noted, MD *and* PhD, had been recruited only six months before, fresh from a doctorate at Oxford.) The efforts of the neurologists had already resulted in important discoveries. A study of computer games was likely to lead to new controls on the industry; another piece of research could help in the efforts to suppress football hooliganism.

'Volunteers taking part in research programmes at the Hall can be confident that their participation will lead to improved conditions for tomorrow's society,' the document concluded. 'We hope they will also enjoy their stay in the lovely Sussex countryside.' More views; picture of a room rather bigger than mine. 'The Hall's resident staff are dedicated to the comfort of our guests.' Amrita Mickleson smiled as she welcomed a guest.

There followed an illustrated list of amenities, tactfully annotated with regulations, much of which Mrs Mickleson had told me the previous night. I read the bits about the facilities for playing tennis and badminton, and about the lovely walks in the vicinity, with some resentment: being confined in a house is bad, but being confined in a house with lots to do outside is worse.

That was the end of the document, and it was still only five to six. I switched over to the computer's entertainment package, didn't fancy any of it at that time in the morning, and shut the machine off.

The image of the patient with the wires in his head at once leapt up before my mind's eye – only this time the patient was me.

I got up and went to look out the window again. I made myself breathe steadily. All right, I admitted, they would start the assessment today. Maybe they would use the machine with all the tiny needles, maybe they wouldn't. Even if they did, it wouldn't hurt me. They wouldn't use it if it was going to hurt a 'participant'. It *wasn't* a surgical device. If it did come down to surgery, it probably wouldn't even be done at Laurel Hall: I'd be packed off to a hospital with a laser-guided robotic surgery programme.

I wondered what sort of thing they were going to find inside my head. Oh God, I admitted to myself, I'm so scared!

I told myself fiercely that there was no reason to think they'd be bothered about the music, even if they found it.

I remembered, though, the doubtful way Dr Spencer had

looked at me the previous evening in the car, after my father had told him . . .

What? He couldn't have mentioned the episodes: he didn't even know about them. I *supposed* that he could have said something like, 'She gets very wrapped up in the music sometimes' – but it seemed unlikely. As I remembered it, Dr Spencer had said something about how the police had treated me. For my father to reply with a comment about lapses of consciousness would've been a complete non sequitur.

So why had Spencer looked at me with doubt, and why had he been so quiet and unhappy for the rest of the evening?

Perhaps, I thought, my father had said something that bothered Dr Spencer for some reason completely private and personal to himself. Maybe it had been something like, 'Look after her,' and the doctor felt uncomfortable at being asked to take on a parent's role. Perhaps that troubled him because . . . because he rather fancied me?

Now *that* was a cheerful and intriguing thought. What was Spencer's first name? Charles. A bit of a stuffy name, but then, he seemed a bit of a stuffy young man. He did have nice eyes, though, and he was only a few years older than me, and clearly very clever, to get a PhD on top of a medical degree, and go straight from Oxford into a job at a well-appointed research institute. Not that I wanted to get involved – I was strictly Arts side when it came to boyfriends, and a scrubbed pink neuroscientist definitely wasn't my type – but it's always flattering to have a clever young man sweating for you.

I felt happier again. I unpacked my things and got dressed, and I won't deny that I put a bit more effort into the job than I usually do. I hadn't brought any particularly good clothes, unfortunately, but I put on a sleeveless blue T-shirt which I knew flattered my chest and some blue-green enamel earrings which brought out the colour of my eyes. I went to examine myself in the washroom mirror.

My hair looked like a duster – a light-brown duster which has just been used to wipe the ceiling. I hadn't had it cut since the fuss over CICNPC first began, and it had grown out over my ears and hung down into my eyes. I combed it back. No good: it showed the wobbly bit at the front right-hand side of my head, where the skull had been reshaped after the accident. I combed it sideways. No, it still looked dim. I remembered that the previous night it had needed washing, too, and that my eyes and nose must have been red and swollen from crying. Maybe I was wrong about Charles Spencer. It didn't seem likely that he could've taken a fancy to such a bedraggled thing.

On the other hand, men are odd, and maybe I'd appealed to his chivalrous instincts. He seemed the sort for chivalry.

It was still only seven in the morning. I checked my nails to see if they needed attention, but, alas, I'd done them only a couple of days before, in an ultra-hard 'black diamond' varnish, and they were still immaculate. (I always use ultra-hard nail varnish: I need my nails for my instrument.)

In desperation, I tidied up. I found places for my clothes, stuck the sleeping bag and the backpack in a cupboard, and stood my guitar case neatly against the wall. Still only ten past seven! I looked through the sheet music I'd brought in the guitar case. It was all stuff I'd picked for busking – *Popular Classics for Guitar* sort of thing, some of it beautiful, some of it complicated to play, but all of it extremely familiar. If I was going to spend the next few days here I'd want something more challenging. I went back to the computer and started checking if there was any way I could download some more music.

No luck: I'd need my own music library, or access to the web. There was quite a lot of recorded music available, though, and I was looking through it when the computer's sound came on with a sudden burst of Beethoven: finally it was eight o'clock, and the quiet-upstairs rule had relaxed.

I rushed for the door without even bothering to switch off the computer. The key now worked before I reached the lock, and I stepped out into the corridor with a sigh of relief. God, if a twelve-hour curfew felt like that, what would it be like to be in a prison?

No one else was in the corridor, though there were sounds of people rising and water running from some of the other rooms. I slipped down the stairs to the ground floor, then hesitated, unsure where to go for breakfast. I tried the door labelled

'Lounge'; it opened, but revealed only (surprise!) a lounge, empty. Another door beyond it led to the games room; beyond that was a conservatory and the laundry room. I retraced my steps to the stairs.

I looked up at the sound of footsteps and saw a small group descending – two women and a man, all about my own age and similarly dressed in jeans and T-shirts. They smiled as they reached the bottom, and one of the girls lifted a hand in greeting.

'Hi,' she said. 'I don't think I've seen you before. Are you in the Ethics programme, too?'

'Uh, no,' I replied. 'I'm here for a, uh, medical review. I just arrived last night.'

Their names were Claire, Jack, and Miriam; they were all studying psychology at Queen Mary's College, and they were all participants in a one-week study of Ethical Decision Making. I had breakfast with them – the dining room turned out to be through an archway beyond the stairs, a bright sunny room with a view of the garden. It filled up quickly while we sat eating our crusty rolls and coffee, and the atmosphere was very like that of a student cafeteria. I found I was enjoying it, though I was careful to keep quiet about the CICNPC. Claire did ask me what I was having medically reviewed – 'I didn't know they did anything like that' – but I satisfied her with the answer, 'I had some treatment for brain damage after an accident, and they're assessing it. I think they've offered to help out the NHS with assessments, since they've got the right equipment for it.' It was all true, as far as it went, but I did manage to imply that the accident had been recent – CICNPC, of course, hasn't been used for nearly twenty years.

Claire had been to Laurel Hall twice before, and was enthusiastic about it. Jack and Miriam were on their first visit, but seemed to be enjoying themselves, though Jack regretted that he hadn't managed to get on one of the football hooligan studies: 'I have a friend who went, and he said it was top score. He said all they did was drink beer and watch football.'

'Ah, they never *all* did that!' said Miriam scornfully. 'Most of the guys on that study must've had *either* the football *or* the beer, and probably there was a control group that drank tea and watched soaps.'

Ethical Decision Making, in contrast, seemed to involve role-playing while wired up to one or another of the brain scanners. 'Some of the groups get drugs,' Claire elaborated, 'to see how it affects them, and I think they tweak the parameters in other ways, too, but we're the control.' There were presently two groups of six at the Hall taking part in the programme, and different volunteers would repeat the study, with variations, over the rest of summer. 'Very much an Apollo Foundation sort of thing,' Claire said cheerfully. ' "How do people make ethical decisions, and how can we get them to do it more *rationally*?" Control freaks.'

'Oh, I think they have a real point!' protested Miriam. 'People *aren't* rational enough. Look at advertising!'

At this we all joined happily in a session of Stupid Ads I Have Seen. We stopped only when Charles Spencer brought his roll and his cup of coffee over to our table.

The doctor still looked tired and anxious, but he made an effort to smile. 'Morning,' he said. 'Mind if I join you?'

Claire smiled back, but glanced at her watch. It was already eight thirty, and she replied apologetically, 'We're almost finished. We're in the first session this morning, and I need to do my laundry before it starts.'

'It's, um, it's really Miss Thornham I need to talk to,' said the doctor, discomfort now showing through his attempt at casual pleasantness.

Claire gave me a look of mixed sympathy and curiosity. 'Oh, that's OK, then,' she replied. 'We'll leave you to it. Val – nice to meet you!'

She and her friends sailed off. Dr Spencer sat down across from me and made another attempt at a smile. 'Did you sleep OK?'

I shrugged. 'Yeah. I woke up early, though.'

The doctor broke open his roll and began to butter it. 'I, uh, wanted to talk to you before we start the assessment,' he muttered, eyes down.

'So you said. When *does* it start, incidentally? Do I get a schedule or something? MRI nine o'clock; psych analysis ten thirty?'

'We don't have a schedule yet,' he replied, briefly meeting my eyes. 'It's one of the things I have to work out this morning. But we will start at nine.'

'Oh.' The roll I'd just eaten congealed in my stomach.

Spencer picked up the strawberry jam pot, saw that it was empty and picked up the marmalade instead. 'Professor Bernet will be in charge,' he informed me, spreading the preserve. 'I'll be assisting him.'

'Professor Bernet?' I repeated, staring hard. 'Isn't he the one in charge of the whole institution? Why's he bothered?'

The doctor put down his marmaladey knife. 'Miss Thornham, I . . . look, I'll be honest with you. When we were notified that you were being arrested for avoiding assessment—'

'I *wasn't* avoiding assessment!' I said. My voice had gone shrill again, and several of the other breakfasters glanced round. I swallowed and continued in a vehement whisper, 'What would have been the point of going to *France* to avoid assessment? It's not like they couldn't arrest me there! I told you: I just wanted to get away for a few days. Last term was horrible, and I wanted a break.'

He blinked owlishly. '*Did* you tell me that?'

I thought a moment. 'Maybe not,' I admitted. 'I told the police, and they didn't believe me. Anyway, this isn't relevant. Why is Professor Bernet bothered?'

'They sent us your medical records,' he said, lowering his voice. 'It's . . .' He grimaced. 'Let me put it this way: Professor Bernet has been looking for someone like you for years. His area of specialisation is the right prefrontal cortex and its role in the integration of personality.'

'Oh.' It was my turn to look down. When the joyrider crashed into my parents' Renault I had been six months old. My carseat had been strapped into the left rear passenger seat, facing backward. The crumpling passenger door had crushed the side of the carseat and fractured the right side of my skull, while glass from the shattered window had been driven into the top front side of my head. I'd ended up with damage to my right

40

temporal lobe and, yes, with my right prefrontal cortex sliced apart.

'The implantation treatment seems to have been unusually successful in your case,' the doctor continued quietly, 'but judging by the scans you had before you were finally discharged, the regeneration process did produce some abnormalities in the region. Nobody seems to have taken any note of them at the time – which makes sense, given that your brain was functioning normally on all the tests of performance – but they are very clear in the scans. The professor is excited about it.'

Oh God. So much for keeping quiet and hoping they didn't spot anything: I was already compromised by childhood scans I'd never even thought to worry about. *Abnormalities in the region.* Nobody had ever mentioned that to *me*. What sort of abnormalities?

'Excited?' I hissed, looking up glaring with eyes that suddenly stung. 'Excited because my brain's abnormal? Jesus!'

'I understand your feelings,' Dr Spencer replied at once. 'But you asked why the professor is involved, and that's the answer. He's a brilliant and dedicated researcher, utterly committed to his subject, and he believes he can learn a great deal from you. And . . .' He hesitated again.

I kept glaring.

'The abnormalities on those scans are the sort associated with lapses of consciousness in other Cicnip-C recipients,' the doctor went on, with the air of a man nerving himself for something unpleasant. 'On the phone last night your father told me you'd never had an episode of lapsed consciousness, but . . . when he said it, I wondered if that was right.'

Oh, hell. So much for romance: Spencer was only interested in my brain. 'What are you saying?' I demanded, from the other side of a growing horror. 'That he was lying to you?'

'I don't know,' he replied evenly. 'It would be understandable if he did: of course he wants to protect you. But it may well be that you've never had anything your father would identify as an episode, particularly after all the negative publicity about what episodes are like. Whether or not you've ever experienced an episode, though, those scans leave you vulnerable – and if there *is* a problem, and you start off by denying it, you'll make things worse for yourself.'

Our eyes met and held. I wondered why I'd thought him nice. 'Are you threatening me?' I demanded.

He blushed. 'No! You've misunderstood completely. You said that you wanted to get out of here as soon as we've done the assessment. OK, I'd hoped you'd be willing to stay longer, but I can understand it that you're not. To get out of here, though, you've got to get us to clear you, and scans like those make that hard to do – particularly if you're perceived as uncooperative.' He put both hands flat on the table. 'Look, you were arrested and *referred to us*. We can detain you for tests indefinitely, and the professor *will* detain you, too, if you give him an excuse. Your best hope of getting away quickly is to be completely open with us. I'm not saying it will be easy even then, but if you get yourself labelled deceitful and uncooperative, it will be much harder.'

I sat silent for a moment, staring down at my empty cup of coffee. My eyes hurt, and it was hard to breathe. I'd never felt so trapped in my life, or so angry.

'You're telling me,' I managed at last, 'that I can be locked up here and studied as long as your precious Professor Bernet wants to study me, and the only thing I can do about it is to open up about everything before he gets round to forcing the lock, is that what you're saying?'

'No, I—'

'I'm talented, you know that? One of my tutors at Dartington said I'm the best he's seen in twenty years. At the beginning of this term, I had friends, I had an admirer, I had a brilliant career in front of me! I have not done *one fucking thing* to change any of that, not *one thing* that ever made anyone question my sanity or my mental competence – but you're telling me I can be locked up here and experimented on like some animal?'

'I'm trying to *help!*'

'Like hell! You're trying to blackmail me into cooperating with your professor's miserable little *private* research programme. Well I say, fuck you! I'm not *going* to cooperate.

I'm going to phone my dad and ask him to get me out of here.' I jumped up and stormed out.

At the access point in the entrance hall, one of the volunteers was on the house machine downloading something off a psychology research site. I stood fuming in the doorway and waited for him to finish. Dr Spencer came up behind me, making me jump. He looked wretched.

'Look,' he said earnestly, 'you've got the wrong end of the stick. Please, can you just let me explain?' He added, with a nervous glance at the volunteer, 'Privately, in my office.'

'I'm not interested in your explanations,' I told him stonily.

'Just listen!' he begged again. 'Then you can call your father. He'll need the full picture anyway – and if you call him while you're in this state, all you'll do is scare him.'

I snorted. 'And whose fault is that?'

'Mine,' he said at once. 'I'm sorry, I didn't know how to tackle the issue, and I did it very badly. Please will you come and listen?'

I hesitated. The volunteer, who'd glanced round with interest, had turned back and was starting to access *another* site. What the hell: I might as well listen to the rest of what Spencer had to say.

We went back to the foot of the stairs, then through the 'Caution!' door. The room beyond it appeared to be nothing more exciting than a small lecture theatre, with chairs in rows and a wall full of screens. Beyond it was a corridor flanked by doors. Dr Spencer went to the far end and opened the last door on the left. It was evidently his office. There was a desk with a computer and a huge stack of papers, a couple of chairs, and four or five shelves of books with titles like *Foundations of Neuroscience* and *The Anterior Cingulate Gyrus*. A half-open door to a second room provided a glimpse of an unmade bed and the top half of a pair of pyjamas.

Spencer offered me the spare chair and sat down at the desk. 'Miss Thornham,' he began, 'I'm sorry if I upset you.'

I snorted. 'Oh, I bet you are. Your prof isn't going to like it one bit that you gave away his *private, personal* research interest, is he?'

43

He winced. 'No, he isn't, but—'

'He can't keep me here against my will,' I said fiercely. 'If he tries, my parents will raise hell, and he'll be *seriously* embarrassed. Even Cicnip recipients have rights. I may be required to undergo assessment, but I am *not* required to take part in somebody's pet research project – *particularly* not when it's privately funded and not even in the public domain!' I glared. 'I have an aunt who's a lawyer, you know.' With a conveyancing firm in Nottingham, but he didn't have to know that.

'Look, I don't think you understand the situation.'

'Don't I?'

'You're right that Professor Bernet isn't going to like it that I gave away his research interest in you. I did it because I was trying to help. What you don't seem to understand is how vulnerable you are. You were *arrested*, you are *in custody*, you are *required* to undergo assessment. If you resist, you can be forcibly restrained and subjected to procedures without your cooperation or your consent. All it needs is a court order, and in the present climate there'd be absolutely no trouble in getting one. Your brain scan records would be enough to convince any competent medical authority that you are likely to suffer episodes of lapsed consciousness, and the fact that you've already been arrested for trying to avoid assessment doesn't help. If you refuse to cooperate, all that will happen is that you won't be assessed here. We don't have the staff or the equipment or the mindset to treat people forcibly. You'll be sedated and carted off to a mental hospital, and the *very fact that that was done* will be used as proof of your mental instability and justify every test Professor Bernet cares to run on you – and he wants to run *lots* of tests. Look, I *believe* you when you say you're stable and competent. I think you probably do experience episodes, but in some form so benign that nobody's ever worried about them, except perhaps you. I don't think it's *right* that you can be treated like this – but the fact is, you *can* be treated like this. Legally. Your aunt the lawyer won't be able to help.'

I stared at him, stunned into speechlessness.

'I'm sorry,' he said again. 'I don't blame you for being

shocked and upset: in your place, I'd be terrified. But, please believe me, I'm not saying this to threaten you. I'm saying it because I'm afraid you could be treated very badly, and I want to prevent that.'

Suddenly, I did believe him, mainly because of the way he looked – angry and earnest and distressed, blue eyes meeting mine with hot sincerity. I'd always found the phrase 'it hit her like a blow to the stomach' incredibly trite, but that's exactly what it was like. I gulped air like a stranded fish and pressed at my face with the heels of my hands.

Spencer jumped up, flapped his hands helplessly a couple of times, then darted off into the bedroom. He came back with a handful of paper towels and a glass of water. I took them and blew my nose, then mopped my eyes and sipped the water. My hands were shaking so much I spilled some down my front. *You can be forcibly restrained and subjected to procedures without your cooperation or consent . . . you'll be sedated and carted off . . . you could be treated very badly . . .*

Spencer took the glass back. 'I'm sorry,' he said again. 'I just . . . I just know how it's going to be if you go in there and say, "Oh no, I've never had an episode." The professor won't believe it, and he's . . . he's an impatient man. He'll declare that you're lying, that you're obstructing the assessment process, and get all indignant and self-righteous. It will make things worse; please believe me, it will.'

I blew my nose and mopped my eyes some more.

'I mean, the way to play it is to go in, very cool, say what you told me – that you weren't avoiding assessment at all, you just wanted a holiday first. Tell him you were planning to make the appointment as soon as you got back, but you're happy to cooperate now you're here. You don't have to say you've experienced episodes – just that you don't know whether you have or not, and you're relying on him to find out. That way he'll be more helpful.'

I wiped my eyes again. Several things about his attitude were starting to become clear. 'You don't like Professor Bernet, do you?' I asked.

He winced. 'He's a great man,' he said reprovingly. 'A very

45

brilliant man. He's read more English literature than *I* have, and English isn't even his native language. He's one of the most respected and admired figures in modern neuroscience. It's an honour for me to be working with him – but it isn't always easy. He's impatient, and . . . and *difficult*. Sometimes he can come across as an arrogant bully.'

I wiped my eyes one more time. 'The volunteers seem happy.'

'They hardly ever see him. Most of the staff are all right – and it is a beautiful place.' He shrugged. 'That's not what we were talking about. Do you believe me?'

I looked at him closely, then nodded. 'Yes. I guess I should say, thank you for warning me.'

He smiled with relief and ran a hand through his tidy hair, leaving it dishevelled. 'That's fine. You're welcome.'

'I'm still going to ask my father to get me out, though. I . . . guess I just won't mention that you told me about the professor's research interests. I'll say I got the information off his publications list in the Hall file.'

He smiled again. 'Fine. Good. Thanks. What I'd suggest is that your father comes down here and asks to talk to the professor. Then he can express concern about how long it's going to take, and ask if the assessment couldn't be done by your local health authority at home. He can let out that he's going to consult your local people and ask what tests they would do and how long it would take. Professor Bernet will be very annoyed with that, but it should make him keep his own tests to a minimum.' He glanced at his watch. 'God, it's gone nine! I'm sorry, but we've got to go and join him. Do you want to wash your face?'

Three

The professor's office was on the first floor, in the staff section of the house. Dr Spencer escorted me there in nervous silence, and knocked hesitantly on the varnished door.

'Come in!' commanded a voice. Spencer opened the door for me, then followed me in and closed it behind us.

It was a big room, and it looked like the Hollywood vision of a professor's study. There were the bookshelves lined with (predominantly leather-bound!) tomes, the oak panelling, the red and gold rug on the parquet flooring, the huge oak desk – and there was the professor himself, suitably grey-haired and magisterial. If his suit was too fashionable for the baggy pipe-smoking stereotype – well, he *was* French. I wondered how much of the decor was an attempt to impress.

Then I noticed his eyes. They were dark, set in hollows of baggy skin, but they were sharp and shrewd – and so cold they made me feel as though I'd just swallowed a snowball. They were fixed on me with a devouring intensity, like the eyes of a pervert I'd encountered once while busking. Oddly, that steadied my wobbling nerves. Tears and terror would do me no good here. They could wait until I had leisure for them.

'Ah. Valeria Thornham,' said the professor severely, still looking me up and down with that perverted lust. His accent was only just strong enough to be noticeable. 'Our CICNPC arrest. You have put everyone to great deal of trouble to bring you here.'

I managed to smile appeasingly. 'I suppose so, Professor. I'm very sorry. I didn't mean to. I really wasn't trying to avoid assessment. I just wanted a holiday.'

The severe look was replaced by irritation. 'What do you

mean? You were arrested when you attempted to flee the country!'

I gave him my wide-eyed innocent look. 'I was only going to Paris! I suppose I should have phoned to make the appointment for assessment before I left – but the letter didn't say you had to respond *right away* or they'd call the trackers. I'd just finished my exams, and I wanted to have a bit of a break. I was planning to make the appointment as soon as I got back. It would only have been a few days.'

He gave me a glare of affront. 'You must have been invited to come for assessment many times before you received the letter which required you to do so.'

'But I didn't want to have it done during term time!' I protested at once. 'There's always masses of work during the summer term – you're a professor, you must know that. I thought if I had it done during the summer vacation it wouldn't interfere with anything. It seems I was wrong to put it off, and I'm very sorry. I didn't mean to cause such a panic. I still think it's completely over the top that they arrested me.'

He stared at me, suspicious and resentful. He'd had the script for this interview all planned: himself the righteous and reproving authority, me the naughty self-indulgent girl. Now he had to find a new script, and he wasn't pleased.

'Whatever the *truth* of the matter,' he at last said stiffly, 'your conduct has caused considerable trouble, both for the police and for my own staff. You should also have had more regard for the safety of the public than to . . . *delay* your assessment for so long. I hope you will be more cooperative in future.'

I gritted my teeth. 'Yes, Professor. But I don't accept that I was, or am, any kind of danger to the public.'

He raised his heavy eyebrows. 'You received the CICNPC treatment as an infant. Your scans show the classic excess foci pattern associated with episodes of lapsed consciousness. Are you claiming that you have never had such an episode?'

'I don't know,' I replied honestly.

A moment of cold silence. 'You don't *know?*' repeated the professor. 'It seems to me that this is something one would be aware of.'

'I've never suddenly come to and found myself somewhere without knowing how I got there,' I said truthfully. 'And I've never suddenly regained consciousness and discovered that half an hour's passed and I have no idea what I did during the course of it. That's what they've been saying episodes are like, and it's never happened to me. On the other hand, sometimes I get . . . sort of abstracted . . . when I'm concentrating very hard. Maybe something abnormal goes on then. That's why I'm here, isn't it? So you can find out?'

The professor frowned.

'When I was twelve,' I continued earnestly, 'the doctors at the brain injuries clinic told my mother that as far as they could tell I was completely normal, and I didn't need to come back for any more check-ups.' My mother, I remembered bitterly, had taken me out and bought me an ice-cream sundae to celebrate. 'Now Dr Spencer says that the same scans those doctors made all those years ago show that my brain isn't normal after all. It's the first I know of it, and I'm still in shock. I can't believe there's anything really *major* wrong with me. Somebody would've noticed. But I guess I'd like to have it checked.'

The professor frowned some more. He tapped the surface of his desk with the index finger of his right hand, a soft noise that seemed very loud in the quiet room. The back of my mind suddenly sounded a counterpoint to it, a rhythm played out on the neck and body of a guitar, with a single bass voice behind it chanting a song without words. I shivered.

'Very well,' said Professor Bernet, and favoured me with a very small, very cold smile. I went limp inside with relief: he'd scrapped Plan A. 'We will see if we can pinpoint what is wrong with you. Dr Spencer, take Miss Thornham to Room 4. We'll start with one of the basic task-sheets and the fMRI. I'll join you in fifteen minutes.'

Spencer shuffled his feet uncomfortably. 'Ah, sir? Suzy is using the MRIs for the Ethical—'

'You tell her she must do without number four!' snapped the professor.

'Yes, sir,' muttered the doctor. He held the door for me, and we left the room.

'He won't tell Suzy *himself*,' muttered Spencer, as we started back towards the stairs. 'Completely screws the schedule, for her and all her participants, and won't even bother to inform her *himself*!' He cast an exasperated glance back over his shoulder.

I'd started to tremble: I felt as though I'd narrowly avoided a nasty accident. 'What happens now?' I asked.

He looked back at me, eyes still hot. 'Like he said. We'll hook you up to an fMRI scanner and give you a series of cognitive tasks. Then we'll use the computer to compare your responses to a paradigm called "normal" and use the Meg to check anything that warrants closer attention.' He noticed the expression on my face, and went on, more gently, 'It's nothing to worry about. It's exactly the same sort of scan you had as a child; the only difference is that our scanner is faster and a bit more sensitive than the ones they were using then.'

I nodded and said nothing. My stomach was churning and I felt faint. Yes, I'd had MRI scans before – and apparently they'd shown abnormalities in my brain. This time, with a more sensitive scanner and doctors who knew what to look for . . .

I would *not* let them cut me, I promised myself – and anyway, they might not want to, and if they did they probably wouldn't do it here, and I would not *let* them do it at all. I would *not* be some wet victim. It wasn't the end yet by any means. Not the beginning of the end. We will fight them on the beaches, we will never give up. Yeah.

We went downstairs. The lecture theatre was now occupied by six volunteers and a dumpy red-headed woman in a lab coat who was standing at the front of the room and pointing to a screen. I recognised Claire, Jack, and Miriam among the volunteers.

'Hi, Suzy,' Spencer said to the redhead. 'Look, I'm sorry: the professor wants the number four fMRI this morning.'

'Oh, *fuck!*' said Suzy in disgust. 'Why?'

'Medical assessment,' replied Spencer, with a nod at me.

Suzy gave me a hostile look. 'Oh, right!' she exclaimed bitterly. 'His Cicnip-C to the right prefrontal cortex! How can a *scheduled* research programme like Ethical Decision

Making compete?' She turned back to her audience. 'Sorry, people. We're going to have to revise the schedule.'

I noticed Claire, Miriam and Jack staring at me aghast. Spencer touched my arm and we went on through the room and into the corridor. When the door had closed behind us, I uttered a vehement, 'Oh, fuck!' of my own.

'Huh?' asked Spencer.

'She didn't have to *say* that I was a Cicnip recipient!'

He paused, taken aback. 'No,' he agreed seriously. 'She didn't, and she shouldn't have. I'm sorry. Normally she wouldn't have – but she *is* upset about losing that scanner. It's going to mess up her experiment for the rest of the week.' He opened a door to the right.

Room 4 had a disagreeably medical look: green linoleum, three bare walls, a couple of ordinary chairs and one that belonged in a dental surgery. One wall was entirely covered by steel, screens, and dials, like the control panel of a spaceship.

'You can sit there,' said Spencer, indicating the dentist's chair. He went to the spaceship controls and started flicking switches.

I stared sickly at the chair. It had, I saw, an enormous helmet affair with sides about fifteen centimetres thick, currently folded back on a stand.

I wasn't frightened of fMRI per se. The acronym stands for 'functional magnetic resonance imaging', if you're not familiar with it, and it's a more sensitive form of the ordinary MRI scanning you may have had instead of an X-ray. The machine works by setting up a strong magnetic field around the subject's head and measuring the tiny differences in magnetic resonance from haemoglobin molecules inside their brains. Haemoglobin is the molecule in your blood which carries oxygen, and the more oxygen it carries, the more it resonates – so the scanner effectively provides a picture of which parts of the brain are using the most oxygen and working hardest at any given moment. It's a non-invasive technique and doesn't hurt at all. I had unpleasant memories of it, but they were of squirming under the helmet and being told by my mother to sit still – that, and the long, tedious sessions in the waiting room beforehand, leafing through a pile of ancient *Blue Peter* annuals while an endless succession of patients went before us to be scanned. MRI machines are expensive, and there was always a queue for them on the NHS.

There was a queue here, too, apparently – but the professor had jumped it. He couldn't wait to get a look at my abnormal brain. I wondered if novice strippers felt this way just before they went on stage. Waiting to be stared at and drooled over, possibly to be pawed and pinched – with rape always a possibility lurking in the background.

Spencer turned back from the controls and found me still staring at the chair. Our eyes met.

He frowned. 'You're frightened?'

I nodded fractionally.

'I'm sorry,' he said, sounding it. 'I do understand. And I'm sorry I was so casual about the abnormalities on your scans; I hadn't realised that you didn't know about them.'

I shrugged.

He looked at me a moment longer, then said softly, 'Excuse me if I'm wrong, but – my impression is that you suspect there *is* an abnormality in your brain, but you haven't admitted it even to your family, because you're too worried about what will happen to you if we find it.'

I swallowed. 'What . . . *would* happen?'

'If it's serious we can write a programme to fix it. Modern laser surgery is very, very precise, and the SGNS treatment is order of magnitude better than CICNPC. It's possible to eradicate a brain defect without changing anything important around it. You would still be you.'

I shook my head. I'd never worried about whether I'd still be me. I'd still be me if I were blind and deaf and paralysed, too. I just wouldn't want to be.

'What I honestly think is most likely, though,' Charles Spencer went on, 'is that the abnormality is trivial. If there was anything seriously wrong with you it would show up in lots of ways – not just in whatever it is that you're afraid to tell anyone about.'

I gazed at him, eyes stinging.

'And if it's a trivial abnormality, you don't have to worry,' he told me earnestly. 'All we'll do then is discharge you with a certificate saying that your minor disorder represents no threat to the public.'

I took a deep breath and climbed on to the chair. 'Thanks.'

Spencer showed me the controls that adjusted the seat's height and angle, waited while I found a comfortable position, then unfolded the helmet. It was supported on a post, like a salon hairdryer. He began to slide it down, then paused and said, 'Could you take off your earrings, Miss Thornham?'

'Call me Val,' I instructed him, unhooking them.

'Val,' he repeated, looking very pleased about it. Maybe he *wasn't* only interested in my brain.

'Can I call you Charles?' I asked, to test this notion.

He beamed. 'Yes please! All the staff here call me Spence, and I feel like I'm back in school – and then the participants call me Dr Spencer, and I feel like I'm turning into my father.' He took my earrings and put them in his jacket pocket, then slid the helmet the rest of the way down.

Professor Bernet came in while he was adjusting the pads that were supposed to keep my head still inside the helmet during the scan. The professor frowned. 'I thought by now we would be ready to begin,' he commented in displeasure.

'I'm sorry, sir,' said Charles woodenly.

'One expects more efficiency, Dr Spencer,' the professor went on coldly. 'Time on these machines is precious. One should not claim it from other researchers, and then waste it in chatting up the female patients.'

Charles made no effort to defend himself. He merely said again, 'I'm sorry, sir,' and finished adjusting the padded clamp at the base of my neck. I remembered that he'd described the professor as a bully. A bully who'd singled out the most junior member of his staff for special attention? It fitted with the way Charles was living at the Hall, running errands out of hours, and playing lab technician for the professor instead of doing any research of his own. I thought about protesting that the delay had been my fault, because I'd been nervous and had

53

needed reassuring – but, in fact, there hadn't *been* any delay to speak of, and to enter into a discussion of who was to blame for it was playing into the professor's hands. Better to handle it as Charles was doing, and cut it short with an apology.

The necessary adjustments were made to the machine, and I presume it produced an image of the inside of my head – I say 'presume' because I was clamped in place staring at a blank wall with my back to the screens, and I couldn't see a thing. Charles got out the 'basic task-sheet' – a list of different cognitive tasks for me to do – and we began to go through it.

I'd done similar tasks before: list all the colour words you can think of; complete these sentences; read this card; add these numbers. There was a flatscreen on the wall I was facing, and they flashed up patterns on it and handed me a mouse to click: which of *these* shapes contains *this* shape? Will *that* shape fit *this* one if it's rotated? Do you recognise this face? (A series of those, some famous, some unknown.) Describe this picture. Look at these three scenes: what do you think happens next? I knew that on the screen behind me, the fMRI would be showing different parts of my brain lighting up as they worked together to complete the different tasks – visual systems, speech centres, auditory systems, spatial orientation centres, face-recognition centres, the diffuse chains of memory and reason. Were the patterns my brain produced the same as those generated in other heads? I listened to the comments of the men behind me, hoping for some clue, but they said very little – merely orders from Bernet and the wooden 'Yes, sir's from Charles.

Then – oh, hell! – the thing I'd dreaded all along: the music started – guitar and woodwinds in A major, *presto vivace* in a shattering 7/8 time.

Apparently it was far from unobtrusive. 'What is *that*?' exclaimed the professor in surprise, and Charles caught his breath with a hiss.

I tried to stop it, to think of something else, but it was no use. I sat there, trapped, listening to the room's silence and the sounds inside my mind.

'Miss Thornham?' Charles asked hesitantly.

'Val,' I told him.

'Val,' he repeated. He sounded very shaken. 'Are you conscious?'

Stupid question! Was I going to say 'no'? 'Yes, of course!' I snapped.

The professor intervened, his voice angry. 'What are you doing?'

Oh hell, oh hell, the bastards had me now.

Maybe it was utterly trivial. 'I'm . . . thinking about music,' I admitted.

'That fits,' said Charles, sounding relieved. 'Yes, yes. Auditory cortex, right-brain cognitive functions, cerebellum and the limbic system and hippocampus. Music. Yes.'

'The activity is *extreme*!' snarled the professor. 'And look, there it involves the motor cortex!'

'It's *guitar*,' I told him, fighting back tears. 'I always think about the fingering, if it's guitar.' I moved my fingers to show him, left hand at shoulder whipping through the fingerings, right hand plucking imaginary strings *presto, presto* . . . change of key, oh God, the harmony from the woodwinds! change of tempo, *down, down,* close. The music stopped, and I sat, staring at the blank wall, feeling the coldness of the helmet around my head, breathing hard.

There was a silence. 'Val,' said Charles quietly, 'do you know what just happened?'

'I told you,' I replied numbly. 'I was thinking about music.'

'That wasn't just *thinking*,' Charles told me, his voice soft, almost awed.

'No,' I admitted.

'Auditory hallucination?' demanded the professor. He still sounded angry.

'No,' I replied. 'I never mistake it for something in the outside world. I know it's inside my head – something I'm creating. It's just . . . a more vivid way of thinking about music. Look, I'm a musician. I think about music a lot.'

'Can you remember exactly what happened just now?' coaxed Charles. 'You started hearing music, and – ?'

'I could probably write out the score.'

'No, no, that's not what I meant!' said Charles. 'I just want to be sure that you remember what happened after the music started. For example, do you remember what I said to you?'

Odd question. 'Yes, of course!'

'What? Repeat it!' snapped the professor.

I raised my eyebrows – pointlessly, since I was immobilised with my back to him – and recited, 'Charles asked me if I were conscious, except he called me Miss Thornham and I corrected him, and I said yes of course I was, and then, Professor, you asked me what I was doing, and I said I was thinking about music, and Charles started muttering about what bits of my brain I was using. Is that all? Oh, no, you said I was using my motor cortex, so I explained that that was because it was guitar, and showed you the fingering. Then the music stopped, and Charles asked me if I knew what had happened.'

The professor let out his breath slowly.

'Think about music,' Charles said softly. 'I mean, just *imagine* you were listening to something, the way anyone else would. Just for comparison.'

I imagined the soothing Largo from the Vivaldi lute concerto – cool rain falling on my hot and swollen heart.

'You really do imagine *playing* it, don't you,' said Charles, after a moment. 'Your motor cortex is lighting up again.'

'It's a piece for guitar,' I told him. 'If you like, I'll imagine something else.' I imagined the Allegri *Miserere*, the high sweet voices calling out the aching melismas of loss: Have mercy upon me, oh God.

'This is *irrelevant!*' shouted the professor furiously. He stalked round the chair, into my field of vision, and seized both armrests, leaning over me. His face was flushed and sweating, and the eyes that glared into my own bulged. 'These hallucinations – you have them how often?'

I shrank back into the chair, as far as I could with my head immobilised. 'They're not hallucinations!' I protested. 'I *know* I'm creating them; I've never mistaken them for something coming from outside.'

'You imply that you do this *deliberately*?'

He was shouting, spraying spit into my face. I wanted to curl up and cry, and I couldn't. I raised my hands to fend him off, then worried that this would make him even more angry, and instead clutched at the clamp at the base of my neck. The vinyl padding was slick under my sweaty fingers, and it was hard to think straight. I had no idea what I could have done to make the man so angry.

Be open, Charles had warned me, or the professor will accuse you of obstructing the assessment process and ask for a court order.

'No,' I gasped. 'No, it's involuntary. It just happens. I—'

'It happens how often? Once, twice a day? At times of stress or of relaxation? It continues for how long?'

He was breathing hard, and I could see the coarse black hairs inside his nostrils blow in and out. 'It probably happens a couple of dozen times a day,' I quavered. 'Sometimes it's just a few bars; other times it's longer. It does tend to happen at times of stress, but it also happens when I'm relaxing – about the only time it *doesn't* happen is when I'm concentrating on some other music or on something routine.'

The professor scowled furiously. The hands clutching the armrests of my chair clenched convulsively, as though he were strangling something. I ached to get away, and fumbled blindly at the clamp – then considered how he'd react if I got up without his permission, and stopped. 'It doesn't interfere with anything!' I pleaded. 'It happens lots of times when I'm cycling, or running, or talking to someone, and nobody ever even notices. It's not like a seizure or anything. I've always thought it was something to do with being very keen on music.'

'It began when?' demanded the professor. 'In infancy?'

'I don't know! I don't remember a time when it *didn't* happen.'

'Professor, please!' protested Charles. 'You're scaring her.' He came up behind the chair gently and firmly lifted my hands off the clamp so that he could get at it himself. I slid my hands up behind my neck, and felt the pulse in my throat hammering against the inside of my wrists.

The professor let go of the chair arms and stood back, glaring at Charles now. 'The subject *lied* to us!' he bellowed.

'Sir, that's outrageous!' Charles replied, in a kind of quiet shout. 'Miss Thornham has given an honest answer to every question we've asked. She told us she had never experienced an episode as described by the media, but that there were some things which concerned her which she wanted us to check. You never even asked her what they were: you just told me to take her down here and put her on a machine. How can you accuse her of lying when you never gave her a chance to say anything?'

The professor drew himself up to his full height and spat out a phrase in French which my school vocabulary text had tactfully ignored. 'You ignorant pink piglet!' he sneered. 'Here you are on your first job, and you presume to instruct *me*? I promise you, *Dr* Spencer, you will keep your mouth shut and do as I tell you, or this will be your *last* job!' He scowled down at me wrathfully. 'You will tell me *everything* about these episodes!'

It suddenly hit me. Charles had asked if I was conscious, had been concerned to establish that I remembered what had happened. 'Episodes?' I repeated in horror. 'But I'm conscious the whole time!'

Professor Bernet looked as though he were about to hit me. Charles quickly slid the helmet up and folded it back. 'Sir,' he said, 'I'm going to take Miss Thornham out and let her calm down. You can review what happened and think about how to proceed. I do think, sir, that we ought to review the data before we jump to conclusions. Maybe the resemblances to an episode were superficial and misleading, and this was another sort of neurological event entirely.'

The professor relaxed slightly. He gazed at Charles for a moment with narrowed eyes, then jerked his head towards the door. 'Go, then!' he ordered. 'I will review the scans. I want her back here in half an hour.'

Charles took my arm and started to help me to my feet. I pulled free, and fairly bolted for the door.

The alarms went off the moment I touched it – a pulsing falsetto shriek that shredded the last fragments of my self-control: *eeyAAA eeeyAAA eeeyAAA*! I recoiled backwards into Charles and burst into tears.

'Keycard,' ordered Charles firmly.

Sobbing, I dug it out of my pocket. He took it and swiped through the lock.

Instantly one of the screens on the spaceship controls lit up to reveal Mrs Mickleson, apparently in the kitchen, and looking worried. 'What is it?' she asked.

'Nothing,' replied Charles. 'Miss Thornham tried to go through a door in front of me, that's all. Please turn that thing off! It's been a very rough morning.'

Mrs Mickleson vanished. The alarm stopped. Charles handed me back my keycard, slid his own through the lock, and opened the door for me. The professor watched us stumble out, his lip curled in superior disgust.

The lecture room was empty, and the sound of voices came from several other rooms along the corridor: Suzy and her volunteers were presumably hard at work making ethical decisions. Charles opened the door that led through into the hall and held it for me. I remembered the way he'd been doing that all morning. It hadn't been as gentlemanly or old-fashioned as I'd thought.

We went through into the lounge, which was empty. 'Would you like some coffee?' Charles asked me concernedly. 'Or a cold drink?'

I sat down on the sofa, swallowing my tears. I found one of the paper towels from the last sob-session in a pocket, and blew my nose. God, I'd always despised wet females who sat weeping on sofas, and here I was turning into a tissue addict. 'Do they have any of those flavoured waters?' I managed.

'No. Mineral water or soft drinks only.'

'Oh . . . mineral water.' I blew my nose again.

Charles fetched me a bottle of Highland Spring and himself a cup of coffee. He sat down beside me and looked at me anxiously. 'Do you have any idea—' he began – then stopped.

'No,' I told him bitterly. 'I don't have any idea. What do I know about brains? Why the *hell* is that *corrupted* pseud so angry with me?'

'You just knocked a large hole in a theory he's been polishing for the past eight years. Look, I think . . . I think I need to explain some of the science, if you can stand it. I know you're kicked up, but he *will* insist on your being back there in half an hour, and . . . and I think it would help if you had some idea what's going on.'

I swigged the water and wiped my nose again. 'Yeah. OK.'

He was silent a moment. 'Probably you do know quite a lot about brains already,' he said apologetically. 'You've had a lot of treatment for brain injuries. But I'll try to keep it simple, and you can tell me if I'm overdoing the simplification.

'First off, the human brain is the most complicated object in the known universe, but we actually understand quite a lot about how it works. People still trot out that "We don't know the function of ninety per cent of our brain" line, but it's been false for a century now. We know how the brain develops well enough to repair it when it's damaged – a thing that was dismissed as impossible right up to the end of the last century. We understand the processes of vision and hearing, we have a pretty good idea how memories are formed, and we even understand something about the action of reason and free will. The thing we don't understand is consciousness. Consciousness has been the Holy Grail of cognitive science for the past forty years: everybody wants to bring it home in triumph, but nobody's managed it yet.'

' "Everybody" including Bernet?' I asked suspiciously.

He nodded. 'Definitely.'

'You said that he was working on . . . on personality integration and the right prefrontal cortex. Is that where consciousness is?'

He grimaced. 'No. There isn't any "centre of consciousness" in the brain, the way there are centres for visual processing or speech. Consciousness seems to be a pattern that can occur almost anywhere in the brain, depending on where we're directing our attention – that is, we are conscious *of* whatever thing we happen to be paying attention *to*, though that thing can be an external perception or an internal image or memory. We know that the brain cells around a focus of consciousness synchronise their firing somehow, forming a pattern on the surface of the brain like ripples from a stone tossed into the centre of a pool – but the stone is continually shifting position so fast that it's hard to detect. We don't know how the brain achieves that synchronisation, or how the epicentre of that pattern is formed. There's input from attentional mechanisms combined with some sort of global process, that's clear, but we don't understand it.

'What Professor Bernet's been working on, for a long time, involves the relationship between consciousness and personality. I suppose you're familiar with the concept of lateralisation?'

'You mean right brain and left brain?' I asked. 'Yeah. The right side of the brain controls the left side of the body and vice versa, right? And the right brain is supposed to be emotional and intuitive, but the left brain is supposed to be logical and verbal.'

'That's the popular cliché,' said Charles, wincing. 'Like most clichés it's got some truth to it, but it oversimplifies drastically. You have emotional wiring on *both* sides of your brain, but the left brain does contain most of the speech centres – though even that's more complicated than people think.'

'Music is supposed to happen in the right side of the brain,' I observed. It was one thing I was aware of, painfully so.

'Predominantly!' Charles said warningly. 'The real trouble with the cliché is that it understates how much of what the brain does, it does globally – and how much brains vary, and how flexible they are. There's practically *nothing* we do that involves only one bit of brain, or even only one side of the brain. But yes, music seems to use a lot of right-brain functions.' He smiled weakly. 'It normally relies heavily on the auditory cortex in the right temporal lobe, one of the parts of the brain which in your case was damaged and repaired.'

'But Bernet isn't interested in that.'

'No. As I said before, he's been working on the right prefrontal cortex. It's known to have a lot to do with personality and with social behaviour, and he's argued that it also has a role in, as it were, modulating consciousness. It can't be *crucial*, because you can lose your prefrontal cortex completely and still be conscious, but it could have a role in integrating consciousness with personality. He's been assembling his evidence for years, and has invested a lot in the idea.

'Now, one problem with most theories of consciousness is that they're impossible to test, because we have no access to any consciousness except our own. I know that *I* am conscious, but I have to take your word for it that you are: I cannot experience your consciousness any more than you can experience mine. Further, there's no observable feature of your behaviour which requires me to posit that you're self-aware. Obviously, I *assume* you are – but I can't prove it. In the last century some philosophers came up with a concept they called a "zombie". Stupid name, really: it makes people think of a living-dead brain-eater from a B-horror flick, when what they *mean* is somebody who has all the normal brain functions but isn't conscious. Some people have even argued that we're *all* zombies – that consciousness is just an illusion generated by the interaction of brain systems, and that we only *think* we possess it.' He paused. 'Most people don't find that argument very satisfying. I don't know, maybe it appeals to zombies.'

'You said you could *see* consciousness,' I objected. 'You said it made ripples of activity in the brain!'

'You can see it with a high-time-resolution Meg,' he agreed. 'It happens too fast to show up on an fMRI. And people who don't believe in it argue that it's just an irrelevant by-product.'

'What's a Meg? And you said that *my* MRI scans showed I had episodes!'

He ran a hand through his hair. 'One thing at a time! A Meg is an MEG – a magnetoencephalograph, a sort of successor to fMRI. A really good one will show the pattern produced by consciousness, if you don't mind your data coming in fast and dirty. You don't get that on fMRI because it takes too long to generate an image. What you can do with the fMRI is identify patterns associated with different states of consciousness in different subjects. For example, where a normal brain might show activity in, say, five places for a given cognitive task, a regenerated brain may show activity in seven or eight – the five needed, and another two or three which have nothing to do with the task and are presumably activated accidentally. That's the pattern which appeared on your old scans. Normally the excess activity is weak and diffuse, but occasionally it becomes abnormally intense, and then, it's believed, lapses of consciousness occur. But let me take things in order.'

He took a couple of deep breaths, frowning as he marshalled his thoughts. I wondered if the pink scrubbed look was really as objectionable as I'd always thought. 'Right!' he began again. 'For a long time Professor Bernet's theory of consciousness, like everyone else's, was impossible to test properly. Then suddenly the media was full of the problems that had resulted from an early and obscure experimental treatment for brain damage with the unmemorable name of Cerebral Implantation of Cloned Neural Progenitor Cells.'

'Cicnip-C,' I said, beginning to understand. 'Lapses in consciousness.'

'Exactly,' replied Charles, nodding. 'A Cicnip-C recipient during an episode of lapsed consciousness is a very good candidate for one of the philosophers' zombies: in possession of all his or her faculties, including speech and reason, apparently normal and coherent – but not conscious. At least, if the people who suffer an episode *are* conscious during it, they have no memory of it afterwards, and everyone inclines to accept their word for it that they weren't. Consciousness researchers have been ecstatic about it. I mean, there are other abnormal states of consciousness, but none of them promise to be as illuminating as Cicnip-C. You can *bet* we offered to help assess it! We would've paid over our entire research budgets for the chance!'

'And I had Cicnip-C to my right prefrontal cortex,' I said slowly. 'The bit Professor Bernet is most interested in.'

'Exactly,' said Charles again. 'Now, the current theory of *why* Cicnip-C recipients are prone to lapses in consciousness centres on the excess of activity it causes in the brain. A Cicnip-C-regenerated brain, it's argued, is just a bit *sloppier* than the home-grown sort, and turns brain systems on when they're not required, like a teenager putting on every light in the house when he only needs the one in the bathroom. When the brain has too many things on at once, goes the reasoning, and when they're on very strongly, then there are too many competing places for the epicentre of consciousness to form, so it doesn't form anywhere. In the resulting unconscious state there's nothing to coordinate and compare conflicting impulses, and the person may choose to act out impulses which would normally be controlled.' He shrugged. 'It's a reasonable theory. Professor Bernet, however, would expand on it. He predicted that a person with a Cicnip-C regenerated right prefrontal cortex should experience particularly frequent and severe defects in consciousness, coupled with a certain amount of 'freezing' from the regenerated part of the brain. His prediction was that such a person would suffer disturbances in personality – perhaps sudden shifts in behaviour, or difficulty in governing impulses.'

'Oh,' I said weakly.

Charles nodded again. 'Of course, when he saw your records, he realised that you couldn't have *severe* disturbances of any sort, or you would never have been discharged by your old health authority – but he thought perhaps you just had numerous small disorders. A spiderweb of fractures, he said last night, rather than a single jagged break. Instead—'

He gave me a sudden look of admiration. 'Instead you've displayed a singularly strong personality, and produced a neurological event that looked like an episode of lapsed consciousness without any disturbance of consciousness at all! It's an almighty spike in the wheels of his theory, and he's furious.'

'Oh,' I said again, and chewed the rim of the water bottle.

Charles was right in that the information was useful – at the very least, I understood why the professor had become so angry – but it also revealed new sources of confusion. If I had an episode of unlapsed consciousness every time I heard the music, then what was happening when I reached for the music and brought it out into the world? And did the fact that I had something like episodes but stayed conscious mean I was likely to be cleared sooner – or later? With or without surgery?

'What happens next?' I asked Charles. 'Presumably the professor will want to do scans with this Meg machine.'

He nodded. 'He'll want to do that, and I'm afraid he's also

going to want to give you a thorough grilling about the episodes – or events, or whatever you want to call them. I'm sorry. I realise you were afraid to talk about them at all.'

I chewed the water bottle some more. All right: I liked Charles. He had warned me. He had been sympathetic. He had stood up for me to his professor, and been threatened for it. He had been unfailingly kind and helpful from the moment I met him. But could I trust him?

Perhaps I had no choice. They'd found the music: who knew what else they'd find? I was afraid. I needed help.

He cut short my inner debate. 'What does it *feel* like?' he asked curiously.

I shrugged. 'It's like hearing music. Well, sort of halfway between hearing and performing it. I've never been in any doubt that it was something I was creating.'

'So what you hear is music you're actually composing on the spot? Not just something you've heard somewhere before? That would explain why the activity in the frontal cortex is so intense! Was it originally simple, and got more complicated as you grew older? – Oh, I'm sorry. I didn't mean to start grilling you myself; it's just I—'

'I don't mind,' I told him. Actually, it was something of a relief to talk about it. I suppose I'd suspected for a long time that there was something abnormal about the music, though I hadn't really worried about it until the Cicnip thing blew up. I'd worried a great deal since, of course.

'It's all music I create,' I told him, 'though there's usually a whole lot of borrowing – you know, a bit of Mozart here, a little Gorecki there. But you're absolutely right, it used to be a lot simpler.' I gave him a rather wobbly smile. 'When I was little it was just little jingles and bleepy tunes like the ones on the nursery programmes. It got more complicated as I started to like more complicated music, and as soon as I started studying guitar it started to involve the guitar a lot. Not all the time, but a lot.' I paused, then added, 'It reflects my mood. You know, loud and fast if I'm angry or upset, sweet and dreamy if I'm feeling lazy and happy, slow and sad if I'm depressed. Sort of a soundtrack for my life, I guess. A funny thing, though, is that it always uses traditional forms – nothing chromatic or atonal or modal. I mean, I *love* Jiang Qi, and once I played the *Five Landscapes* for a concert. I was rehearsing them for hours at a stretch for *weeks*. You'd think it would soak in – but no, there's never been anything that wasn't composed strictly according to the formal Western canons.'

He looked utterly nonplussed.

'Don't you like classical music?' I asked, with a sinking feeling.

'I don't really know much about it,' he admitted. 'I sort of thought . . . that is, you were carrying a guitar, you were studying at a media arts place—'

I gave him a look of disgust. 'What?'

'I assumed you were doing something more . . . I don't know, popular. Theatrical.'

'You thought I did *musicals?* Pop-rock-metal? Dartington *isn't* just theatre and media arts. The music department has been growing for years, and is one of the most prestigious in the country!'

'I wouldn't know,' said Charles humbly. 'I'm just an ignorant neuroscientist. I *like* musicals.'

'Oh, horror!' I exclaimed, and unexpectedly found myself laughing. 'I am trapped in a cognitive research institution, menaced by a malevolent professor, and my only helper is an Andrew Lloyd Webber fan!'

'Gilbert and Sullivan fan,' Charles corrected me, straight-faced. 'And I like Sondheim and Cindy Levi, too.'

'Oh, that's all right then.'

We grinned at each other.

'Actually,' I admitted, 'I like Gilbert and Sullivan too. And some pop. That's one reason I went to Dartington: because you get a bit of everything there. I just like classical *most*.'

Charles nodded, then sobered suddenly as he remembered what we were supposed to be talking about. 'Look,' he said resolutely, 'I'll try to . . . that is, I'll do everything I can to see that the Department of Health is aware that you don't suffer from lapses of consciousness and accepts that you aren't dangerous and don't need treatment. But the fact that your brain isn't behaving the way the theory says it should is going to make it harder. It will take longer to clear you. I'm sorry.'

'The thing I've really been afraid of,' I confessed, slowly, 'is that somebody will decide that the part of my brain that does the music is dangerously defective, and cut it out. I don't see how they could do that and leave me with any musical ability worth thinking about, and I couldn't stand losing it. I'd rather be deaf and paralysed. If that happens I . . . I couldn't stand it. But anything else – if it takes a long time, if there are a lot of tests, if that horrible man shouts at me – I won't like it, but it's something I can endure. I only want to come out intact in the end.'

'I understand,' said Charles, looking at me earnestly. 'I promise you, you will.' He looked at his watch. 'We ought to get back. Do you want to use the washroom first?'

Four

V aleria Thornham vs. Prof M. Bernet, round two: two hours' slogging, no blows landed. I went back to Room 4, and, as Charles had predicted, the professor grilled me about the 'anomalous brain events'. I answered him honestly: they'd been going on as long as I could remember, they typically occurred a couple of dozen times a day and lasted between a few seconds and ten minutes, they never involved any loss of consciousness. I felt a bit uncomfortable about saying the last, but it was true, as far as hearing the music at the back of my mind went. I might decide to confess the whole truth to Charles, but it seemed better to exercise caution even with him, and I certainly wasn't going to tell the professor any more than I had to. I might be mistaken about Charles, but I was already certain that I was not mistaken about Professor Michel Bernet. He was a horrible man.

We did some more fMRI scans, this time with tasks involving the right prefrontal cortex. The professor wasn't happy with the results, but at least he didn't scream at me, and at twelve thirty we were allowed to break for lunch.

The professor wanted to speak to Charles, no doubt to give him some more work, so Charles escorted me to the hall and then went wearily back to his master. I continued to the dining room, feeling highly indignant. I remembered that Charles had missed his breakfast on my account, and, for that matter, probably hadn't had time for supper the previous evening: it was unfair for the professor to make him miss lunch!

The dining room was already crowded. I went over to the sideboard and helped myself to some of the mouth-watering array of salads – then hesitated, looking for somewhere to sit.

Claire, Jack and Miriam were sharing a large table with three others I didn't know. Claire was staring at me – a stare I knew all too well, the compound of curiosity and revulsion I'd stayed in my room at Dartington to avoid. When she realised I'd noticed, she looked hastily away and pretended to be deeply engaged in conversation with her neighbour. Damn.

Then I noticed the dumpy red-headed staff member, Suzy, waving at me from another table. As soon as she was sure she'd caught my eye, she pulled a spare chair over from the neighbouring table and nudged it towards me invitingly. Maybe she wanted to apologise. I went over and sat down.

It appeared to be a staff table: the five men and women sitting at it were all older than the student 'participants' and less casually dressed. They all gave me speculative looks that made me feel like an elk being inspected by a wolf pack. They definitely knew why I was at Laurel Hall, and they were professionally interested. The salads no longer seemed so enticing.

Suzy, however, was brash and casual. 'Hi,' she said. 'I'm Dr Susan Jones. I didn't catch your name earlier.'

'Valeria Thornham.'

'Right. Look, do you know if Professor Bernet is going to want the MRI this afternoon, too?'

So much for apologies. 'He wants the Meg this afternoon,' I informed her, and tried the pasta salad.

One of the men at the table – a younger Asian man – groaned, and asked 'When?' I noticed that he seemed fed up, certainly, but also resigned. There was no question of protesting his prior claim.

'He told me to be there at two.'

The man scowled. 'To finish when?'

I shook my head and shrugged. 'I wish I knew.'

That renewed the speculative looks. 'You're the right prefrontal Cicnip assessment, yeah?' asked another of the men, this one bearded and about forty. 'How's it going?'

You see wolves doing it on wildlife documentaries: just a casual run at the elk, to see what sort of shape it's in. Just out of interest, not because they're hungry.

'One thing I don't understand,' I said loudly, 'is how come Professor Bernet can throw the rest of you off an MRI or a Meg any time he likes, even when it completely messes up your schedules and the schedules of your volunteers. I mean, you must have to pay them to sit around doing nothing while he uses the equipment.'

There was a moment of surprised and uncomfortable silence.

'Is it because he's the head of the institute?'

The Beard shifted uneasily. 'He's also on the Apollo Foundation Board.'

I looked around the table at the wary faces. 'You mean he controls who gets funds?'

Nobody said anything, but I knew I'd got it right, and they knew I knew.

'He's a really horrible man, isn't he?' I remarked conversationally, and took another forkful of salad. 'He threatened Dr Spencer.'

'What?' asked Suzy sharply.

I met her eyes: they were concerned. Well, why *not* make trouble for Bernet? 'You know Professor Bernet has a pet theory about consciousness and the right prefrontal cortex? This morning all the results he got from me contradicted it, and he lost his temper. He started shouting at me and saying that I'd been lying. I was in the MRI helmet, with my head clamped, and he came over and grabbed the chair and screamed right into my face. I was really scared. Charles – Dr Spencer, that is – told him to stop, and said that it was outrageous for him to accuse me of lying when he hadn't let me tell him anything to begin with – which he hadn't; he'd just told Charles to hook me up to the machine. So Professor Bernet swore at him instead, and said, "I promise you, you keep your mouth shut and do as I tell you, or this will be your last job."'

'My God!' murmured the Beard, very shocked.

Suzy's eyes were hot. 'That's going too far!'

'Now, Suzy!' said the third man of the party, a plump jolly man with a bald spot. 'Bernet was just mouthing off.'

'Stop making excuses for him!' snarled Suzy. 'He's been bullying Spence ever since the poor guy got here, and we've all just looked the other way. He has him up all hours of the night collating data, he sends him off on personal errands, he has him on call twenty-four hours a day! I don't think Spence has had as much as a day off since Easter. It's disgraceful!'

I noted, with some horror, that her indignation was all for Charles Spencer. The way Bernet had treated *me* barely seemed to register.

'Spencer can take it,' replied Baldie. 'And it was his choice. The job was advertised as assistant to Bernet, and he was sweating to come work with the Great Man even *after* he'd met him.'

'So you'll just sit by while Bernet exploits a promising young researcher, then kills him with a stinking reference?'

'He hasn't *done* it,' protested Baldie. 'There's no reason to think he will. He just lost his temper.' He glanced at me. 'And if his longed-for Cicnip-to-the-right-prefrontal-cortex subject has just made his theory go pear-shaped, you can understand why.'

Suzy fumed. The fifth member of the party, a dark-haired younger woman, asked me curiously, 'So you *don't* have particularly severe lapses of consciousness?'

'No,' I said savagely. 'In fact, I have never had a lapse of consciousness in my life. And I am not Professor Bernet's *subject*. Legally, I'm here under the Mental Health Act, being assessed as to whether I'm a threat to the public – and, incidentally, I'm absolutely certain I'm not. I didn't volunteer *or* consent to take part in research into consciousness, and I hate it that all of you just casually accept that I can be hijacked, detained against my will, experimented on *ad-lib* by the head of your institution, and shouted at and called a liar when I fail to support his pet theory. I am going to complain to the Medical Research Council and to the Apollo Foundation. What are your names?'

The elk turns out to be a cougar. The researchers all stared in surprise and misgiving.

'Hi,' said Charles, turning up behind me with a tray of macaroni cheese. He looked round the table, and added nervously, 'Is something wrong?'

'What are these guys' names?' I demanded.

He stammered, then introduced them. The Asian was Ahmed Uzin; the Beard was Simon Kozetsky; the dark-haired woman was Bernice Silves, and Baldie was William Hammond.

'Right,' I said sweetly. 'I will be sure to mention you all by name.'

'Look,' began Hammond.

'Look at what? It's perfectly clear that you all *know* that Bernet wants to use me to research consciousness: he took your equipment out from under your noses to do it! You accept it. I told you how he behaved towards me. None of you expressed the least surprise or concern. If he wants to experiment on human subjects without their consent, that's perfectly OK by you; the only thing that worries you is the possibility that he might give a colleague a bad reference.' I picked up my plate and stood up. 'I'm going to phone my father and start complaining. I *very* much hope that the result is a black mark permanently affixed to the record of each and every one of you.'

'Val, what—' began Charles.

I turned and fixed him with the coldest look I could muster. Reason, crawling after the explosion of emotion like sound after light, told me that the fact that he'd desperately wanted the job of Professor Bernet's assistant didn't mean that he wasn't genuinely disillusioned with the man now. It wasn't *necessarily* true that he'd been stringing me along, playing nice cop to the professor's nasty one, in order to persuade me to cooperate with their joint programme of research. But I remembered how he'd begun to look worried as soon as I'd announced that I wouldn't go along with anything more than the bare assessment, and how his discomfort had grown after my father had spoken to him – telling him, I was now certain, that I'd never had an episode, and hence that his mentor's theory was wrong.

I could believe that he wanted the research to proceed in a nice, gentlemanly fashion, with the cooperation of the subject. But I also believed he was determined it *should* proceed, and to that end had duped me. Dear God, I'd almost told him everything!

'I think we'd better go back to "Miss Thornham",' I told him. I took my plate of salad and walked out.

Nobody was using the computer in the entrance hall: they were all at lunch. I puzzled over it for a minute or so, then gave up and used the videophone to get Mrs Mickleson. She swept in from somewhere in the back of the house and set up the clearance for the outside call. She didn't seem to mind that I'd interrupted her lunch, and chatted happily.

'Really it has to be cleared by a member of the research staff,' she informed me, 'but it's all right, I remember Dr Spencer said he was going to arrange it. I'll type in his code . . . there! Now you can phone that number as often as you like, and the charges will go to your name. Do you want to set up some Internet access as well?'

I did, but I was worried that Charles might follow me again. It seemed very likely that he'd never actually intended to give me the clearance, and I wanted to get my phone call in fast. 'Maybe later,' I said, 'or maybe I'll just wait until I have my own phone back. Thanks a lot.'

It was no use phoning home – my parents would both be at work. I'd got the clearance for my father's work number. When I rang it, all I got was his answering machine. I left a message explaining the situation as well as I could, and asking my dad to contact the local health authority and to get legal advice. Charles came in just as I was hanging up.

'Look—' he began – and stopped.

'I'm looking,' I replied, doing so.

'The others say that you're threatening to complain. I thought . . .'

'What?'

'I thought we'd agreed that you'd cooperate until I could get you cleared.'

I picked up my plate of salad and rested it on my knees. 'I am going to cooperate until I'm cleared or referred back to my own local health authority for assessment.' I scooped up a forkful of food. 'I'm also going to do everything I can to ensure that one or the other of those events happens soon. You never had any intention of doing the same, did you?'

'That's grossly unfair!' His face was flushed.

I shrugged, finished chewing. 'If you say so. But I don't trust you, Charles. You never mentioned that you were Professor Bernet's research assistant, that you'd come here specifically to work with him – that this research programme you were so *very* eager to get me to cooperate with was one you were working on yourself.'

Emotions warred on his face: anger, fierce disappointment – guilt. Ah. I'd thought so. I hadn't thought getting confirmation of it would hurt so much.

'Look, Val, please . . .' he began.

I got up. 'I'm going to finish this in my room,' I informed him, hefting the salad. 'You can come and fetch me at two. I've told you, I'll cooperate until I get out of here: I'm going to assume that your warning wasn't *complete* bollocks, and I'm not going to give anybody an excuse to play rough. But I *will* get out of here just as soon as I possibly can. I prefer grotty NHS wards, queues and callbacks to self-serving *liars*, thank you very much.'

I left him saying, 'Val, please!' which was at least some satisfaction.

In fact, I wasn't in my room at two. I thought of another safeguard I could use: I phoned Mrs Mickleson and asked if the house had any videomatic cameras I could borrow.

'I'm sure your sessions are already being recorded,' she informed me in surprise. 'Test sessions are always recorded, so that they can be analysed and compared afterwards.'

'But I want an *independent* record!' I said fiercely. 'One that can't be edited afterwards.' And I told her what had happened that morning, and explained about the professor's private research project.

I was relieved to see that, unlike the researchers, Amrita Mickleson was shocked and dismayed. Oh, all right: I did play up to her quite a lot. I did the hapless-young-female-student act, and wailed about how *horrible* the professor had been to me, and how *scared* I was. Competent, motherly women reliably go all protective about frightened girls, and Mrs Mickleson genuinely was a competent motherly woman. She told me she would speak to her husband; at quarter to two she phoned back to say I could borrow the Mickleson's own videomatic. When I went downstairs to collect it, I discovered that she had also opened a file on the house computer system, logged my call to her, and locked it with a dated tamper-proof seal.

'We'll put the file from the videomatic in next to it,' Mrs Mickleson told me warmly. 'And my husband agrees with me that if that man tries to bully you again, we'll use it as evidence when we file a formal complaint about him. You make sure he knows that.'

'Thank you very much,' I said, meaning it.

She smiled nervously, then squared her shoulders and announced, 'I'll walk you to his office.'

I hesitated. I badly wanted help and support, but her demeanour made it clear that she feared that supporting me could get her into trouble. I was already feeling a bit guilty about the way I'd taken advantage of her, and I didn't want to be responsible for getting her sacked. I nerved myself and did the Right Thing. 'I don't want you to get into any trouble because of me,' I declared nobly. 'I mean, the other researchers were saying that Professor Bernet isn't just head of the Laurel Hall Centre, he's on the Apollo Foundation Board and controls the funding.'

'I'll just walk you through the security systems, then,' she said, with evident relief. Then, however, *she* hesitated, nerved herself, and did the Right Thing. 'But if you do need help, dear, you *can* call.'

'Thank you very much,' I said again.

V. Thornham vs. Prof M. Bernet, round three. Amrita Mickleson walked me through the security systems to the professor's office, and left me there. There was a low murmur of voices behind the door. I knocked tentatively, but apparently nobody heard. I was about to knock again, when the professor's voice was raised and he said, 'There are major abnormalities!'

I paused. The other voice murmured a reply I couldn't make out.

'*Ça ne coute pas!*' snarled the professor. 'Anyone looking at the scans would say she suffers lapses. There would be no difficulty obtaining it.'

'Sir, she's already telephoned her father!' said the other speaker, more loudly – and yes, it was Charles. 'He *is* going to make trouble if he finds out that you've put his daughter in a mental hospital. And if there's an enquiry, you *can't* justify it. The evidence is *not there*, sir.'

'Her father!' sneered Bernet. 'And who is he? A shop manager, a bank clerk?'

Charles's voice dropped again, and I put my ear against the door. Classic stupid-eavesdropper position, compromising as hell if I were caught – but I needed to hear.

'. . . professional people. She mentioned an aunt who's a lawyer. There's her college to think about, too: when I phoned them they said one of her tutors had already been in an argument with the Department of Health about whether she should even be assessed. Sir, I'm telling you: there *will* be an almighty stink if you do it. And correct me if I'm wrong, but I have the impression that you left the CNRS' – he said the initials in French, *say-en-er-es* – 'under a cloud. Would you be able to *survive* an enquiry?'

There was a silence. I wondered when Charles had phoned Dartington. I wondered which of my tutors had been arguing with the Department of Health on my behalf. Probably Montero, my guitar coach – though it would be more satisfying if it were Prof Frasier, whom I had for composition. I wondered what the CNRS was, and what Bernet had done there.

'Why did you *allow* her to telephone, you imbecile?' demanded the professor at last.

'She'd already phoned from the police station. And, sir, she was referred here and is officially in our custody: our involvement is a matter of public record. If her father didn't hear from her and turned up on the doorstep demanding to know what we're doing to her, what were you planning to tell him?'

There was another silence, and then the professor admitted reluctantly. '*Tu as raison* . . . You suggest what, then?'

A pause, and then Charles said, 'Just that we do a very

thorough assessment, sir. We can certainly justify that, and I'd say it would cover eighty per cent of what you want anyway.'

'But you say she is threatening to have herself transferred!'

'Sir, we have reasonable grounds to oppose it. The brain events are anomalous and puzzling. We have the equipment to study them; the NHS doesn't, unless it diverts some from critical care. If there's no question of abuse, sir, there shouldn't be a problem. If there *is* a question of abuse, though . . . sir, don't you see that you have to take what you can get, or risk losing everything?'

There was a silence, and in it, I heard footsteps. Abruptly terrified that I'd get caught, I leapt back from the door. I glanced around anxiously, but there was nobody to be seen in the corridor: the footsteps must have been from one of the rooms, or from upstairs. Still, I felt I'd better take what I'd got, and not risk anything more. I backed off to the end of the corridor in silence, then began to walk back down it, as though I were just arriving.

Good move: Charles opened the door when I was about halfway there. He saw me and recoiled.

'Hi,' I said. 'It was two o'clock and you didn't come, so I asked Mrs Mickleson to walk me through security.'

'Oh,' said Charles, glancing back up the corridor. 'She shouldn't have just left you in the corridor.'

'I don't think she likes Professor Bernet any more than I do,' I told him coldly. '*I* wouldn't actually speak to the toad if I didn't have to.'

Charles grimaced and escorted me back to the professor's office.

Bernet was sitting behind his desk looking angry and tired and a bit unwell. He greeted me with a sneer of intense dislike.

'She got Mrs Mickleson to bring her through lab security,' Charles informed his master.

I switched the videomatic on, looked through the viewfinder and focused on the professor.

'What is that?' demanded Bernet, affronted.

'Videomatic camera,' I informed him evenly. I set it down on one of the bookshelves, noting in passing that the leather-

77

bound tomes were an elderly encyclopedia in several volumes. Ha! I'd *known* he was a poseur. 'I borrowed it from Mr and Mrs Mickleson. I'll feel more comfortable about these sessions if I have a record of what happens.'

Bernet glared. 'There is no need for that machine! We have a recording system.'

'Excuse me,' I told him coldly, 'but I want my *own* record.'

Charles covered his eyes with his hand. The professor glared harder.

'You shouted at me,' I told him. 'You accused me of lying. I was terrified you were going to hit me. When Dr Spencer tried to intervene, you swore at him and threatened to ruin his career. When I spoke to your staff at lunch, I found out that you've been desperate to get hold of someone who had Cicnip to the right prefrontal cortex, and they all take it absolutely for granted that you aren't assessing me, you're using me as research fodder for your own theory about how consciousness works. As a result of all this, professor, I have lost confidence in you, and I want my own record of these sessions.'

He opened his mouth, and I went on ruthlessly, 'I am *not* trying to avoid assessment for Cicnip. I'm perfectly willing to have that done, and I'll cooperate with the process – and since I don't know what you need to do for it, that means I'm bound to cooperate with whatever tests you say are necessary. But I also want it on record that I have not consented, and do not consent, to taking part in any purely scientific research—'

'You ignorant bitch!' exploded Bernet. 'You do not *consent* to take part in finding a solution to the most important mystery known to humanity?'

'No,' I replied, looking him in the eye. 'I don't. Ignorant bitches aren't interested in anything like that.'

The professor began to swear, then glanced at the videomatic and stopped himself with a visible effort. He sat and looked at me with the fixed glare of a tomcat facing an intruder on its territory.

'An educated and intelligent woman ought to be interested,' Charles said suddenly. 'Particularly when the mystery is inside her own head.'

'An educated and intelligent woman would be treated with respect!' I told him fiercely. 'She'd have had the whole situation explained to her, she'd have been kept informed, she'd have been consulted. So I must be an ignorant bitch, mustn't I?'

He had the grace to look away and blush.

'Anyway,' I went on, with a shrug. 'I've borrowed the videomatic. If the sessions are being recorded anyway, you should have no objection to me making a record, too – unless you've been intending to edit your recordings or withhold them from public scrutiny, which I hope you haven't.'

The professor's glare became murderous. God, the man scared me.

'I've said I'm willing to cooperate,' I added. 'You wanted me at two. What do we do?'

What we did was use the Meg, which was down the corridor. In appearance this machine was very much like the MRI, except that the helmet was bigger and thicker and you had to lie down on a specially designed couch to wear it. You also had to wear a little cap full of sensors. The controls, in contrast, were smaller and simpler. I submitted to being clamped in, fixed my eyes on the ceiling, and waited while the two men adjusted things until they were satisfied with the reception. (No, I did not forget the videomatic. It had a good view of the proceedings.)

'When are you likely to have another anomalous brain event?' asked the professor gratingly, as though it hurt him to have to speak to me.

If he'd been American, I thought, he would've started to call them ABEs. I was glad he was French.

'I could try to make one happen now,' I offered.

There was a moment of silence, and then Bernet cried indignantly, 'You said they were *involuntary!*'

'I *tried* to explain,' I replied angrily. 'You wouldn't let me. You wouldn't let me *tell* you anything: you just wanted answers to your questions, *vite vite*, and no backchat.'

'I'm sorry,' said Charles quietly. 'Can you induce these events?'

I stared up at the light fixture. It was very boring: an institutional low-energy bulb on an institutional white panel ceiling. I supposed that the Georgian elegance of the common areas must be unhygienic or something. 'Some of the time I can get the music to start by thinking about something I heard before and trying to get it to continue,' I informed him grudgingly. 'Sometimes I can make it stop, too. It doesn't always work, though, either way.'

'What makes it stop?'

'Putting on some other music, or trying to play something different. Writing an essay. Playing tennis. That sort of thing. It doesn't always work.'

'Try and induce an event,' said Charles, then added awkwardly, 'Please.'

I thought about the music I'd heard that morning. Guitar and woodwinds, in A major . . . no, that piece had had a definite closure: there was no way I could make it go on. On the other hand, there'd been that piece with the cello, *andante cantabile*, very pretty, probably heavily influenced by Beethoven, and it had just trailed off. What it *needed* was a bit of dialogue . . . say a violin, coming in just *there* . . .

The violin sang out fiercely at the top of its range, hard against the fading melody of the cello; another followed, and then the viola joined them. The cello replied, deep and slow, no longer *cantabile* but *sostenuto*, with a deep burning anger. I closed my eyes, listening to it. I was aware of the two men exclaiming and adjusting in the background, but once again their utterances revealed nothing.

The music ended. Charles said quietly, 'Val?'

'Miss Thornham!' I insisted.

'Miss Thornham,' he agreed unhappily, after a pause. 'Were you conscious?'

'I certainly thought so,' I replied acidly. 'I suppose your sweet Meg tells you otherwise?'

'No,' he told me. 'According to the Meg, you were fully conscious. Can . . . can you tell me anything about the music?'

I opened my eyes and stared at the ceiling again. 'It was a string quartet in G. It grew out of a cello solo I heard the other evening, and I got it to start by deciding it needed another instrument.' I hesitated a moment, then added, 'I don't think the two pieces really fit together. If I were going to write it up, I'd have to alter one or the other fairly drastically.'

And I knew which of the two pieces I'd chuck. The cello solo had been pretty, but not very interesting. I thought about the the way the violins had come in, hard and high, and the way the cello had argued with them. If I moved that argument back, made it softer, used it in place of the too-facile melody . . . well, all right, I had the makings of a nice second movement there. What to do for the first?

'What are you doing?' demanded the professor harshly.

I'd temporarily forgotten I was still clamped to the Meg. 'I was just thinking about how to shape the music up into something.'

'You weren't trying to induce another event?' Charles asked disappointedly.

I snorted. 'No. Anyway, I'm pretty sure I couldn't. It's too soon.'

'There's a period to them?'

A 'period'. As though music were a kind of mental disorder. Jesus Christ! 'Look,' I told him, 'this is *music*, not a random succession of notes! I don't just *babble* it. Its order and structure have to be *created*. It may be involuntary but, as I've told you all along, I *know* I'm creating it. It takes *effort*, and I can't keep it up for too long at a stretch.'

'Please!' protested Charles. 'We are aware that your brain is working very hard during the events. The scanners show that very clearly. But we can't know what it *feels* like, unless you tell us.'

There was a silence. I flexed my fingers and stared up at the ceiling. An integral part of my being was being isolated and teased out as though it were a deformed and unnatural growth. Misery tightened my throat so that I was afraid I'd start crying again.

'*Do* you ever write out any of this music?' asked Charles.

I shrugged, as well as I could lying on a couch with my head clamped. 'I use ideas from it all the time.'

'Ideas?'

Talking was at least a distraction from the abominable

feeling. 'You really don't know much about music, do you? Look, when you're doing science, you must get ideas about a subject, but it's not the same thing as a . . . a . . . whatever you have when you've worked on them and sorted them out and written them up.'

'Research paper,' said Charles.

'Right. It's the same with music. You get ideas – melodies, contrasting instrumental effects, rhythmical tricks and so on – but if you're going to do anything with them, you have to work on them. You have to find a way to fit them together into a coherent shape – a song with a beginning, middle and end, say, or a string quartet in four movements. The music I hear at the back of my mind contains lots of ideas, but mostly they're short and not very original. If I hear something I like, I may use it, but it's always going to need a lot of deliberate shaping if it's going to be worth anything.' Except on the occasions when I reached for the music and brought it out of the back of my mind without any intervening passage through consciousness – and I wasn't going to talk about them.

'Oh. You're talking about composing?'

I rolled my eyes. 'Are there music degrees which *don't* include some composition?'

That was an evasion, of course. But it's a hard thing for a young woman to say she wants to be a composer. There aren't *any* really great female composers, unless you count Clara Schumann, and I'm afraid I don't. I have ambitions, sure, but I don't know how good I am, and I've always wanted to be certain I know what I'm doing before I come forward. The trouble with the limelight is that it shows up everything that's wrong with you.

The professor gave a harsh snort of amusement. 'So,' he said, 'you make good use of these events. You adapt the music you hear and submit it to your composition classes!'

I set my teeth. 'I use *ideas* from it, Professor Bernet. Other people get ideas from other composers, or from folk songs and pop songs and things they hear on the radio. I get ideas from the same things, only I get them subconsciously as well as consciously. I put just as much work into *shaping* my ideas as

82

anybody else. If I submitted some jumble of bits and pieces from the back of my mind, I'd fail the course.'

Whereas in fact I was far from failing the course. I wondered again if it could possibly be Prof Frasier who was trying to take on the Department of Health for me. He was a vague, reserved, scholarly man who didn't seem to care about anyone much, but I knew that he did like the things I'd been composing recently. My thoughts went to a piece I'd entered in a national competition. The results would be announced in August. What if I'd won – and no longer possessed the part of my mind that had created it?

It was stupid still to be so afraid of that. I did not suffer from episodes of lapsed consciousness. Not from just *hearing* the music, anyway. As for the other business, the experience of reaching for it and bringing it out – I wouldn't even *think* about that.

Professor Bernet sneered slightly, but did not challenge me. Instead he asked, 'How soon will it be before you can induce another event?'

I 'induced' three more 'events' that afternoon, and did cognitive tasks in between them. It was numbingly stressful and grindingly depressing, and when they finally unclamped me and let me up I was trembling and unsteady on my feet. Charles tried to take my arm, but I knocked his hand away. I picked up the videomatic and let him escort me back to the residential part of the hall.

'Can I get you a cup of coffee or anything?' he asked, with a look towards the lounge.

'You can leave me alone, is what you can do,' I snarled, and continued on towards the stairs.

'Look, Val, please,' he began, trying to take my arm again. 'You don't understand. I really was trying to help. If you had—'

I shook him off. 'Leave me alone!' I told him again. 'Get it into your head: I am not some sweet little snail who's going to say, "Oh well, he was totally dishonest with me, but he really was trying to help me as well as himself, so I'll forgive him." I *don't care* if you were genuinely concerned to see that nothing terrible happened to me while the research went ahead: the main thing is you lied to me to ensure that it *did* go ahead. You're trying to have your cake and eat it, and you're willing to lie to both sides. I would have to be completely turgid to trust you. You can get screwed.' I marched up a few steps, then turned and looked back at his angry face. 'And not by me, either!'

I climbed the stairs the rest of the way to the second floor, stumbled along to my room, and collapsed on the bed.

After a little while, the back of my mind produced a solo guitar playing something very slow entirely on the D string. I listened to it with my eyes wide open and stinging. *My heart and soul, are you nothing more than a warping of the fabric of my brain?*

The music ended. I closed my eyes and listened to my own breathing and the soft sound of the breeze around the roof slates. What has music ever been but a creation of the mind? Birds don't sing like humans, let alone violins: they do nothing but proclaim a territory and a willingness to breed. To suspend the deepest conceptions of the spirit in a web of sound – that requires a human mind. Did it matter if the brain which produced that mind had been torn and inexpertly patched together? Surely the mind's power to create music was the ultimate proof that all was well?

The Megs and MRIs didn't seem to see it that way. They saw a damaged and abnormal brain generating mysterious and anomalous 'events'. Oh God, would I ever feel whole again?

Through the window came the sound of voices and laughter, followed, faintly but unmistakably, by the sound of ball on racket: some of the 'participants' were playing tennis. I didn't want to listen to them. I went over to the computer and selected some Gorecki, then lay on the bed listening to it. After a while I checked my watch and saw that it was nearly seven. If I wanted some supper, I should go downstairs.

To hell with supper. I couldn't face the stares of the participants, the protests of the staff – if they were still around, which I supposed was unlikely if they only came in during the day. Charles would be around, though, and I wanted to see him least of all. I stayed where I was, feeling hungry and desperately sorry for myself.

My parents phoned a little later. Mrs Mickleson routed the call up to me without comment, and I was relieved to see that incoming calls were accepted. I was also relieved to see my parents' images filling the videophone screen – but disappointed, too. I'd been hoping fiercely that my father at least would arrive in person. I wanted a shoulder to cry on.

He had a good excuse for not making the drive, however: he'd got my message, and had spent the afternoon talking to the local health authority and the Department of Health, consulting the Citizens' Advice Bureau and looking for a lawyer. Everyone wanted more details. He'd tried to phone me back during the afternoon, he said, but Mrs Mickleson had told him that I was busy having tests. So, he said, now that he'd got hold of me, could I give him a detailed rundown on the situation so he could get back to the other people first thing in the morning?

It was better than a shoulder to cry on, though it didn't feel that way at first. My parents were angry and indignant, prepared to fight and expecting to win. (And no, my father isn't a shop manager or a bank clerk: he's Head of Music in a large comprehensive school in Birmingham. Not, perhaps, a job that the likes of Prof Bernet would recognise as powerful and important, but one which nevertheless requires a great deal of toughness and organisational skill. My mother, however, *is* a shop manager, and Bernet's apparent belief that such people are spineless and easily dismissed is egregiously mistaken.)

I talked to my parents for quite a long time. I even told them about the music, though perhaps I misrepresented it. ('Sometimes I kind of do impromptu compositions in my head, and apparently when they look at it with an MRI scanner it looks like an episode of lapsed consciousness, only of course I *don't* lose consciousness, so they're treating it as something abnormal.') That made them even more indignant, which made me feel better: maybe the abnormality really was all in the eyes of the beholder! I told them about the videomatic and said that I thought Prof Bernet might be backing off a bit, and I told them that there was a suggestion he'd had to resign from his last post,

85

with something called the CNRS, because of some kind of trouble. My father at once suggested that we contact the Medical Research Council or the General Medical Council; I supplemented the proposal with the Apollo Foundation Board.

'We'll take it to the European Court if we have to,' vowed my father. 'But I expect they'll back off as soon as they realise we won't take it lying down.'

'From what Val said, they're backing off already,' agreed my mother with satisfaction. 'But don't worry, darling, we'll keep up the pressure.'

They assured me that they would phone again the following day, once they'd established the legal position. In the meantime, I was to keep my chin up and not let the bastards grind me down. I promised I would, and wouldn't, respectively, and they said goodnight.

When the screen had gone dark, of course, I felt worse than ever. I sat staring at it for a while, then went and picked up my guitar. I didn't play anything, just sat holding it, stroking the smoothness of the wood.

I was tired, of course, after getting up so early and after the stresses of the abominable day. I was getting ready to go to bed at about half-past nine when there was a knock at the door.

'Who is it?' I asked suspiciously.

'It's me,' said Charles. 'Charles Spencer. I came to return your earrings.'

My hands flew involuntarily to my earlobes. Oh, yes. The blue-green enamel earrings which I'd put on so early that morning to accentuate my eyes and impress Charles Spencer, and which he'd asked me to take off for the MRI. I glared at the door.

'I can't open it!' I reminded him. 'It's after eight.'

The door buzzed and opened. I yelped and grabbed the bedspread: as I said, I'd been getting ready for bed, and I was only wearing a T-shirt.

'Sorry,' said Charles, averting his gaze and holding out the earrings in one hand.

I hauled the bedspread round me. 'How come you can open my door?' I demanded indignantly.

'I'm the doctor on call,' he explained apologetically. 'My key has to be programmed for all the rooms, just in case there's an emergency.'

I snorted. He was still holding out the earrings. I marched over and snatched them. 'OK, you've returned them. Now get out.'

'Look. Please. You keep saying I lied to you, but I haven't. You don't realise—'

'That you're actually a knight in shining armour? No, I don't.'

'Everything I told you is true.'

'And a lot of things which you *didn't* tell me are also true.'

'Look. Professor Bernet is one of the most distinguished figures in modern neuroscience. He *invented* the method of chemical guidelining used in SGNS, and his work on personality integration could be ground-breaking. When this job was advertised, there were dozens of people applying for it. If you had the opportunity of working with a musician whose music you deeply admired, you'd take it, wouldn't you? Even if you didn't like him personally. The fact that I assist the professor doesn't mean I agree with the way he treats people! I've been trying to protect you since we got you. I—'

'Shut up,' I said tightly. 'I don't want to hear it.'

'You're being completely inconsistent! You got angry because we didn't inform you or consult you, but when I try to establish enough communication with you to do that, you don't want to hear it!'

'You've been trying to protect me since you *got* me,' I repeated bitterly. 'Sounds like you're talking about an experimental animal. Yesterday I was a human being. Now I feel like a freak. You want a full programme of research into my fascinating right prefrontal cortex, but that bit of brain happens to belong to *me*, and it's something I use all the time. It's not just an . . . an *object*, a thing you can take out and photograph and put back again: it's something central to what I *am*, and you've been poking it and prodding it and twisting it all day, and tonight I hurt like hell, do you understand that? I feel like

87

I've had GBH to the spirit. I don't want to hear your justifications. I want you to go away.'

He looked shocked. 'I'm sorry.'

'Just go away!' I shouted tearfully, sitting down on the bed and wrapping the bedspread more tightly around myself.

'I'm sorry,' he said again, and left.

I sat there for a while longer, trying to calm down. All right, maybe I was being a bit unfair. I did want to be informed and consulted: perhaps I should have listened. I knew Charles was telling the truth when he said he'd been trying to protect me: after all, I'd overheard him talk the professor out of applying for a court order to have me committed. He had never had any intention of cutting me off from contact with the outside world, either: my eavesdropping had shown that, too. He *had* lied, though. He'd persuaded me to cooperate with a programme of research without letting on that he was an interested party in that research, and I still believed that if I hadn't caught on he would have delayed clearing me for the health authorities for as long as he could, assuring me all the while that he was doing everything he could to hasten the process. Not, perhaps, an unforgivable sin if he didn't think the delay would do me any harm – but the fact was it *hurt*. It hurt so much it was hard to think.

I picked up my guitar again and played a Bach sarabande and an Elizabethan pavane – then, very carefully, plucked out the piece on the D string that I'd heard earlier. It felt good deep down, like a shot of local anaesthetic on a stinging wound. Music hath charms to soothe the savage breast, never doubt it.

Five

The next day, though unpleasant, was quieter and far less stressful. (Well, it could hardly have been any worse.) I had sessions on the Meg and the MRI and the differential angiograph – which turned out to be a kind of ultrasound scanner that measured blood flow inside the brain and represented it in 3-D. Charles was unfailingly anxious and polite and made strenuous efforts to keep me informed about what they were testing; Professor Bernet was foul-tempered and resentful, but said very little. I recorded each session on the videomatic, but in fact there were no more instances of anything I could take to a medical tribunal and complain about.

'But that's just what we want,' Amrita Mickleson told me, smiling, when I informed her of this. 'Who knows what would happen if you *weren't* recording things? You keep the camera a bit longer.'

I didn't talk to anyone much apart from Mrs Mickleson. I didn't even eat in the dining room with the others: I collected my meals as soon as they appeared, and ate them alone in my room upstairs. I know, I know: I should have faced down the starers – but I was feeling far too miserable and insecure for that.

I did decide, however, that I ought to get my own phone and laptop asap, and that evening I got clearance to phone my best friend at Dartington, who had a key to my room there.

It was only when I talked to Alicia that I really began to appreciate how much I'd been living a lie.

Alicia and I had been friends since secondary school. She was a small, vivacious black girl with a voice like gold velvet; we'd met each other in a school production of *Cats*, where she was a star and I was in the orchestra. She'd decided, in her usual enthusiastic born-leader way, that we ought to publicise our production by performing some numbers from it in the city centre, and to that end had rounded up several cast members to sing, and me to play accompaniment. I'd been far too shy and proper to do anything like that before and she had to twist my arm a bit – but I'd enjoyed it enormously. We sold thirty tickets and earned eighty-five euros, which we put in the kitty for the cast party. I'd never been to a cast party before, either, but I enjoyed that too.

After that, Alicia pretty much adopted me. She sang, I played guitar; she talked, I listened; she was the extrovert adventurer, I was the cynical voice of caution. She'd decided to get a degree in Music and Theatre Studies because of me (her initial plan had been simply to go off and become a rock star); I went to Dartington because of her. We were best friends, and everybody around us had known it. I'd always thought I could talk to Alicia about *anything* – and now I found that I'd never been honest with her at all.

'Yeah?' she asked brightly when I phoned. The familiar sound of her voice made me feel instantly better.

'Hi,' I told her. 'It's me.'

'Where've you *been*?' she shrieked. 'I was worried!'

I told her. She was very upset. She reminded me that she had *told* me to go in for a check-up when CICNPC first hit the news. I agreed that she had told me, and said I wished I'd listened. This made her even more upset, but she tried to reassure me. 'Don't worry,' she urged. 'I'm sure they'll prove you're perfectly normal and discharge you in no time.'

That was when I realised I'd been lying to her. I knew that it wasn't going to be that simple – and I couldn't tell her that, because I'd never told her anything to the contrary. Nor could I explain now.

Instead I pretended that one of the doctors wanted to talk to me, gabbled out Laurel Hall's address, then hung up and regarded myself and my lies with horror.

My parents phoned again later the same evening to give me a progress report. The Department of Health and local health authority had been unhelpful: typically eager to shuffle off responsibility on to anybody else, said my mother. The Department of Health had informed my father that Laurel Hall was a respected centre for brain research, that it had been approved for assessments for CICNPC recipients, and that no one else had complained about it. However, my father had chased about after various officials, and had at last succeeded in extracting a grudging promise that someone would enquire whether Professor Bernet was conducting any unnecessary tests in support of his own research, and remind him that he could not do so without the written consent of his subject.

My mother, meanwhile, had been chasing around the local health authority, but had failed to find anyone there who knew what tests a CICNPC assessment should actually involve. A prim and officious young man had informed her that the object of such an assessment was to 'determine whether a recipient has any abnormality in brain function that represents a danger to the public, and to recommend a method of treatment if such an abnormality is found' – but there was no definition of when a brain function is dangerously abnormal and when it isn't, or what you had to do to prove it.

'I must have spoken to a dozen people,' said my mother wearily, 'and – you know? – I think they *really* don't have any idea what they're supposed to be looking for. I mean, I think it simply hasn't been defined, that there *isn't* any file of guidelines or anything. The whole business of sectioning Cicnip recipients was just a gesture to calm public hysteria, and they didn't even bother to follow it up. I'm sorry.'

My father was still looking for a lawyer, and my parents were both planning to descend on the Hall the following evening, which was a Friday. 'We haven't been able to get hold of your Professor Bernet,' my father informed me. 'But we've left a message saying that we're very concerned by what you've told us, that we want to discuss it with him, and that we'll be arriving at quarter to five.'

'Thanks,' I said weakly.

'Till tomorrow, then! And keep your chin up.'

'I will.'

The next day, Friday, dawned grey and rainy, and was scheduled to be full of more tests. I was partially consoled, however, by the fact that the participants whose stares I was avoiding would soon be gone. Laurel Hall's research programmes, as I knew from the desktop file, normally ran only during the week, with participants arriving Monday morning and departing Friday afternoon.

'The Hall is usually very quiet over the weekend,' Mrs Mickleson told me. 'Sometimes one or two of the research staff come in, but apart from that it's just me and George. The cook doesn't come in, so there aren't any fixed mealtimes. The researchers generally bring their own food, but I can make you sandwiches – and you're welcome to have supper with me and George. I hope you like curry.'

'Are there people who don't?'

She smiled. 'Not many. Oh, and I hope you've left your room neat this morning. We do the housecleaning today, and the girls will be in at about nine.'

Sure enough, when I went back to my room at lunchtime, it was beautifully clean, with fresh sheets on the bed and new fluffy towels. I was feeling too dispirited to take any pleasure from it: the cleanliness merely functioned as a reminder that I'd have to do my own laundry soon.

I wondered how long I was going to be stuck at Laurel Hall being 'very thoroughly' assessed. Three days, Charles had said originally, but it had been almost that already and there was no end in sight, despite the fact that there was no wait for access to the scanners. I'd tried asking Charles a couple of times, but he'd just looked unhappy and told me that they had to prove that a pattern of brain activity which would be abnormal in most people was normal for me, and that this was complicated.

I wondered if they were going to keep on testing over the weekend. I hoped not, even if that did mean I had to stay at the Hall for longer. I felt so emotionally battered that I only wanted to curl up and be very quiet for a long time – or alternatively, pull the music out from the back of my mind and rest in it.

Not a good idea at the Hall.

I got out my guitar and played a few things, but it wasn't very satisfying. Musicians cannot live by popular classics alone: I needed to have a long session with something that really made me work. Perhaps my laptop, with its collection of scores, would arrive in the morning.

We had more Meg that afternoon, and when the session ended I came out to find the Hall silent and deserted. Feeling a sense of release, I went into the lounge and sat down in front of the television, just to show that I could, even though there was nothing remotely interesting on.

My parents arrived promptly at a quarter to five. Amrita Mickleson led them into the lounge: my mother, tall and thin and elbowy in a blue cotton dress, and my father, bull-necked and gorilla-armed in the black trousers and white shirt he wore to teach. I leapt up so fast I almost fell over my own feet, and ran to hug them. With their arms around me I felt safe. With them to help me, I was sure to get out of this in one piece.

'Well, then,' said Mrs Mickleson comfortably. 'It seems I don't need to find your daughter for you. I'll go tell Dr Spencer you're here.'

At that we all stopped hugging and looked around. 'Professor Bernet, you mean!' I protested.

Amrita Mickleson made a face and shook her head. 'I'm afraid the professor went home immediately after his last session with you.'

'We *asked* to speak to Bernet himself,' said my father, looking Mrs Mickleson up and down.

She rolled her eyes. 'I know you did, and Professor Bernet knows too, but he's gone home – and don't look at me like that: I don't approve of it any more than you do. Dr Spencer is his assistant. I'll go find him.'

She left. 'Isn't Spencer the one I spoke to on the phone?' asked my dad.

'Yeah,' I agreed. 'He's Professor Bernet's downtrodden lackey. I'm not surprised that the professor has fobbed you off with him: he seems to assign him all the dirty work.' I paused, then found myself adding, 'He's OK.' I was a bit surprised at myself at that.

Mrs Mickleson returned with Charles, who looked even

93

more anxious and unhappy than usual. He shook hands with my parents. Mrs Mickleson offered them coffee and biscuits.

When Mrs Mickleson had supplied the company with caffeine and departed, my father opened the proceedings.

'We are very concerned about what Val's been telling us,' he declared levelly. 'She has never experienced any problems resulting from her Cicnip treatment, and there is absolutely no reason why she should be detained here.'

Charles flinched. 'I'm very sorry,' he replied humbly. 'I absolutely agree with you that your daughter isn't any sort of danger to the public, and that she *shouldn't* be detained, but we simply cannot release her without doing enough tests to satisfy the Department of Health. If they aren't happy, they'll just ask somebody else to assess her.'

My mother rolled her eyes. 'So what do you actually have to do to satisfy them? Because I haven't been able to find out.'

'I agree, they haven't published any criteria, and that does make it harder,' replied Charles frankly. 'What they actually want, though, is an assurance that the person assessed isn't going to suffer lapses of consciousness in future. Normally what happens is that we assemble a package of evidence and a conclusion which we send to them, and they forward it to a panel of three who review it independently. In practice, many of their panelists are non-specialists, which means that we have to make our evidence as clear-cut and unambiguous as possible. With all our other Cicnip assessments this has been time-consuming but otherwise pretty straightforward. If the subject doesn't suffer episodes, we do a whole lot of brain scans during a whole range of different tasks to prove that brain function is normal; if they do, we do other scans to pinpoint which bit of brain is triggering the episodes, and provide a 3-D model to guide the surgery. In Miss Thornham's case—'

'Her brain function is normal!' declared my father forcefully.

He stared in surprise. 'No, I'm sorry. It isn't.'

I'd been longing to see my parents ever since I was arrested. Now all at once I wished they hadn't come. I had misrepresented myself – I'd been no more honest with them than with Alicia – and now they were going to discover the truth. I pushed myself deeper into my chair and twisted my hands together, feeling sick. Why hadn't I realised even enough to be scared?

My father made a dismissive gesture. 'I understand her brain patterns look unusual when she's composing music – but composing music on the spot isn't something most people *do*, is it? She doesn't suffer from lapses of consciousness: haven't you managed to prove *that* yet?'

Charles cast a worried look at me, then looked back to my father. 'I'm sorry, Mr Thornham, but the pattern of activity in your daughter's brain during one of these events is *not* that of someone composing music. Researchers have made scans of people doing that, and they're in the databanks. I looked them up and compared them, and when your daughter is composing music in the normal way, her brain patterns match those scans fairly well. During one of these anomalous events, however, the pattern is much closer to an episode of lapsed consciousness, at least on the fMRI. Now, we know that in her case there *is* no lapse of consciousness, but if we discharged her without an impressive stack of evidence to support that conclusion, somebody would be sure to call us on it. They'd say, "Ah, but how do you know there aren't other occasions where she *does* have a lapse?" After all, most people who suffer lapses don't have them very often. Nothing like as often as a couple of dozen times a day.'

I could feel my parents looking at me, but I couldn't meet their eyes. The back of my mind began a rapid and complicated beat on the timpani. A flute joined in.

'We could, of course, recommend treatment,' Charles went on. 'Professor Bernet and I have been able to pinpoint the sections of brain which are involved in the abnormal activity, and it would be perfectly possible to devise a surgical and SGNS procedure to replace them. But Miss Thornham is strongly opposed to this – and I entirely support her on that. The procedure would require the replacement of a comparatively large amount of cortex, and I can't see that there's any justification for it on the grounds of clinical need. She's never suffered any impairment from this abnormality; on the contrary, she seems to have used it to strengthen and extend her natural musical abilities. I think she's correct to fear that surgery might damage those abilities, and there is absolutely no reason to inflict it on her.'

I found I could meet *his* eyes OK. They were urgent and concerned. A double bass came in under the timpani, emphasising the beat.

'Val—' said my mother.

'Well, I don't know anything about brains, do I?' I burst out miserably, finally daring to look at her. 'This is what *they're* saying.'

'What does he mean by "events"?' asked my father in bewilderment.

'Music,' I said wretchedly. 'Hearing music. No, well, sort of part hearing it and part performing . . . composing . . . it. How was I supposed to know that something that happens to me all the time isn't normal?'

'It *is* normal,' Charles interrupted, surprising me. 'It doesn't interfere with any of your other brain functions and it's a well-integrated part of your normal life: for *you* it's normal. It's just that it's going to take time to establish that in such a way that nobody's going to question it. I know you believe the professor wants to do a lot of unnecessary tests on you just to investigate his theory of consciousness, I'll even admit that you're *right* to believe that – but still, it is genuinely going to be difficult. We *can* do it, I think, but it's going to take time. And I'm sorry, and I *know* you don't like it, and I *know* you think I lied to you before and you probably think I'm lying again – but it *is* going to take time, and I can't change that.'

'Dr Spencer,' said my father, 'could we speak to our daughter privately for a moment?'

Charles got up. 'Certainly. I'll be in my office. Call me when you want me – the number's on the house phone system.'

My parents watched him leave, then both turned back to me. I tried to hide in my chair like a tortoise in its shell, and stared miserably at my hands. The black diamond polish still wasn't chipped. I had sent my parents out to fight for me, and not told them that their guns were loaded only with blanks.

'You knew about this,' said my father, very quietly. I'd been terrified of that quiet voice as a child: it always made me feel small and stupid. It made me feel that way now. 'This is why you were so reluctant to go in for a check-up.'

'I didn't *know*,' I said defensively. 'I just . . . sort of started worrying about it after all the publicity, and I . . . I didn't *want* to know.'

'How many times do I have to tell you,' cried my mother in exasperation, 'that problems don't go away because you put off facing up to them? Val, we talked to *all those people*! We told them that you had no problems from the Cicnip, that your brain was completely normal, that this Professor Bernet had no cause whatsoever to detain you!'

I scrunched deeper into my seat and tried not to cry. '*I* don't know anything about brains!' I protested again. 'I didn't know mine was abnormal. I didn't *want* it to be abnormal!'

'Oh, God!' groaned my father. 'We were so damned *pleased* when they said you could have that treatment!'

'Steven!' said my mother reproachfully. 'She would've ended up in an institution without it. And it worked; the man just *confirmed* that it worked. He said that for her it was normal.'

At that I lost my battle with myself, and started to cry. I hadn't expected Charles to say that – and I knew, I knew, that I hadn't told him the whole truth. I wasn't going to tell it to my parents, either. Not now, anyway. Not here.

'Oh, Val!' my father cried in exasperation, and came over to put an arm around my shoulders. He never could stand to see me cry. I don't know why this made me reluctant to cry in front of him: it had got me off hooks all my life.

I told my parents about hearing the music. They told me I'd been a fool to worry about it in silence. I snuffled and agreed, and had a glass of mineral water and a chocolate biscuit.

'I don't think we're going to be able to make a complaint stick,' my mother said thoughtfully, when we had all calmed down. 'Not if your scans are as . . . abnormal . . . as the doctor was saying. What's this about him lying to you? He seemed very helpful and straightforward.'

I wiped my nose. 'I suppose it wasn't a *big* lie. He just didn't tell me that he was Professor Bernet's assistant, that he had an interest in the research he was pushing me to cooperate with.'

My father frowned. 'What about the thing you were so afraid of? *Are* they giving you any tests that have nothing to do with the Cicnip?'

I shrugged irritably. 'How would I know? *I* don't know what tests are necessary and which aren't!' Then I admitted, reluctantly, 'I do think, though, that they've given up on doing any of the pure research. I told you that.'

My father sat frowning for a moment, cracking the knuckles of his big pianist's hands. 'Let's see if we can get some more hard information,' he concluded, and went to call Charles back.

Charles still looked worried and unhappy. He still couldn't say how long the assessment would take. 'At the moment we're doing what we do with Cicnip recipients who don't suffer episodes,' he told my parents. 'Running brain scans while the subject performs a whole range of different cognitive tasks. We're using the Meg more than we normally would, because that demonstrates that Miss Thornham is conscious during these events. In her case, though, I doubt that's going to be enough. Professor Bernet wants to analyse the architecture – that is, which bit of brain is actually connected to what. The central problem is that we don't really understand consciousness, so we're trying to prove that something works when we have no idea *how* it works. We may stumble on a convincing explanation, but . . .'

'A week?' said my mother impatiently. 'Ten days?'

Charles blinked for a moment without replying. 'To tell the truth, I think we'll have run out of tests by the end of next week,' he said at last. 'If we haven't been able to prove anything conclusively by then, we'll have to discharge Miss Thornham under a supervisory order. That will mean she has to report to a health worker at regular intervals, and may be referred back to us for further evaluations. For her sake I'd like to avoid that if we can, but . . . I just don't know what we're going to come up with.'

Actually, having to report to some dreary clinic every month or so sounded . . . bearable. Much better than the mental hospital I'd been imagining. And getting out in a week, come what may – that *glowed*.

My parents were relieved as well: I saw them exchange glances. 'Thank you very much,' said my mother. 'You've been very helpful.'

Charles blushed. 'I wish I could do more. I, uh, I've been . . . that is, I'm very sorry Miss Thornham has been treated so badly, first by the police and then by my superior. Professor Bernet . . . he's a very brilliant man, but he can be very insensitive and he has a one-track mind. He also suffers from a chronic illness, and he's often in considerable low-grade pain, which makes him very irritable. I don't say that excuses his behaviour, but I think it helps to explain it.'

It did, actually. It turned the whole situation into something intelligible and ordinary and *real*, and ended the sense of being trapped and helpless in a nightmare. I remembered, though, that I'd felt like that before.

That was pretty much the end of the discussion. My parents wanted to take me out to dinner – they'd booked a room for the night at a nearby hotel, and apparently it had a restaurant that looked decent. Charles, however, informed them that since I was officially in custody, I wasn't supposed to leave the Hall. We ended up all having supper with the Micklesons. It was a dhansak curry, and very nice, too.

After the meal, my parents hugged me and said goodbye. They would be back in a week to pick me up, they said; meanwhile, we could phone each other regularly.

I watched them drive off, then went up to my room. Now that they were gone, I felt certain that Charles had once more been lying to disarm us. My parents had surrendered their weapons and accepted a peace settlement – and the enemy would no longer hold back.

The next morning, however, I was able to sleep in undisturbed until nine o'clock, and when I came downstairs it was to discover that my phone and laptop had arrived: Alicia, bless her, had sent them first class. I had a quick cup of coffee and a piece of toast in the kitchen, then took my things upstairs and greedily accessed my laptop's supply of music.

There was a piece I'd been working on before I left Dartington, 'Intifada' by the contemporary composer Dani Gorvenko. It had a long central section which I hadn't yet mastered: it was entirely percussive – varied taps and blows against the neck, sides and body of the guitar – and calculated to tangle the most agile fingers. I took out the guitar, tuned it, propped up the laptop's screen and set it on scroll-to-cue, then embarked.

First attempt: hopeless collapse in the percussive section. Second attempt from the beginning: same place, same outcome. Rethink: I started the percussive section at half speed and managed to stumble through to the end. Second go, still at half speed: better. Third go, speeding up: success. Ha! Third attempt from the beginning: I had to slow down for the percussive section, but I made it – only to fall down over a perfectly straightforward bit of *laqueada* in the final section.

I sucked a knuckle with which I'd struck the guitar rather too enthusiastically and glared at the computer screen. My hands were sore. I examined them: the black diamond nail polish had finally acquired some chips. Not enough practice over the past few days, that was the problem. Two hours a day, it should be, and what had I been doing? Half an hour, perhaps, of popular classics!

The back of my mind suddenly contributed a percussive section of its own – but instead of the rich drumbeat of wood, this rhythm glittered with chords. Strings rippled out a melody, making me shiver.

I knew that if I reached for it, it would come out. It *wanted* to come out – and I wanted to bring it out, and hold it in that moment of stopped time that occurred when such things did emerge into the light of day. Couldn't I do that? I was alone in my room. Even if the phone rang or someone came in, they'd think I was just concentrating hard. Surely if—

There was a knock on the door. I gave a guilty start, staring at it in alarm, then quavered, 'Who is it?'

'Me,' said Charles.

God, I'd nearly been very stupid. I set the guitar down. 'Come in.'

He opened the door. I saw at once from his face that he was particularly unhappy about something. 'I'm sorry,' he said quickly. 'The professor is ready to start the next test now.'

It was like the moment when the break in a long journey ends, and you have to force your stiff and aching limbs back into the weary confinement of the car. 'Oh,' I said stupidly. I looked at my computer, then picked it up and shut it down. I set the guitar in its case. 'I didn't know if he'd want to work over the weekend.'

'He prefers the weekends,' said Charles. 'Ordinarily he takes a couple of days off during the week, but I think this week he's planning to work through until Friday.'

Until I left, in other words. Dirty old encephalophile. Yuck. I sighed, closed the guitar case and got up. 'OK. Back to the salt mines.' I picked up the videomatic.

'I'm sorry,' said Charles, and held the door for me.

We walked along the corridor and started down the stairs. 'That thing you were playing before I knocked,' said Charles. 'That was . . . very impressive. Did you write it?'

I shook my head. 'It was by Gorvenko, a better man than I. I was just practising it. What's the next test, then?'

Charles hesitated, looking more unhappy than ever, and I stopped, halfway down the stairs. 'What?' I demanded. 'Something I'll like even less than the Meg?'

He grimaced. 'I'm afraid that's probably right. Most people don't like the neuropharmacological sampler – it's more . . . intrusive . . . than the other scanners we use. It is a very useful device, though, and it could possibly help you a lot.'

Oh God, the thing with the needle-wires. I *hate* needles. I swallowed queasily. 'What are you going to do with it?'

'As I said last night, Professor Bernet wants to check whether your neural architecture is normal – that is, how the different regions of your brain connect. Cicnip-C usually produces extra, non-functional connections alongside the normal set. If we can show that all your extra connections are functional, it would be a big help.'

'And that thing with the needles could tell you that?'

Another hesitation. 'Not on its own,' he admitted. 'But if we

101

stimulate a particular area of brain, the sampler can tell us what responds.'

Worse and worse. 'Stimulate how?' I asked faintly.

'The normal method is a weak electrical current applied by a nano-probe. One can also use a micro-dose of neurotransmitter. It doesn't need surgery; either can be applied through the sampler itself.'

Stick a needle right down into the *brain* and inject stuff. Oh God. I caught and held his eyes. 'Is this really necessary?' I demanded. 'Or is it consciousness research?'

When he didn't answer at once, I declared fiercely, 'I'm not having it!'

'No, no, don't get me wrong!' said Charles. 'This is entirely defensible as assessment. I just—'

'Wouldn't do it yourself?' I finished angrily.

He winced. 'Wouldn't ordinarily use the sampler *at this stage*. I'd bring it in later, to confirm something I suspected from what I could see with the other scanners. But it will save time, and you want to get out as quickly as poss—'

'I'm not having it *now*, then!' I declared.

Charles was silent a moment. Then he asked, in a neutral voice, 'Do you not like needles?'

My turn to wince. 'Does anybody?'

'Some people dislike them *more*,' he said drily. He took a deep breath, let it out slowly. 'Look . . . I'll talk to the professor. If you don't like needles, it makes no sense for you to suffer them any more than you absolutely have to.'

'Oh,' I said weakly. 'Thanks.'

We continued on down to the landing. I started on the next flight, too, and Charles had to call me back and hold open the door to the first-floor section of the lab.

The neuropharmacological sampler was in the room at the end of the corridor. It looked just like its picture: there was the table, the helmet, the green surgical cloth. There was a wall full of controls, too, and – oh, God! – it had one of those tunnels they slide people into for whole-body scans.

Professor Bernet was there too, fussing with the machine. When we came in he turned to greet us, and I noticed at once that there was something different about him today. The sullen air was gone, and had been replaced by malicious triumph.

'Miss Thornham,' he said.

'Professor Bernet,' I replied, and began the now-familiar ritual of switching on the videomatic and finding a place for it.

'That will not be necessary!' said the professor sharply. He marched over and snatched the camera.

I was startled, but not so startled that I let go. Guitar playing makes your hands very strong, and the professor found that he couldn't just take the camera out of my grasp. For perhaps a second we wrestled for it – and then Bernet apparently decided that such behaviour was undignified, because he let go. 'Put it off!' he commanded. 'The session is already being recorded. Your camera is unnecessary, and I find it distracting.'

'No,' I said, shaken. 'I've explained that I want a private record.' I checked that it was on and tuned to him.

'Professor,' began Charles. 'About this test . . . Miss Thornham is afraid of needles. Given that, it seems to me that—'

'She is refusing to cooperate with this procedure?' asked Bernet sharply.

'No—' began Charles.

'Yes!' I snapped.

Bernet's eyes glittered. 'Miss Thornham, I am no longer inclined to tolerate your behaviour. Since you arrived here your attitude has been hostile and uncooperative. You have refused to participate in basic research which might have helped others as well as yourself, and you have been deluging the authorities with groundless complaints about the staff of this establishment.'

So, he was getting feedback from some of the complaints? Good! 'Not all the staff,' I pointed out. 'You. But you can't say I've been uncooperative; I said I would cooperate with the assessment, and I have.'

'Yet you refuse this test? You wish to dictate the procedures by which you are assessed? Let me remind you, Miss Thornham, that you were arrested because you tried to avoid assessment. You are in our custody until that assessment is complete. If I say that this test is necessary – which I do! – you are not *permitted* to refuse it.'

103

'I don't believe that!' I proclaimed. 'I don't believe you're allowed to stick needles into somebody's brain against their wishes when there are alternative procedures you could be using instead. And you don't *need* to use that machine at this point. Dr Spencer was just saying so.'

Bernet turned an evil look on Charles, who flinched, but said clearly, 'Professor, being scanned by the sampler is an experience *most* people find frightening. In my opinion it's better to—'

'I am not interested in your *opinion*, Dr Spencer,' snarled Bernet. 'You do not have the clinical experience to make it valuable. I am shocked. You have been speaking to the subject behind my back, undermining her confidence in me and in the procedures. If you had any professional ethics at all, you would know that such behaviour is grossly improper.'

'Professor, I didn't—' began Charles again.

'If there is any repetition of this incident,' interrupted Bernet softly, 'you will be dismissed – and I will make certain that everyone understands why.'

Charles went red and stared wordlessly at the professor. Bernet turned the glare back on me. 'Miss Thornham, I repeat: this test is necessary for your assessment. Will you cooperate with it?'

I squared my shoulders. 'Only if you can justify it! I want you to explain to me, on the record, why it is necessary for you to use that machine *now*, when the standard practice would be to use it only to confirm the results you obtained from the other scanners.'

He stared at me a moment, fingers twitching. Then he smiled. I didn't like that smile at all. 'Miss Thornham,' he said softly, 'if you will not cooperate with the assessment programme, I will have to abandon it. Since you will not let me determine whether or not the abnormalities in your brain represent a danger to the public, I will have to recommend to the Department of Health that all the affected regions be treated by surgery and SGNS.'

I felt cold and numb. I stood there a moment, unable to speak. A thought coiled through my mind: *Charles has told him how desperate I am to avoid surgery.*

'You couldn't do it,' I managed at last. 'You'd need a court order.'

'Given the abnormalities on your scans,' he replied smoothly, 'there would be no trouble in obtaining one.'

The bastard had me. He *had* me. I'd do anything he wanted – and he knew it.

He came over, took the videomatic out of my hand, and smiled more widely as he switched it off.

'B-but s-sir!' stammered Charles. 'There's no *need* for surgery. You *know* that.'

'I know nothing of the sort!' snapped the professor. 'I cannot know that unless I have been allowed to complete the assessment – including all the tests that *I* believe necessary.'

'OK,' I choked. 'OK. I'll cooperate with the test. But. Put the videomatic back on.'

The smile of triumph grew, and he shook his head. 'No, Miss Thornham. I've told you, I find it distracting, and I do not want my concentration disturbed. This session, like every session, is being recorded on our own machines: you will have to be content with that.'

I wasn't content with that; looking at the way his eyes glittered in their hollows, I knew that it would be a very great mistake to be content with that. Submission would not appease him. Bullies feed upon submission. My mind suddenly went very clear. If I gave in now, he would crush me.

'I want my own record,' I insisted. 'I already have recordings of our previous sessions logged in sealed and dated files, and as soon as this session ends I will go and log a verbal report of what happened here and explain why there isn't any record of it. I will seal and date that, too. I think any fair-minded judge would find it pretty damn suspicious that after tolerating the videomatic for three days, you found it too distracting just on the occasion when I'm claiming you blackmailed me. I doubt very much, too, that any expert witness would give you a guarantee that your own recording wasn't doctored.'

The smile vanished, and was replaced by a glare of outrage.

'You *are* blackmailing me,' I told him flatly. 'And OK, the threat scares me, and I'll give in – but don't push it too far. I warn you, don't push it. I am going to get out of here in the end, and if you give me anything to use against you in court, believe me, I'll use it. Furthermore, if you have me mutilated, you son of a bitch, I will *kill* myself, and I will leave a very long letter explaining exactly why. There would *damn* sure be an enquiry after that, and you'd be in front of it with blood all over your precious court order and your sweaty hands.'

His eyes widened in shock and indignation. 'You would not do such a thing!'

'I *would*!' I exclaimed fiercely. 'If you destroy my ability to do music, I *will*.'

He gave me a seething look that said both that he didn't believe me and that he feared he might be wrong. Then he glanced at Charles, who was looking quite horrified. There'd be no support for him from that quarter if it came to a trial, he could see that as well as I could. He began to scowl.

'Put the videomatic back on,' I said, hearing my own voice shake a little. 'Leave it on. We both have a lot to lose if we push one another too far – so we won't push, OK?'

Bernet opened his mouth, closed it, swallowed a couple of times. 'You spiteful little bitch,' he managed at last, low-voiced and furious. He switched the videomatic on. 'We will proceed with the test.'

I had not lost – but I was a long way from winning. I took the videomatic back, arranged it on top of a cabinet, and submitted to proceeding with the test.

It wasn't surprising that most people didn't like the sampler, even if they didn't have a phobia about needles. It entailed a lot of mess and discomfort. The hairlike wires that covered the helmet were not, in fact, the needles of the sampler: they were merely the *mountings* for the needles of the sampler, which were so fine as to be almost invisible. Charles assured me that the needles themselves were made of a protein that would degrade and be absorbed by the blood if they were accidentally broken off inside the body – but it was nonetheless considered undesirable that they should do so, and every precaution had to be taken so that the head of the person being scanned did not move.

What this meant was that first I had to change my T-shirt for a plastic tunic affair. (There was a changing cubicle *en suite*, with a toilet, which I used.) Then I had to rub my face, neck and shoulders with a lotion that smelled like a citrus washing-up liquid: this was to stop my skin from sticking to the quick-setting aerosol foam which would be used to form an immobilising mould around my head and shoulders. After this, I came back into the scanning room and had my hair doused with an antiseptic/anaesthetic lotion which smelled like nail-varnish remover, and which made my scalp tingle unpleasantly. When my hair was well soaked, I was given a tight vinyl bathing cap to put over it. It muffled my ears and came halfway down my forehead. Next Charles brought out a syringe.

It had all been bad, and I'd hated it, but the sight of the needle was the last straw. I squeaked, 'No!' and dashed towards the door. The professor, who'd been looking at something on one of the machine's screens, looked round indignantly.

Charles lowered the syringe. 'It's a muscle relaxant,' he informed me, very calmly. 'It won't paralyse you, just loosen the major muscle groups a bit, so that you don't make any involuntary movements. It will also stop you from getting cramp from lying so still. It wears off in about an hour.'

I looked at his face, my heart pounding. He took a step closer, leaned towards me, and whispered, 'Please. He's in a foul temper. If you have another fight with him now he might do something stupid.'

I knew that I should not trust Charles – but I couldn't help it, I did. I drew a deep, unsteady breath. 'All right.'

I looked away when he gave me the injection: it barely stung at all. He sprayed the foam all over the inside of the helmet, and I lay down and put it on. There was a kind of nylon net that went over the top half of my body, securing me to the trolley, and then more aerosol foam went around my neck and shoulders.

I lay there, feeling the plastic tunic slick and hot against my skin and the foam prickling as it set. I was completely immobilised, utterly helpless, and half deaf. I wanted to scream and jump up, and I swallowed repeatedly to ease the ache in my throat.

107

'Try not to move,' Charles warned me. His voice was muffled. 'I'm going to put a mask over your face and spray that, too. There's an air hose in it that goes over your mouth and nose, so you won't have any trouble breathing. Don't try to speak or you'll damage the mould and we'll have to do it over. It may make you feel better to know that this stuff isn't strong even when it's set, and if you panic and jump up the whole lot will break apart like styrofoam – but it's better if you let us take it off. If you start to feel panicky and want out, raise your right hand.'

Strangely, I was no longer feeling panicky: a blurry numbness was creeping over me, as though this were all happening to somebody else. It didn't seem natural. 'Was it *just* muscle relaxant?' I asked muzzily.

He hesitated. 'No, there was a mild sedative as well. It's the normal procedure.' He glanced sideways, then lowered his voice again and said, 'Don't worry: I will *not* let him switch off the camera or wipe its memory while you're out of action. And . . . if I could talk to you after lunch—'

'OK,' I mumbled.

He put the mask over my face and sprayed it, leaving only my eyes free. I felt like an Egyptian mummy. I was starting to be befuddled enough that it seemed funny.

Charles pulled the green surgical cloth up over my chest. 'Now, what will happen,' he told me, moving his head close to mine, 'is that first we'll put your head and shoulders inside that tunnel in the wall, which is another MRI scanner. We always use the sampler in conjunction with another scanner, so that we can see what we're doing. We've also programmed the MRI's computer with all the results of your previous scans, so that we have quite a detailed map of the surface of your brain: again, this is so that we know where to put things. Once we've got a good image on the MRI, we'll insert the needles. They're designed to rotate like very tiny drills, but the sound they produce is extremely high frequency, too high for humans to hear, so you should scarcely even be aware of them. They take about five minutes to get through the skull, and it will prickle a little, but the anaesthetic in your hair rinse should ensure that it doesn't do more than that. Just remember that the needles are so extremely fine that they don't do any damage: there should be no blood at all, and they won't harm any brain cells. Once they're in place we'll let them get a reading, which will take another fifteen minutes or so, and then we'll deliver a mild stimulus to your right prefrontal cortex, and see what responds. Again, if you get frightened and want out, raise your right hand or kick with your right foot. OK? Raise your left hand for "yes", or your right hand for "no".'

I raised my left hand, pushing it against the restraint net. My muscles felt like jelly.

'OK,' said Charles again. 'Here we go.' He patted my hand. 'Cheer up: the worst is over. The rest is just tedious – and it should be over in about an hour.'

Into the tunnel I went, like a roast into an oven. I lay there feeling drunk and staring up at the metal curve of the roof. I could not hear anything.

After a while my scalp crawled with pins and needles: the invisible threads of the sampler were drilling their way into my brain. Despite the drunk wobbly feeling, the situation no longer seemed funny.

Distraction, that was what I needed. I thought of the Gorvenko piece. At once my own piece of percussion leapt up in my mind, glittering and beautiful. It still wanted to come out, and the prospect of letting it, of being inside it instead of in this horrible tunnel with needles in my brain and a filthy pervert salivating over what they showed him – it was almost unbearable. Oh God, no, no, *no*! Not here. Something else . . .

I went back to my string quartet. It would start with the argument on the solo cello; then the violins would come in, and . . . it still didn't have an ending. I prodded my memory of how it went, trying to encourage the back of my mind to make it continue – but my subconscious was still stubbornly engaged on percussion. I would have to do my composing the hard way, and I didn't have any bright ideas just at the moment.

Well, I needed three more movements if I was going to stick to the classical canons. I had part of a slow movement, an Adagio, though I suppose it could be speeded up to *andante*. At least one of the other movements ought to be fast, *allegro* or even *presto*. Start off with a bang, maybe some fierce rhythmic effect on the violins . . . on the first violin, with the second doing a counterpoint, while the cello and viola came in on a soft, swooping, ever-so-slightly dissonant glide . . .

For a moment I found myself looking at the tunnel above my head and having no idea what it was. I blinked, and it seemed to come back into mental focus – then wavered again; steadied again. I realised that Bernet had applied some stimulus to a touchy area of my brain. I swallowed, feeling . . . as though I'd been groped. *Yuck.* I thought about flapping my right hand frantically – but what would happen if I did? He could have them go in there with knives.

Lie back and think of music. *Allegro molto* in G: the violins come in . . .

I worked at it for what felt like weeks. There were probably stimuli which I didn't feel, but what I did feel was bad enough. At last my musical daemon came to my aid: the whole quartet played a Scherzo in G, hot and furious. I blinked at tears, and . . .

Time stopped. I was conscious of the music not as a sequence of notes, but as a simultaneous whole, an architecture of sound that enclosed me completely. It was transparent to me, and all else was opaque. I hovered bodiless in the centre of a jewel, able somehow to perceive every facet of it at once, to contemplate each note separately at the same time as I grasped the whole. A string quartet in G. Three movements: Allegro molto, Adagio, Rondo: Allegro. It was passionate and angry, but as orderly as the movement of stars.

I took a deep breath, still contemplating the fierce beauty of what had moved through me. There were voices nearby.

'. . . proves nothing of the sort!' Charles was shouting.

'The stimulus was tiny!' replied the professor. He sounded shaken and defensive. 'If the connections respond so violently to such a small stimulus, it's because the pathways are habituated!'

I looked round at them, saw that they were both a few feet away, in front of the sampler's controls. It was only then that I realised that I was out of the tunnel, the helmet, and the foam.

'There's no record of it!' cried Charles. 'Not of seizures or . . . or whatever it is, and—'

'She has been evasive and hostile from the start!' Bernet shouted.

'She was frightened and disoriented and you screamed at her and bullied her!' Charles shouted back. 'What did you expect her to do: kiss you?'

'I? No! It is *you*, Dr Spencer, who wants to kiss her. That has been *very* clear.'

'I—' began Charles – then stopped abruptly and spun round, because I'd sat up. He hurried over to me. 'Val!' he shouted, and caught my hands. I thought he was about to burst into tears. 'Are you all right?'

'Yeah,' I said. I pulled my hands free and rubbed my face – and got citrus washing-up lotion into my eyes. 'What happened?' I asked, trying to wipe it out again.

I realised even as I asked that I knew: the professor had given my brain a stimulus while I heard the music, and it had made the music come out. It was strange, really strange: it had never come out before unless it was something I could play.

'We don't know,' said Charles. He sounded frightened. 'You . . . one of the stimuli . . . we don't know. Please, lie down. You should take it easy until we have a better idea what happened to you.'

I had no intention of lying down on that table again. 'Do you have a paper towel?' I asked, shutting my stinging eyes and putting my hands over them. 'I've got that lotion stuff in my eyes.'

Charles dashed into the changing cubicle and came back with a handful of paper towels. I sat there mopping my face. I realised I was still wearing the bathing cap, and took it off. At once the room stank of nail-varnish remover. My hair felt horrible.

'How are you feeling?' Charles wanted to know.

'Shaky,' I told him, which was certainly true. 'What happened? Was . . . was that an episode of lapsed consciousness?' I might as well ask: they had the whole thing on record.

111

To my surprise, Charles shook his head. 'Whatever it was, it was *nothing* like an episode. Are you feeling OK? Do you remember anything?'

I put the paper towel down and stared at him. It *hadn't* been an episode? Then what the hell had it been?

Not what the hell: what the heaven, maybe. I contemplated my three-quarters of a string quartet again. God. I had to get that down. I had to programme it into a computer and hear what it sounded like. It was good. I was sure it was very good.

'What do you remember?' asked Professor Bernet, coming over. He seemed comparatively subdued. 'You experienced one of the anomalous brain events immediately before this seizure—' Charles gave him a filthy look, and he broke off.

'It was a seizure?' I asked, trying to make sense of it.

'No,' answered Charles at once. 'It was . . . we don't know. You . . . when we took you out of the scanner you were just lying there smiling, you didn't seem to see or hear anything. I thought we'd done something terrible.' He caught my hand and squeezed it.

The professor returned his filthy look, with interest. 'What do you remember?' he demanded again.

'Leave her alone!' ordered Charles angrily. 'She should . . . she should go lie down. Someone should stay with her.'

'You?' sneered Professor Bernet. 'How touching! She *should* have another scan, to ascertain that her brain function is normal again.'

I glanced at the tunnel. 'No,' I said flatly. 'Not now.'

To my surprise, the professor did not argue. 'Miss Thornham,' he said instead, 'what do you remember?'

I bit my lip. 'You had me in that horrible tunnel,' I told him. 'I was trying to compose music for a string quartet, to distract myself. I'd got most of two movements, and I'd got the music to . . . to *play* for me. Then . . .'

I was not going to tell him. It wasn't even because I wanted to protect myself any more: it was an almost religious sense that one should not give what is holy unto dogs. I shrugged. '*I* don't know what you did, do I? What time is it?'

'Quarter to one,' said Charles.

It had been about eleven when the session started. I scrubbed at my face again. My skin felt too tight, and my eyes were sore. My hair was manky and stinking. I wanted food and quiet, but I wanted a bath first of all. I pushed myself off the trolley and balanced on unsteady legs. 'I'm going to wash and lie down,' I told the professor. 'I don't . . . I don't want to do any more tests today.'

Again he did not argue. I realised that he had been afraid that his application of a stimulus at the wrong moment had done irreversible damage to my brain, and that somebody would call him to account for it. He'd been frightened. Good. That made two of us.

Six

C harles fussed. There is no other word for it: he insisted on helping me up to my room, and did not want me to take a bath, in case I passed out in the tub. When I agreed to take a shower instead, he fetched Mrs Mickleson to wait outside the washroom while I did, so that I could be rescued decently in case of need. He ran back to the sampler room to fetch my T-shirt, and had Mrs Mickleson pass it in. When I emerged from the shower, I found that he'd fetched me a plate of sandwiches and a glass of orange juice, and arranged them on a tray beside the bed. There was also a rose from the garden, in another glass. I ought to lie down, he told me solicitously, and have a rest. He would come up in an hour to check on me, unless I felt giddy or ill and phoned him first.

Actually, he was very sweet.

I thanked him, thanked Mrs Mickleson, promised that I would rest, and sent them out of the room. As soon as they were gone I got out my computer and set up my composition programme. I selected the string quartet scoring and began to set down the parts, pausing only occasionally to devour a mouthful of sandwich and wash it down with a swig of juice.

Charles knocked on the door while I was still in the middle of the third movement. I told him to come in, and he sidled in carrying a plastic bottle misted with condensation.

'I thought you might like one of those flavoured waters,' he explained.

I was sitting up on top of the bed with the computer on my lap and the selecterpen in my hand, but I put the pen down. 'Oh!' I said in surprise. 'I thought you said there weren't any.'

He flushed. 'I got it in the village. How are you feeling?'

'Much better, thanks.'

'Do you want some of this now? Or shall I put it downstairs in the lounge?'

'I'll have some now, thanks.'

He picked up my empty orange-juice glass and went to rinse it out in the bathroom sink. I saved my quartet-so-far and moved the computer out of the way as he came back with the glass.

'Would you like some?' I asked, as he opened the bottle.

'No thanks. I'm not thirsty.'

So he'd walked or driven over to the nearest village to fetch it just because I'd asked for some *once*? That was very pleasing. That was, in fact, top score.

The water was strawberry-flavoured. Not my favourite – but I had no intention of telling him so.

'Thanks very much,' I said, taking the glass and giving him my very best smile.

He smiled back. He turned the desk chair around and sat down. 'Do you feel up to talking about what happened?'

Why did he have to go and spoil it? 'Not really,' I said, without enthusiasm.

'No. Well,' said Charles, with disappointment, 'I can understand that.' Then he burst out, 'I was so frightened when you . . . when we took you out of there and you were just *lying* there . . . and the way he coerced you into cooperating, that was *disgraceful*!' He leaned forward, regarding me intently. 'That was what I wanted to talk to you about. Do you want to file a formal complaint? Because I'll join you in it if you do.'

'He threatened to sack you,' I said, looking at him questioningly. 'With a killer reference.'

He shrugged. 'Frankly, that isn't as dire a threat as he thinks.'

I looked at him closely. 'Cognitive neuroscience is littered with his former research assistants?'

He smiled. 'Well, no, not *littered* – but he has had more academic quarrels than most. I have a good degree and I can get references from my profs at Oxford. A bad reference from him might set me back a bit, but it can't ruin me.' He frowned.

115

'I'd prefer it, though, if he didn't sack me until after you'd left.'

I hadn't really focused on that before. The prospect of being trapped with the professor all on my own was quite terrifying.

'Maybe we'd better wait on the formal complaint,' I said weakly.

He nodded. 'At the moment he's confident that even if you do complain, nothing will come of it. Even what he did this morning – he could argue that if you wouldn't allow him to complete the assessment, public safety required him to take the cautious option of recommending you for treatment.' He hesitated, then looked me straight in the eye and asked, 'You wouldn't *really* kill yourself, would you?'

I looked away, then decided I owed him an honest answer and looked back. 'If it meant I had to live without music, I would,' I told him flatly.

Our eyes held for a long moment. 'You mustn't think like that,' he said quietly.

I shrugged. 'Maybe. Other people manage to live fulfilling and happy lives with nothing more than canned music in shops and what they hear on the radio. Me, I'd rather be a paraplegic. Can you understand that?'

'That's not what I mean. It's *very* unlikely that you would end up unmusical even if you had some fairly drastic surgery. Brains are changed by what we do with them, and you have a culture and habit of music already in place. With surgery and SGNS you'd lose the episodes of hearing music, and you might have to learn new ways to do a few things, but you'd probably be able to take up your music degree again after only a year off.'

Perhaps I'd have *something* left – but I was instinctively certain that it wouldn't be what I'd had before, and I'd have to go through the rest of my life knowing that. Still, I supposed I could just about bear to contemplate living on like that – which was, I imagined, what Charles was trying to achieve. 'You sound like you're trying to talk me into it,' I said queasily.

'No,' he replied at once. 'I don't want it to happen, and I'll try to ensure that it doesn't. I promise you that. I just . . . just don't want you to write off your whole *life* as the product of a

116

few cubic centimetres of grey matter. Cicnip isn't responsible for making you who you are. There's a great deal more to you than that.'

That, frankly, rather took my breath away. I gaped at Charles stupidly, and he looked back. God, he had wonderful eyes.

At last he looked away again and said, 'Anyway, I don't think Professor Bernet will do anything extreme at the moment. He probably has a lot to lose if he gets into trouble. On the other hand, if he thought he was *already* in trouble, he might—' He stopped, biting his lip. 'To tell the truth, he worries me. One moment he'll be a man you can talk to; the next he behaves like a paranoid dictator. He's had the reputation of being arrogant and impatient for a long time, but I have the impression that the way he's been behaving recently is different. It's not just the way he's treated you; he was very nearly as bad with some of the other Cicnip assessments. They've all arrived here confused and frightened, and he's bullied them unmercifully.'

'Maybe it's because of his chronic illness?' I suggested. 'What's wrong with him, anyway?'

'He has Crohn's disease,' replied Charles dismissively. 'It's an auto-immune disorder of the intestinal tract, controllable but not curable. No, I don't think it's just that: as far as I know he's had it for years – though it has flared up recently, I think. He was off work for a couple of weeks last month. My guess is it's something to do with the way he left the CNRS.'

'The what?' I asked quickly.

'The Conseil Nationale pour la Recherche Scientifique. It's the French equivalent of the Science and Medical Research Councils combined – only it's bigger, better funded, and more powerful. He was in charge of allocating all its funds for medical research, but he resigned suddenly and came here. It's a big demotion, and I don't know why he took it. My guess is that there were complaints about him from his previous re-search post and he decided to jump before he was pushed – but that's just a guess, based on the way I've seen him treat subjects. Anyway, that's neither here nor there.' He smiled at me shyly. 'I was very impressed by the way you stood up to him.'

I felt my face heat. I shrugged. 'I was . . . glad you were there.'

'I was no use at all,' he said unhappily. 'I let him coerce you into going along with a procedure that frightened you and which was *not* necessary, and you nearly . . . I was so scared. Thank God you're all right!' He sighed, glanced around, and noticed the quartet on the computer. The screen was displaying the bit I'd been scoring when he arrived. It was the middle of the Rondo movement, and the same series of triplets was sprinkled down the screen, marking the entrance of each instrument in turn. 'What's that?' he asked, leaning forward to look at it.

'My string quartet,' I told him proudly. 'I wanted to get it down while it's still clear in my head.' I picked up the selecterpen and used it to copy a sequence from the viola part and move it down to the cello line further back. I pulled an A up to a C, lengthened it and cut two notes in lieu. I inspected what I'd done: yes, that was right.

Charles laughed. 'You're writing that out *now*? If anything remotely like what happened to you had happened to me, I'd be completely bits!'

'It's *good*!' I protested, looking up at him. A thought occurred to me. 'Here, you want to hear it?'

His eyes widened. 'I'd love to. Can your computer do it justice?' He eyed the machine – a battered three-year-old student Mac with a bright blue case – doubtfully.

'It doesn't sound anywhere near as good as the real thing,' I admitted, 'but it isn't actually *sour* to listen to. I've got a lot of dedicated software.' I saved my newest addition, then whizzed back to the beginning of the document. 'Here,' I said, quitting 'Write' and selecting 'Play'. 'This is going to be the first time anybody hears this but me, and I've only heard it inside my head. String quartet in G by V. Thornham: first movement, Allegro molto.'

I clicked the pen, and the two violins stormed into life – a fierce rhythm, a guitarist's rhythm with a hint of flamenco in it and a hint of Africa, transformed by the strings to something harsher and more austere. The viola and cello came in with that ever-so-slightly dissonant glide, just as I'd imagined them in my foam and metal prison. Perfect. Oh God, perfect!

The length was good, too. Early compositions tend to be either too short or so swollen as to be unperformable, but this was just right. I timed it, and found that the first movement took about eight minutes, while the second, the Adagio, was slightly shorter. The third, the Rondo, only played for about three minutes before it reached the end of what I'd written out, and stopped abruptly. I sat there for a moment, gloating.

'That was *beautiful*!' said Charles, in a stunned voice.

I beamed. 'Yeah.'

I considered my work again, trying to be critical, then set the computer back to 'Write' and started on the next section of the first violin part. 'You know, it's the first longer piece I've done that isn't for guitar. I suppose it's still a *bit* derivative, but I think I'm finding my own style. At least it doesn't sound like Jiang Qi.' I marked out another phrase for the first violin.

'You worked out all of that while you were in the sampler?'

'Not all of it. You remember the first time I was on the Meg? That was when I got the idea for the main part of the second movement. The rhythm in the first movement is the bit I was working on in the sampler. Then there's a bit in the Rondo – this bit here – that I've had floating around for a few months. I tried to do it for guitar, and then I tried to do it for piano, but *this* is how it works.'

I started on the second violin part. I'd marked it out for the next section, and was about to start on the viola line, when it dawned on me that Charles had become very quiet. I looked up and found him watching me with a strange expression, both hurt and anxious.

'What's the matter?' I asked, my heart sinking.

'When you came out of the sampler,' he said slowly, 'you said you'd done *two* movements. Now you're writing out a third movement as fast as you can move your pen.'

I knew I should say, 'Oh, but I'd already done the third movement for piano, so it just needs transcribing.' I couldn't say it, though. That hurt, worried look silenced me.

'Professor Bernet said that the fact that there'd been such a

119

dramatic response to such a small stimulus meant that the pathways were habituated,' said Charles.

I set the pen down. We looked at each other.

I'd played him the quartet: the best creation of my soul, alive in the air for the very first time. I saw – and somehow it seemed something I'd known for a while – that I'd done it because I'd wanted to tie him to me with something so striking and so extraordinary that he would never forget it. Him and his silly little moustache and his delicious blue eyes and his quiet voice and his stuffy and absolutely sincere courtesy. Oh, yes.

The last young man I'd had, I'd lost because he didn't want anything to do with a girl with a patched-up brain. Charles, though, understood about brains. Perhaps I could make him understand this. I had to try, anyway. Telling the lie too late would be no use – or so I told myself then.

'All right,' I admitted at last, from some huge distance. 'I guess the pathways, whatever they are, could be habituated.'

'Oh, God, no!' he said in horror.

'Not like that, though! In the past it's always been something I've had to *work* to make happen, and it's always been a piece for guitar.'

His face moved in bewilderment. 'That . . . *that* – was something you *wanted* to happen to you?'

'Yes. Oh yes, very much. It's . . . it's like getting behind the *sound* of the music and into the thing that *is* the music, the structure and the pattern of it and the way it . . . it glows in the mind. Time stops, and I see it all at once, like a painting, instead of in a sequence of one sound after another. I . . . always felt it was an incredible gift. I never really felt that just *hearing* music in my head was very important, and if it hadn't been for the other business I never would have worried about it at all. I was poleaxed when you said it looked like an episode. No, when the publicity started about Cicnip and I started getting worried, what I started worrying *about* was what happens when the music comes out. I thought, my God, maybe I've been driving myself to have episodes. But *these* episodes don't happen unless I make them, and they're solely to do with music. The music comes out, and I sit inside it, and then it ends and time starts up again. And apart from what happened this morning, the music only comes out when I *make* it come out. And anyway, you said it wasn't an episode of lapsed consciousness after all. So I don't see how it can be dangerous.'

He was looking more bewildered than ever. 'Val—'

'It never has come out without me working at it,' I insisted.

'How . . .' He swallowed, looking frankly stunned. 'How do you work at a thing like that?'

'It has to be a piece for guitar. I get the music to play in my mind, and then I play along with it, concentrating on it completely, trying to do it *perfectly* – and if I succeed, it will come out. It doesn't have to be my own music. I've managed to do it with Bach and Mozart and Vivaldi, as well.'

He was now frankly stunned. 'You can *play* in that state? You were . . . you were completely unresponsive . . . that is, your reflexes were functioning, but you didn't seem to see or hear or . . . you're saying you can play the guitar like that?'

'I play it very well like that,' I told him. 'Or so I've been told by people who've heard me. But obviously, I couldn't play a whole string quartet.'

'This has happened before in front of *other people*? And they didn't even *notice*?'

I was beginning to feel exasperated and hurt as well as frightened. 'I was playing *music* for them, and they were listening! You don't start testing the reflexes of someone who's playing a Bach Prelude with all their heart. You *expect* them to be concentrating very hard. It's normal.'

'Normal!'

'Look,' I said urgently, 'once I went off on holiday without my guitar, and when I got home I hadn't practised for two weeks. I sat down and worked hard at it, and after about an hour I noticed the strings were wet and slippery. When I looked at them, I saw they were covered with blood. My fingers weren't used to the strings any more, and I'd cut them so badly they'd started bleeding – but I hadn't noticed. That's *normal*. Other classical guitarists I've spoken to have said the same thing has happened to them. Ditto harpists. A sitar player wouldn't be taken seriously if he'd never made his fingers bleed.'

121

He looked appalled.

'Music isn't like a job in Tesco,' I told him. 'You have to give it everything you have, and even then you can only hope that what you have is enough.'

'No,' he said suddenly. 'Val, please can we not make this a matter of music?'

'It *is* a matter of music!'

'It's a matter of abnormal wiring in your brain! Do you have any *idea* what was going on in your head when you had this wonderful musical experience?'

'Yes! I was composing three movements of a string quartet!'

'The activity in the affected areas of your brain suddenly became so intense that on the MRI they looked black. Your levels of glutamate and acetylcholine and enkephalin went off the scale, and the neurochemistry of your whole brain went haywire.'

'What does that mea—' I began, but he went on ruthlessly, 'I went over to the scanner and called you, but you didn't hear. I checked your pulse, and it was racing – a hundred and forty beats a minute! Bernet started trying to apply more stimuli, to snap you out of it, but all the parts of your brain that were working were so full of excitatory hormones that it was like trying to stop a flood with a bucket of sand, and all the rest of your brain was so frozen with inhibitory neurotransmitters that the stimuli just rolled off. I pulled you out of the tunnel and shouted at you, but it had no effect. We got the sampler needles out and tried to revive you, but *nothing* we could do made any difference.'

'But, look,' I said helplessly, 'that's not what *normally* happens. Normally I'm playing the guitar, and nobody even notices!'

He snorted and rolled his eyes. 'Maybe! All your reflexes were working normally, and we *knew* that there was cortical activity, *extreme* cortical activity – but for all you responded, you might have been brain-dead. It went on and on, and we were afraid to do anything in case we made it worse. I was sure that the next step was going to be an epileptic seizure – and I was afraid that even that wouldn't stop it; I was imagining *status epilepticus* and death. Val, this was not a benign and harmless event that you can just shrug off; this was something acute and dangerous – and I don't mean dangerous to the public, I mean dangerous to *you*.'

'How long did it last?' I asked him coldly.

He blinked.

'Just over twenty minutes?'

He blinked again. 'It felt like years.'

I pointed at the computer. 'About as long as those three movements would take to play?'

He looked at the computer dazedly. 'I don't know,' he said at last. 'Perhaps. But—'

'If you were looking at the body of an athlete who was running a marathon, you'd see all sorts of alarming things, wouldn't you? Thundering heart, lungs working, energy consumption right off the scale. But you wouldn't be worried, because you know that that sort of activity is normal for what the athlete's doing. Well *I* think that all those things you were saying happened were normal for what *I* was doing. The only real difference is that you didn't know what it was: for all your scanners you can't see the thoughts in a brain. Is there anything in your list of my terrifying symptoms that means more than that I was concentrating and working very hard?'

'You mustn't brush this off!' said Charles urgently. 'Val, I'm sure this thing is very bad for you.'

'Oh, you know so much about it!' I scoffed. 'You don't even know what it is, but you know it's bad for me! The only reason you think so is because it scared you.'

'Brains aren't designed to work like that!'

'My brain isn't normal. You've said so yourself. It *does* work like that!'

'Oh God, I wish you trusted me! I know I wasn't honest with you at first, but I didn't know then what you were like, I thought I needed to *reassure* you. There were abnormalities on your scan, the professor had been talking about fractured awareness, and I expected someone confused and frightened and a bit stupid. I didn't expect *music* to be an issue at all. I've been trying to understand – I've been trying *hard*. Can't you believe that I'm not saying this because I want to make trouble, but that I really am very, very frightened of what this thing might do to you? That was not a harmless event! That was a tiger.'

'You *don't know* that!'

'Don't I? Well, I bet you this sort of event isn't like the other. It isn't something you grew up with and can't imagine life without. This is something that started fairly recently, and has been growing more frequent. I'll bet that at first it was very, very difficult for you to make it happen, but now it's much easier. I'll bet the first incidents were short, and that they've grown longer.'

'Ha! It first happened about three years ago . . .' I realised he was right. The first time the music came out, it had been like pulling teeth, and the piece had been very short. I'd been rehearsing for a school end-of-year concert, and I'd worked and worked and worked at it, until I was in a sort of a daze of exhilarated exhaustion – and then the music had come out. I'd tried to make it happen again, but I hadn't been able to, not for months. It was much easier now.

But *anything* gets easier if you practice. The first Jiang Qi piece I studied had taken me two weeks of steady practice to master; the second, three days. 'That doesn't mean anything,' I told Charles resentfully. 'The first time I rode a bicycle didn't last long, either.'

'Val, people take opiates to mimic the effects of enkephalin and the other endorphins; they use nicotine to mimic acetylcholine. During this event, your brain was flooded with those neurotransmitters. *Sure* it felt good. *Sure* you wanted to make it happen again. And every time you tried, and every time it happened, you strengthened the neural and chemical pathways that allow it – which are not normal pathways. Soon you'll feel as though it's *trying* to happen – and then it will start happening whether you want it to or not, perhaps when you're driving, or crossing a road. This is *dangerous*. It is too powerful. It could swamp you.'

'You *don't know that*,' I said again. 'You say my brain was flooded with feel-good neurotransmitters: did it never occur to

124

you that that might be because I was doing something I loved, and it felt good? I don't think this could have happened when I was little, but that's not because my brain was normal then and isn't now: it's because I didn't understand music well enough, and certainly couldn't *play* it well enough, to reach into the heart of it like that. This has never hurt me or anybody else: in fact, nobody else has even been aware that it was happening at all! It has never shown any sign of getting out of control, and any idea that it might is pure speculation.'

'But—'

'What are you going to do? Send me to the Department of Health with a recommendation for immediate surgery *as a precaution*, and sign the court order so that they can sedate me and do it without my consent? Any prostate gland *might* become cancerous: would you recommend that every man over the age of thirty be *forced* to have his removed, as a precaution? And, if he objected to having his perfectly healthy genitals sliced up, would you tell *him*, "A few square centimetres of tissue aren't your whole life"?'

He winced. 'This isn't the same! Prostate glands are *normal*!'

And my brain was not. Yes, I realised with horror, he did want to recommend the knife. He wanted the thing that had frightened him eliminated.

This was the thing I'd been afraid of all along, but coming face to face with it was worse than anything I'd imagined. Beforehand, my anxieties had always lumped the two things together: hearing the music, reaching the music. Now I was suddenly, horribly aware that hearing the music was unimportant compared to what happened when I reached the music. If I lost this, I lost everything. What was more, it was *Charles* who would condemn me to the knife, and that hurt horribly. I caught my breath, then wailed, 'You *promised* me that you'd do everything you could to ensure that I came out of here intact!'

'That was before I knew about this problem.'

'This isn't a problem! How do you *know* it's a problem? You don't! You don't know anything about it at all!'

'And you don't want me to find out!' He was shouting now. 'You never told *anyone* about this: you said so yourself.'

125

'And I wish I hadn't admitted it!' I shouted back. 'I *could* have said that third movement was just a transcription of something I'd written before, but I didn't – because I wanted to trust you. I *did* trust you, and, oh God, I was wrong, I was wrong! You're going to tell them to *do* it.' I caught my breath with a sob. 'Bernet was just making a threat, but you're really going to tell them to *do* it. You *liar*, you fucking *liar*! Why the hell did I ever talk to you? Get *out*!'

'Val, I'm not—'

I jumped off the bed and slapped him across the face as hard as I could. 'Get *out*!'

He got up. The mark of my hand was scarlet on his cheek, and my fingers were tingling. 'Val, don't you understand? I'm afraid you're going to be hurt; I want to protect you!'

'You are not God!' I shouted. 'You do *not* understand what I need better than I understand it myself! You're condemning me to a mutilation so horrible that I'd rather be dead!'

'I'm not *going* to recommend surgery!' he shouted back.

I caught my breath. 'You're not?'

'I never said I was recommending surgery. Not . . . not now, not when you feel so strongly about it. You're right, it would be wrong to do anything drastic when we don't actually *know* that this . . . this condition is harmful. But you *can't* expect us just to ignore it! It has got to be investigated!'

'Us?' I repeated slowly. 'You and . . . Bernet? You're going to tell him?'

'I *have* to! Val, this is a potential threat to your life and sanity. I'm a doctor; I can't just ignore—'

'No, no, *no*! You *know* what Bernet is. How can you invite that loathsome toad to put his filthy paws all over—'

'Now you're being totally irrational!'

'It's not *your* brain he's groping.'

'This is pointless!' exclaimed Charles furiously.

'Then get out! I already told you to get out! Just get out and leave me alone!'

He got out. I sat down on the bed and burst into tears.

When I had cried until I had a headache, I played the guitar for an hour, and when I'd done that, I finished writing out the

126

Rondo. If it was the last thing I did, there was all the more reason to complete it. What had happened had not changed it: it was still perfect.

Amrita Mickleson came up a little later. She had a sober, concerned face, as though I were ill. She set a cup of tea down on the bedside table. 'I thought you might like this,' she told me. 'And I thought you might want some paracetamol.' She dug a packet out of her shirt pocket.

'Oh,' I said heavily. 'Thanks.'

'Dr Spencer says they've found a serious abnormality in your brain. I'm very sorry. I hope—'

'That's Dr Spencer's view,' I said angrily. 'It isn't a *problem*. It never has been a problem.'

She obviously thought Charles knew more about it than I did. 'Whatever. I'm sure they'll find a way to treat it.'

'They don't *need* to treat it! It never did any harm! All they have to do is leave it *alone*!'

She shook her head doubtfully. 'You must realise that Charles Spencer in particular wouldn't have told you anything you didn't want to hear unless he really couldn't avoid it. He's a decent and conscientious young man, and I'm sure you've noticed how much he admires you.'

I looked at her despairingly. 'He doesn't understand what's involved. If they . . . if they go in there with the knives . . .'

'They use lasers and microwaves,' she told me soothingly. 'With great precision, and without damaging anything but the tissue they need to remove. And they can regenerate—'

'Stop!' I told her, feeling my eyes sting again. 'Please! You don't know what you're talking about. This abnormality they've found involves the whole of my talent for music.' Even as I said it, I knew I was wrong. Those moments of stopped time involved even more than that: they involved my awareness of time and sequence and order, the integrity of my very self.

'Oh,' said Mrs Mickleson. 'Yes, I see that's a problem.' She hesitated, then went on, 'But I'm sure there's no need to despair. They can do wonderful things these days. I'm sure they'll find a way to treat the abnormality that doesn't involve destroying your talent for music.'

I was sure they couldn't – but how I could explain my certainty, when I didn't know myself why I felt it? I snuffled, then blew my nose disconsolately.

'Charles will certainly do everything he possibly can,' Amrita Mickleson added meaningfully.

Charles, was it, now? 'Did he ask you to say that?' I demanded.

'No,' she replied at once. 'I just thought I might be able to help. I like Charles very much: of all the research staff who've used the Hall, he's the kindest and the most considerate. I hate to see him so miserable. It really isn't his fault, and you shouldn't blame him for it.'

'I don't want to talk about it!' I exclaimed desperately. 'Tomorrow morning there are going to be more tests, and Professor Bernet will be all over me, and it makes me feel sick. I don't think I can stand it. Please, I don't want to talk about it any more.'

'I'm sorry,' she said quietly. In the doorway, she paused. 'Will you be joining us for supper?'

'Oh. No, thanks. I couldn't. I'm sorry.'

'Don't worry. It's very bad news, and it's natural to be very upset. I'll bring you up a sandwich.'

She left, and I lay on the bed listening as the back of my mind played a mournful Adagio for solo guitar in E minor.

Perhaps I was wrong about the music, I told myself. Perhaps what happened when it came out really *was* a dangerous illness, and the fact that I couldn't see it that way just meant that I was hysterical and deluded. After all, what did I know about brains?

But I couldn't believe that, and the more I thought about it, the more certain I became that if they tried to cut the music out of me I wouldn't even *need* to kill myself: it would be a mutilation so devastating that it would destroy my mind. Even telling myself that this conviction was irrational didn't dull it.

Charles had said he wasn't going to recommend surgery – yet. It was absolutely clear, however, that in the end he might very well do just that.

So where did that leave me? I could refuse to cooperate: I could go on hunger strike, demand to speak to officials from

128

the Department of Health, try to phone news reporters and get my story into the media. I doubted, though, that media or health officials would be sympathetic, and if I became an uncooperative embarrassment to Professor Bernet, he would probably condemn me to the surgery at once.

I longed for a way out so much it made my throat hurt. I thought about trying to escape.

The glow that filled me at the thought of being *out* of the Hall, *away*, clean and clear, took my breath away. I told myself that it would be pointless: if I ran away, I would never be able to go back to my course and my plans for the future.

Then I realised that I no longer cared. Oh, of course I wanted my bright future – but not more than I wanted the integrity of my mind and soul. Even if I had to spend the rest of my life as a cleaner, hiding in a strange city under a false name, it would still be better than submitting to the knife. Besides, if I stayed hidden for a year or two, until the hysteria over Cicnip had died down, I might be able to go back to my music safely.

I had to get away. Surely my parents would help me hide, once they understood the full horror of what threatened me?

I couldn't walk out the door, of course – not unless I could steal a valid keycard, and I was no pickpocket. Could I make one, then, or change the one I had, using the computer terminal downstairs? I had watched Amrita Mickleson make one, and it hadn't looked *too* difficult.

I dismissed that notion. Everything I'd seen of the security system said it was pretty good: it *couldn't* be so limp as to let just *anybody* make up a card to please themselves. The fact that I hadn't noticed what Amrita Mickleson had done to identify herself meant only that I hadn't noticed the system's safe-guards, not that they didn't exist.

All right, then – what? Climb out the window?

I got up and went over to the window. It was a beautiful window, with little diamond-shaped panes of glass set in lead; it really might be original Georgian. It was fixed very solidly into its wooden frame, however, and the side window, the bit that opened, was far too small for me to squeeze through, even if there hadn't been a two-storey drop the other side.

I could smash the glass, of course. If I did it at night, probably nobody would hear: I was alone on the second floor, now that the student participants were gone. I felt squeamish, though, about smashing something so old and beautiful – and the little panes looked as though they would be very hard to smash, too. I pressed at one, dug at the lead with a fingernail: God, it would take *forever*, and even somebody on the ground floor might notice a screech-thump-smash that went on for half an hour. There *must* be a bigger window somewhere.

The windows on the ground floor were probably not a good idea: they were undoubtedly locked and alarmed against burglars, and I knew that the Micklesons had their private rooms down there somewhere, to say nothing of Charles. Were there any other windows I could get at?

I went down to the first floor and had a look at the bathroom with the 'proper bath'. It was a small room in the middle of the residential corridor, and it had a single diamond-paned window set high above the toilet. It wasn't a *big* window, but it was big enough, and it hinged open with one of those post-and-pin affairs, now open a single notch to allow in the clean summer air. I stood on the toilet seat and looked out: it looked out on the area at the front of the house, and I thought it must be above the lounge. There was a long drop to a flowerbed and the gravel of the drive, much further than I wanted to jump. I supposed I could make myself a rope of knotted sheets, like some runaway heiress in a Victorian romance, and tie it to the towel rack – no, too flimsy; to the bath taps – and let myself down. My heart began to speed up again, and I forced myself to sit down and think it through calmly.

I would have to pick my time carefully. I couldn't do it at night, since I couldn't leave my room after eight in the evening. I couldn't do it now, because Amrita Mickleson was going to bring me up a sandwich at suppertime, which was – I checked my watch – only about an hour away. It seemed likely that in the early evening either Charles or the Micklesons might be in the lounge watching television, so I couldn't do it then. The best time, I decided, would be when the Micklesons were eating supper.

I went back to my room, put the Mozart Requiem on very loud, and lay back on the bed to wait.

Amrita Mickleson came up with the sandwich at ten to seven. I put it on the bedside table and thanked her listlessly, and she went out, frowning.

As soon as she'd gone, I stripped the sheets off the bed and knotted them together – at the corners, where they weren't too bulky – then added on the floral-print bedspread for good measure. I tugged at my improvised rope: the knots didn't slip. I glanced around the room, wondering how much I dared take with me. The backpack of clothing and the sleeping bag might be useful, but they'd be cumbersome to get out the window. Perhaps I could throw them out first, and then follow them? That would be noisy, and might attract the attention of somebody else in the house: better to leave them. I should leave the computer, too: I was already going to have to carry my guitar – I couldn't leave *that* behind – and I wanted to have at least one hand free.

I pulled on my black cotton jacket, put my phone in my pocket, picked up the guitar, and went downstairs to the first-floor bathroom with the sheets bundled in my arm. I locked the bathroom door behind me, hoping that it might cause at least a little delay. Then I tried to tie the sheets to the bath taps.

It was immediately apparent that this wouldn't work: the tap set was one of those short shiny ones that looks like it's been designed to be aerodynamic on take-off, and the sheets were too bulky to fit round them. I could rip them, of course – but then they might not be strong enough. I looked around some more, checked the towel rack again and concluded that no, it really would just pull out of the wall. Eventually I settled for looping the sheets around the pedestal of the toilet. I tied them, tugged to see if they slipped. They did, so I tied the knot again: this time it seemed to be OK, though it did take up a lot of bedspread. I climbed up on top of the toilet and opened the window.

The lawn was green and calm and empty, and there was a smell of wisteria. I threaded the sheet through the handle of my guitar case and lowered it slowly.

It didn't reach the ground: the rope of sheets wasn't long

131

enough, particularly with so much of it wrapped around the toilet. The guitar case dangled, three or four feet in the air, between the rosebushes and at just the right height to bang into a lounge window. I bit my lip, but told myself that it would be OK. I started to climb on to the window sill – then realised that the window was too small for me to crouch on the ledge. I stared at it, realising that I couldn't go out feet first: I would have to throw myself over the sill and wriggle out on my stomach until I started to fall, and only then get my legs under me.

I began to wonder if this was really such a great idea. What could I expect, even if I did get away? I would be not merely a CICNPC recipient evading assessment, but a CICNPC recipient with a serious brain defect who'd escaped from custody. The police wouldn't wait for me to turn up: they'd go out looking for me.

But if I stayed . . . I thought of Bernet getting his dirty hands on the music in my mind – and then I tried to imagine what it would be like if they ripped out that glorious mystery. No, no, no, no, *no*!

I reached through the window to grab the sheets and twist them round both wrists, then started to wriggle out.

The guitar below me swung about wildly, then, to my relief, snared itself and the sheets in a rosebush. The bush shook madly, but nothing hit the window. I wriggled on, upside down like a bat, staring sickly at the ground below me, and finally got a leg out of the window.

I fell. The twisted sheet bit hot and hard into my wrists, and I banged my hip against the wall. Fabric dragged along my skin, burning; there was a hollow thud as I bumped the guitar case – and then my feet hit the ground.

I staggered, staring through the ground-floor window into the empty lounge through tears of pain. Then I let go of the sheets and looked at my forearms. I had friction burns on both, red and sore but not actually very bad. I glanced up at the open window, then swallowed and unknotted the sheets from my guitar case.

I tried to toss the sheets back through the bathroom window, but I couldn't get enough of a bundle to make it work: they kept catching stupidly against the frame and falling back. I was terrified that somebody would come to see what was causing all the noise, and in the end I left them fluttering there and hurried off across the front lawn with my guitar.

At the end of the rhododendron-covered drive I hesitated. I knew there must be a village somewhere nearby: Charles had bought the strawberry-flavoured water there. Whether it was to the left or right, though, I didn't know, and I had no idea where the main road was from here. I had only the vaguest idea of what to do next. Get away, I supposed: get well away from the Hall, and then phone my parents.

I turned right and began to walk along the narrow lane, pushing myself to take long, rapid steps, guitar swinging. Somebody was bound to notice those fluttering sheets before very long. I needed to put enough distance between me and the Hall that Charles or George Mickleson couldn't just cruise up and down the road until they found me. I should hitch a lift, I decided. Not on this lane, of course – there was too much danger that any car coming up behind me would be from the Hall. When I reached a larger road would do. It didn't matter where I hitched to: all I needed was a place I could safely wait for my parents to come to collect me. I was sure they would help; they would never allow anyone to mutilate me just as a *precaution*. They would find me a place to hide, and then . . .

I would need a fake ID – one good enough to let me get an unexciting job, open a new bank account, and start a new life. Maybe I could get one of my Fine Arts friends from Dartington to make me one.

I followed the lane for about half an hour, dodging into the bushes whenever I heard a car approaching from behind me – though none of the cars turned out to be the Laurel Hall van. At last I reached a larger road which was signposted 'Arundel'. I turned left and walked slowly along the verge, sticking out my thumb hopefully whenever a respectable-looking car went by.

I got a lift into Arundel with a middle-aged couple who were going out to an open-air concert at Arundel Castle. 'Classical music, I'm afraid,' the man told me with a smile and a glance at the guitar case. 'Probably not your sort of thing at all.' I told them I was making my way back from a party with some student friends, and they accepted it without question. They dropped me off at the turn to the castle, and I walked back to the nearest bus stop, sat down on the bench, and telephoned my parents. It was twenty past eight by then, on a mild, overcast June evening. The streets of Arundel were quiet, and there were still hours to go before it got dark.

My mother answered the phone. 'Yes?' said her voice into my ear, anxious and urgent and distressed. A lump formed in my throat at the sound of it, and once more I longed for her to put her arms around me and make everything all right.

'It's me,' I told her, choking on the words.

'Val!' she exclaimed in relief; and then called, 'Steven, it's *her*! – Oh, darling, are you all right?'

'Yeah,' I said, fighting not to cry. 'Sort of. Look, a really horrible thing has happened—'

'Dr Spencer told us they found a serious abnormality,' said my mother, sounding as though she, too, was fighting not to cry. 'He says you've been having some kind of seizures for years. Why didn't you—'

'They're not *seizures*!' I exclaimed angrily, stung out of my tears. 'They're . . . a way of making music. It's never done me any harm at all, and nobody else ever even *noticed* it! Charles Spencer is just full of crap because it scared him. Mum, they're talking about surgery, and if they take this out of my mind, I'll be a vegetable, I know I will. Please, you've got to help me!'

'Where are you?' came my father's voice, patching into the line.

'Arundel,' I told them, starting to shake with relief. 'The bus stop by the castle. I had to get away; I climbed out of a window. Please, please come and get me out of here!'

'Calm down!' ordered my father, though he sounded very far from calm himself. 'It'll be all right. Are you OK? In yourself, I mean.'

'Yes,' I told him, swallowing. 'I'm kicked up, obviously, but I'm OK. I could wait for you here. Or there's a pub just down the road.' I could see it from where I sat, an oldish brick building with a trellis covered in clematis and yellow climbing roses: it was called, inevitably, the Castle. I remembered that I still had the money I'd earned busking in London about a century ago last Tuesday. I could buy myself a drink while I waited. I could use a drink.

'Look, Val,' said my mother seriously. 'I think you should go back to Laurel Hall.'

'No!' I exclaimed, in anger and dismay. 'No! That *foul* Professor Bernet will . . .' I didn't know how to explain the way I felt about letting Bernet ogle the part of me that did music, so I changed it to, 'They'd send me for surgery just as a *precaution*, Mum! They don't *know* anything about this thing, they don't even have a *name* for it. They have absolutely no reason to believe that it'll hurt me, but they want to take it out anyway, just because it's *different*. If they do that, it'll *destroy* me. I'll *kill* myself before I let them do it!'

'Calm down!' said my father again.

'This isn't what Dr Spencer was telling us,' said my mother doubtfully. 'Darling, I think you're panicking unnecessarily. He was very insistent that they were going to study this thing carefully, and that they wouldn't know what to do about it until they had.'

'They don't need to do *anything* about it!' I said shrilly.

'Val, he was saying that this was—'

'They're going to cut my head open and burn all the music out of my mind!' I screamed. 'That's what they're going to do, and I'd rather *die*!'

'Calm down!' said my father, for the third time. 'Please!'

'Please get me out here,' I begged, beginning to cry. 'Please. I want to go home.'

'All right,' he said. 'All right. You're at the bus stop by the castle at Arundel, you said.'

'Yeah,' I sobbed. 'B-but I think I'll wait in the pub. It's called the Castle.'

'OK,' said my father. 'I'll drive right down. Expect me in three or four hours.'

'Thanks,' I said, and clung to the phone as if it were his hand.

When he'd cut the connection I sat at the bus stop for a few

135

minutes, fighting to regain control of myself. A few late arrivals for the concert at the castle went past: they gave me looks of concern, which gave me the impetus to push the tears back inside. When I was sure I wasn't going to break down again, I went down the road to the pub.

It was a very Olde Worlde place, with exposed beams and inglenooks lined with horse brasses. The few other customers were sitting out in the garden, chatting cheerfully over their pints. I bought a glass of red wine and took it to a table in a dark corner inside; I wanted to gulp it all down, but I knew I had to make it last, to give myself an excuse for staying put, so I sipped it decorously. After a little while I took the sheet music out of my guitar case and pretended to study it so that nobody would try to talk to me.

About five minutes after I'd finished the wine, Charles walked in.

I stared at him in horror, too shocked even to move. He looked around carefully and saw me.

I understood, in one appalling instant, that my parents had told him where I was. 'Where are you?' my father had asked – before I'd told him that I'd left the Hall. Charles had telephoned my parents to enlist their help as soon as he'd realised I'd escaped. He'd succeeded, that was the worst thing. They had believed him and not me.

'Val,' he said, coming over to me.

I jumped to my feet and screamed, 'Go *away!*'

'Just let me talk,' he replied quietly. 'I don't want to have to call the police.'

I stood there, clutching the edge of the table and staring at him.

'If I have to call the police,' he went on, in a whisper, 'you will certainly end up being committed for treatment at a secure hospital.'

'Is he bothering you, miss?' called the landlady suspiciously from behind the bar.

'I just want to talk to her a minute,' Charles replied, half turning to her, then turning a sober face back to me.

The landlady frowned. She had obviously jumped to the

conclusion that he was my ex-boyfriend, and for a moment I had a wild idea of taking advantage of that – of playing the frightened victim of a stalker, and getting her to throw him out.

But then he would call the police.

I sat down slowly, still gripping the table edge. I felt utterly sick and betrayed. The landlady frowned again, but left us to talk it out.

Charles sat down carefully on the stool facing me. 'You've got to come back at once,' he said in a low voice. 'Luckily we hadn't actually phoned the police when your parents phoned me back to say where you were. If you come now we can hush it up. Bernet won't even know.'

I stared at him blindly, unable to frame a coherent reply.

'Look,' he said, very gently, 'you panicked. I understand why, but it *was* panic. Running away won't help anything. The thing causing the problem will still be inside your head.'

'I *want* it inside my head!' I snarled.

'You don't know—'

'Shut *up*!' I buried my face in my hands.

'Val, please!' Charles reached across the table to touch my shoulder. I recoiled back into the corner and glared miserably into his unhappy face.

'Look,' said Charles doggedly, 'I can't let you go: you must see that. You have an unheard-of and potentially dangerous abnormality of the brain, and you're already in custody for trying to avoid assessment for the Cicnip. If the police get involved they'll probably decide that since we couldn't keep you secure, you'll have to go somewhere that can. God knows what will happen to you then. Your parents are very worried about you—'

'Because you *lied* to them,' I said bitterly. 'You told them it was dangerous, when it's not.'

'Val, I don't want to argue about it now! I just want you to come back quietly. If you get arrested and committed, I can't protect you.'

'And just how have you been "protecting" me?' I demanded. 'You're the *threat*!'

'It's the thing inside your head that's the threat!'

137

'The thing inside my head is my *brain*, Charles, it's where I *live*!'

'If you're so sure this abnormality isn't a threat,' he said reasonably, 'let us prove it. Let us *study* it. Val, that's all we're going to do for the foreseeable future!'

I pressed my hands together. 'You're going to prove that it's *abnormal*, I know that. Abnormal is *wrong*, isn't it – even if it works.'

'Nobody is going to do any surgery until we understand this thing a lot better,' he said soothingly. 'Please. I really, really, really don't want to have to call the police.'

I sat there staring at my hands and shaking. I had no choice: I'd known that from the moment he walked through the door. I had no money to speak of and no refuge: if even my own parents refused to help me, I had no way to hide.

I got up in silence and picked up my guitar. Charles stood warily.

'Are you OK?' asked the landlady, with another suspicious look at Charles.

I nodded, not trusting myself to speak, and let Charles escort me out to the car park.

The Laurel Hall van was parked neatly in the half-empty lot. Charles opened the front passenger door for me, then closed it again and got into the driver's seat. He switched on the central locking with a clunk, then got out his phone.

'It's OK,' he told the person on the other end of the line. 'She was there, and she came quietly.'

Seven

We arrived back at the Hall at about quarter to ten. It was still only beginning to get dark, but the shadow of the Downs had fallen over the big house, and lights were already burning in a couple of the ground-floor windows. Security lighting came on as we pulled into the drive, and when Charles parked the car, George and Amrita Mickleson both came hurrying out of the house.

I stayed sitting in the front passenger seat after Charles had got out and opened the door for me, pointlessly putting off the moment when I re-entered my prison. Charles offered me his hand. I shook my head and climbed out heavily on my own, clutching my guitar.

'Oh, you silly girl!' Amrita exclaimed in relief, coming over. 'I understand that you were scared, but what a *stupid* thing to do! Never mind, you're back safely and no harm done.'

I dug out a tissue and wiped my nose. I didn't trust myself to answer. When I looked up at the house I wanted to be sick.

'You'd better come inside,' said Amrita, taking hold of my shoulder. 'Your father should be here in a few hours.'

I'd forgotten that he'd said he'd drive down – or rather, I hadn't realised that he would still drive down even though he wasn't going to help me get away. I swallowed, realising that if I saw him, I would undoubtedly scream at him and end up feeling even worse.

'I don't want to see him,' I said in a choked whisper.

Amrita looked shocked. 'He's very worried about you,' she said reprovingly.

'I don't want to see him, OK?' I said, more loudly. 'We'd only have a row.' I hugged my guitar and started towards the house. 'I'll phone him myself and tell him so!'

Amrita had to let me into my room, of course. It was too late for my keycard to have worked, even if I hadn't left it on the bedside table. The sheets had been put back on the bed, slightly creased where I'd knotted them but otherwise none the worse, and the sandwich Amrita had brought me a few hours before sat drying on its plate.

Amrita picked up the keycard and looked me in the eye. 'Probably I ought to just take this away. I'm sure it's what the police would recommend.'

I shrugged and sat down on the bed.

She set the keycard down, frowning. She'd evidently been planning a lecture and decided to abandon it, because she went on, 'I'm not a prison warder, though, and I'm not turning my house into a jail. You were scared and you panicked, and we'll leave it at that. Would you like a hot drink?'

I shook my head.

'I'll get Charles to give you something to help you sleep,' she said. 'You're overwrought.' She went out.

I phoned my father. He was on the M40, and asked me to wait until he could pull over. I told him he should turn around and go home, there was no point coming down to Sussex, I was back at the Hall. Then I cut off, phoned my mother, and told her the same thing.

She was *relieved*, that was the worst thing. She was relieved that I was 'safely' back at the Hall.

My father patched into the line from the hard shoulder, and I had the most painful phone conversation I've ever had in my life. Charles had told my parents that I had a serious and potentially life-threatening brain defect and that I'd panicked and run away when I found out about it. They were utterly dismayed, firstly because of the news itself, secondly because I'd kept my 'seizures' secret from them, and thirdly because I was trying to fight the people who wanted to help me. The possibility of surgery, which they'd previously opposed as wholeheartedly as I had, was suddenly something that they were urging on me as my salvation. In the end I couldn't stand it: I told them flatly that I didn't want to see them, and hung up.

Charles came in as soon as I did so, and I guessed that he'd been standing outside in the corridor waiting for me to finish.

I stared at him miserably. He hesitantly proffered a little foil pill pack. 'To help you sleep,' he whispered.

'Leave me alone,' I replied.

He broke off a strip of the pills, broke the strip in half, and set the tablet down on the foot of the bed. 'I think you should take it,' he told me, and turned to go.

In the doorway he paused, looking back at me. 'It's not my fault,' he said. 'Don't you believe I wish your brain was normal?'

'Go away!' I ordered, and he went out.

When I'd first arrived at Laurel Hall, I'd felt isolated. I saw now that I hadn't known what the word meant. I'd been able to count on the support of my family, I'd recruited help and sympathy from the staff of the Hall, I'd been confident that I could fight. Now I was entirely on my own.

I took the sleeping pills. Then, because I didn't know what else to do, I turned to God – in my own way. I put the Bach *Matthias Passion* on the house computer, and lay on the bed listening.

I fell asleep in the glory of it, and woke again at five to birdsong and the light of dawn through my window.

The computer was still on, its screen pale and unreadable in the sunlight. Once again I went over to the window and looked out at the view of woodland, field and hill. No trumpets, this time. I leaned my head against the pane.

I could try again to escape, but I knew it would be no use. Even if I succeeded in getting out of the house a second time, where could I go? My own parents had turned me in; nobody else was going to help me. I'd just get caught – and, as Charles had pointed out, if I were caught I'd be committed to a secure mental hospital and probably sent for surgery right away.

The only option I had was to cooperate with Bernet. Perhaps I could convince him that whatever the abnormality was, it didn't merit anything more than a supervisory order.

141

That was indeed the most sensible course. Only it felt like prostitution, and I ached for another way out so much that it was hard to breathe.

I went back to the computer and put on another requiem mass – Verdi, this time. The noise controls on the computer must have been relaxed on weekends, because I managed to crank the volume up to deafening.

Charles and Mrs Mickleson came up together at about half-past eight. By then I was on to Beethoven: the Prisoner's Chorus from *Fidelio* was a bass thunder shaking the window-panes. Amrita Mickleson rolled her eyes and Charles stared at the computer in disbelief. He had a bruise on his face that puzzled me for a moment, until I remembered how hard I'd slapped him the day before.

I got up and turned the music down.

'Thank you,' said Mrs Mickleson. 'Would you like to come down and have some breakfast?'

'No,' I told her. 'I don't think I could eat right now.'

She frowned, went to the bedside table and picked up the untouched sandwich from the night before.

'I couldn't eat last night, either,' I explained.

'You ought to have something,' she said with concern.

'Why?' I asked bitterly. 'So I'm in good shape for the next test?' I looked directly at Charles. 'When does the professor want to start screwing me?'

He winced. 'Val, please . . .'

'Please *what*? I'm going to cooperate. I don't have any other choice, do I?'

Mrs Mickleson's mouth narrowed the way my mother's did when she thought I was being obstinate and self-indulgent. 'We are trying to *help* you,' she said reprovingly.

I choked back the bitter response: she, at least, had been helpful and kind beyond the call of duty from the moment I set foot in her door. 'I understand that,' I said instead. 'But I feel awful. I wish I were dead.'

At least it made her sympathetic again. 'You'd feel better if you had something to eat – or at least drink,' she coaxed. 'What about some hot chocolate?'

'Honestly, I couldn't. Maybe later. When *does* the professor want me?'

Charles looked miserable. 'Half-past nine,' he whispered. 'We haven't told him about what happened last night, and we don't plan to let him find out.'

'I'll see you then.' I turned up the sound again. The chorus was over, so I jumped the recording forward to Florestan's first aria, with that clear, desperate, impossibly long cry out of the dungeon: *aaaaach, Gott!* I'd never really appreciated before how good it truly was.

'What is that?' asked Charles, startled.

'Shhh!' I told him sharply. 'Beethoven.' I lay down on the bed to listen to it, and didn't look up when he left.

In fact it was nearly ten when he returned to fetch me. I looked up at the opening door from the depths of the *Winterreise*, then took a deep breath and got up. I switched off the computer.

'Um,' said Charles nervously. 'Um. Could you bring your guitar?'

'What?' I asked in suspicion and surprise.

He swallowed. 'The professor and I both agree that we don't want a repeat of what happened yesterday, so we want to avoid artificial stimulation if we can. You said you could induce these events by playing the guitar, so—'

'I said *sometimes*,' I corrected him sharply. 'It doesn't always work.' The thought of having my guitar with me was painfully sweet, and I warned myself fiercely that it was too much to hope for. 'How am I supposed to play guitar lying on my back with my head in a clamp?' I demanded.

'We've, uh, been rigging the Meg so you can sit down under it,' he replied. 'That's why I'm a bit late. Um. I thought you'd prefer this to more needles.'

I would, of course. It was *infinitely* better than another session in that horrible sampler. It would've been a comfort just to hold the guitar, and to be allowed to *play* it . . . I could block out all the rest, even the professor's slavering look. I wanted it so much that I couldn't trust it. Warning myself again that something would go wrong, I picked up my guitar case and my computer.

'Why do you need the computer?' asked Charles.

'It's where I keep musical scores,' I explained impatiently. 'If I'm going to try to reach the music, I'll have to warm up first.'

'You can't use the computer in the same room as the Meg!' protested Charles. 'It's fantastically sensitive, and even a small computer generates enough interference to swamp the signal.'

'Oh?' I demanded. 'So why didn't the videomatic screw it up, too?'

I realised only then that I hadn't picked up the videomatic after the session on the previous day.

'You put that in the safe zone, on the wall next to the controls,' said Charles. 'You'd need your computer in front of you. Besides, we've had to detach the helmet, and that affects its screening. Can't you get your computer to print some of the music?'

I could, of course, though it entailed a trip down to an office on the ground floor, and sheet music won't scroll to cue. I wondered about the videomatic all the time the music was printing. In a way it no longer seemed important – I was so entirely at the mercy of my doctors now that all my efforts to protect myself seemed pointless. On the other hand, I didn't like the thought that the professor could have been editing its record. Besides, it was the Micklesons' camera, and I would need to return it to them.

I could, of course, have asked Charles if he knew what had happened to it – but I didn't want to speak to him any more than I absolutely had to.

By the time we turned up in the Meg room on the first floor, it was twenty past ten and Professor Bernet was fuming.

'I'm sorry, sir,' panted Charles. 'Miss Thornham needed to print up some music.'

Bernet glared at me and my armful of paper with distaste. 'What does she need music for?'

'Dr Spencer said you wanted me to try to reach the music,' I told him, feeling stupid and humiliatingly weak, 'to induce one of the brain events, that is. I don't know if I can do that, hooked up to a Meg, but it would help if I could play some other music first. To get in the right frame of mind.'

He snorted in disgust. 'Very well.' He hesitated a moment,

and then his cold eyes narrowed and he said softly, 'We have discovered some substantial structural anomalies in your brain, Miss Thornham.'

I didn't know what to say to that. I looked at the floor, running my thumb over the catch of my guitar case.

'Why didn't you inform us that you were subject to these extreme events?'

'Extreme' events. When most people say that, it means 'very good'. Not Professor Bernet. I swallowed. 'They're harmless,' I quavered. 'It's just . . . just that people have been so irrational about Cicnip-C, and I didn't want anybody to cut up my brain. I was frightened.' Even as I said it, I knew it wasn't true. I'd never told anybody about it because I'd wanted it to be normal.

'Your attitude,' Bernet continued, like snow falling, 'has been evasive and hostile all along. You have admitted to brain abnormalities only after we discovered them ourselves. I think you know very well that they are dangerous.'

I swallowed again, reminded myself what was at stake, and forced myself to say, 'I'm sorry. I can see I should have said something. It's just that I was scared about what would happen. I'll try to be more cooperative.' I swallowed one more time, then forced myself to say, 'I'll cooperate with any research you want to do.'

There was a silence. 'Very well,' Bernet said again, this time with satisfaction. His eyes gloated. 'Sit down there, and we will see if we can adapt the sensors.'

They'd brought in what looked like a footrest from the lounge, and the Meg's huge helmet had been turned around on its stand. I sat down, then had to get up again so that the two men could fetch books and insert them underneath the footrest to raise it enough that my head would fit inside the helmet. Eventually, however, the Meg and I were at the right height for one another, and I sat down uncomfortably on the footstool with the sensor cap on my head and the helmet hanging over it. Charles fastened a strap under my chin, then fixed another strap from the Meg's table across my shoulders to stop me from moving about too much. Bernet, muttering to himself, began checking the read-outs.

I edged my head down and moved my eyes about, checking whether I'd be able to play. It was not comfortable – but then, neither is the average shopping mall. I would recommend busking expeditions to any aspiring musician purely as a way to improve concentration in difficulties. If I thought of this as just a particularly bad pitch next to some malfunctioning escalator, I ought to be able to manage.

'You want me to find any particular piece of music to start with?' asked Charles helpfully.

'Yeah,' I replied. 'The *Three Gorges*. I think it's in the middle.'

The professor stopped muttering. 'Jiang Qi?' he asked angrily.

'Yeah,' I agreed. 'He's a contemporary Chinese composer. He's written some very beautiful things for guitar.'

'I know who he is,' said Bernet. 'I was not aware that you played music of *that* sort.'

Loathsome man. *Naturally* a toad wouldn't like Jiang Qi.

Charles shuffled through the papers. 'This one?' he asked at last.

The *Three Gorges*, first and longest of the *Five Landscapes*, an elegy for ravished beauty and corrupted innocence. 'That one,' I said with satisfaction.

Charles set the sheet music aside, then fumbled with the guitar case until he got it open. My Segovia came out into the sterile room like a messenger from another world: honey-coloured curves and a glitter of strings. I reached out for it and was caught by the strap across my chest. Charles came nearer and put it into my outstretched hands. I pulled it on to my lap and trailed my fingers over the strings, listening to their rich sweet voice. This was my one true friend, the only supporter I could trust to stay loyal, no matter what – and I had it with me. I tuned it carefully, no longer caring so much about the enclosure of the helmet round my head.

'Do you ever sing?' asked Charles suddenly.

I tried to shake my head, found I couldn't, and said firmly, 'No.' Not for you, anyway, I added silently. I adjusted a couple of keys on the Segovia, and let it sing for me.

146

To my surprise, Bernet came over with one of the chairs which had stood by the controls. He moved it up against my knees, then picked up the *Three Gorges*, secured some of it to the chair back with sticky tape and arranged the rest on the seat, so that I could see the whole piece. Then he retreated out of sight.

I'd chosen the *Three Gorges* as a warm-up because it was a piece I knew very well, and because it had never failed to move me. It didn't fail this time, either. A fusion of Western and Chinese styles, slow, deep, complex and achingly sad, it made everything around it quiet. When I stilled the last lingering note with the palm of my hand across the strings, the silence reverberated.

Bernet broke it. 'Very fine,' he said sarcastically. 'Now try to induce one of the events.'

I picked out a ripple of notes, struck a chord. I was not angry or frightened, as I would have been without the guitar: however much he tried to bully me, I had in my hands the one thing over which I possessed absolute mastery. I picked out another phrase, then played the little thing on the D string. It still felt very good.

Should I try to reach the music through something of my own, or through the creation of another mind? It was harder to do through someone else's work, but it was also more controlled: with a written composition I knew exactly what was going to come out. I needed to impress the observers with my control: I should try it.

Besides, I was pretty sure that the back of my mind didn't have anything appropriate ready. It had gone quiet back there, stunned – along with the rest of me – by the prospect of destruction.

'Can you give me the Mozart piece?' I asked Charles. 'The Williams adaptation of the C major piano sonata.' I'd reached the music through that one before, and Peter Shaffer got it right: Mozart really is the voice of God. If anyone could take me outside of time and space, he could.

He found it and propped it up against the chair back; I picked it up and looked through it carefully, renewing my memory of it, trying to hold the whole thing in my mind. It was beautiful, as always – the same profound perfection that had transported me before. OK. I set it down, fanned out the first movement against the chair back, then began to play, *allegro moderato*, letting the notes I played resonate against the ones in my mind. The helmet, the machinery, the men watching – gradually they all ceased to matter. The music filled all my awareness, until I wasn't sure whether the sounds I heard were the notes which sprang from the page directly into my mind, or the ones made by the strings beneath my fingers.

Nobody said anything when I finished. I shuffled the pages together, and set out the second movement in their place. The melody began to glow in my hands – and then it happened: the notes in my mind and the notes in the air fused. Time stopped. I floated in the Andante cantabile, a thistledown drift of shadow and infinite light.

Time started again. I paused, caught my breath, then stacked the pages together and set out the final Allegretto. The music did not come out again for that – but even so it remained exquisite.

When I finished, there was silence. I set the guitar down across my lap, then flexed my fingers and rotated my wrists. I felt as I usually did after I'd managed that communion: heavy and sleepy and satisfied in some place deep inside.

My shoulders ached, though. 'Can I get up now?' I asked. My voice seemed very loud and rough in the stillness.

There was a pause, and then the professor sighed slowly – satisfied and heavy, like me. 'We will try again after lunch,' he decreed.

I hesitated – but I was tired, and I knew there was no point in trying again after lunch: I wouldn't be able to reach the music twice in such rapid succession. Normally I wouldn't try to reach it even on two successive days – I had done it a couple of times, but it was tiring. 'I don't think I'll be able to do it again so soon,' I said humbly.

Charles appeared in my field of view and began undoing the straps. 'That . . .' he said breathlessly. 'I've never heard music like that.'

'Do *what* again?' asked the professor, beginning to sound his normal irritable self.

I shrugged my newly freed shoulders. 'Reach the music.' I wriggled out from under the helmet and set the guitar down carefully in its case.

'But you did not reach it,' declared Bernet in a supercilious tone.

'Yes, I did,' I corrected him. 'During the Andante cantabile – that was the second movement.'

'But we were watching—' began Charles – when the professor exclaimed '*Merde!*'

'What?' asked Charles, hurrying over to him at the Meg's controls.

'She is right,' said Bernet grimly, gesturing at a screen.

'What?' exclaimed Charles again. 'But we were *watching*!'

I regarded their astonishment with a feeling of unspeakable triumph. 'You didn't notice,' I pointed out. 'The music must have really got you.'

Eight

W e didn't have another session after lunch. Charles and Bernet, so far as I know, didn't even eat lunch: they stayed in the Meg room, going over the record of the 'event'. I went on to the kitchen on my own, found Amrita, and let her show me where things were so I could make myself a sandwich. I was feeling more cheerful – I couldn't imagine that the scientists would be so worried about a brain event they hadn't even noticed.

After I'd eaten, I contacted them on the videophone to ask whether they wanted me back. Charles, who answered, looked flustered. 'We're not ready,' he stammered. 'We're not even sure what to do next. Anyway, I don't . . . I don't think you should try to do that too often.'

That made me feel less cheerful again. 'So what am I supposed to do?' I snapped.

'Um . . . take the afternoon off. Try to relax.'

I felt like snarling, 'With the threat of radical brain surgery hanging over me?' – but in fact I was glad enough not to have to get back in the cage that I contented myself with hanging up.

In the end I managed to get out of the house: the Micklesons invited me to join them for a walk, 'if you'll promise not to do anything silly.' Very probably it was Amrita's idea: I can just see her having decided that I needed some healthy activity to take my mind off things. I don't know whether or not it breached the rules about keeping me in custody – probably it did, but nobody raised the subject. Anyway, I promised, and was allowed to walk with them through the oak woods, then across some fields of wheat – marigold-scented GM, to keep off pests, and almost overpowering in the hot sunshine – and up on

150

to the Downs. From the top you could see half of Sussex: a patchwork of field and farm, with the towns scattered across it like toys, and the sky miraculously blue from horizon to horizon – except for towards the south, where it paled above a distant azure glimpse of sea. The air smelled of grass and chalk, and the sun was hot against my face.

'This is *extreme*,' I told the Micklesons gratefully – and remembered Bernet characterising what happened when I reached the music with the same word. Yeah, I thought, it *is* extreme – like this!

They both smiled. 'Why we took the job,' agreed George. 'Fabulous bit of country.'

They had, they explained as we walked on, formerly run a pub in Swindon, but they had felt like a change after their son grew up and went off to university. 'He's at Brighton,' said Amrita. 'Studying hospitality management. Well, except this summer he's off touring Europe with some friends.'

They told me about their son and about the countryside and about the garden at the Hall as we walked a long circle back to the house. When we were nearly there again, I worked up the nerve to tell Amrita that I thought I'd left their videomatic in the room with the sampler.

'Oh, I'll fetch it for you,' she said, unconcerned.

Back at the Hall I did my laundry and had a long bath (I noticed that the bathroom window had been closed and locked). Then I sat back to watch a programme off the house entertainment package in my room. I was in the middle of this when the door buzzed.

'Who is it?' I asked, suddenly tense again.

'Me,' came Amrita's voice.

I got up and opened the door, and there she was, holding the videomatic. Unfortunately, there was Professor Bernet as well. I gazed at him in surprise and apprehension. It was nearly six, and I'd assumed he'd gone home.

'Here's the camera,' said Amrita cheerfully. 'It was right where you said it was. Supper's at seven.'

'Thank you,' I told her, taking the videomatic.

'I wish to speak with you,' said Professor Bernet.

Amrita looked sideways at him, raised her eyebrows, and looked significantly at the camera. I nodded, and she headed off. I backed away from the door, switched the videomatic on, and tuned it to Bernet as he entered.

He snorted. 'That is unnecessary.'

'So you keep saying,' I replied, putting the camera down on the bedside table. I did not sit down, nor invite him to do so. I wanted to keep the meeting short.

'I merely wish to talk. Miss Thornham, you have presented me with a dilemma.'

'I'm ever so sorry,' I answered sarcastically.

He eyed me coldly. 'It seems that your cooperative attitude was short-lived. Miss Thornham, why were you not at the Royal Academy of Music, on a scholarship?'

The question was so unexpected that I answered it honestly – or, at least, with part of the truth. 'My best friend was going to Dartington.'

He gave a snort of pure contempt.

'And,' I went on, beginning to feel angry, 'I didn't want to be hothoused. I . . . I wanted to take my time about things. See what I really have in me.'

'You retreated to a remote college in the wilds of Devon, more famous for theatrical arts than for music, because you knew that there you would not be promoted as a guitarist before you had determined whether you had it in you to become a composer.'

I couldn't answer. I could feel my face going red. How the hell had the vile snob worked *that* out?

'I have received a long e-mail from one of your teachers. A Professor Frasier. In fact, I received it two days ago, but I had not troubled to read it until after the events this morning. I had assumed that the music you studied was popular and undemanding – guitar music for a theatrical college! – and I was not interested in what your teachers had to say about you. I assumed that even if we were compelled to recommend you for surgery, the loss, to you and to others, would be minor. I have now been forced to revise that assumption. Your Professor Frasier thinks you are a genius.'

I could feel my heart pounding in my ears. 'Professor Frasier said that?'

Bernet made a small, contemptuous, 'Huh!' of agreement.

I'd known Professor Frasier thought highly of me, but . . . *genius*? He wasn't a man who threw that word around casually. He'd never even applied it to Corelli, for example, or Villa Lobos or Rodrigo . . . *genius*? Oh God, oh God, oh God . . . of course, he'd use it more loosely of one of his own students, but still . . . *genius*?

'He did not mention this opinion to you? I suppose not: he said that you were wary of your own gift, and he did not wish to alarm you with a heavy burden of expectation. He did, however, take it upon himself to warn me against damaging what he believes to be a major talent. Yesterday I would have dismissed his letter as nonsense, but today I heard you play.' Bernet shrugged. 'Of course, ability to play an instrument is not evidence of merit as a composer – but you undoubtedly possess a profound musical ability. There are very few guitarists who can do justice to Jiang Qi.'

'I thought you didn't like him!' I mumbled.

Bernet's eyes widened. 'Why?'

'You were so angry and disgusted when I said I was going to play him.'

He was silent a moment, then said, very slowly, 'No. I consider him to be one of the greatest of living composers. I was merely surprised to find *you* playing him. I was expecting to have to endure something . . . popular. But I have never been good at communicating with other people, and recently . . . I have become worse.' He looked at me grimly. 'I regret it if this contributed to your uncooperative attitude. I hoped for so many answers from you, but all you have done is create more questions. And now there is this . . . dilemma.'

He moved closer, dark, bloodshot eyes still regarding me intensely. He reached out one big, knotted hand very slowly and touched the right side of my forehead, on the wobbly bit where the skull was patched. I stood frozen. His fingers felt their way through my hair along the ridge of thickened bone

153

that ended above my right ear, and his palm cupped my forehead almost reverently.

'There have not been any great female composers,' he said in a low voice. His thumb stroked the ridge in my skull, making my skin crawl – but somehow I could not push it away. 'Great performers, yes, certainly, many; a few capable composers of the second rank – but *greatness* . . . it seems to be something to do with the differences in the way neural circuitry is recruited on the right side of the brain during development. Except in your case the normal pattern was disrupted. The abnormalities in your brain are substantial, Miss Thornham. Dr Spencer believes they represent a threat to your life and sanity, and he wishes to treat them. His understanding of music, however, is trivial, and the only dilemma he sees is over your own strong opposition to receiving treatment. He does not understand that the gift which the abnormality bestows on you may be worth more than the things he wishes to preserve – but I think you do. What would you say if I told you that the abnormality in your brain will kill you within three years if it's left untreated? Which would you want saved – your life, or your yet-to-be-written music?'

The beat of blood in my ears was suddenly joined by a solo voice, *basso profundo*, crying a long, African-style chant without words. Three years to compose, and I was a *genius*? Three years – and if they operated, I would have *nothing*, nothing at all. 'The music,' I whispered.

He moved my head back and forth, jarring my teeth. 'As I thought. As I thought.' He let go. 'Music is a fearful thing.'

I put my own hand up against the skull and tried to rub away the touch of his hand. Did I really have only three years? What would happen to me during those three years? Would I start having seizures? Would I rave and hear voices? Would I end up losing everything – except the music?

How did he *know* I was going to die? Everything else he had said implied that he didn't understand what was happening at all! 'Where does this figure of three years *come* from?' I demanded suspiciously.

He grinned at me malevolently. 'My invention. It was a hypothetical question, Miss Thornham.'

154

I lowered my hand and glared, my heart now beating very fast. 'You *bastard*!'

'I have no idea how this abnormality in your brain works or how it may develop. It may be entirely benign – though, like Dr Spencer, I doubt it.'

'But, but . . . you're not going to recommend treatment?'

He laughed. 'I have no *wish* to, Miss Thornham, and if you continue to cooperate, I will have no *need* to.'

In other words, he was reserving his power to blackmail me – and now he was fully aware of his threat's potency. 'You *bastard*,' I muttered again, hating him more than I'd ever hated anyone in my life.

He bowed slightly. 'That little piece you played this morning just before the Mozart – what was that?'

I swallowed. 'Which little piece?'

'It was all on one string of the guitar.'

'Oh, that. That's mine.'

'Ah? I had wondered. It was very effective. Play it for me now.'

I swallowed again. Then I got out the guitar, sat down on the bed and played my comforter on the D string. He stood in the doorway, listening, his cold eyes downcast. When I finished he looked up, and for a moment our eyes met. Then he bowed slightly and walked out, closing the door behind him.

I sat on the bed, hugging the guitar. He should not have asked for the piece on the D string: he'd given himself away. He hadn't won, after all. His threat was empty. He *loved* music, and he would be no more willing to destroy me than I would be to smash my Segovia. It was *Charles* who was the threat now – Charles, who valued me above the music, and was willing to recommend surgery to preserve me, even if I hated him for it.

What was strange was that I despised the professor more than ever, and found myself rather admiring Charles. He was wrong, I was sure of it – surgery would not preserve me – but it wasn't really unreasonable for him to think he knew more about it than I did.

Was I *really* in any danger? I'd never felt it, and nobody had provided any evidence of it. I couldn't help feeling that Charles and Bernet both had simply been so frightened by what happened in the sampler room that they had assumed the worst.

I set down the guitar and picked up the videomatic. I presumed I had a record now of the events in the sampler room, and I supposed I might as well have a look at it – and check whether it had been edited, while I was about it.

The beginning of the videomatic record, however, was the scene just past. I realised with surprise that *everybody* must have forgotten that the camera was in the sampler room: it had just sat running until it reached the end of its memory, and when I restarted it for the professor's visit, it had begun to overwrite its previous recording, as they will if nothing's saved. I watched it for a couple of minutes with distaste, then began to fast-forward. Presently the image jumped, and I was watching the scene in the sampler room as Charles got me ready for the scanner. I slowed the recording, listening again as Charles reassured me about what would happen. I hadn't realised I'd looked so scared sick. The camera, though, was focused on the professor, who was busy checking over the scanner, casting occasional looks of disgust over his shoulder.

My foam-encased head and shoulders disappeared into the tunnel, and Charles went over to the professor and began examining a screen. He looked angry, and the glances he cast at Professor Bernet were furiously indignant. He and Bernet said very little to one another as they began the scan. I fast-forwarded some more, through a long passage of flickering indecipherable images on the scanner screens and no discussion from the men. Then everything changed, and the two started shouting at one another. I slowed the recording.

Charles rushed over to my recumbent form, caught my hand, shouted my name, checked my pulse. He whirled back at the professor and cried, 'It's a hundred and forty beats a minute!'

Bernet shook his head and jabbed at some controls.

'What have you *done*?' demanded Charles in distress. 'I *knew* you shouldn't have stimulated that link during an episode!'

'It was a *tiny* stimulus!' replied the professor, jabbing at something else. 'It couldn't have caused *this*! I'm going to give her some noradrenalin.'

'Stop that!' Charles shouted. 'It *did* cause it, you *saw* it cause it! No, no, don't touch anything: you'll make it worse. Val! Val, can you hear me?'

'There's no response,' said Bernet frantically, gazing at the screen. 'Acetylcholine and enkephalin are still climbing.'

I watched as Charles hauled me out of the tunnel, as Bernet disengaged the sampler and Charles got the helmet off, slapped my cheeks and chafed my hands. My own face was disquieting: wide-eyed, smiling, passionately intent and completely blind to everything around it. Charles began checking my reflexes – knee-jerk, eye-blink, palm-curl – then stood a moment blinking at tears. 'Val!' he said again, and caught my unresponsive hand. 'Val, please wake up!' The anguish in his voice tore at me.

I stopped the recording. Charles was at least twenty-six, probably a couple of years older: he must have had lots of girlfriends. Oh, all right, Mickleson had revealed when I'd first arrived at Laurel Hall that he was single right now – but there must be people in the background back at Oxford. Yes, all right, I'd suspected he fancied me, then confirmed it; all right, everyone else at the Hall seemed to have noticed. But it couldn't be serious. He barely knew me!

That note in his voice, though, implied rather more than casual interest.

I was, or had been . . . interested . . . in him in turn, but suddenly I found myself blindingly angry. I'd never asked him to fall in *love* with me, to suppose that he had a say in my whole *life* . . .

That wasn't why I was angry, I saw suddenly. If he felt like that about me, and knew how I felt about surgery, and *still* he urged it . . . that was frightening. And it looked as if at first he'd blamed Bernet for what had happened. It couldn't have been easy to go back to the professor to enlist his help, but he'd done it without hesitation.

Maybe there really *was* something wrong with me. *We have discovered some substantial structural anomalies in your brain. What* structural anomalies? What was wrong with me?

Angry, frightened and resentful, I fast-forwarded the recording. The two men argued silently at speed, gesticulating in jerks,

157

trying this and that to reach the plastic-draped dummy on the table, then finally just shouting at one another until the dummy abruptly sat up.

I almost put the recording off and downloaded it into its sealed file at that point, but it wasn't quite seven yet, so I just sat staring at the screen as Charles and the dummy fast-forwarded out, and the professor sat down and put his head in his hands – then jumped up and whizzed at high speed through a check of what the scan had recorded. He sat down once more; jumped up again, whizzed into something else . . .

Something peculiar. I slowed the recording, then froze it. The videomatic had been on the table to the side of the sampler controls, and didn't have a good view of what was on the screen, but what I could see didn't look like the indistinct images I'd glimpsed before. It was an MRI scan, I realised – but it looked . . . different. After a moment, I realised that was because the front edge of the brain it showed was missing.

I reversed the recording, let it play forward, froze it again, zoomed in until the image went grainy, then stared sickly: there was definitely something very wrong with the front edge of that brain.

Nobody had said anything about a part of my brain being *missing*. Abnormalities, they'd said, inappropriate connections, excessive activity, affected areas going black on MRI – but nothing about bits *missing*! And that bit – the prefrontal cortex – wasn't that the part that Charles said controlled social behaviour and empathy and sense of reality?

Oh God, what was happening to me? Was my brain beginning to dissolve away? Was I going to lose my faculties, slowly becoming blind and dribbling, incontinent and paralytic? I'd said I preferred music to life – but I'd assumed I would be facing a *clean* death.

Maybe that scan wasn't mine. Maybe it was a record of the inside of someone else's head, and the professor was looking at it because, because . . .

It would have to be because he suspected that it showed what was going to happen to me if I didn't receive treatment. That would have been why he'd come to check with me what I wanted – except how *could* he suspect that? Everything every-one had said so far implied that the way CICNPC had affected my brain was completely unique, and that nobody had any idea what was really going on, let alone what was going to happen in future.

I could ask Charles about it – if I could trust him to answer me honestly, and not exaggerate the danger. Perhaps I could phrase it so that I caught him off guard. I could be crafty, and—

The phone buzzed: Amrita, to say that supper was ready. I thanked her, left the recording as it stood, and stumbled hurriedly downstairs. I had no appetite, but I found I did very much want company.

We were still eating in the big dining room, though only one small table had places set out. I hurried into the sunny elegance to find a smell of curry, and George and Amrita and Charles already sitting around the table. I sidled in and edged round to the other side of the table, muttering a general greeting. Amrita smiled back, heaped a plate with curried new potatoes and lentils, and passed it to me before going on to serve everyone else. I stared at the curry sightlessly. I realised that the last thing I wanted to do was eat.

'Val?' said Amrita, and I looked up to find everyone staring at me. I blushed and looked down again.

'What did Professor Bernet want?' Amrita asked with con-cern.

I frowned at the curry. 'I think he was sounding me out,' I admitted. My voice sounded far away. 'He wanted to know how much I really care about music, and how good I really am at it. Apparently Professor Frasier, my composition tutor, e-mailed him that I . . . that I'm very good.' I picked up my fork – then put it down again and found myself saying, 'He asked me what I'd want to do if the thing in my head was going to kill me within three years – whether I'd rather keep my life or the music. I said I'd rather keep the music, but . . .' I saw that degenerating brain again, and suddenly I was so scared I could barely stand it. I pressed both hands to my face. Damn, damn, damn: I should've stayed upstairs.

Amrita jumped up, rushed over, and put an arm around my shoulders. 'Hush!' she said. 'You'll be all right.'

'I don't want to be mutilated, and I don't want to die!' I cried, and fought against the tears.

'You'll be all right,' Amrita told me again, patting me on the back.

'No I won't,' I replied, but I grabbed her arm and held on to it. The fear, now that it had started to come out, was sweeping through me in hot howling waves: needles, knives, the horrifying unstoppable collapse of body and mind, the loss of reason, the disintegration of the soul.

'Val,' said Charles urgently, 'nobody's going to mutilate you, and you're not going to die!'

'Yes I am,' I said. '*You* want them to mutilate me. But if nobody does anything, then my brain's just going to shrivel up and I'll turn into a drooling idiot!'

'Val!' he said, very distressed. 'Your brain is *not* going to shrivel up. There's absolutely no reason for you to be afraid of that. It isn't happening. It isn't even a risk. And nobody's going to operate on you without making absolutely certain that it won't do significant damage. Nobody's even going to recommend treatment without having a much better idea of what's going on.'

I stared at him, swallowing sobs. Amrita rubbed my shoulders gently. 'You hear?' she asked. 'It will be all right.'

I swallowed again. 'My brain isn't sort of . . . crumbling away at the front?'

'Not at all,' declared Charles, his face darkening. 'Did Professor Bernet tell you it was?'

'No,' I admitted, looking away. So much for craftiness: I was about as crafty as a raincloud. I had my answer, though. 'No, he admitted it was just a hypothetical question. It's just . . . I was looking at the record from the videomatic, from the sampler room, and there was a bit where the professor was looking at some scans, and it looked like the brain he was looking at had a bit missing at the front.' I managed to let go of Amrita and find my table napkin. I wiped my nose. 'I was afraid it was what was happening to me. I guess I just . . .

started to panic. I'm sorry.' I looked down at the curry again, then looked up at Amrita, who was hovering anxiously.

'I'm sorry,' I told her again. 'I can't eat this. I'm too upset. It looks lovely, and you've been very, very kind, and I really do appreciate it, but I'm just . . . I just can't eat until I've calmed down. I'm sorry.'

'No, I'm sorry,' she said. 'I should never have left you alone with Professor Bernet. How *could* that man say something like that to you when you were already so upset? It was *wicked*!' She glanced round at the men, who both looked as though they agreed entirely, then turned her attention back to me. 'If you want to go upstairs and lie down for a bit, I'll bring your supper up to you later. Would you like me to come and sit with you?'

'No, thanks very much,' I told her wiping my face again. 'It's very kind of you, but I'll be OK. I'm sorry: I didn't mean to . . .'

'Val,' said Charles, 'would it help if I went over your scans with you and explained them?'

I looked at him, and he looked back. Actually, I realised, it would help a lot. I couldn't bring myself to say anything, but I nodded.

Charles got up at once, looking relieved. He glanced down at his untouched plate, then at the Micklesons. 'I'm sorry,' he said. 'Would you mind if . . .'

'I can warm yours up, too,' said Amrita at once. 'Go ahead.'

We went up the stairs in silence, me occasionally dabbing at my eyes with the napkin. I now felt a total snail.

When we reached my room, Charles went over to the computer. It was still frozen on the image of Professor Bernet looking at the MRI of a damaged brain. Charles frowned at it. 'He seems to be looking at a case of prefrontal degeneration,' he remarked. 'I don't remember him doing that.'

I sniffed and sat down on the bed and explained where the image came from. 'What's prefrontal degeneration?' I asked when I'd finished.

'A rare brain disorder. The cells in the front of the brain start to die off for no reason that anybody's ever been able to discover. Sometimes they can halt the process with SGNS, but sometimes the new cells that are grown in just die off as

161

well, and the degeneration continues, eating away more and more of the brain until the sufferer dies.' He swallowed. 'It's a horrible way to die. Because the prefrontal cortex is the part of your brain that handles your social skills, when you lose it you lose your ability to identify with the feelings of other people. You can have been kind and thoughtful all your life, but once the degeneration's started you can break the heart of everyone you love most and not care. You can't care: the bits of your brain that do the caring are dead.' He looked up at me. 'It's definitely not you, Val. There's nothing wrong with your prefrontal cortex, despite all the implantation treatment you had on it. The professor must have looked this up because of some other feature. The prefrontal cortex *is* his field, remember: he's probably looked at more deranged prefrontal systems than normal ones, so there's nothing sinister about him looking one up in connection with you.'

'Oh,' I said, deeply relieved.

'I'll show you,' offered Charles. 'Can I quit this?'

'Better save it first,' I advised him.

He nodded, saved the videomatic record, then quit. He sat down at the desk, accessed the house system, then keyed in his password and placed his right hand flat against the screen. 'We use a dual-key identity check for access to medical records,' he explained, when he saw me staring. 'Password and palmprint – there.' The computer had chimed and granted him access. He typed in my name and got a menu up. I moved round on the edge of the bed so that I could see better – the room was small enough that I didn't have to stand over his shoulder. Charles selected 'Map', and the screen went dark for a second. Then a 3-D outline of a brain appeared in gold. Surface contours unfolded rapidly across it, and then blood vessels appeared in deep red, branching out from its centre like time-lapse footage of a tree flowering. It was unexpectedly beautiful. Another menu appeared to one side.

'This is our composite image of your brain,' Charles told me, glancing over his shoulder to be sure I was watching. 'It's actually a huge file. We started it the first time we scanned you, and the results of every scan you've had since have gone into it, along with all your medical records – and, as you can see, there are no bits missing.' He traced the front edge of the image with one finger. 'All healthy tissue. In fact, we were surprised at how completely normal your prefrontal cortex turned out, seeing that it was the part of your brain that sustained the worst trauma. All the abnormalities are elsewhere – and there's absolutely no sign that any tissue anywhere in your brain is degenerating. OK?'

'What are the abnormalities?' I asked, then cleared my throat: my voice had come out very rough and choked.

Charles sighed and shook his head. He went to the menu, pressed some keys, and a green tangle appeared on the image of my brain. At the very front there were only a few spiderwebby threads, but a thick verdant bar ran from just behind them down to a bulb at the side – the spot just above my ear – and tendrils curled out from either end, deep into the brain and across the top to the other side. 'Those are connections your brain has which normal brains lack,' he told me. 'Most of the information behind this image comes from the sampler data, though we were able to reinterpret some of the data from the other scanners to sharpen it up once we had some idea what we were looking at. This is the real surprise.' He touched the green tendril which crossed the top of my brain. 'In most people, the two cerebral hemispheres communicate through the corpus callosum, which is here.' He touched a spot in the middle of the brain. 'But the regenerated area in your right frontal lobe seems to have decided that it wanted a direct line to its counterpart in the left frontal lobe.'

'Why?' I asked faintly.

He shook his head again. 'I don't know. I really don't. Those areas are both normally associated with higher cognitive functions, that's all I can say. With most Cicnip recipients I'd say that the connection just grew that way at random, but in your case, I doubt it. An abnormality that substantial is very unlikely in anyone who had the treatment as young as you did, and all the other unusual connections you've made seem to have been driven by your brain's own activity. This very strong one, for example.' He touched the thick green bar along the side of the

163

image. 'It goes from your right frontal cortex to your right auditory cortex. No mystery about what drove *that*.'

'Music,' I agreed. I got up so that I could touch the green bar, then traced the tendrils from it. They followed the contours of the rest of my brain, reassuringly natural. 'Charles, what does it *mean*? Why are you so convinced it's dangerous?'

He let out his breath slowly, then turned in his seat to look up at me, his face unguarded. The bruise where I'd hit him stood out on his cheek. 'Val, I'm sorry. I shouldn't have told you it was – or not like that, anyway. I was kicked up, and I handled it very, very badly.'

'I wasn't exactly calm,' I admitted. 'I'm . . . sorry I hit you.'

He ventured a very small, very hesitant smile. '*You* had every right to be kicked up. And you had a real point, too: I *don't* really know that your episodes, or seizures, or whatever you want to call them, are dangerous. Probably you're right, and a lot of how I feel about it stems from the fact that I was so scared when you . . . when you passed out like that. All I can really say is that structural abnormalities in the brain are usually bad news, and the way your whole system jumped into a very extreme state in response to a single stimulus, coupled with the sort of levels we were seeing on those neurotransmitters – I don't like it at all, and I think I'd still feel that way even if all I knew of it was an anonymous case history. But please, please don't believe I'm some kind of knife-happy butcher. I would *never* recommend you for any kind of treatment unless I was as certain as humanly possible that it was necessary.'

This actually made me feel worse: it didn't sound like there was much chance of me just walking away. 'How do you define "necessary"?' I asked him coldly.

He took another deep breath, then said, with great determination, ' "Required to avoid significant mental and physical impairment" – but, please, I don't *know* that there's a real risk of that. It's what I'm afraid of, but I may be worried about nothing. I hope I am.'

I met the desperate sincerity in his eyes and felt queasy. 'Look, I've seen the image: you can ease up on the reassurances. Just what do you think is going to happen to me if I don't get treatment?'

'The thing I'm afraid of,' he replied slowly, 'is that your neural systems are becoming so habituated to this experience that they're beginning to crave it. Let me repeat it again: I *don't* know this, it's just what I'm afraid of. If it's true, then these events could soon start happening involuntarily. The neurochemistry is so extreme that it makes me worry that it could cause neurological damage, and the physical demands must be considerable, too. That sort of heart rate must place a real strain on your cardiovascular system – and I don't even know what your blood pressure was doing while it was going on. There's a real risk, too, that you could have a seizure in some circumstance where it would be life-threatening – while bathing, for example, or crossing a road. At best it would be impossible for you to live a normal independent life and at worst you could end up with epilepsy, a heart condition and God knows what cognitive defects. But this is all speculation. I could be wrong.'

I winced as I considered that. It sounded horribly plausible, but . . . 'But what if the *surgery* leaves me with a significant mental and physical impairment?' I asked wretchedly.

He was taken aback. 'Why do you think it would? This is the twenty-first century: people aren't lobotomised any more, and we have SGNS.'

'But you don't know what those extra bits of my brain are doing,' I pointed out. 'How do you know it wouldn't do terrible things to me if you took them out? I think it would. I'm *sure* it would.'

To my surprise, Charles didn't just dismiss that: he sat silent a moment, frowning deeply. Then he asked quietly, 'Can you explain *why*?'

'No,' I admitted miserably. 'I can only tell you what I feel when I reach the music – that it uses so much of me that if you pulled it out, there wouldn't be enough of anything left to work.'

Charles's frown grew even deeper. 'It's not just that you . . . that is, Professor Bernet was saying that for you it was a choice between great music and a dull normal life, and that it was a dilemma I wouldn't understand. Are you saying that's *not* your dilemma – that you're afraid of something more?'

I bit my lip. 'It is *partly* that. But what I'm really afraid of is . . . is losing *me*. When I first came here I told myself that if I lost the music I'd kill myself, but now that I'm staring the possibility in the face, I don't think I'd even be able to. There wouldn't be enough of me left to kill, and if they put in a lot of new tissue with SGNS it wouldn't matter, because whatever they brought back, it wouldn't be me. And I'm sorry, I can't explain why I think that, except that the music goes in so deep.'

Charles started to speak, stopped himself, then burst out, 'Val, why didn't you *tell* me that before? It's very important. I don't have any way of knowing things like that, unless you tell me.'

I stared at him. 'You mean – you believe me?'

He grimaced. 'That's not the point! I believe you *feel* that, and I believe that there's probably a *reason* you feel that. I don't know what the truth is, but you don't, either. What you *feel* is one of the most important clues we have. If you don't tell me what that is, then I'm working blind. It's conceivable that you have a point. The frontal lobes *are* involved in personality integration, and their normal functions could be entwined with the abnormal ones. Now you've told me about it I can think up some way to check it – but if you hadn't told me, I wouldn't have thought to worry. You can't go on keeping secrets! You haven't been telling *anyone* about things that are desperately important – you hadn't even told your own parents that you were hearing music! You've got to trust me more, for your own sake!'

'Why should I trust you?' I responded, angrily. 'I tried to, yesterday: I went and told you my last secret – and you took it straight to that foul old brain-groper.'

'Val, he's one of the world's leading authorities!' Charles cried in exasperation. 'He can *help*! Can't you see that I'm not out to get you, that I'm on your side?'

'Huh! You've lied to me. Bernet wants to use me as an experimental animal. I've been locked up and scanned and bullied and had needles stuck into my brain, I'm threatened with the prospect of having radical brain surgery against my will, and the only reason – the *only* reason! – is that Michael Torrington shot eighteen people and some government minister decided to calm the public about Cicnip-C. In case you've forgotten, the reason I was sent here was to be assessed as to whether I was a danger to the public. We all know I'm *not*, so why can't you just let me go?'

He took a deep breath. 'Do you really, truly believe that this thing is harmless?'

'I *used* to!' I cried. 'I did until you and Professor Bernet got to work. I *used* to be a very promising young musician. Now I'm some sort of cloned-brain freak tottering on the verge of complete mental breakdown. Everything I tell you gets twisted around into a proof of how sick I am.'

'That's not true!'

'Yes it *is*!'

'How can you *possibly* claim that I think of you like . . . like that? My God, I think you're the most fabulous girl I've ever met: everybody else can see that, if you can't!'

That stopped me short. I picked up the sodden napkin and wiped my eyes again. I thought of saying, 'In spite of the fact that I've been pretty horrible to you?' – but I didn't. The fact that I didn't trust him could not be swept aside so easily. It wasn't that I disbelieved his protestations; it was simply that he was part of the monstrosity that had trapped me here, and ultimately he would serve it, and not me.

'I shouldn't have said that,' Charles said, suddenly ashamed. 'I'm sorry.'

I stared in bewilderment. He was *sorry* that he thought I was fabulous?

'I don't want to harass you,' he continued seriously.

Oooh my, sexual harassment. Doctors can be struck off the register for that. 'You think *that* was harassing me,' I croaked resentfully, 'but betraying me to Bernet wasn't?'

He reddened. 'Val, I told Bernet because I don't know what this will do to you, and he's one of the few people in the world who might be able to work it out. But I'm sorry: I shouldn't have started this. You're already standing with your back to the wall, and I didn't come up here to fight with you. If you can't trust me, don't. But, please, tell me as much as you can – for your own safety. Please.'

I blew my nose and chucked the napkin at the bin. He had a point. 'OK,' I conceded grudgingly. 'I'll try. But don't ask me any questions right now. They make me feel deformed, and I'm not up to it.'

He relaxed slightly. 'I'm not going to,' he said warmly. 'You've already had far too much grief from the professor. But is there anything you'd like to ask me, while I've got your records up?'

'Yeah,' I said slowly. 'What happens when I . . . when I reach the music?'

In answer he turned back to the computer and selected some more things off the menu. A network of regions across the gold-outlined brain on the screen lit suddenly and brilliantly white, and the rest became a shadow.

'I thought you said it went black!' I protested.

'On the fMRI,' he agreed. 'This graphic shows activity by increasing brightness. It's just computer graphics, Val: all the real events are invisible. It's very, very intense activity, though, however you represent it. Your heart has to work like a sprinter's to get enough blood to the region, and the rest of your brain virtually hibernates.'

I looked at the image some more. The lit regions weren't in the places I expected them. There was a bright spot in the place above my right ear, yes, but the very front of my head – the much-discussed prefrontal cortex – was only hazed with light. There was a clump of three brilliant lozenges behind it, with another cluster across from it, over on the left side of my brain, and another one curling around into the very centre of my head. I pointed at the last two. 'Those are what I have extra connections to, aren't they?'

'Yes,' agreed Charles, looking unhappy about it.

'Does it look as dramatic as this on the scanner?'

'It's very dramatic, however you look at it.'

'But when it happened this morning you didn't even notice it.'

'That is the weirdest and most frightening thing of all,' said Charles grimly.

I stared at him.

'You know how much it scared me the first time I saw it happen,' he said levelly. 'Don't you think I was nervous this morning? I was watching the screen and waiting for something to happen like ... like an expectant father! And then ... all I remember is the music. I've never even been interested in classical music! It's not that I don't like it, it's just that I don't know anything about it – but when you played, I forgot about everything else. The professor and I had a long list of things we were going to try and check, but we missed the whole event – you *know* we did; you had to tell us that it had happened! The professor thinks—' He stopped abruptly.

'What?' I asked, dreading the reply.

He seemed to decide that he ought to answer. 'He thinks you induced some sort of abnormal brain state in us, too. He wants to rope in some volunteers from the next Ethical Decision Making programme, fix them on the MRI, get you to induce one of these events and see what happens inside their heads when they listen.'

I wasn't sure whether to be offended or amused. 'For God's sake! Of *course* music affects people's minds! That's why we like it!'

'This was excessive,' said Charles flatly. 'You said you've had these episodes when you've had an audience before. What sort of reaction did you get then?'

'They told me it was extreme, total, top score!' I snapped impatiently.

I remembered one occasion at a party the previous year, just before the end of term. It had been held in the common room of my residence hall, and everyone had been getting drunk and rowdy. Sometime after midnight the building superintendent came by and told us we had to shut up and shut down. Alicia, who'd organised the thing, and who'd been standing on one of the tables singing silly versions of Christmas carols, got down and announced to the mutinous revellers and angry superintendent, 'And now, to close, my friend Val will play the guitar!' I complained that I was too drunk, but Alicia dragged me into the middle, sat me down on her table, and I played some Bach. I was intoxicated and happy and still glowing from the singing, and the music came out easily.

Nôw I remembered the absolute silence that had filled the room when the last chord stilled, and the hushed wonder on the faces around me. Nobody was laughing any more; nobody spoke. Everyone shuffled off to bed in a stunned and breathless silence. They had not, I realised now, told me it was extreme: that had been next day, and in the following weeks. 'That was magical,' Alicia had said. 'Absolute Christmas Eve. *Never* do it in the middle of a party, though, OK? You'd kill it dead.'

Could that have been excessive, unnatural? Music has always done things like that. I'd seen similar expressions on other faces on occasions when the music stayed firmly in the back of my mind – most recently in a police cell with the bag lady and the wildgirl. The world's folktales are full of magic flutes and drums, of tunes that bewitch their hearers to drop everything and dance, of singers who can tame the wild beasts or still the storm or open the gates of hell. We who create music have always acknowledged its power – a power that has nothing whatever to do with CICNPC.

'It was very beautiful,' Charles said quietly. 'But it still worries me.' He sighed. 'I wish I knew more about music. People have studied how it affects the brain, but nobody seems to understand why. Professor Bernet was talking about it a lot this afternoon.'

'What did he say?' I asked curiously.

He gave me a hopeless look. 'That every known human culture produces music, that they've found fragments of bone flutes and rattles that show it goes back as far as our species does, that we all take it for granted that it's a multi-billion-euro industry and that the top performers should be fabulously wealthy, without ever asking what it does for us that's so valuable. Almost everybody feels that music is worth spending money on, not just in theory, but in practice: more than that, we seem to regard it as one of the best and noblest creations of the human species – but nobody can explain why we do so.' He paused, then added dispiritedly, 'He told me all that when he was explaining why I wouldn't understand your dilemma.'

170

I made a face. 'He's a horrible man.'

Charles winced and nodded. 'I'm sorry, Val. I wish there was someone better I could call on – someone *kinder*. But at the moment I think he's the one man who might be able to understand you well enough to help.'

'Assuming I need help!' I muttered – but my heart was sick. I was beginning to accept that they were right, and I did.

Nine

I had trouble sleeping that night, and when I eventually succeeded in drifting off, it was to dream of being chased down a maze of twisting red-lit tunnels to the frantic thunder of a drum. Eventually I came to a dead end and turned, sobbing in terror. Charles and the professor stood behind me, scalpels glittering in their hands. I cringed away from them, pressing my back against the wall, and cried, 'No!'

Suddenly they weren't there, and in their place stood the figure of Apollo, golden and beautiful, as he'd appeared in the Laurel Hall history file. With a ripple of harp strings, the god stepped forward. In his right hand he held a mirror, which he extended towards me. My terrified eyes met those of my own reflection, and I saw that veins of green had pushed through my scalp and hung in leafy tendrils among my hair, while my skin oozed blood. I screamed, and woke.

It was three in the morning, and everything was hushed. I turned over a couple of times, trying to shake off the sense of horrified recognition. It was no use. I knew what that dream was about, and waking was no escape.

I got up and went over to the window. The moon shone chalk-white on the high ridge of the Downs, and the oak wood was like black velvet. I thought about smashing the window and throwing myself out, diving head-first into the moonlight like a swimmer casting herself into an infinite dark ocean.

I leaned my forehead against the pane: it was cool and calming. Dreams, I told myself, are something you wake up from. They have no more authority than any other panic-stricken midnight maundering. *It wasn't real*. The thing inside my head had been there since I was eight months old, and there was no real reason to believe it was about to burst through my skull and reveal me as a monster. Nor was anybody recommending surgery yet. There might be other options. There might be a secret doorway about to open in the wall against my back, and a path that led away from the tunnels and the knives.

I took a shower, trying to wash the dream from my mind with torrents of hot water. Then I went back to bed.

I slept late next morning, and woke at about eleven to the sound of voices and laughter in the corridor. It was Monday morning, and a fresh collection of volunteers had arrived at the Hall for the next stage of Ethical Decision Making.

These were undoubtedly a new group who didn't know that I'd had CICNPC, but I felt no inclination to go out and introduce myself. The way I'd slotted myself in among Claire, Jack and Miriam only the previous Wednesday morning now seemed ludicrous and unreal. I'd thought I was one of them – just another middle-class university student – but I'd been mistaken. All my life I'd worn a mask called 'Normal' and believed it was my face, but now the mask was off. I didn't understand what was underneath it, and didn't know how to put it on again.

I wondered why I'd been allowed to catch up on sleep. Presumably the professor and Charles had to corral some participants for the proposed new test. I wondered what Suzy and the other researchers would feel about the professor's new incursion into their research programme. They would not be happy, I was certain – but I was equally certain they wouldn't do anything about it.

I got up, washed, dressed, and went downstairs to get some coffee.

There were people in the lounge, and a couple of them smiled at me when I came in. One of the girls asked me if I were in the Ethical Decision Making programme too, and I said no, I was a medical assessment. That was the end of the conversation: the others went back to discussing Ethical Decision Making and the views of some of their lecturers in the Sociology department of University College London. I sat in a corner to drink my

173

coffee, then went back upstairs and practised the guitar until lunchtime.

When I went down to lunch, Charles was sitting with the other researchers, and everyone else was sitting in groups with their friends. I decided that I didn't want any lunch – I felt queasy anyway – and went back upstairs. I was redoing my now very chipped nails when the videophone chimed. It was Charles.

'Have you eaten anything at all today?' he asked in exasperation.

I shrugged. 'I'm not hungry.'

'You came downstairs. I saw you. I waved for you to join us.'

I shrugged again. 'How'm I supposed to share a table with your colleagues? The only time I spoke to them, there was a row, and I don't imagine they're feeling very pleased with me just at the moment.'

'No, no, you're quite wrong about that! They're intrigued.'

'That's worse. Look, I was only going downstairs anyway so you and Amrita wouldn't pester me. I really am not hungry. You're doing the next test this afternoon, aren't you?'

'At two,' he admitted. He hesitated, then asked quickly, 'Would you like to go for a walk?'

'What?' I stared at him, surprised and taken aback.

'We could go for a walk,' Charles offered again awkwardly. 'There's about half an hour before we have to start the session. We couldn't go very far, but it's enough time to get down the lane to the village and back.'

'I'd love to,' I told him, before he could change his mind. 'I'll meet you downstairs right away.'

On the way downstairs I started to worry that Charles would ask me questions and we'd end up having another fight, but in fact he said very little as we walked down the dark, rhododendron-flanked lane to the nearest village. It was to the left, of course, the way I *hadn't* gone when making my abortive escape – a small place, basically a London dormitory settlement, and at this time of day empty apart from a clutch of young mothers wheeling pushchairs home from some nursery school or playgroup. I bought a packet of crisps and a bottle of lemon-and-elderflower-flavoured water from the post-office-cum-general-store, and we started back. Getting outside the Hall had eased the hollow queasiness in my stomach, and I opened the crisps and devoured them.

'I was thinking last night,' said Charles, watching the lane in front of his feet, 'about what you said – that the questions we ask make you feel deformed. I decided you had a real point. So far this whole thing has been driven by an assumption that there was something wrong with you. I mean, first off the Department of Health decided you were a potential danger to the public, and then Professor Bernet and I started looking for abnormalities in your brain function. If you look for abnormalities you can always find them. We looked at you and we started categorising what was going on in terms of the Mental Health Act and the questions and problems of modern neuroscience, and you've hated it, and resisted it, and . . . and suffered from it – and none of it's helped us, because none of the questions are leading us towards an answer, and none of the categories really seems to fit. I was complaining last night that you hadn't told us anything, but after I said goodnight I wondered if that was our fault – because we were asking questions you could only answer by using our terms, and our terms make assumptions which you can't accept. The fact is that you were managing this thing so well that nobody around you had noticed anything amiss: your strategies for coping have obviously *worked*, at least up till now.'

I stopped dead in the lane, staring at Charles with a mixture of hope and suspicion.

'What I'm trying to work round to,' he continued hesitantly, meeting my eyes, 'is that I want to investigate this thing on *your* terms, but to do that I need you to help. What are the questions *you* have? You must have wondered about what was going on. You're not stupid, and you don't just let things pass unquestioned. You must have your own way of thinking about it. If you could share that, maybe we could tackle this thing as allies.'

It was like a door opening, like fresh air in a suffocating prison. I gaped at Charles in astonished gratitude. He looked back, uncertain and doubtful, afraid he'd offended me. I flung my arms around him, dropping the empty crisp packet and accidentally hitting him with the bottle of water, and kissed him.

It was relief and gratitude, not passion, but after standing rigid with amazement for about half a second, Charles started kissing me back, and that changed things. He was strong and solid in my arms, and his face was slightly rough and smelled of shaving cream. Where he touched me, every nerve started to hum like the string of a guitar. We came up for air and stood with our arms around each other, looking into each other's faces. Fabulous alpine-lake eyes!

He was pink. 'This is what I get for asking the right question?'

I kissed him again. 'Uh-huh.'

'Like the Holy Grail,' he muttered, and kissed me. 'Why didn't you *say* we were asking all the wrong questions?'

'I didn't know,' I told him, and stroked his hair. It was short and very soft and fine. Now that I'd touched him, I wanted to go on touching him. 'All I knew was that I hated everything about the questions you were asking. I hadn't put it to myself like that – that they put everything in the wrong terms. They do, though . . . What do you mean about the Holy Grail?'

He laughed and pulled me closer. 'That's how Perceval wins the grail, in most of the myths. He has to ask the right question. It's always struck me as a very *scientific* myth: most good science is a matter of finding the right question. God, I can't believe this!' He brushed my own hair back from my forehead, smiling at me. 'I wanted to do this the moment I saw you, but I couldn't seem to do anything except hurt you and make you miserable. It was like being under a curse.' He kissed me again.

He had his hand on the wobbly bit at the front of my skull, but it didn't bother me in the least. He wasn't just interested in what was underneath it: he was interested in *me*. I snuggled up against him, massively comforted. I wasn't on my own any more. I had him on my side now.

Maybe. Caution suddenly sounded an alarm: what had he actually offered to do? Pay attention to my view of things. It was an improvement, certainly, but hardly a conversion. The fact that I *wanted* him on my side should just make me twice as cautious about leaping to the conclusion that he had taken up station there. I began to detach myself.

He didn't try to stop me; in fact, he was detaching himself, too, looking guilty. Was that because the GMC frowns upon doctors kissing their patients, or because he knew that he was going to betray me to the system imposed by the Department of Health and all its minions of darkness?

As soon as he was loose, however, he caught my hands, including the one holding the bottle. 'So,' he said earnestly, 'what are the questions I should be asking?'

'Let me think.' I pulled away and started on up the lane towards the Hall, looking at him sideways. He was hurrying to keep abreast of me, and now wore the worried expression again. He *wanted* to be on my side: that much I did believe. It would undoubtedly help us both if we could work out what in hell my side actually *was*. What were the right questions?

'I suppose the first question *I* have,' I said slowly, as we turned into the drive, 'is about the way I can reach into the music of some great composers. I first reached the music with the stuff that comes out of the back of my mind, but then I found I could make it work with other people's compositions. Is it the same thing or isn't it? And then I want to know, why can I do it with Bach and Mozart but not Jiang Qi or Purcell?'

Charles frowned. 'You said something a bit like that when you were talking about *hearing* music,' he pointed out. 'That you were surprised that you never heard anything that sounded like Jiang Qi, when you like him so much.'

'I think I do sort of understand that.'

'Oh?'

'Mmm. I learned music according to the Western rules: octave scale with sharp and flats, tones and semitones, major and minor keys and so on. Even before I started studying it, nearly all the music I heard was traditional classical – or rock and pop and so on, which are written to the same canons. I didn't learn about other traditions and musical systems until much later. Jiang Qi tries to synthesise Western and traditional Chinese music. My subconscious can't accommodate that. It thinks Western musical rules are the only ones that are real.'

'Like a native language,' said Charles, his face clearing.

'Huh?'

'Your native language usually has a privileged position in your mind. Temporary loss of a second language is very common in cases of shock; loss of a native language nearly always means there's been severe brain damage. If the musical part of your brain has adopted Western rules as its native speech, any other rules you learned would be equivalent to a second language.' He regarded me with interest. 'When you're composing *consciously*, do you ever sound like Jiang Qi?'

I rolled my eyes. 'Last year I had trouble *not* sounding like him.'

'So the unconscious system only uses the oldest and most basic musical pathways,' said Charles. 'That's probably significant.'

We reached the Hall, and stopped. Charles was now looking unhappy again. He checked his watch.

'Don't tell me,' I said. 'We have to abandon this and go do Bernet's test.'

Charles winced. 'He spent all morning setting it up. He's using all the MRIs and three students from the Ethical Decision Making programme, and he's enlisted Suzy and Ahmed to help. Suzy's livid. I wish we weren't going to do this, Val, at least not now; I wanted to give it a rest and just *talk* to you for a few days, but the professor is very . . . that is, he wouldn't listen to me at all. I'm sorry.'

'I'll fetch my guitar,' I said resignedly.

He nodded. 'Yes. You can bring your computer this time, too: the MRIs aren't as sensitive as the Meg, and they're properly screened for people who're sitting up. I'll come with you and walk you through the security systems.'

When I'd collected the guitar and my computer, we went down to the lecture theatre in the ground-floor section of lab. The others were already there: Professor Bernet standing at the front; dumpy red-haired Susan Jones and slim young Ahmed Uzin sitting in the front row; three students – one of whom I recognised from the group in the lounge that morning – just behind them. Everyone looked round irritably as Charles and I came in. I smiled feebly, and sat down in the nearest available seat. Charles sat down behind me.

Bernet gave me a disdainful glare. 'Now that we are all here,' he announced to the assembled party, 'we should commence as soon as possible. If we are efficient, you should be able to complete your scheduled programme session when the special investigation is finished.'

Suzy scowled at him, Ahmed Uzin looked resentful and the volunteers regarded him with polite interest.

'We are, as I hope Dr Jones has informed you, looking at the effects of music,' Bernet went on. 'Miss Thornham here will play several pieces on the guitar while being scanned by fMRI; the rest of you will listen, also while being scanned. One of you will be in Room 2, which is equipped with two MRI scanners, together with Miss Thornham, myself, and my assistant, Dr Spencer. The others will be in Room 3 with Dr Uzin, and Room 4 with Dr Jones. All three rooms will be in continuous connection by videophone. Is this clear?'

'I guess so,' agreed one of the students, a plump blonde. 'But, uh, can you tell us what the investigation is trying to prove?'

'No,' replied Bernet shortly, glaring at her. I clutched my guitar in relief: I was not going to be named and shamed as a CICNPC recipient this time.

'That's a standard precaution,' Charles put in hurriedly. 'If you knew what we were trying to show, it would distort the result.'

The blonde nodded sagely, then glanced over at me. 'You take requests?' she asked, with a hopeful grin.

I shrugged. 'Depends on what they are.'

' "Rainy Day, Sweaty Night"?'

I bit my lip. Her and the wildgirl. 'No. Sorry. I don't sing, and I do mostly classical.'

'Oh, shit!' said the blonde, with a smile. 'No offense,' she added hurriedly.

Her name was Liz Potter – I learned it because she ended up in Room 2 with me, Charles, and the professor. She was cheerful, chatty, and studying Sociology. She had never seen an MRI scanner before, and wanted to know all about it.

Bernet evidently found her extremely irritating. He kept giving her venomous looks, which led me to feel friendly towards her.

Eventually, however, she and I were both locked into our respective scanners, and the videophone showed that the two other volunteers were ready as well. Charles handed me my computer so I could choose some music.

I looked through my collection. I was no longer feeling quite so sick about the whole thing. Charles had offered me the hope of a way out, none of the students expected anything other than ordinary music, and I had the prospect of that deep communion before me. I had no doubt that I could reach the music that afternoon. I *was* tired, it was true, but the emotional hammering I'd taken left me wanting music, and I was certain that it would not fail me.

In deference to the more populist tastes of the volunteers I started off with some dances for Spanish guitar, very lively with a good strong rhythm. Liz seemed to like them. Bernet just scowled. I thought at first it was because he didn't like anything with a strong beat, but then I noticed that he was wearing ear plugs. God. He really believed I could cast some kind of *spell* on them.

I thought about doing the Gorvenko piece next, but decided against it: I still hadn't got it mastered. I did some Purcell instead, and once more debated whether to try to reach the heart of the music through someone else's work or my own.

What the hell. I had told Charles I wanted to understand the difference between the two ways of going about it. I would try to give him something to compare with the Mozart. I plucked a few strings thoughtfully, feeling my way, then embarked on the percussive thing that had come to me while I was working on the Gorvenko, which had wanted so much to come out before.

No, no, not quite right. I stopped, fumbling, then tried it again. Still not good. I played a little of the Gorvenko, then tried again. Yes! The sound caught fire in my mind, and I let it burn, reaching for it, reaching . . .

Time stopped. I hung in the middle of a frozen bonfire, a rush of thundering power which had scattered sparks everywhere. The rhythm chequered the flames: a touch of tango, a dash of flamenco, a large dollop of West Africa. Play it in a concert and everyone would be twitching and tapping the arms of their chairs; play it at a party, and they'd be on their feet dancing. When it was finally over, I contemplated the energy and excitement of it with delight. Not great stuff, no – but one hell of a lot of fun.

My hands hurt. So did my neck. I was so exhausted that I wanted to lie down on the floor. I took a deep breath, relaxed my grip on the guitar, and extended my right hand so that I could see it. The fingertips were bright red, and the layer of black diamond polish was chipped to pieces. I'd broken a thumbnail, too. I put the sore digit in my mouth and felt at the edge of the torn nail with my tongue.

Across from me, Liz stirred dazedly, then met my eyes and grinned.

'Wow!' she exclaimed. 'Wow!'

' "When the last and dreadful hour," ' came the professor's harsh voice from somewhere to the side of us:

> ' "This crumbling pageant shall devour,
> The trumpet shall be heard on high,
> The dead shall live, the living die,
> And music shall untune the sky." '

There was a startled silence. I moved one of the pads and managed to wriggle my head out of the scanner. Bernet was standing by the bank of controls, watching me, an expression of obscene satisfaction on his face. His eyes met mine, and he grimaced, looked away, and began taking out his ear plugs.

Abruptly I felt like a whore watching her client dispose of his used condom. Sickened, I got up, still holding my guitar by the neck. My legs were wobbly and the exhaustion hit even harder when I stood up, but I was so desperate to get away that I was able to ignore it. 'Do you need me any more this afternoon?' I asked, my voice thick with disgust.

He shook his head impatiently and waved me towards the door.

'Hey!' said Liz, struggling to undo her own clamps. 'That was *extreme*! I don't usually like classical music, but that was top score. Have you cut a disc?'

'No,' I replied, taken aback.

'Shit! Well, let me know when you do, OK? I'll buy it. That was *extreme*!'

It helped. It did help – but I still felt an urgent need to wash.

Charles opened the door for me and escorted me back along the corridor to the main Hall. He said nothing and would not meet my eyes, but when I reached the stairs he murmured, 'I'll tell you as soon as I can' – then turned and went back to help the professor.

Back in my room, I put my guitar and computer on the bed and went straight into the washroom. I tore off my clothes, turned the shower on hot and hard and stood under it, eyes shut, face turned towards the cleansing flood. I fumbled around for the little plastic packet of shampoo, ripped it open, and began rubbing it into my hair.

My fingers encountered the familiar ripples in the bone on the right side of my skull, and I saw again the look of satisfaction on Bernet's face, and shuddered with a fresh wave of hot shame and nausea.

What *was* it with Bernet? Charles thought I was just being irrational, that Bernet was simply a crass and insensitive man with a strong professional interest in my brain. I had felt from the first moment we set eyes on one another that he was a pervert – that there was something twisted and repulsive in what he wanted from me. *Was* that irrational? I had twisted anxieties of my own about what was inside my skull. Perhaps I was projecting them.

I remembered the way he'd touched my head the day before, the way his thumb had stroked the scar on the bone, and the delight he had taken in frightening me. No, I was not projecting: there really was something *wrong* about the way Bernet regarded me.

I scrubbed my hair, rinsed it, and climbed out of the shower. My clothes were lying in a crumpled heap, the jeans half in, half out of a puddle from the shower. I left them there, went back into the bedroom, and crawled into bed.

The sheer *bliss* of being clean and warm and curled up in bed alone!

What *was* wrong with Bernet? What did he want from me, if it wasn't just confirmation of some theory he had about consciousness? Something sexual?

That was certainly what it felt like – and of course it's the first and most obvious thing an older man wants from a young woman. Bernet had sniped at Charles about me right from the beginning and, now that I thought about it, I was sure it represented a kind of jealousy. And yet, I couldn't believe that what the professor wanted was anything so straightforward as the yob's 'good fuck'. If anything, he seemed disgusted with every bit of me except my brain – which he wanted to gaze upon and fondle and caress.

I shuddered again and pulled the bedspread closer. Yeah, that was what he wanted, all right. I'd known it from the start, but I hadn't completely believed it even when I thought about it that way. Bernet wanted me sedated on an operating table with my skull split open so that he could have full and unhindered access to my brain. From the beginning he had wanted that. He had wanted to apply for a court order so that he could get it without interference; he'd been in a hurry to get me on to the machines so he could see inside my skull. Sex has a habit of insinuating itself into places where it has no legitimate business, and Bernet's longing to understand the brain had morphed into something strange and horrible. From the beginning I'd felt he was dangerous, and now I didn't want him near me at all.

Particularly not with that satisfied look. What had he seen, while I was letting off those musical fireworks on my guitar? Was it only that he'd been able to play peeping Tom with *two* female brains, to watch one acting upon the other – a cerebral lesbian spectacular, played out for his personal delectation? All those venomous looks he'd cast at poor Liz every time she'd opened her mouth . . .

I wanted Charles. I wanted him to put his arms around me, and I wanted to talk to him, make him understand what his boss was, get him to protect me. Charles, however, was undoubtedly working with Bernet at that very moment – going over the recordings of the session just past, analysing and evaluating whatever it was that had satisfied Bernet – and Charles thought I was being irrational. I was on my own. I still had no way out, except through a carefully calculated cooperation. My only consolation had to be that so far I'd succeeded in forcing Bernet to abide by the rules.

I spent the rest of a miserable afternoon in my room – in fact, I went to sleep for about an hour. When I woke up, I dressed, hung up my wet jeans, redid my nails (gluing a false thumbnail over the broken one) and vainly endeavoured to find some distraction among the entertainment programmes. My parents phoned at about half-past five: the conversation was marginally less traumatic than our previous one, but only marginally. They still wanted me to have treatment. In the end I told them to talk to Charles about it.

Charles himself knocked on the door just before seven. When I opened it and found him standing there my first impulse was to throw myself into his arms – but I checked it. We stood a moment looking at each other. He seemed tired and ill at ease.

'Please come down for supper,' he asked quietly.

'Oh . . .' I said, and swallowed. I was very hungry, but I didn't fancy company: my nerves were one raw bruise.

'The research staff have all gone home. The volunteers have been told that you're getting medical assessment because of injuries you received in a road accident, and the participants from this afternoon have been spreading the word that you're the greatest guitarist since Segovia. They're all interested, but nobody's likely to want to talk to you about anything but music.'

'Oh!' I said again. 'OK.'

We started along the corridor. 'What was Bernet so pleased about?' I asked, before we'd even reached the stairs.

He made a face. 'He was pleased because he was proved right, and when you . . . reached the music, you induced a trance state in everyone except him. He was wearing earplugs.' He paused at the top of the stairs, looking anxiously into my face. 'I was under too, at first, but he shook me and I snapped out of it. The three volunteers all exhibited identical patterns of brain activity involving the auditory cortex and the frontal and prefrontal cortices on both sides of the brain. Suzy and Ahmed . . .' He shook his head. 'There was a list of things they were supposed to check if anything happened, but they didn't: they were under as deep as the volunteers. Val, it scares me.'

It scared me, too. I saw again the green tendrils bursting through my skull, and fought the urge to bolt back to my room. I gazed wordlessly at the steps that led down to the dining room, and I felt as though the whole human world lay on the other side of a vast gulf, beyond a bridge I could never recross. I wanted to weep.

Then Charles touched my arm, and I looked quickly back at his face. The emotion there was raw and vivid. 'I'm sorry,' he said. 'I shouldn't have said that. I think probably I'm much more scared than I should be, simply because this thing involves *you*.'

I held his eyes. 'You're not scared of . . . of *me?*'

He closed his eyes a moment, then opened them again. 'Of course not. I'm scared *for* you – and, like I said, probably more scared than I should be. Your brain function is normal for all ordinary purposes, and this effect must be a form of audially induced hypnosis. That's been around for generations, even if we don't understand it very well. We were all *listening* to the music, even before you . . . reached it, and you sort of worked all of us, including yourself, into a state where we were receptive. It's not *magic*. Come on: I think we both need something to eat.' He started down the stairs.

I followed slowly. 'Maybe it *is* magic,' I suggested unhappily. 'Have you thought of that? Maybe all the stories about enchantment worked by music were talking about this. Maybe it's something that's been around as long as music itself, only nobody's ever looked at it this way before.'

He paused, startled. 'Maybe!' He smiled at me tentatively. 'Just the extreme end of the normal spectrum of the human use of music, huh, and not a clinical problem? It *could* be. You're right: there *are* lots of stories, they may reflect something real. I hope so.'

'Me too,' I whispered.

Supper was actually rather pleasant. The food was good, and I felt much better when I'd eaten it: I'd been very hungry. The volunteers all seemed to be under the impression that I was an up-and-coming star who was receiving private medical treatment in exchange for help on a special investigation into music. They all wanted to know who was going to publish my first disc and if I were part of a group. I admitted I hadn't got as far as a disc yet, but I told them about Alicia's plans – which were multiple and ambitious – and they promised to look out for us. It felt false from beginning to end, but it was a relief to discover that I could at least still *pretend* to be normal.

After supper I suggested to Charles that we go out for another walk. I wanted to tackle him about Bernet.

We started off along the path through the oak wood. It was nearly eight o'clock, but there were still a couple of hours of daylight left. The sky had clouded over during the course of the afternoon, however, and the air was muggy and close. The forest was a hazy green dusk full of insects. From behind us came the sound of the volunteers playing tennis and badminton on the lawn.

'Look,' I began uneasily, fanning gnats away from my face, 'about Professor Bernet . . .'

Charles paused, looking guilty, and I stopped, turning to face him.

'I know you think I'm irrational about him, but I really do think there's something *sick* about the way he looks at me. I think he gets a sexual kick out of looking inside the skulls of young women. I think that's why he was in such a rush to get me on the machines, why he was so insistent about using the sampler when he didn't need to. I don't have any faith at all in his clinical objectivity or his goodwill, and he scares me.'

There was no reply. Charles gazed at me, stricken.

'What happened?' I demanded, suddenly cold.

'Nothing,' he whispered. He shook his head. 'Nothing. It's just . . .'

He knew the professor better than I did. He had seen him treating other young women. He had commented on how the

186

man had bullied other CICNPC recipients – and I was suddenly sure that the ones he bullied tended to be female. 'You know I'm right!' I exclaimed triumphantly.

He winced. 'No! I don't know. He . . . I don't know. I hate the way he talks about you, but . . . well, you know how I feel, and I *shouldn't* feel like that about a patient, so probably I'm being unreasonable. Probably . . . probably I feel secretly jealous of him, because he is so brilliant and so cultured and so much better at everything than I am.'

'*I'm* not jealous of the toad, and I'm *not* being unreasonable!' I declared angrily. 'The look on your face already gave it away, you know: I'm not the only one he's harassed. What do you mean, the way he talks about me? What does he say?'

He looked away. 'Nothing. I mean . . . sometimes he talks as though you and your brain were two different things. As though your brain was treasure trove. As though he found it, and it belongs to him.' He looked back, confused and angry. 'Val, he's a *genius*. I've been reading his papers since I was nineteen; I can't . . .'

I saw it at last. He was trying desperately to retain the Bernet he had admired at nineteen. He had made excuses for him – he's got a chronic illness, he's just impatient – and he had scurried about trying to repair the social damage Bernet wreaked in all directions. He had learned to disapprove of Bernet's conduct, he had quarrelled with him about me, but he had still clung to the notion of the professor's clinical brilliance. Naturally loyal, he struggled to prop up his fallen idol. He did not want to believe his one-time hero would conduct tests on vulnerable patients simply to satisfy a perverted lust.

'Maybe he's ill,' I said slowly. 'Maybe he can't help it.'

That seemed to be even worse: Charles went white. 'Oh God.'

'What?'

'Those scans . . .'

'*Which* scans?'

'The ones you caught him looking at on the videomatic. The case of prefrontal degeneration.'

I made the connection with a horrid cold lurch. We stared at one another. 'You think those might have been *his*?'

'I . . . I don't know. He has the symptoms – complete lack of empathy, increasing social ineptitude, growing impulsiveness and disregard for the consequences of his actions . . . oh God!' He was silent a moment, then said, 'It would explain why he resigned from the CNRS, too. He would've been forced to step down as soon as people knew about it, and he would want . . . he would want to achieve something, some last really striking piece of research, before the end. So he stepped down *before* people found out about it, and took up a post here. He's on the Apollo Foundation Board, and nobody would've checked whether there'd been trouble at his last post. He probably didn't even need an interview.'

We continued to look at one another, aghast.

'Charles, it scares me sick that he's in charge,' I said at last. 'I don't like *any* of this, it *all* terrifies me, but he scares me most of all. If you're right about this, there's absolutely no check on what he might do.'

He might open up my head, stick probes into my brain; he might explore the pathways of my personality with drugs and electrodes; he might slash and burn the very foundation of my soul.

Charles took a couple of quick steps forward as though he meant to hug me – but he stopped and put his hands behind his back. 'I wish we were away from here,' he said in a low voice.

'Oh, God, I wish we were!' I cried miserably. 'God, I wish!'

'I don't know what to do!' he admitted, twisting his hands together behind his back. 'Even before this . . . this new trouble, I thought things were getting out of hand. You've been coerced into cooperating, and this afternoon the volunteers weren't even informed about what was going on. There was no way that experiment could be represented as part of your assessment process or the research they'd signed on to do. I should have protested it, but . . . but I've been distracted, I didn't really focus on it, until afterwards, and then . . . I tried to imagine what he would have done if I had protested, and—' He stopped, then began again. 'He's been getting harder and harder to reach. It used to be I could get through to him, say, "Look, you've upset her," or "That isn't necessary" – but recently if I say anything, he takes it as a challenge to his authority and squashes me flat. If I try to stop him, he'll dismiss me, and then . . . oh God, he should *not* be in charge of vulnerable people, and I don't know how to get him out of here! Even if I go straight to the authorities, and even if they listen, it would be weeks before anyone took any action, and in the meantime . . . he isn't responsible; he might do *anything*.'

The last came out in a choked rush. I moved towards him, and his arms came out from behind his back and folded round me. I pressed my face against his shoulder, finding comfort in the strength and solidity of his body. 'I'm scared,' I whispered.

He began to kiss the back of my head. 'Me too,' he admitted.

I raised my head so that he could kiss me on the mouth, and he did. I loved the way his mouth tasted, the feel of his skin, the hesitant reverence in his touch.

He stopped abruptly, however, shook himself out of my arms, and stumbled back several steps in alarm. 'We mustn't,' he told me earnestly.

'I'm not going to sue,' I told him, trying to get close again. I desperately wanted comfort.

'That's not the point,' he said firmly, catching my hands and holding them in front of me. 'We may have to take on Bernet in the courts, and if I . . .'

'He could use it to blow you out of the water,' I said, and stopped trying to get back into his arms.

Charles nodded unhappily. 'It's a bad idea anyway,' he whispered miserably. 'A clear breach of professional ethics. You're legally in custody. You're scared and vulnerable. I . . . I think afterwards we would both regret anything that happened.'

'You're so *sensible*!' I said in disgust. My nerves were still tingling where he'd touched me.

'I can't help it,' he replied humbly. 'It's the way I am.'

I rolled my eyes in exasperation, and we stood looking at each other a moment longer. I wanted so much not to be alone, to be loved, to be safe. It hurt.

'We need to talk about what to do,' said Charles at last.

'Not here in the woods!' I snapped irritably. 'It's too buggy.'

We walked to the end of the woods, then stopped where the track crossed up on to the Downs and sat down on the stile. Charles went over the gate and sat on the opposite side of the fence.

'If he has had treatment for prefrontal degeneration,' Charles began unhappily, 'he must have been manoeuvring to keep it secret. The records to prove it will be hard to get.'

'He can't legally be *allowed* to keep it secret and stay in charge of other people!' I objected. 'I mean, *my* medical records should've been private, and look what happened to me!'

Charles brushed that aside. 'Prefrontal degeneration isn't sectionable. It's true that if it were known he had it, he wouldn't be allowed to hold a supervisory position, but he wouldn't be considered a danger to the public. There's no obligation for the medical authorities to report him to the Department of Health.' He chewed his lip. 'He must have gone for treatment, though. There must be a specialist clinic somewhere who advised him. Maybe he told them that he was retiring, and when he quit the CNRS they believed him. That might be a way – find out who was treating him in Paris, and get them to intervene.'

'Can't we just go to the GMC? Say, "We think this guy may be really sick, can't you suspend him while you investigate it"?'

Charles shook his head. 'We'd have to mount a legal challenge, saying that he is unfit to be in a supervisory position owing to his degenerative brain disease. Then he would have the right to produce records, if he can, showing that he doesn't suffer any such disease. There's a real risk that we're wrong – that those weren't his scans after all and that he's just *naturally* insensitive. That would be a disaster, because after that nobody would listen to any other accusation we cared to make. Even if we're right, though, it could be dangerous. He'd be allowed a couple of weeks to assemble his evidence, and I don't think the Apollo Foundation would stop him from working in the meantime. If he were working for the NHS or a government research body, he'd be suspended, but he's a member of the Foundation Board, and if he swore that it wasn't true, they'd believe him. And I think . . . I think that the worst case scenario would be if he does suffer from prefrontal degeneration and was left in charge pending the investigation. He would know that he was about to be exposed. He'd be aware that he'd be unlikely to be punished for anything he did, because he can be certified as having diminished responsibility. And he's incapable of caring about how much other people get hurt. He would probably decide to pursue his research ruthlessly in the time available.' He gave me a frightened look. 'He might *cripple* you!'

I licked my lips, feeling sick again. 'How could he do anything drastic? People wouldn't let him!'

'People here at the Hall wouldn't. But he'd be sure to apply for his court order and move you somewhere else.'

'No, no, no! He'd never be granted one, would he? Not while he's accused of being psychologically unfit for command or whatever!'

Charles shook his head doubtfully. 'If the court knew what was going on, obviously he wouldn't get his injunction. But they wouldn't know what was going on unless somebody told them, and he might be able to slip it through on the sly. You're entitled to representation when he applies for the order, but that can just mean a spokesman appointed by the court. He's a widely respected authority, and you're a Cicnip recipient who appears to suffer from episodes of lapsed consciousness, in custody for trying to evade assessment. If he claimed that you're mentally incompetent, that you're resisting treatment which you need urgently, he could probably get an order without anyone even consulting you. There'd probably be some conditions attached, but if he didn't care what happened to him afterwards, he'd simply ignore them.'

I swallowed several times. 'Oh.' After a minute, I said, 'So you're saying that we should do nothing? Go along with him?'

'No!' he said vehemently. 'I'm saying we shouldn't do anything to alarm him until we're in a position to have him suspended.' He thought a minute, then went on, 'What I want to do is contact my PhD supervisor at Oxford. He might be able to find out who was treating Bernet in Paris, and I think that has to be the safest and surest way to get him suspended quickly. But I'm also going to check what the procedures are for the GMC, and get something started, if I can. You

191

had your parents up in arms before: you should certainly get them started again. You shouldn't tell them *all* of this, though, not at this point: you should just say that he's been harassing you and that he's conducted experiments which have nothing whatever to do with assessing you.'

'My parents phoned this evening,' I informed him. 'I told them to talk to you. They . . . they don't trust my judgement any more, they want me to have treatment. They'd probably pay more attention to you than to me.'

The words hurt unexpectedly, and I had to look away.

'I'll speak to them, then,' he said neutrally. 'Yes, that's the best way to do it. He knows they were making a fuss before, so he won't be too alarmed if they start to do it again.' He got to his feet. 'We should go back to the Hall and start at once.'

In the end, Charles and I both spoke to my parents. I told them about how Bernet had threatened me and what he'd said when he came to my room; Charles confirmed it, and added that the afternoon's experiment had been completely unjustified. They were consolingly outraged, and promised to take up the matter at once.

The clouds thickened during the night, and I was woken in the small hours of the morning by a thunderstorm. I went over to the window in the dark and watched it. Rain roared on the roof and rattled against the pane, and the grounds leaped out in vivid white, then vanished with a roll of thunder. I opened the window to get the smell – wet slates and damp earth, ozone and broken greenery. It was cheering.

When the storm receded I went back to bed and slept soundly, waking at a quarter to ten. I stretched and rubbed my eyes, surprised that I'd been allowed to sleep so long. When I dressed and went downstairs I found the participants all hard at work making ethical decisions, but no sign of Charles or the professor. Amrita was in the kitchen, discussing lunch with the cook.

'Oh, yes!' she agreed. 'They're both out. Apparently Professor Bernet isn't feeling well, and Charles has gone to run some errands. He left a message for you on the house machine.'

I thanked her, collected some coffee, and went back to my room to look at the message.

192

It was a video recording: Charles, with the familiar slightly worried look, holding a large manila envelope. 'Hi,' he said breathlessly. 'Val, Professor Bernet has phoned to say he isn't feeling well and isn't going to come in today, so I'm going to Oxford. If my PhD supervisor doesn't know who treated Bernet in Paris, somebody else might. He would've had to go to a specialist, and somebody in Oxford must know who it would've been. I'll, uh, be back this evening, before five o'clock. Try and relax, OK?'

The image ended with his nervous smile. I smiled back, stupidly, then sat a moment looking at it and thinking how much I liked his face.

Where was this going? I'd known Charles a week. I'd dismissed him at first as scrubbed, bland and boring: if I hadn't been, as he put it, frightened and vulnerable, would I even have given him a second look?

Probably not – but it would have been my loss. He was much better value than my last admirer – intelligent, decent, conscientious, genuinely kind . . . loyal, too: he'd tried so hard to be loyal even to Bernet.

He was right, I supposed, not to start anything now. I was too powerless, too entirely at the mercy of the system of which he was a part; the inequality between us, like a fungus, would rot away anything else. But what was going to happen after I was free?

That was something I couldn't conceive of any more. I might never be free. In another week I might not even exist any more, not as the person I was now. Charles hadn't said anything about treatment recently, but I was sure he still wanted me to have it, and I would still prefer to be dead.

I sighed and shut down the computer. I had a day off: I could 'relax'. It was what I'd been hoping for at the weekend. I might as well make the most of it.

I spent the rest of the morning writing out my percussive piece for guitar – I decided to call it 'Danza', even though that's what everybody else calls theirs – then went downstairs for lunch.

Liz and her friends were just sitting down; they waved for me to join them. I heaped my plate with salads and did so. They asked me what I'd been doing that morning; I asked them about the Ethical Decision Making. They were still telling me about it when Susan Jones came over.

'Hi.' She smiled brightly, but her eyes were wary. 'Could I have a word with you, Miss Thornham?'

'Now?' I asked unhappily.

'When you've finished your lunch,' she conceded.

I considered saying, 'No,' but I didn't have the guts. I nodded, and she went back to the staff table. For the first time I noticed all the eyes on me, and I lost my appetite.

I spent the next ten minutes toying with my salad and only half listening to the ethical decisions, then gave up, muttered excuses to the others, and left the table. Susan Jones at once got up and followed me, and Ahmed Uzin followed her. They caught up with me at the foot of the stairs.

'We can talk in the office,' said Suzy. She led the way upstairs and along the first-floor lab corridor, opening the door of the room next to Professor Bernet's.

It was much more the sort of room that real, as opposed to Hollywood, academics possess. There were two desks shoved into opposite corners, both covered with computers, discs, and papers. Battered books, of all shapes and sizes, overflowed the bookcase and stood in stacks on top of it and on the floor beside it. A poster for a neuroscience conference in Rome, with a spectacular picture of the Colosseum, adorned one wall; on the other was a still life of some flowers. More flowers – roses from the garden – were dropping pink and yellow petals on the mess on one of the desks.

Suzy pulled out the chair of the rose-littered desk and offered it to me, then cleared a space on the desk itself and perched. Uzin took the chair at the other desk. I guessed that they shared the office.

I sat down stiffly. The two researchers watched me as though I were a dangerous animal, liable to leap up and attack at any moment. The back of my mind began an angry piece of *laqueada* on the guitar.

'Um,' said Suzy. 'Um. Miss Thornham, the, um, event yesterday . . .'

'What event?' I said coldly.

'The music you produced while in an abnormal brain state,' Uzin put in quietly, 'which induced a hypnotic trance in everyone who heard it.'

I set my teeth. 'The dance piece I played on the guitar. What about it?'

'Professor Bernet hasn't told us very much,' said Suzy. 'To be honest, if I'd known he was expecting something like that to happen, I would never have cooperated with the experiment. Exposing unwitting volunteers to a powerful, abnormal and mysterious stimulus without their express consent is illegal.'

I could feel my face getting hot. 'My music is not some kind of dangerous drug!'

'It affects the brain like one,' she replied flatly.

'Oh, for God's sake!' I jumped to my feet. 'I'm not going to take this! Music has *always* affected the brain! That doesn't make it the same as heroin!'

'Please!' interrupted Uzin. 'We didn't invite you here to accuse you.'

'You could've fooled me!' I snarled.

'Please!' said Uzin again. 'We understand that you're angry and unhappy, and I'm sure you've got reason, but we're not the ones to blame! When we talked to you at lunch that first day, we all assumed that you'd consented to take part in Bernet's consciousness research: we were shocked when you said you hadn't. Maybe we should've been tracking better, but Bernet is so degradedly touchy that, to tell the truth, we prefer not to ask. All we know is bits and pieces from Charles Spencer. He's never happy to discuss patients with people who aren't clinically involved, and Bernet never wants him to discuss anything at all. Yesterday Bernet sprang a bizarre experience on us without warning, and we're both still kicked up about it. We would be very grateful if you could tell us what's going on. Bernet certainly won't.'

He looked anxious and sincere. Suzy Jones was looking disgruntled, but did not dissent. I sat down slowly. The fierce guitar playing in the back of my head stilled with a sweet, sweet lingering chord. 'OK,' I said grudgingly. 'But I don't really know what's going on. As far as I can tell, nobody does.'

'This abnormal brain state isn't an episode of lapsed consciousness?' asked Suzy eagerly.

'Apparently not.'

'You're conscious during it?'

'No. Yes. I'm conscious of the music and nothing else. Look, this abnormal-brain-state neuroscience language makes it hard. The terms are all wrong.'

She ignored that. 'Spence told us that you had episodes of what looked like lapsed consciousness, except that instead of suffering any interruption in consciousness, you heard music.'

'Yeah,' I agreed, starting to feel hot and weak with embarrassment. 'That happens all the time. It's different from what happens when I reach the music like I did yesterday, though.'

'What happens then?'

'I . . . I don't know. Not in neuroscience language.'

'You haven't seen any of the scans?'

'Charles showed me some,' I admitted. 'Apparently my brain isn't . . . isn't like most people's.' I couldn't make myself say 'is abnormal'. 'It's got these extra connections, mostly between here and here' – I touched the front of my head and the right side – 'and one across here.' I drew a line across the top of my head. 'Apparently when I reach the music, all those areas work very hard. Charles told me the neurochemistry goes wild, too, and he's worried that it's going to hurt me, but it never has. It's never bothered me at all, in fact, and nobody else has ever even noticed. As for it hurting your volunteers somehow – that's crashed. It's never done anything to anyone who heard it before.'

'That can't be true,' said Suzy sharply. 'It had a clearly visible effect on the brains of our volunteers, both while they were listening and afterwards.'

A swallow of ice water. I stared at her, then at Uzin. They both gazed back soberly. 'What?' I asked weakly. 'Afterwards?'

'We did a session of our own research after we finished that imposition of Bernet's,' Suzy told me bitterly. 'The three students who'd participated in Bernet's programme showed a

196

marked difference in cognitive function compared to the nine who had not. It was strong enough that we can be completely confident it's not coincidence. The difference was still there this morning, though much weaker.' She regarded me grimly. 'What I really hate is that I *know* that Ahmed and I were exposed to the same stimulus. Whatever you did to their brains, you did to us, too.'

I swallowed. They were saying that the Department of Health was right: I was indeed a danger to the public. I saw again the figure of Apollo from my dream, holding out the mirror that showed my transformation. Oh, God. 'I didn't know about this,' I said at last. 'I've never . . . people I've played for before haven't . . . it's not like they've ever seemed *drugged* or anything, and all they've ever said to me afterwards is how much they liked the music!'

The other two continued to regard me grimly, and after a moment I added guiltily, 'The volunteers who heard me play . . . what happened to their . . . cognitive function?'

Uzin stirred. 'There was an increase in activity in the frontal and prefrontal cortices and an inhibition of the limbic system. It isn't obviously dangerous, but it is *very* disturbing to see such a clear-cut effect resulting from fifteen minutes of hypnosis by guitar.'

'I didn't know anything about this,' I told him faintly.

'You've played for an audience in that abnormal brain state often?'

'No,' I said, and swallowed again. 'Only a few times.' At heart I had always known that there was something very strange about what happened when the music came out. I'd never been afraid of consequences for others, though – only of consequences for myself, if someone noticed. I had blithely assumed that if music did anything, what it did was good. 'Nobody ever *worried* about it,' I offered hesitantly, 'and nobody's ever *noticed* anything wrong afterwards.'

'That's reassuring,' said Uzin.

'As far as it goes,' Suzy corrected him.

Ten

I spent the rest of the afternoon in my room, vegetating and talking on the telephone.

Vegetating: painful word, in the context. I spent about an hour looking up images of Daphne and Apollo on the Internet. There were lots, from ancient Greek to modern, and I queasily regarded each one, watching the girl turn into a tree in the arms of the god she had tried to escape. I couldn't work out which, if any, had prompted my dream.

My friend Alicia phoned at about three: apparently she'd tried to phone several times before, and hadn't been able to get hold of me. I dismayed her by bursting into tears when she asked me how I was. I couldn't explain why, either, except to say that I'd been told there were serious abnormalities in my brain and I might have to have surgery. She tried to comfort me, but how could she, when I'd never told her anything that would let her understand? Eventually I told her that I didn't want to talk about it – that I would cope OK if I didn't have to talk about it. At that she promised to come and visit me. I begged her not to, and hung up.

Around four, my father phoned to check how things were going; he was relieved to hear it had been a day off. He said that he and my mother had been chasing the same officials at the local health authority and the Department of Health whom they'd contacted before, and had extracted exasperated promises to investigate the matter. 'I said, "At once?",' my father said triumphantly, 'and they hemmed and hawed and eventually agreed to make it urgent. So if you don't see any results soon, let me know, and I will hammer them.' He tactfully did not bring up the question of treatment.

When there was a knock at the door shortly before five, I leapt up and opened it eagerly, expecting Charles back with the result of his search in Oxford. It was Bernet.

I should have slammed the door, but instead I recoiled, and he pushed his way in. He looked a bit tired, but not ill in the least. 'What do you want?' I demanded, glaring.

He shrugged. 'I could lie, and say to you that I wished to discuss your case, Miss Thornham. But the truth is that that piece you wrote all on one string has been in my mind incessantly since first I heard it, and of course I have no other way to hear it again, except to ask you to play it for me.'

It wasn't the answer I'd expected, and I floundered in my response. 'I thought you weren't coming here at all today,' I said at last. 'I thought you were ill.'

Another shrug. 'I am ill, and I was not going to come here today. But, as I said, that piece on the guitar has exasperated me. Please.' He made a little pushing gesture towards the guitar.

I didn't know what else to do, and I was, frankly, flattered that he'd come in just to hear that piece of music – if that was his real reason. I got out the guitar and sat down on the bed. Bernet settled himself at the desk, turning the chair to face me, and watched as I tuned the instrument. When I began to play he closed his eyes. His face, bereft of the pervert's gaze, had an expression of deep suffering.

When I'd finished the piece, he sighed. 'It is one of those pieces that calms the heart,' he said in a low voice. 'It reminds me a little of some of the Bach cello solos.'

I was once more taken aback. I hadn't noticed the influence before, but he was right. 'Oh . . .' I said stupidly. 'Yes, I suppose so. Not as good, of course.'

That brought a nasty smile. 'Great composers should be more egotistical, Miss Thornham, whether they have cause to be or not.'

I drew my false thumbnail across the strings discordantly. 'Stop it,' I ordered sharply. 'You get a kick out of needling your female patients, don't you? You *really* get off on sticking things into our brains, but you like it if you can make us cry, too. Well, you can go off and . . . and *play with yourself*, instead: I'm not going to let you play with me.'

He stared back at me in complete silence for a long moment. 'You are extraordinary,' he said at last. 'I beg you, do not settle for that fool Charles Spencer.'

'He isn't a fool!' I replied, startled and angry.

He waved that off impatiently. 'He is beneath you. A man with no fire in him. I can see him at forty, with that fat face and that moustache, a hospital consultant with a big house in the country who grows roses. What would he do with a woman like you?'

'Maybe women like me need men like him,' I said, without considering what I meant by it. It was true, though. I needed stability and strength. Nerves and imagination I had plenty of myself.

'People like you die young, in chaotic circumstances, of syphilis or tuberculosis – or obscure conditions of the brain.'

'I don't accept that!' I said fiercely. 'Just because Mozart and Schubert died in an unholy mess doesn't mean that it was inevitable or *creative* or anything. Plenty of composers have lived perfectly respectable lives. Besides, if somebody had stepped in to save Mozart or Schubert the way Nadezhna von Meck saved Tchaikovsky, God *knows* what they might have produced!'

'And you think Charles Spencer will save you?' Bernet sneered. 'He wishes to destroy you, and keep your ghost as his pet.'

'You're wrong!' I told him hotly. 'You're dead wrong!'

'Why? What has he been plotting with you?'

Abruptly, and almost too late, I saw where this was heading. 'You're paranoid,' I improvised hastily, and struck a chord. As though the sound was a switch, the back of my mind began something fast and furious in B minor.

'And you're still trying to upset me,' I added, and played some of it.

'Touch the music,' he said quietly.

My hands stilled. The music in my mind played on, darker now, rich-toned, almost frightening.

200

'The gift you have is beautiful beyond words,' Bernet said in a low voice. 'Yesterday I did not allow it to reach me. I wished to, but I also wished to observe. Now I am oppressed by my own soul, and I ache to escape. Please. This is nothing to do with research or explanation or understanding. I ask this because I am alone and ill and you can show me the face of God. Please.'

He was sincere. I was absolutely certain he was sincere. I hated him, feared him, despised him; he had probably come to my room expressly to bully me, he had God knew what foul plans for me – and he was begging me to share with him a thing so holy that I hadn't even wanted him to know about it.

I wanted to refuse. I opened my mouth to laugh, to say, 'No' – and I couldn't. He was a man dying slowly in a foreign land, and he was begging me to give him music. He had called the thing inside my head a gift beautiful beyond words, and yes, it was, and I, as the possessor of it, had an absolute obligation to grant its power to anyone who understood to ask. If I failed that condition, I would lose the gift. I *knew* that, even though I knew that my knowledge was irrational and superstitious. Whatever he was, however much I hated him, I could not refuse what he had asked.

I set my hands on the guitar and began to play along with the music which still resounded in my mind. It was slower now, wild and deep and dark. It matched with my fingers almost at once, and time came to a halt.

In the silence afterwards, I stretched my fingers, then set the guitar down carefully on the bed. My hands were trembling, and I felt desperately tired. Bernet was sitting with his eyes shut. He drew his breath in slowly and let it out again, then opened his eyes. For once they were calm – the calm of a man who has been in agony, and is lying spent now on its far side.

'Thank you,' he said quietly.

Then he drew a folded piece of paper from his jacket pocket and silently set it down on top of my Segovia.

I looked at him a moment, then picked the paper up and unfolded it. It was a court order committing me to a secure mental hospital for treatment of CICNPC-induced abnormalities of the brain.

'I obtained it this afternoon,' Bernet told me.

I looked up from the paper into his dark stare.

'It was easy,' he informed me. 'I went to the court in the morning and informed the judge that you urgently needed treatment, and that your parents wished you to have it, but that you yourself adamantly opposed it, as you feared it would damage your musical abilities. The court administration was sympathetic, and an emergency hearing was convened that afternoon. I presented my evidence – do you know that Dr Spencer had recorded a telephone conversation with your parents in which they expressed their wish that you should have treatment? He stored it in a private file, but I have no doubt he made it for the same purpose for which I employed it. The court did appoint someone to represent your interests, of course, but I do not believe the woman responsible for the task even believed herself that music is more important than life. As for the medical evidence—' He shrugged. 'Courts never understand the details. Your brain is abnormal, and you have had CICNPC, that deadly thing: that was enough.'

My hands were shaking, and I was afraid I might faint. Bernet reached over and took the paper back, then folded it again and ran it through his fingers.

'I know that Spencer has begun to scheme against me, you see,' he explained. 'He has hovered on the edge of it for months, and now he is infatuated with you. Does he think I haven't noticed all his attentions – the walks, the private conversations? He is trying to steal you from me and direct the research himself. He intends to devise some plan to mutilate you only slightly, so that he can keep what is left and say that he has saved it. I knew that if I wanted to proceed unhindered, I needed to ensure that no one could interfere with me. Now I have this. I could take you away now, if I wanted.' He put his hand in his pocket and drew it out holding a capped syringe. 'If I gave you this, you would not be able to struggle. I can call on the police to assist me, and if we acted quietly, no one here would know you were gone, until too late. There is a clinic for the criminally insane in Oxfordshire which would be willing to assist me. Its head is delighted to think that a man of my distinction might work with him.'

'No,' I croaked. 'Please.'

'Please,' he repeated. He folded the court order over on top of itself, smoothed it carefully with the side of the syringe. 'Please.' He looked up and met my eyes. 'Shouldn't you be pleading with Spencer? He is the one who wants to *cure* you.'

'No!' I said again, more shrilly this time. 'No, please!'

'Calm yourself,' he said wearily. He put the syringe back in his pocket and ran the court order through his fingers again. 'I am not going to use this, Miss Thornham. Not even if it means letting Spencer have you. I could not expunge that piece of music from my mind, and when I realised that, I realised that I could not touch you. "Thou art too dear for my possessing, and like enough thou knowest thy estimate."' Still holding my eyes, he folded the order over again. ' "The charter of thy worth gives thee releasing; my bonds in thee are all determinate."' He folded it over once more, then tossed the small wad of paper neatly in the dustbin and stood up.

I was shaking all over. 'You're not . . .'

'No,' he agreed, with a curl of the lip. 'I am not going to use that. The assessment will be completed here at Laurel Hall – which will create its own problems, *bien sûr*, but you have nothing to fear from me. I am not going to harm you in any way, because what would become of your music if I did?' He moved forward suddenly and leaned over me. 'You are right: I do like to make pretty girls cry. I see them smiling and talking, so charming, and I think of my Yvette, and I long to hurt them. It is an urge I regret but cannot master. When I came here this evening, I did not want to distress you, and I apologise that I have. Thank you for playing for me.'

'I . . .' I began, then realised that I had no idea what I meant to say, and changed it to, 'Thank you for . . . for . . .' I did not know what word to use to describe his sudden surrender when he had the means of victory in his hands.

'You are welcome.' He touched my cheek, then turned to walk out.

203

Charles was standing in the doorway, his face red and his eyes blazing. Bernet started, then stepped back, facing him.

'What are you doing here?' Charles demanded furiously.

'I might ask the same of you,' said Bernet coldly.

'It's all right!' I exclaimed hastily.

From the look of him, though, it wasn't all right with Charles. 'I'm not going to tolerate this any more!' he declared loudly. 'I won't allow you to harass Miss Thornham!'

'Charles, it's all right!' I cried again. 'He wasn't, he just—'

'You think that she is *yours*, then?' sneered Bernet. 'Women like her do not end up with men like you, Dr Spencer. They do not fall in love with flat-footed eaters of porridge. You are a very boring man, Dr Spencer, and women like her hate boredom above all else.'

Charles went from brick-red to white. 'You *toad*!' he said; then more loudly, 'That's what she calls you, you know, a—'

'Stop it!' I shouted.

'You know I am right,' Bernet told Charles, ignoring me completely. '*Now* she is frightened, she wants safety, she looks to you.' He fluttered his eyelids and added, falsetto, 'Please help me, Charles! . . . It is sweet, isn't it, to have those beautiful eyes looking up at you pleadingly? That you have taken advantage of her fear is not in doubt; the only question is how *much* advantage you have taken.'

'You—' gasped Charles faintly.

'Ah, but you are prudent: you will have been careful to do nothing which could lead to your being struck off the register. Still, you must be tempted. You know in your heart that if she is out of danger, she will want nothing more to do with you. That is why you want to keep her here until you can make her safe and tame and small, like yourself. Have you considered whether you will still find her so desirable when you have?'

Charles hit him. Bernet staggered backward, and I managed to jump up and catch his arm in time to stop him from falling on to the bedside table. I thrust myself between him and Charles – but in fact there was no need for me to do anything. Charles was still standing in the doorway, stunned and pale, looking down in amazement at his own fist.

Bernet sat down heavily on the bed, pressing a hand to his nose and glaring venomously at Charles. Blood oozed between his fingers and trickled down over his lips.

'I—' Charles began blankly.

'I think you'd better get out,' I snapped in exasperation.

Charles looked as though he might cry. Bernet was now dripping blood down his shirt. I dashed into the washroom, ran some cold water on the facecloth, wrung it out. When I got back to the bedroom, Charles had gone.

I gave Bernet the facecloth, and he wiped his face and pressed it against his nose. '*Cochon méchant,*' he muttered, looking daggers at the empty doorway.

'Yeah, well, you didn't come off smelling of roses, either,' I snapped. 'You were *horrible* to him. Jesus! What a *stupid* display!'

Bernet smiled at me from under the bloody cloth. 'It is entirely your fault.'

'Rubbish!' I said, with feeling. 'I accept no responsibility whatsoever because you and he decided to act like drunks when the pubs close. God, I don't believe he hit you.'

'Nor does he,' replied Bernet, and laughed. It was the first time I had ever heard him laugh, and it was a surprisingly easy sound. He looked surprised that he had made it, and also rather alarmed. He got to his feet, still pressing the cloth to his face. 'Thank you for your assistance,' he said formally. 'Goodnight.'

He left. I sat down on the bed, shaking a little. I noticed that there were splotches of Bernet's blood all over the bedspread, and I got up, stripped the cloth off and dumped it on the floor. I ought to get some cold water on that . . .

I realised that I was much, much too tired to do any such thing. I was sick-tired, nearly ready to faint. I collapsed on the half-stripped bed and curled up.

I lay there in silence, listening to the sound of my own breathing. One very odd thing stood out in my mind: I didn't hate Bernet any more. Or perhaps the thing itself wasn't odd, but what definitely *was* odd was that I hadn't stopped hating him when I realised that he wasn't going to hurt me, but when he'd begged me to reach the music. It was as though that was

205

another magic question, like Perceval's in the quest for the Holy Grail. It rendered the asker sacrosanct.

One reason I was so exhausted, I realised slowly, was that this was the fourth time in as many days that I'd called the music out into the world. I'd never before done it so often, and I was drained – totally wrung out, limp and empty.

Another very good reason for being exhausted, of course, was a week of emotional stresses such as I'd never suffered in my life, followed by the abject terror induced by the sight of Bernet's court order, and then the stress of the ludicrous and ridiculous confrontation.

Poor Charles. I ought to go and find him, reassure him that he wasn't a boring flat-footed porridge-eater, and find out what, if anything, he'd discovered in Oxford. I would just rest here for a little bit longer first.

When I woke it was dark, and I was cold. I sat up, fumbled around until I found the bedside lamp, and put it on. My watch told me that it was half-past twelve.

God. I'd intended to eat supper: I was very hungry. I went to the door, but of course it was locked. I thought of phoning Charles or Amrita, but decided not to wake them. Instead I had another shower, cleaned my teeth, and went back to bed.

I woke early the next morning, and had to sit at the computer waiting for eight o'clock. When it finally arrived, I hurried downstairs with a rumbling stomach. Amrita was still putting out the breakfast things in the dining room.

'Good morning!' she said cheerfully. 'We haven't seen you down here so early for days. Would you like a cooked breakfast?'

I was so ravenous that for a moment I actually considered it. Then I thought of what I'd really do if confronted with a fried egg, and shuddered. 'No, thanks,' I told Amrita. 'But I am hungry.'

That pleased her. 'Help yourself!' she said, gesturing at the laden table.

I helped myself. Liz Potter and a friend turned up while I was tucking into my fruit salad and croissants, and joined me. 'What've you got on for today?' asked Liz.

I shrugged. 'I have no idea. It depends on Professor Bernet. He was ill yesterday, so we didn't do anything.'

'It looked like he'd had some kind of accident,' agreed Liz. 'He came in yesterday evening, and I saw him talking to Suzy and Ahmed.' She grinned. 'To tell the truth, he looked like he'd been in a fight. He had blood all over his shirt and a cold pack on his nose. Who d'you think could've clobbered him?'

I considered telling her that it had been Charles, then dismissed the notion: it would require too many explanations I wasn't willing to make. 'All I know is that he called in sick,' I mumbled. I wondered what he'd been talking about with Suzy and Ahmed. Probably they'd been telling him that they wouldn't cooperate in any more dubious enchantments. 'What've *you* got on?' I asked Liz hurriedly.

She told me – it was more ethical decisions, of course – then continued, 'Some of us were thinking about having a little party this evening. Joshua and Mick are going into the village at lunchtime to buy some things for it, and the rest of us are chipping in. You're welcome to join us, and if you play that dance thing on the guitar again, we'll let you off paying for anything.'

I was pleased to be invited, of course, but . . .

'I'll see how I feel,' I told her. 'Last night I was so tired I fell asleep at six, and missed supper. But thanks for asking.'

'Sorry!' she said at once. 'I keep forgetting that you're here for medical reasons. Come if you can make it, and if you can't, don't worry.'

Charles did not show up during breakfast. I hung around hoping for him, talking to the participants and drinking too much coffee, until they all left to prepare for the next session and Amrita and the cook came in to clear the breakfast things.

'Where's Charles?' I asked Amrita.

'Hasn't he been in for breakfast?' she asked in surprise. She frowned. 'He wasn't at supper last night. He did get back from his errand, didn't he?'

'Yeah,' I agreed, then added – guiltily, because I knew I should have spoken to him, 'He got in some time after five, and came up to talk to me. But Professor Bernet was there, and they had a really stupid row. Charles punched him on the nose.'

Amrita set down the empty coffee pot and stared at me, wide-eyed. 'What?'

'It was one of the stupidest things I have ever seen,' I told her, suddenly relieved to be telling somebody. 'I'm surprised nobody else seems to have heard, because they were both yelling. Bernet said some very nasty things, and Charles hit him.' I mimed the punch. 'I went to get a washcloth, and then when I got back, Charles had gone. Bernet bled all over the bedspread, incidentally. I was going to try to get it in cold water, but I was too exhausted.'

'He told me he'd hit his face on a piece of lab equipment,' Amrita said numbly. 'He came into the kitchen to get a cold pack. Oh *no* . . .' Her expression suddenly sharpened. 'Professor Bernet went up and bothered you *again*? And Charles found him doing it?'

'Yeah,' I agreed. 'Except Bernet *wasn't* bothering me.' I met her doubtful look, and added, 'Not this time. He wanted me to play him some music. He even apologised to me.'

'Really?' Amrita asked in astonishment. 'He *apologised*? He must really like—' She stopped, with a look of shocked conjecture.

I felt a strange desire to protect Bernet. So he was a pervert who harboured unnatural desires towards women's brains: it still wasn't fair to punish him now that he was actually trying to behave decently. 'I think he's ashamed of the way he's behaved,' I said. 'He was in the middle of swallowing his pride when Charles turned up, which is probably *why* it was such a disaster: he blew up and said horrible things, and Charles blew up and punched him on the nose. I think I ought to find Charles.'

'Yes,' agreed Amrita. 'Oh, dear.'

We tried to reach him on the videophone, but there was no response. Amrita took her housecleaning keycard and marched along the corridor to his room.

It was empty. The bedroom behind the small office was disordered and cold, pyjamas dumped on the rumpled bed and an empty coffee cup standing in a brown ring on the bedside table. Amrita pressed through into the small washroom: there was a toothbrush on the shelf above the sink, together with an electric razor and a bottle of shaving foam. She gazed at them a moment, frowning, then touched the toothbrush with a delicate forefinger. 'It hasn't been used this morning,' she observed unhappily. 'Oh, dear.'

I went back to the office and switched on the computer, hoping that there would be some kind of message. All that happened was that the operating system asked me for the password. I shut it down again. '*Stupid* man!' I said angrily.

'How can you say that?' Amrita demanded angrily. 'He's just lost his job because of you!'

'He hasn't—' I began – then realised that yes, he probably had. He could hardly go on being Bernet's research assistant after punching his elderly and infirm boss in the face, and he could expect an utterly damning reference, if not a charge of assault. I don't know why I hadn't seen it before – probably only because I'd been so utterly drained.

'Oh, *nooo!*' I wailed in dismay. I remembered again some of the things Bernet had said to him, and how I hadn't corrected them. 'Oh, *fuck!*'

'Oh fuck, indeed!' agreed Amrita tartly. 'I've got his personal phone number on the house machine somewhere; I'll try to reach him.'

She went into the entrance hall, found the number, and tried it, with me leaning over her and fidgeting miserably. There was no answer. 'Oh, dear!' said Amrita again. She glared at me. 'Why didn't you *stop* him?'

'I tried!' I exclaimed wretchedly. 'Neither of them would listen to a word I said. But I didn't think, I . . . Oh, God, I should've realised what it meant!'

Amrita gave a snort of contemptuous agreement. She didn't do more than that, however, and after a moment she said resolutely, 'From what the professor said, he doesn't mean to publicise what happened. Probably Charles can salvage something. He'll have to come back here for his things. We'll try to see how much can be sorted out before he does.'

'You think he's all right?' I asked anxiously.

'You mean, do I think he's killed himself?' asked Amrita

bluntly. 'I'm quite certain he hasn't: he's far too responsible to inflict something like that on his family. Is he *all right*, though? No. It was his first real job, and he has no idea how much trouble he's going to be in. He must be feeling utterly degraded. He's probably walking along the top of the Downs, wondering what to do next and how to break the news to his family and his friends.'

I could imagine it. 'Oh, God!' I said miserably.

'Why didn't you—' Amrita began angrily, then looked at the expression on my face and stopped herself. 'Very well, we have to think what we can do to help. Can you talk to the professor, explain to him that Charles misunderstood the situation, and persuade him to take a soft line?'

'I'll try,' I said in a small voice. 'Is Professor Bernet coming in today?'

'He hasn't phoned in sick,' said Amrita. She gazed at me soberly. 'If I know Charles Spencer, one of his greatest worries will be about you.'

'I'll be all right,' I told her. 'Bernet isn't going to hurt me.'

'You sound very sure of that.'

'Yes.' I met her gaze and answered the implied question honestly. 'Yesterday he got a court order to have me committed to a mental hospital so that no one could interfere with what he did to me. But he threw it away and told me that he couldn't hurt me, because he likes my music too much.'

Her eyes widened. 'A court order? How could he get that?'

'He told the court I was refusing to have treatment I needed urgently.' And, I realised, he'd pillaged evidence from Charles's private records, and perhaps from elsewhere as well.

'But . . . but you *don't* need any treatment urgently, do you? I thought they were still assessing what's wrong!'

It made me realise how little I'd actually told anyone about what was happening – and how much I'd trusted Charles. 'Yeah,' I agreed, boggling at it. 'He said—'

The outer door buzzed, and we both spun round eagerly, hoping for Charles. It was Bernet.

For the first time since I'd met him, he looked cheerful, even though his nose was swollen under a red-purple bruise. He was wearing a particularly fine blue-grey suit and a dark blue tie patterned in gold, and there was a bounce in his step. He noticed us crouched over the house machine in the corner, and smiled. 'Good morning! Miss Thornham, I need to speak to you. Is Dr Spencer about?'

'No,' said Amrita nervously, getting to her feet and knitting her hands together. 'As a matter of fact, Professor, Miss Thornham and I were just talking about him. We don't know where he is. I understand there was a problem yesterday evening—'

Bernet gave a sharp bark of laughter. '*I* was going to ignore that small matter. Spencer has gone off to brood over it, has he? Well, when he comes back, tell him I want to see him, but *not* to discuss yesterday evening. *Alors*, Miss Thornham . . .'

Amrita gaped. 'You're not going to sack him?' she asked, more bluntly than she probably intended.

Bernet smiled crookedly. 'No. Not at this juncture. Miss Thornham, please will you accompany me to my office?'

I exchanged a bewildered look with Amrita, then shrugged and followed Professor Bernet.

Bernet strode over to the desk and seated himself behind it, still smiling. He looked at me standing awkwardly before him and gestured expansively. 'Please. Close the door and sit down.'

I did so, uncomfortably.

'Last night,' he began, 'after I spoke to you, I was caught by Dr Jones and Dr Uzin. They had some very startling information about the after-effects of the experiment on Monday.'

'They told me,' I admitted.

He was surprised and indignant. 'They did?' He looked at me more closely. '*What* did they tell you?'

I swallowed. 'That the, uh, music I played had had an effect on the brains of the participants who heard it. They'd noticed it during the next session of their own programme. They were, um, very kicked up about it.'

Bernet hit the desk angrily. 'The small-minded, short-sighted *imbeciles*! Yes, they took that tone with me, too: "How could you subject us and our participants to this dangerous stimulus?" and "We refuse to cooperate any further!" Idiots! Potentially the most important discovery in neuroscience for twenty years, and all they can do is complain!'

'It's what?' I asked incredulously.

He slapped the desk again. 'Don't be a fool! And don't let fools interpret your experience for you! Miss Thornham, you *know* what your music is, do you not? You *know* it is not a "dangerous stimulus"!'

'I *used* to know that I was a talented young musician,' I snapped back. 'Now I'm in custody as a danger to the public, and I'm waiting to learn how much has to be done to my brain before it's considered safe to let me go.'

He was startled, and sat back in the chair, regarding me with surprise and a touch of shame. '*Touché*,' he remarked, after a moment. 'I apologise. Let me reinterpret what they said, then, as *I* see it. The music you produce while in the . . . trance state . . . has a beneficial effect on the brains of those who hear it. It improves the clarity of their thoughts, calms their emotions, makes them become more sensitive to others. It achieves this without the use of drugs, psychological therapies, or anything remotely akin to hypnotic suggestion; it seems merely to stimulate each brain individually, and it does this so powerfully that the result is immediately apparent and endures for at least a day.'

'B-but they said—' I began – then realised that yes, they'd said that it 'increased activity in the frontal and prefrontal cortices' and 'inhibited the limbic system', and that *meant* what Bernet had just told me.

I stared at Bernet stupidly, and he leaned forward across the desk, his eyes shining. 'We need to know more, of course. How is the effect achieved? Is it reproducible? Are there side effects? How long does it last? Would repeated exposure to the stimulus cause permanent changes in the brain? If that is the case, Miss Thornham, it will be the most significant advance in psychotherapy since the discovery of neuropharmacology! The potential benefit to humanity is enormous!' Too excited to sit still, he jumped to his feet and swept his arms out dramatically. 'Just think! A victim of clinical depression could sit down for twenty minutes of Mozart every day and *voila!* his suffering ends – without drugs! A schizophrenic could be cured by regular applications of Bach! Just *think* what it could mean!'

I gaped. He rested his hands on the desk and leaned forward again, beaming at me. 'Miss Thornham, I know you said that you did not wish to participate in any research, but you must see that this is entirely different. This is so significant, so potent, so . . . I cannot believe that you are indifferent to the magnitude of it! To cure the mind's ills by music – surely *that* prospect moves you?'

'You don't know that it would,' I managed at last.

'No,' he agreed eagerly, 'but I don't know that it wouldn't! The preliminary results are so extremely promising that it would be *criminal* not to follow them up!'

I was stunned and staggered. 'I . . . I don't . . .' I began; then managed, 'W-what are you suggesting?'

He licked his lips, eyes very bright. 'A course of experiments to explore this effect. Perhaps six weeks, to begin with. I can get funds from the Apollo Foundation. For something like this, *millions* would be available.'

'But . . . but the assessment—'

'*Fuck* the assessment!' he shouted – a surprising and totally unexpected use of obscenity. 'What do the stupid demands of the Department of Health matter, compared to *this*? But, *bien sûr*, we can finish the assessment. We can say, as we hand in the scans, "Yes, this woman has an abnormality of the brain – but not one that is dangerous, one that is beneficial and valuable. It is precious beyond your miserable little bureaucratic dreams. So-many million euros have already been invested in this abnormality." *That* is language they understand and respect; they would back away *genuflecting* after that.' He smiled again. 'This is your *liberation*, Miss Thornham! This is something so great, so valuable, that petty little Mental Health Acts become irrelevant!'

It was too much. 'I . . . I don't know,' I stammered.

'You *don't know*?' he exploded indignantly. 'How can you *not know*? This is . . .'

'*Too sudden!*' I shouted back, losing my temper as well. 'I need time to take it in.'

He subsided. After a moment, he sat down again. 'We could get you a salary,' he offered, after another moment. 'A very large salary. Enough to pay for the rest of your university course – if you want to continue it.'

'Of course I want to continue it!' I said angrily. 'Why wouldn't I want to continue it?'

'It will be an irrelevance to you. You are not someone who needs a piece of paper to say who you are. But if you want it, you can have it. You could negotiate a contract to your liking.'

'You're going too fast!' I complained. 'Can you just explain, first off, what sort of experiments you want to do?'

He took a deep breath. 'The most obvious beginning must be to find out what it is about the trance-state music in particular that creates the hypnotic effect. I would ask you to play the Mozart C major sonata in the ordinary fashion, so that we could compare that performance with the recording we made before. We would build up a library of recordings, the same pieces performed in the two different states, until we can identify which features are crucial. We would also recruit volunteers to test it, of course. We need to know exactly what the effect of the music is, and see how long it lasts, and how it operates, and whether some people are particularly resistant or susceptible to it, and whether it has any side effects. We would presumably need at least two groups – one that was exposed to the trance-inducing performances, and one that was exposed to the same music played in an ordinary state of mind . . . and perhaps a third group, too, as a control, which had no music at all. A standard research programme, in other words. Nothing *outré*.' He tried to smile. 'I expect that we will be using the scanners *less* than hitherto.'

'I . . . I don't know how often I *should* reach the music,' I said hesitantly. I realised that what I'd just said implied tacit acceptance of the proposal. Too fast! And yet . . . *liberation*! If this were true, if it was *real*, it didn't just release me from the threat of mutilation and the constraints of the Mental Health Act. It did more: it lifted the music I loved from its unnatural role as Child of Disease and Parent of Madness, and restored it to its rightful place as Queen of the Arts and Mirror of Heaven. It put the world right way up again.

'*Spencer* told you that!' snarled Bernet, starting to lose his temper again. 'He has made you afraid of yourself. Three days ago you were saying it was harmless!'

'It's not just that!' I snapped. 'I've *never* tried to reach the music four days in a row before, and yesterday after you left I was so exhausted I was almost sick. I fell asleep where I sat, and didn't wake up until after midnight. Reaching the music is *hard work*. I love it, but it takes it out of me. I don't think I *can* do it on demand once a day, and I think it would kill me to try!'

That startled and sobered him. He studied me anxiously for a long moment. When he spoke again it was in a much more moderate tone. 'How often would you induce one of these events, in the normal course of things?'

I shrugged. 'I don't know. For a long time it was hard to do, and I used to try a dozen times for every time I succeeded. Now it's easier. I suppose that last term I was reaching the music a couple of times a week, depending on how I was feeling. I have done it two days in a row before, but never three, let alone four.'

Bernet frowned. 'You should have informed us of this.'

'Now who sounds like Charles? You never asked, and I was afraid that if I said anything, you'd blow up and accuse me of obstructing the assessment.'

'I'm sorry,' he said. After a moment he went on, 'It should cause no problems. There is every reason to believe that the effect would work through a recording – the volunteers exposed by the videophone link reacted identically to the young woman in the room with us. We could put it in your contract that you were not obliged to induce one of these events more frequently than once a week, and still run a full course of experiments with the volunteers.'

'You really think,' I said slowly, 'that this is . . . that when the music comes out, it *helps* anyone who hears it?'

He gave me a smile that took my breath away, because it was astonishingly sweet. In a way that was even more unexpected than his swear word. 'Yes,' he said, without hesitation. 'Isn't that what you would *expect* of music?'

'Yes,' I agreed dubiously. 'But . . . it doesn't, normally.'

'But it does!' exclaimed Bernet. 'There has been considerable study of the effects of music on the brain. For example, it's been known for forty years that exposure to certain types of music in infancy improves a child's intelligence, and, in particular, its temporal and spatial abilities.'

'The Mozart Effect,' I agreed; like most musicians, I'd heard all about it. 'But that's tiny. It's barely even statistically significant.'

'Agreed. But it *is* a well-known example of the effect music can have upon long-term brain function. It's also long been known that music can alter mood.'

'Yeah, well, everybody and his brother takes advantage of that. You can't go into a shop without somebody trying that game. But—'

'But the effect goes far beyond that!' said Bernet contemptuously. 'Certain types of music will reduce aggression not just while they are being played, but for several hours afterwards; other types trigger the release of stress hormones, and improve alertness. Music can speed up or slow down the metabolism; it can improve recovery rates after surgery, raise or lower performance on tests of intelligence or dexterity, dull pain, promote healing, grant mobility to Parkinson's victims barely able to walk, provoke or reduce epileptic fits, rouse accident victims from a coma. It has profound effects on mind and body. The difference between ordinary music and the sort you produce while in one of these trance states isn't one of kind, but of degree.' He frowned slightly, gazing at me intensely. 'I wonder . . .'

'What?' I asked sharply, disliking the stare.

He was not offended. 'I wonder if the key might not be the music itself, but some aspect of the playing that manipulates the attentional mechanisms of the brain, and thus allows the music to exert its ordinary influence more completely. I wonder if . . .' He trailed off again, still staring at me.

I shifted uneasily. 'What?' I asked again, more loudly.

He didn't answer this time, just sat there staring. The bruise across his nose stood out spectacularly against his pale face, and for once his gaze held not that pervert's mix of lust and contempt, but a solemn darkness that was almost awe. Then he shivered and looked away.

'You are right, I am going too fast,' he said. He looked back and smiled appeasingly. 'Miss Thornham, can I take it that you agree to participate in the programme of research I am proposing?'

I was silent for a moment. 'I . . . need to think about it.'

He scowled impatiently. 'Why? You have an opportunity to escape the stupidity the Department of Health has been inflicting on people with your history, and, at the same time, benefit humanity and explore the power of music. Why should you need to *think* about it?'

'Because it's very sudden, and because I haven't been exactly happy with how you've treated me,' I replied instantly. 'You're lucky I'm not saying, "No, I couldn't possibly work with you again." There's plenty who would.' I returned his stare. 'Why are *you* in such a hurry?'

He blinked.

It dawned on me that he really *was* in a hurry, and the reason wasn't hard to guess. 'You're worried about the trouble my family have been stirring up,' I said slowly. 'You're afraid somebody is going to come along and say, "You've abused your position, so we can't let you continue this assessment." Oh, God! You're worried about what Charles has been doing, too. That's why you aren't going to sack him: if he's involved in the programme himself he's not going to be off accusing you to the authorities. You're going to offer him a place in this research programme *provided* he doesn't make trouble!'

To my surprise, Bernet smiled. 'You are a clever young woman. However, I am *also* impatient because this is an astonishing and marvellous thing. Last night I could not sleep. I kept thinking about what Dr Jones and Dr Uzin had told me, and I promise you, I longed for the morning as though it were the beginning of a child's holiday.' He leaned forward. 'Please. I want to go and speak to the Apollo Foundation Board today. I need to be able to tell them that you have provisionally agreed to take part in my research programme. You do not have to commit yourself irreversibly at this point. You can change your mind when you are presented with the contract; you can negotiate and demand.'

'I want Charles to help plan the programme,' I told him.

He scowled. I was instantly certain that he'd planned to shunt Charles as far to the fringes of things as he could.

'I trust him,' I said.

'That is a mistake,' he told me angrily. 'Oh, certainly' – with scathing contempt – 'he is *in love* with you, but he does not understand you, and he knows nothing about the things you love. He is capable of doing you great harm – yes, and telling himself complacently as he does it that it's for your own good.'

'I think,' I said slowly, 'that *I* am capable of doing me great harm if the music requires it, and that *you* are capable of doing me harm if the neuroscience requires it. I want *somebody* in this programme who is going to worry about *me*. Charles will. Besides, he's already agreed to try and answer the questions *I* have about the music, and I want somebody to work on that, too.'

'He has *agreed* to work on *your* questions?' repeated Bernet indignantly.

'Uh-huh,' I agreed, and met his eyes. 'You *said* you knew he was scheming with me. I think I'm willing to have all three of us scheme together, if this thing is what you say it is. But I trust him, and I'm sorry, but I don't trust you. I certainly wouldn't want to be left alone on a project with you in charge. I think you would *try* to act responsibly, but you might not succeed.'

Bernet scowled and clenched his teeth a few times – then sighed. 'Very well. You agree to participate if he *is* part of the programme?'

I swallowed, then nodded. 'Yes. I do.'

He smiled. 'Good! Excellent! We should set off for London at once.'

'We?' I repeated blankly.

'Of course,' he said blandly. 'If we are to get money for this research project, it is essential that you accompany me. Do you have any clothing suitable for a formal occasion?'

Eleven

I did have some good clothes, of course – but not with me. When I came back downstairs in the best I could manage – my black jeans, blue T-shirt and black cotton jacket – Bernet, who was waiting for me in the hall, rolled his eyes in exasperated disgust.

'We wish to ask for money!' he pointed out. 'You would not wear *that* to apply for a scholarship, would you?'

'No, I wouldn't,' I agreed. 'But I didn't stuff anything really smart in my backpack to take to Paris for a holiday, either, did I? And I didn't plan on being arrested!'

Bernet snorted, then looked speculatively at Amrita, who was hovering anxiously by the house computer. He evidently concluded that it was no use trying to bully her into lending me something: she was too much shorter and rounder. 'Very well,' he said resignedly. 'Perhaps it is for the best; I doubt you possess anything truly suitable anyway. You have your guitar and the computer?'

I hefted them. 'Just let me write a note for Charles.' He still wasn't back, and I was worried.

Bernet looked pointedly at his watch. I ignored him and turned to Amrita. She looked relieved, and at once dug out pen and paper from the drawer under the house computer.

'Dear Charles,' I wrote, on the Laurel Hall headed stationery.

PLEASE DON'T DO ANYTHING DRASTIC!! YOU HAVE NOT BEEN SACKED, and the whole situation has changed. Apparently when I reach the music it has a <u>good</u> effect on the people who hear it, and Professor

219

Bernet thinks we can get money for a new programme of research into how it works. He thinks that will help me with the Department of Health. We are going to London to see the Apollo Foundation Board. He is going to ask you to help him plan the programme. He had already given up any idea of hurting me even before we found out about this – that is what he was doing in my room y'day. I am quite certain he's sincerely trying to behave. If you found anything in Oxford, <u>don't act on it</u>! I'm going to ask my parents to call off the hunt: I think *this* is the way out. <u>I AM NOT BEING COERCED. PLEASE, PLEASE DON'T DO ANYTHING UNTIL I'VE TOLD YOU ALL ABOUT THIS</u>.

Don't worry about what Bernet said yesterday; he was just jealous. I <u>don't</u> think you're boring. Talk when we get back, OK?

Love, Val

I looked through the letter, underscored the 'don't do anything's a second and third time, added my phone number under my signature, then folded the paper in quarters and handed it to Amrita. 'Could you give this to Charles when he comes in?' I asked her. 'And tell him he can phone me if he's worried. And tell him it really is OK.'

She nodded, smiled weakly, and cast an uneasy look at Bernet, who was standing by the door tapping his fingers on the handle impatiently.

'You can also advise Dr Spencer to telephone me,' he said curtly in reply to the look. 'He has the number. He should also consult Drs Jones and Uzin about the results of some of their experiments. Miss Thornham, we must go. I told the Board I would meet them at lunchtime, and now we have some errands first.' He flung open the door, and I followed him out into a grey and sullen morning.

Bernet's car was parked in the turning circle directly in front of the door. It was exactly the sort of car I would have expected of him, a very sleek silver BMW hybrid. He opened the passenger door for me, then waited impatiently while I stowed my guitar and computer in the back. I got in, and we purred off down the drive and along the lane.

'You already told the Board you'd meet them, huh?' I remarked. 'What would you have done if I hadn't agreed?'

'I assumed you would agree,' Bernet said dismissively. 'You would have been a fool not to, and I knew you were not a fool.' He gave me an approving glance.

I gave him a disapproving look in reply, then sat back in the deep bucket seat and worried. It had occurred to me while I was changing that perhaps Charles had gone to London to begin proceedings against Bernet. In one way, that made a lot of sense. He would assume that he needed to find a way to restrain the professor as quickly as possible. I *hoped* he wouldn't actually do anything drastic without talking to me first – he was the one, after all, who'd insisted that we dared not alarm Bernet – but I couldn't be certain, and the possibility frightened me. I couldn't bear the thought that Charles might destroy my fragile new spring of hope with a wintry blast of ill-timed accusation.

After a few minutes of uncomfortable silence, Bernet put on Radio 3. It was early music – a Gregorian chant – and we wound our way on towards the M23 to the sonorous chanting of monks.

I worked up the nerve to phone my parents about the time we reached the motorway. I was worried about saying much to them, with Bernet sitting right next to me, but I told them about the effect of the music and about Bernet's plan to investigate it, and added that he'd apologised for the way he'd behaved to me.

'So he should!' exclaimed my mother. 'But he has no business trying to rope you into yet another of his research projects!'

'No, no!' I told her. 'This one is different. I *want* to work on this.'

There was a silence, and then my father asked, 'Why?'

'Dad! It's . . . it's about a new way for music to connect with the world and make it better! Of *course* I want to be involved with that! If something solid comes out of this, I'd be incredibly proud.' I realised, with a shock, that I was telling the truth.

'It seems to me,' said my father tightly, 'that you're hoping this will let you escape treatment. I don't like it one bit that Professor Bernet is pushing it at you: it's already clear he doesn't give a damn what happens to you, so long as he makes a name for himself out of the research.'

'Charles is going to be working on it, too,' I told him desperately.

'Oh,' said my mother: obviously, that was different.

My father asked, 'He's happy about it? He doesn't think it would hurt you?'

'Yes,' I agreed, and told myself that it was only a sort of lie, that Charles *would* be happy about it, when I told him. 'Look, can't you just phone up the people you were talking to, tell them that there's been a surprising new development, and ask them to hold off for a week or two, until we all have a better idea what's going on?'

They both groaned, and I felt guilty. They had, after all, gone clamouring to those people twice already, demanding that they *do* something, and cancelled once. 'You weren't just crying wolf!' I protested. 'The situation has *changed*! It really *has*. Surely they have to understand that?'

They both sighed, and agreed to call off the hunt.

When I switched the phone off, Bernet turned the radio up again and gave me an ironic sideways look. 'I see that Dr Spencer does, after all, have some uses.'

I didn't know how to answer that, so I just snorted.

When we reached the M25 we turned right. I gave the professor a questioning look, and he turned the radio down. 'I am going to take the A2 East route in,' he informed me. 'One of my fellow Board members is based in Greenwich, and another will come down from central London, with a third who happens to be in the City on business. That provides a quorum sufficient to grant provisional approval to our project. It will allow us to draw up contracts and hire staff.'

'Oh,' I said, rather blankly. I hadn't even considered that this would be a 'project' which 'hired staff'. Despite the fact of our errand, the whole idea of grant applications and documentation in connection with the music at the back of my head seemed unreal.

222

Of course, to Bernet it must seem absolutely natural. He was a member of the Apollo Foundation Board. He'd got money from it before, and probably decided whether or not to give money to other people. So: three or four members was a 'quorum' sufficient to get things started. Would they all be scientists, like him, or would they be educationalists and people who worked in the media? 'Who are we going to meet?' I asked uneasily.

He smiled nastily. 'Sir Peter Lethering, who is chairman of the Greenwich Museums Trust; David Henderson, who is executive director of Telnet; and Heinrich Schellmann, who is a deputy at the European Bank. We are lucky that Schellmann is available; two members who are normally based in London happen to be away at the moment. The Foundation's headquarters is in Rome, as I'm sure you are aware, and the next Board meeting will be in September. Applications for funding for new projects, however, are usually made to a local quorum, and, because I am a member myself, this request has been expedited.' He pulled out to overtake a string of lorries.

'Oh,' I said again, this time with misgiving. Not scientists; not educationalists and media people either: a high-powered pair from the world of business and finance, and one high-powered quasi-governmental administrator. I hadn't realised that I was going to be presented to people like *that*. I looked down at my jeans and my scuffed sandals and my chipped black-diamond-polished toenails. I was *not* dressed for the occasion. Oh, hell, I was *ludicrously* underdressed for the occasion, and completely unprepared for it mentally! I suddenly felt as though I were going into a concert hall to perform a piece I'd barely even rehearsed, in front of an orchestra rigged out in black and white formality.

I looked over at Bernet with incipient panic. He was watching the road, his foot keeping the BMW hard against the electronically enforced limit. 'This is going to be a disaster!' I wailed. 'Why did you want me to come?'

Bernet passed the lorries and pulled back left in front of them before answering. 'Because you are the source of the project,' he announced deliberately. 'You will be central. They will have

223

questions about you – and doubts. They have already been contacted by the Department of Health as a result of your complaints, and will need proof that I am not *abusing my position*.' He spat out the phrase with distaste. The traffic control panel of the car lit up with the 'excessive speed' warning; Bernet swore and slowed down. 'That will be a secondary consideration, however,' he continued. 'The principal concern will be that I am proposing to expose healthy volunteers to a powerful and completely unstudied stimulus emanating from the abnormal brain of a recipient of Cicnip-C.' He gave me another sideways look of irony.

I bit my lip. I wanted to protest, but what would be the point? I looked down at my jeans again. 'You made a mistake, then, didn't you?' I managed at last. 'They're not going to be impressed by me!'

'I think they will be,' Bernet announced smugly. 'We will stop at the Dome Mall, where we will buy you something suitable for the occasion. We can also see to it that your hair is rescued from its current derangement.'

I stared at him, then went red with embarrassment – I couldn't help it – and blurted out, 'I don't have any money!'

'Calm yourself,' replied Bernet. 'I know very well that no student ever has any money left over at the end of a year – not even medics, who, I am very certain, are far more competent in such matters than musicians. I will pay.'

I didn't like that; I didn't want any sort of debt to this man. On the other hand, I didn't want to go in front of this Apollo committee dressed the way I was. 'I'll pay you back when I get the salary,' I said uncomfortably.

Bernet only shrugged. 'If you wish.'

I'd never actually been to the Dome Mall, but I knew it was supposed to be big and comprehensive. Bernet pulled into one of the underground car parks on the south bank of the Thames, and we took a series of lifts and walkways into the Great White Moneyspinner. I reluctantly left my guitar and my computer in the car: the professor assured me that BMW hybrids have state-of-the-art security systems.

We emerged at last under the vast white tent with its collection of tired old Millennium exhibits and its glittering new shops. There was a BHS near the entrance and I headed towards it. Professor Bernet caught my arm. '*That* is not the place for what we want,' he informed me, curling his lip at it.

'They have some nice stuff!' I protested. 'I got a good concert dress there once for only seventy euros!'

'Indeed,' he replied, a disdainful lift of the eyebrows making it clear he didn't believe for a moment that any dress from BHS could deserve the epithet 'good'. 'Miss Thornham, please. It is essential that my colleagues should decide that you are a charming young woman of *their own class* – that to regard you as a potential psychotic and source of dangerous stimulants would be frankly ridiculous. I know these people, and I know what will impress them. Permit me to instruct you.'

I made a face, but yielded. He did, after all, know these people.

Bernet turned left and strode quickly through the throngs ambling along the perimeter of the mall. About a quarter of the way around he stopped at a fairly small and subdued place which had in its display window only two mannequins, a male and female, both in elegant suits. The name painted on the window in dull gold lettering was 'Skye'. I'd never heard of it before. It certainly wasn't a chain.

The professor pushed his way confidently into the shop. There was nobody there except a middle-aged salesman sitting behind the till reading. Racks of clothing lined both walls; men's on the left, women's on the right. No walk-around racks, and nothing on sale. I had a bad feeling about this.

The sales assistant got to his feet at once and came over, eyeing my jeans with doubt and distaste. 'May I help you?' he asked.

I gaped. I mean, you don't *expect* shop assistants to come over and offer to help, do you? In most places you have to start throwing things on the floor before they'll even look at you.

'Yes,' said Bernet smoothly. 'We are on our way to an important business meeting, and my client needs to impress our prospective colleagues as a person of substance.'

The sales assistant's expression cleared. 'Aha!' he said, with knowing pleasure. He eyed me again, this time with professional interest. 'May I ask if it's about an acting or a publishing contract?'

'My client is a musician,' said the professor at once. I had the distinct impression that he was enjoying this.

'I see, I see . . . you don't play double bass, I hope? Ha ha ha.' The salesman directed his expectant laugh at me.

I swallowed. 'Classical guitar.'

'Oh, good. It would be *very* difficult to find something that would still look elegant on someone playing a double bass, ha ha ha. Hmm. You're a size ten? – no, taller; a twelve.'

He strolled down the rack on the right, pulling out suits or dress-and-jacket sets and showing them to me. None of them looked like anything I'd ever worn, and none of them had price tags.

'That one!' Bernet said decidedly, about two thirds of the way down.

'That one' was a silk dress of a peculiar shade of green somewhere between fern and olive, with a jacket of a darker green fastened by little gold buttons. All right, yes: I thought it was very pretty.

'Very good!' exclaimed the sales assistant, casting an approving look at Bernet. 'It matches the young lady's eyes. Would Miss . . . like to try it on? Ah, she'll need some nylons. We have a few packs . . . here.'

I took the outfit into the tiny changing cubicle on the right and tried it on. It was unbelievably svelte. It made me look like the sort of woman who strolls out of airport VIP lounges to the flashing of paparazzi cameras. I pulled the jacket straight and struck a pose: EMINENT COMPOSER V. THORNHAM ARRIVES IN NEW YORK FOR THE PREMIERE OF HER LATEST SYMPHONY.

Perfect. Damn. I *wanted* it. Oh God, how much did the damned thing *cost*? It certainly wasn't going to be machine washable!

Well, Bernet had said I might get a *very large* salary. I came out into the main aisle of the shop again, and Bernet and the

226

attendant applauded. I smiled inanely and struck another pose. Bernet took his credit card to the till.

'Good luck with your contract,' the sales attendant said contentedly, handing Bernet his copy of the receipt. 'I will watch out for Miss – ?'

'Thornham,' said Bernet, with satisfaction. 'Miss Valeria Thornham. Yes, watch out for her.'

'How much did it cost?' I asked apprehensively as we left the shop, me feeling very self-conscious in my finery.

Bernet gave a smile of genuine amusement and showed me the receipt. It wasn't as bad as I'd feared, but it was still more than I'd ever spent on clothing in my life. I swallowed. 'I'll pay you back,' I said resolutely.

'Please, don't,' urged Bernet, smiling more widely. 'If an old man like myself is able to buy a dress for a pretty girl, he congratulates himself. Besides, I am the one who insisted that you come to this meeting, and that you buy that outfit, rather than one from your' – scathingly – '*British Home Stores*.'

'It's too much,' I insisted uncomfortably.

'It is not *expensive*,' he told me, still with amusement. 'That was a shop run by an amateur, an enthusiast. The truly expensive shops are never in shopping malls.'

'It's expensive enough by *my* standards.' I told him. 'And I *will* pay you back.'

'We still need to buy you some shoes,' he said, dismissively changing the subject.

To my relief, he allowed me to buy shoes in an ordinary shoe shop. (I got a pair of black low-heeled things with little gold buckles, which unfortunately proved to be excruciating to wear for more than about three hours.) Then we continued on to a hairdresser's, where I got a cut and blow-dry while Bernet sat and waited, impatiently clicking through the standard-package e-mags.

The hairdresser kept giving him doubtful looks, so many that she didn't even comment on the wobbly patch in my skull, which they normally do. About halfway through she asked me if he was a relative.

I considered confirming her suspicions and replying, 'No,

he's my latest sugar daddy.' Instead, however, I followed Bernet's lead. 'No, he's my manager,' I said airily. 'We're off to negotiate an important contract, and he wanted me to look good.'

'Wow!' said the hairdresser, reassured and impressed. 'You with a group or, like, solo?'

'Solo,' called Bernet, and buried his face in the e-mag. 'Solo guitar.' I had the impression he was laughing.

He was still smiling when we walked back to the car. It was now about half-past eleven, and the lifts and walkways were crowded. I was conscious of the way most of the passers-by gave us second looks, wondering at our un-Mall-like elegance – unless they were simply wondering what had happened to Bernet's nose.

'I am sorry now that I am not taking you out to lunch, just the two of us,' he remarked lightly, as we passed a pub. 'Another time, perhaps?'

I looked over at him. He was still smiling to himself. I wondered how serious this semi-flirtation was. It was one hell of a lot pleasanter than his previous bullying, but I suspected it sprang from the same root: that he genuinely did find me attractive. I felt, for no reason I could explain even to myself, that the current approach was a kind of surrender – that he was acknowledging the attraction because he knew and accepted that nothing would ever come of it. I worried, though, that I might be wrong, and that if I failed to slap him down, he'd be encouraged. 'Can I ask you a personal question?' I said.

He blinked. 'What?'

'Yesterday you said you bullied girls because they made you think of Yvette. Who's Yvette?'

His smile vanished. He did not reply.

I looked down at my feet. 'Don't answer if you don't want to.'

'Yvette is my *wife*,' said Bernet savagely. 'She left me a year and a half ago.'

'Oh,' I said, surprised. I'd wondered if she were, perhaps, a daughter who had died tragically.

'We were married for *thirty years*,' Bernet told me, his voice choked with rage. 'I *adored* her. She was the only one, you understand? For thirty years, the only woman. I never wanted anyone else. Then . . .' He fell silent, then continued, very quickly, 'I have a chronic illness, you understand. For a time it was controlled. Then the treatment began to fail. I am going to die, Miss Thornham. By this time next year I will probably be confined to a hospital, if I am still alive at all.'

He was talking about the prefrontal degeneration: I was sure of it, and I felt a chill on the backs of my arms. A solo flute soared in the back of my mind, sweet, slow and desperately sad. 'I'm very sorry,' I said quietly – and, to my surprise, I was.

'Yvette left me because of it. She left me to die alone. I . . .' He didn't finish the sentence, only scowled.

'Maybe she couldn't bear to see you suffer,' I suggested hesitantly. 'It must be horrible, watching someone you love grow worse and worse and not being able to do anything. Maybe she just couldn't take it.'

Maybe she couldn't bear to watch the man she'd loved, with whom she had lived for thirty years, slowly turning into a misanthropic monster she could only despise. Maybe she'd wanted to remember him with love.

'I miss her terribly,' said Bernet in a low voice. 'Every day and every night, I wish for her.' He swore and wiped his hand over his eyes. 'You should not have asked that, Miss Thornham.'

'I'm sorry,' I told him sincerely. Even knowing that his response to losing her had been to bully attractive young female patients and to play peeping Tom with their brains couldn't dull the pity I felt. I remembered how I'd felt when I'd thought that degenerating brain was mine. He *knew* it was his; he *knew* what was going to happen to him – and he had to face it alone. How could I go on blaming a soul in mortal anguish for the strange contortions it performed to ease the pain?

The car was still securely locked, and no one had touched my Segovia. Bernet unlocked it, logged on to London Traffic Control, and we purred out of the car park and up on to the road. We drove the rest of the short distance into central Greenwich in silence.

Bernet's colleague had an office in the old Royal Observatory, near to the National Maritime Museum. Bernet parked the BMW next to the beautiful Palladian building, in a slot labelled 'Official Visitors Only'. When I opened the rear door to get my guitar, he stopped me. 'Not now,' he told me. 'After lunch, if they want it.'

I shrugged and closed the door again. He locked the car, and we walked past the carefully tended flowerbeds into the building.

There was a reception desk, where Bernet presented his ID and had his car registered as official, and then we climbed a carpeted stairway flanked by portraits of deceased Astronomers Royal, and made our way along an oak-panelled corridor to a heavy oak door labelled 'Chairman' in thick brass lettering. Bernet knocked, then went in without waiting for a response.

'Ah, Michel!' exclaimed the man sitting at the desk in the bright, high-ceilinged office inside. He spoke into the phone he was holding. 'He's here now, David. Yes. Yes. *A bientôt*, then.'

He switched the phone off and turned back to Bernet, smiling. He was thin, with a long nose and dark hair that had gone theatrically grey at the temples, and his dark suit was at least as fine as Bernet's own. 'That was David,' he explained. 'He and Heinrich are at the Riverside, and they suggest we meet there. That way we can have an, uh, informal discussion over lunch first, and see whether we need to hold a formal meeting. Good Lord, what have you done to your nose?'

'An accident with a piece of lab equipment,' Bernet replied smoothly. 'Peter, this is Miss Valeria Thornham. Miss Thornham, this is Sir Peter Lethering, of the Greenwich Museums Trust.'

Sir Peter's congenial expression vanished, and he stared at me in shock and embarrassment. I saw at once that he knew exactly who I was, but had never expected Bernet to bring me along.

I made myself smile. 'Hello.'

Sir Peter gave Bernet a look of shocked reproof, which the professor blandly ignored. 'Umm,' said Sir Peter. 'I, uh, told the Riverside there'd be *four* of us.'

Bernet shrugged. 'They will hardly decline to produce an extra chair, surely?'

'Is there a problem?' I asked uncertainly. 'Professor Bernet thought it might be helpful if I came along, but if . . .'

'No, no!' Sir Peter said hastily. I wasn't sure whether he was declining my implied offer to leave because he didn't want to be impolite, or because he didn't want to be responsible for the escape of a dangerous CICNPC recipient. 'Umm. I suppose they can squeeze in one more. Umm. Well, I guess we'd better go and meet the others.'

We walked down through the grounds of the Royal Naval College ('Quicker than trying to find parking near the river'). Sir Peter said very little at first, but he kept giving me uncomfortable looks. He was obviously one of those terminally well-bred men who find rudeness physically painful. When we reached the Thames, however, he gathered himself up and said, 'I'm very surprised to see you here, Miss Thornham. I understood that you've been complaining about the treatment you've received from Professor Bernet.'

'Yeah,' I agreed. 'He wanted to do lots of scans on me to test a theory he has, and I just wanted to get my assessment over as quickly as possible. We both got pretty angry about it. But this new project he has is different. I'm happy to be part of this one.'

Sir Peter gave me a worried frown. 'I hope I, uh, won't offend you if I just check that I've got the situation straight. You, um, received CICNPC treatment as an infant, is that right? And Michel has been assessing you under the provisions of the Mental Health Act?'

'Yeah.' I met his eyes. 'I've never had any problems from the Cicnip, not that anyone ever noticed. My local health authority discharged me when I was twelve. But apparently my brain's ended up wired differently from most people's.'

Sir Peter turned the worried frown on to Bernet.

'We are still studying her case,' the professor murmured. 'However, you should be aware that Miss Thornham's brain function is entirely normal on all tests of performance. In particular, she does not suffer from episodes of lapsed consciousness.'

'Oh!' said Sir Peter, taken aback. 'She *doesn't* have episodes? I thought these, uh, musical episodes you mentioned were—'

'They are *not* lapses of consciousness,' Bernet declared firmly. 'They are a completely different phenomenon. Miss Thornham is able to control them and remains conscious during the course of them. We are still studying them to see whether they might represent a danger to her, but I'm already completely confident that they represent no danger whatever to the public – unless you consider it dangerous to play Mozart extraordinarily well.'

Sir Peter smiled obligingly, then at once resumed the frown.

The Riverside was a very posh restaurant with a view over the Thames. When we arrived, a waiter ushered us through the white-linen-and-crystal interior and out on to a riverside terrace under a canopy. Two other men were sitting at a table there, sipping cold drinks and watching the boats gliding up and down the river under the cloudy sky. They both got to their feet when we appeared, and Sir Peter introduced them to me.

David Henderson, the industrialist, was stout, bullet-headed and red-faced; Heinrich Schellmann, the banker, was tall, rugged and good-looking: they were both about fifty and their suits were both exquisitely tailored. When Sir Peter told them who I was, they were both aghast, and both shot looks of reproach at Bernet, who once more ignored the reaction. A waiter brought over an extra chair and some menus.

'Michel, this is out of order!' Henderson said bluntly, as soon as we'd sat down. In contrast to Sir Peter, he was clearly the sort of man who thrives on rudeness. 'We agreed to have a quiet discussion of this proposal of yours in order to *avoid* the embarrassment of a formal meeting about it. You have no call to go bringing your precious Cicnip recipient *here*, for God's sake.'

Sir Peter winced and shot me a look of apology, but he did not disagree.

'Why?' asked Bernet coolly.

'Why what?' asked Henderson in confusion.

'Why have I no call to bring Miss Thornham?' Bernet clarified, with exaggerated patience. 'She will be at the heart of the project when it proceeds.'

Henderson glanced at me, then said, even more bluntly,

'She's a *Cicnip recipient*. She's supposed to be in custody! What if she has a, uh, an *episode*?'

'She does not suffer episodes of lapsed consciousness,' Bernet told him calmly. 'And the fact that she is legally in custody is the result of a misunderstanding.'

I cleared my throat. 'That's right.'

All three Board members looked at me.

'I was, uh, intending to get the assessment done during the summer vacation,' I told them. 'I'm doing a music degree at Dartington, and I didn't want to take the time off during term. I got a letter telling me I had to go in for assessment just on the day I finished my Year Two exams, but I thought it would be OK if I took a few days' holiday first. I still think it was utterly crashed for them to arrest me for going to France. It's not like I was trying to leave the EU or anything. I was going to make the appointment as soon as I got back.'

They looked as though they couldn't work out why a lunatic was pretending to be sane. I began to feel less nervous and embarrassed, and more angry.

'What Professor Bernet says is true,' I told them. 'I've never had an episode of lapsed consciousness in my life. I've never had *any* mental health problems, and the reason I was sent for assessment isn't because of anything *I* ever did, but because I happen to have had the same form of medical treatment as Michael Torrington. I've always thought I was normal. That's one reason why I complained so hard about Professor Bernet when he wanted to use me for consciousness research: it seemed so outrageously unfair that I could be arrested and detained like that when I'd never done anything.' I glared at the three men. 'If I've understood right, you three decided to meet Professor Bernet here for lunch so you could talk him out of applying to do this project and avoid the "embarrassment" of a formal refusal – and the reason you want to turn him down is because you think I'm dangerous. I know I'm not, and he says I'm not: what makes you think *you* know better? You think you know more about neuroscience than he does?'

Schellmann looked baffled. Sir Peter looked embarrassed. Henderson's face turned a darker shade of red. 'Now, see here, young lady!' he exclaimed sternly. 'You were not invited here—'

'Excuse me, but I was!' I replied hotly. 'Professor Bernet invited me, and I assumed that it was OK, until we got here and everyone started looking at me like I'm some kind of monster!'

'That's true,' Sir Peter told Henderson quietly. 'There's no need to take it out on the girl.'

They all looked accusingly at Bernet, who gave a very Gallic shrug, lifting both hands in the air. 'I assumed you would want to meet her!'

Liar, I thought. He'd known perfectly well that they didn't, and he had chosen not to warn them or me.

'You've been behaving pretty damned erratically for the past couple of years,' Henderson told Bernet harshly. 'First quitting the CNRS for no good reason, and now this business!' He tapped the table, scowling. 'We all got official notices about those complaints that you were experimenting on this Thornham person without her consent – and now you haul her up here and spring her on us at four hours' notice! What's the rush?'

I tensed at that question, but Bernet merely gave a superior sigh. 'The "rush", David, is a result of Miss Thornham's position under the Mental Health Act. She is legally in my custody until I submit an assessment to the Department of Health. A preliminary assessment is normally envisaged to take not more than three days; because of the complications of Miss Thornham's case, she has already been in custody a week. I cannot in conscience keep her much longer without making some recommendation for her further treatment, and I would like to be able to mention this project when I do.'

Henderson grunted. 'Because of this crashed suggestion that she can treat mental illness with *music*?'

'I have the preliminary results,' said Bernet sharply. 'They are quite clear-cut. David, the beneficial effects of music in mental illness are already well known and well documented. The novelty here appears to be something about Miss Thornham's playing, when she is in a particular trance state, which makes the listener more receptive to those beneficial effects. Let me

234

stress that this is not some kind of science-fiction "mind control". The trance state for both performer and audience is confined to the appreciation of the music, and the effect is entirely consistent with standard musical influences – only much more intense. I think this phenomenon has immense potential as a drug-free therapy for mental disorders. It would be criminal not to investigate it!'

Henderson gave him a flat stare of disbelief. 'This "phenomenon", as you call it, is the result of abnormalities in a Cicnip recipient's brain!'

'It has been discovered because of that, yes,' said Bernet. 'I hope, however, that we will be able to determine its neurological and psychological basis and use that to employ it more widely. Miss Thornham finds the effort of "reaching the music" – as she terms it – extremely tiring, and would never be able to meet the probable demand for this treatment by herself.' He spread his hands flat on the table. 'As to your assertion that I have been behaving erratically during the past year – yes, you are right. I have personal reasons for it which I do not wish to discuss. I also admit that I am guilty of trying to conduct investigations on Miss Thornham without her consent, and of behaving badly towards her when she refused to cooperate. I have apologised to her, and I hope that we can set that case behind us, and concentrate on this one, which is quite different.'

'Because this time she's willing?' demanded Henderson sarcastically.

'Because of that, yes – and because this time, the potential benefits are much greater. I have been engaged in research in neuroscience for over thirty years, and I have never encountered anything so wonderful before.'

That made them blink, but after a moment, Sir Peter shook his head. 'Yes, but, Michel,' he objected painedly, 'you're proposing to expose human guinea pigs to a totally new and unknown form of stimulation created – I apologise, Miss Thornham, but I have to say it – created by what you admit is an abnormal brain! You say that you haven't even finished assessing Miss Thornham. How can you possibly justify ex-

235

posing a whole raft of student volunteers to a powerful stimulus when you have no idea what it is or how it works?'

'It vould be very bat publicity for the Foundation effen to conzider such a thing,' Schellmann agreed, nodding. He had a strong accent, but didn't seem to have any trouble with fluency.

Bernet fixed each one in turn with a steely glare. 'I do not see that it is my task to discover the nature of *music*,' he stated coldly. 'That is the stimulus involved, gentlemen, and I agree that it is powerful and hard to explain – but I don't believe that the Medical Research Council would be as anxious about it as you are. I would not anticipate any difficulty with the regulations regarding the employment of human volunteers. We are not planning to use drugs. We are not planning to use any form of subliminal or hypnotic suggestion – and my colleagues in neuroscience are aware, as you apparently are not, that brain abnormalities are not *contagious*.'

Sir Peter winced, Henderson flushed, and Schellmann frowned.

'Let us be clear on this,' Bernet continued. 'Miss Thornham's musical technique may be able to affect the fine-tuning of her listeners' brains, but it could not alter their basic neural architecture – not unless her listeners had themselves been injected with cloned neural progenitor cells or were undergoing a course of SGNS at the time. Any side effect this new technique may have on the brain's fine-tuning would probably wear off quickly, and would certainly be reversible with modern drugs. These investigations pose far less risk to the participants than a standard drug trial. No: the only reason I can see for you to turn this proposal down is blind prejudice against a recipient of Cicnip-C – a prejudice that was created by ignorant hysteria after a single well-publicised tragedy.

'Heinrich mentioned "bad publicity". Should we allow our course to be dictated by media hysteria? Our foundation was set up to promote rational thought and the love of learning, to encourage reliance on knowledge instead of superstition. Will you yield to prejudice yourselves, and allow superstition to go unchallenged?'

They all three of them looked abashed. I realised, with a

sense of shock, that they *really believed* in the principles of the Apollo Foundation.

Of course, it shouldn't have been a shock. They were all successful, powerful men, and successful, powerful men are always very busy. They wouldn't have taken time off their regular jobs to be on the board of a charitable foundation if they didn't believe in what that foundation was trying to do. Nonetheless, the idea that rich and powerful men are motivated solely by the desire to become richer and more powerful is so deeply ingrained in the public psyche that I was surprised, and then ashamed of myself.

'Are you ready to order now, sir?' asked the waiter, appearing suddenly at Bernet's elbow.

Everyone jumped.

'Give us a little longer,' said Bernet. He caught my eye and quirked his eyebrows disgustedly, and I had to smile.

Everyone looked through the menu and placed an order. I asked for the toasted goat's cheese with mediterranean vegetables. The waiters brought more cold drinks. The Apollo Foundation quorum watched one another, and me, uneasily: they appeared to have given up on persuading Bernet to drop the whole idea, but were uncertain how to proceed now. Only Bernet seemed unperturbed.

When the waiters had gone off again, Schellmann leaned across the table and asked Bernet about CICNPC.

The professor spent the next few minutes explaining about cerebral implantation and episodes of lapsed consciousness. 'Miss Thornham, as I said, does not suffer them,' he continued, 'though, intriguingly, she does display the classic excess foci pattern associated with them. I strongly suspect that the abnormal connections in her brain developed specifically to *prevent* such lapses. Our scans indicate—'

I caught my breath. 'Wait a minute!' I interrupted, and Bernet stopped and looked at me in irritation.

'You never told me that,' I told him incredulously.

'No?'

'No! Not that you think the abnormal connections in my brain are actually there to *prevent* episodes of lapsed consciousness!'

He gestured impatiently. 'It is a theory I have only been developing in the last few days. I will explain it to you in due course.'

'But—' I began.

Schellmann leaned across the table again and said, 'Vy not explain now? You know that ve are all uneasy about the young lady's condition.'

Bernet looked annoyed, but shrugged. 'Very well. Miss Thornham was involved in a car crash at the age of six months; she sustained damage to her right prefrontal cortex and right temporal lobe; she was treated by CICNPC over the following two months. The treatment repaired the damaged areas, but also had the usual side effect of producing extra, non-functional connections between the affected areas and unaffected portions of the brain, causing regions of the brain to become active without any appropriate stimulus.

'Miss Thornham, however, had a resource most Cicnip recipients lacked: music. She was, I suspect, born with a very considerable musical talent and inclination, and this was reinforced by her family background – your father is a teacher of music, is that correct? The strong stimulus of music on a receptive mind influenced the new cells as they grew, so that the random connections were co-opted into functioning as part of a developing musical awareness. One very illuminating feature of Miss Thornham's case is that the excess foci pattern never appears in the weak, diffuse form in which it is common in other Cicnip recipients. The weakness of *that* activity is, I think, a sign that the patient's brain is attempting to suppress it – which, incidentally, it usually does: the episodes occur only on the infrequent occasions when the activity becomes too strong to suppress. Miss Thornham, in contrast, exhibits only the *strong* excess foci pattern, which in anyone else is only observed during the actual course of an episode – but in her case, there are no lapses in consciousness. Instead, she reports hearing – or rather, composing – music. More than a dozen times a day, yes? Reflecting her mood at the time, but in no way interfering with anything she might be doing. Her brain makes no attempt to suppress the events – and why should it?

A neurological liability has been converted into a psychological asset.'

The quorum looked at me, and I looked down, my face going hot. I nodded, wishing I'd kept my mouth shut.

'Integrating this level of musical activity, however, must necessitate control networks which normal neural architecture doesn't provide. That, I think, is why Miss Thornham's neural architecture is unique: it is a *control* on the underlying, Cicnip-induced abnormality, and not a further example of it. That is my hypothesis, and the *pattern* of the unusual neural connections bears it out.'

I looked up again, heart beating fast. He was saying that I was *normal* – or that I'd gone out one side of normal and come back in the other, which was much the same thing.

'And the musical trance states?' asked Schellmann.

'Are completely unlike anything I've seen before,' said Bernet composedly. 'However, I do not for a moment believe that we are dealing with anything so simple as a CICNPC-induced defect. Miss Thornham is a profoundly gifted musician – her composition tutor, who contacted me shortly after her arrest, used the term "genius". I would not care to make hasty pronouncements about what is normal for a genius, let alone one who restructured her own brain to accommodate her musical inclinations. I suspect the trance states have far more to do with music than with neuroscience.'

Everyone stared at me again, and I squirmed. 'Look,' I muttered, 'I . . .'

'So. You compose music, Miss Thornham?' asked Schellmann politely.

'Yeah,' I admitted, face still hot. 'And I play classical guitar. But, look, this "genius" business is premature. I've still got a year of my course left at Dartington.'

Bernet snorted derisively.

Waiters arrived with the food and distributed the plates among us. When they'd gone again, Schellmann resumed. 'Michel has declined to tell us in any great detail about these musical trances,' he observed. 'I think, though, that ve all vant to know more about them, if ve are to be happy about expozing student volunteers to their effects. How vould *you* describe vhat happens?'

I hesitated. 'I don't know what's going on in neuroscientific terms.'

'Just describe it in your own vorts, then. Please.'

I shrugged. 'I . . . concentrate very hard on a piece of music. It can be some of my own music, or it can be a piece by somebody else. It's as though I get the music playing in the back of my mind, in an ideal state. I don't know if you've ever done any music?'

He blinked. 'I haff played the bass guitar a little. Not classical – electric and metal.' He smiled. 'I vass in a group with some frients, a long time ago. Ve called ourselfes "Katastrophenknaben". Ve vere *schlecht*, but ve enjoyed ourselfes very much.'

'Oh. Well, you know how you can hear the music in your mind sometimes, the way it *ought* to sound, without any struggle for the right timing or fingering or pauses to catch your breath?'

He nodded, surprised by his own recognition.

'I get that to happen, and I try to play along with it. And then I concentrate on the music in my mind, try to make it more *vivid,* and I keep trying to match it, to reach it and make it come out. If I get it right, it's like it . . . like it catches fire, and time seems to stop, and I'm aware of the whole piece at once, as though the whole structure existed in space instead of time. It's incredibly beautiful and fulfilling. It's very tiring, though. I only learned to do it in the last few years, but I think that's because before I just wasn't *good* enough. Anyway, that's what it's like for me. For people who're listening to it . . . I don't really know, but nobody's ever told me that they noticed anything funny about it. All they've ever said is how much they liked it.'

Schellmann looked puzzled. 'I know that feeling, as though the music catches fire! I haff never felt time stop for it, but . . . I can imagine such a thing.' He stared down at his plate, then up again. 'That is odd! I can think of occasions with that very bat student bant, and imagine such a thing.'

'Why is it odd?' Bernet asked at once. 'If the trance states have more to do with music than with neurology, it is exactly what one would expect.'

Schellmann looked at him sharply. 'Michel, the CICNPC treatment is not an irrelevance.'

Bernet shrugged. 'The first time I heard Miss Thornham play in this trance state, she played three movements of a Mozart piano sonata, adapted for classical guitar. During the first and third movements, her brain state was normal; the second movement was played in a trance. I did not notice any difference until I checked the record of the scanners. Without that record, I could have said only that the whole performance was exquisite, but that of the second movement was particularly profound.' He smiled. 'I have asked Miss Thornham to bring her guitar today, so you may hear for yourselves, if you wish, but I must insist that you not ask her to "reach the music". She has done so recently more than is normal for her, and it is apparently very tiring.'

It was perfectly clear to me that far from pressing me to reach the music, these three men would run away if they thought I might. I was sure Bernet was aware of that as well. He was merely using the ban to belittle their fears. He was a clever, clever man.

I thought about that during the rest of the lunch, watching him work on the others. Charles had said that the professor was 'brilliant', but I'd never really seen it before. Now I could believe it. The three other men were all very intelligent and all strong personalities, in their different ways, but they weren't anything like a match for Michel Bernet.

I thought about his analysis of the abnormalities in my brain. That offhand hypothesis tossed off to pacify his colleagues had been more illuminating than all Charles's pondering. Was Bernet right?

I wanted him to be right. I wanted, with a gulping intensity, to know that the abnormalities inside my head were there to support the pressure of my unwieldy self, and that nobody was going to take them out. It *felt* right. Maybe I really was going to escape.

Twelve

By the end of the meal, the three Board members were beginning to be excited about the potential of the new 'technique'. There was no more mention of 'avoiding' a formal meeting; instead it became assumed that the next step on the agenda was to hold one, and that no one was going to be embarrassed by a refusal.

I suppose it did help that I was there. I looked like a friend or girlfriend of the quorum's own children, and, as Professor Bernet had predicted, they soon began to feel that to regard me as a potential psychotic and source of dangerous stimulants would be frankly ridiculous. By the time they had paid the bill they were talking warmly of how they might 'combat media prejudice' against CICNPC recipients, as if they hadn't shared that prejudice only an hour before.

We walked back to the old Royal Observatory talking about Schellmann's rock band, Henderson's daughter's piano lessons, and Sir Peter's nephew's experiences playing the trumpet. Bernet did not add to this musical conversation, but when I looked at him, I noticed that he was very pleased with himself.

We arrived back at the museum in a loud and cheerful mood. As we came into the entrance hall, Sir Peter was telling us that we could use his office for the formal meeting, and that it had recording equipment, when the receptionist at the desk, a grey-haired woman in a suit, interrupted. Her strong voice cut across Sir Peter's with determined anxiety: 'Sir, there's a young man here who says he has urgent business to do with the Apollo Foundation.' I looked round, and there was Charles.

He was a mess. His face was unshaven, pale and hollow-eyed, his hair was matted, and there was mud on his trousers and one side of his jacket. His expression of rather desperate resolution turned into astonishment as he recognised me. 'Val!' he exclaimed, in a strangled croak.

'Charles!' I replied. 'What are you doing here? Did you get my message?'

'Dr Spencer,' said Bernet, with great displeasure. He glanced at the quorum, who were gazing at Charles in bewilderment, and completed the introduction. 'My research assistant.'

'Ex-research assistant,' said Charles, drawing himself up. 'Are you the members of the Apollo Foundation Board? There's something you should know.'

'Don't!' I ordered, all at once certain what he was going to say. I realised that he had not phoned me or Bernet – that probably he hadn't even been back to the Hall – that he hadn't got my message.

'Professor Bernet has—' began Charles, ignoring me.

'Do not make a fool of yourself,' Bernet told him sharply. He once again caught the eyes of his fellow Board members and went on, 'Dr Spencer and I had a disagreement yesterday: I told him he was behaving towards Miss Thornham in a way that was professionally inappropriate, and he lost his temper.'

They all looked at me, then at Charles, and instantly decided that the charge was true, but not entirely Charles's fault. Henderson laughed. 'Oh my God! That's not what happened to your nose, is it?'

'It is,' said Bernet, with a thin smile. 'I was not tactful, and he was horrified when he realised what he had done. He is a talented researcher on his first posting: I was not planning to take any action. Spencer: go back to the Hall, clean up, read the messages we have left for you, and then, if you wish, come back.'

Charles swayed as though he'd been slapped, but glared back grimly. 'No,' he said. 'God knows what you'd do in the interval.'

'Charles, *don't*!' I said, more urgently. 'Please stop! Things have changed!' But there was no stopping him. He faced the amused and intrigued quorum squarely, shouldering aside my plea as easily as he had the evident disapproval of the receptionist.

243

'If Professor Bernet has been asking you to approve any research proposals,' he declared deliberately, 'you should be aware that he is not fit to be any supervisory position, let alone one that puts him in charge of vulnerable—'

'Stop it!' I shrieked.

Charles turned the grim look on me. 'What's he promised you? That if you cooperate, he'll see to it that you don't receive any treatment? Val, you *need* treatment, and he just doesn't care. He *can't* care.' He looked back at the quorum, who were beginning to sober, sensing his seriousness. 'I have every reason to believe that Michel Bernet is suffering from a degenerative brain disorder affecting his prefrontal lobes, and that his responsibility is diminished to the point where he is unfit for his position. He has been receiving treatment at the Clinique Broca on the Rue de Rivoli in Paris, an institution specialising in SGNS for degenerative brain disorders, and his most recent visit to them was in May. They believe there that he has retired from clinical work, and were concerned to hear that he has not. I have not been able to confirm his condition with his doctor, who is on holiday, but I have left an urgent message for him and expect to hear from him soon. In the meantime, I can vouch for it that Professor Bernet exhibits many of the symptoms of prefrontal degeneration, including lack of empathy, irresponsibility, and indifference to the consequences of his own behaviour. I am very concerned for Miss Thornham, who has a brain condition which is of particular interest to him, and who he has been trying to coerce into cooperating with his research without any regard to her own needs. I believe he should be suspended from his position immediately.'

There was a profound, shocked, precarious silence. Bernet stared at Charles, his face skull-like, white around the dark hollows of his bloodshot eyes. 'Judas,' he whispered.

Charles flinched, but gazed back steadily. 'I couldn't let you hurt Val.'

'He wasn't *going* to!' I cried wretchedly. 'Everything had *changed*! You *idiot*! Why the *fuck* couldn't you have answered your telephone?'

'Michel,' said Sir Peter, in quiet horror. 'Is this right?'

Bernet slowly drew himself together. He took a deep breath. 'I have received treatment for prefrontal degeneration, yes,' he admitted. Then some of the glare came back into his eyes and he added, 'It was, however, *successful*. I have been cured and discharged. I have not mentioned it because of the stigma attached to brain disorders, but it is of no relevance. Dr Spencer has brought it up, as far as I can determine, to protect his own reputation, in the belief that I intended to publicise his assault on me.'

The other three looked at him wordlessly – remembering, no doubt, his 'erratic' behaviour, remembering the complaints.

'I don't know,' said Sir Peter, at last. 'Michel, what is this "prefrontal degeneration"?'

Bernet made a fierce impatient gesture of brushing something away. 'A rare condition where the cells at the front of the brain begin to die off. I first began to suffer it eight years ago – it was that which sparked my interest in the prefrontal cortex. It was treated then, successfully – and when it recurred two years ago, it was somewhat more stubborn, but eventually yielded to SGNS. My visit to the clinic in May was just a check-up. Yes, I stepped down from the CNRS while I was being treated! But I had long wanted to spend more time on my research, and I saw no reason to go back to an administrative post after I was cured. I tell you, this affects nothing! There is no reason to abort this wonderfully promising programme!'

Henderson looked at Charles. 'You said something about Miss Thornham needing treatment. What's wrong with her?'

Charles barely hesitated. 'She has substantial structural abnormalities in her brain, and she is subject to brain events which are extreme both in the levels of cortical activity and in the levels of neurotransmitters released – so much so that I am very concerned for her safety if they continue. She is vehemently opposed to receiving any treatment, though, because she's afraid that it might damage her musical abilities. Professor Bernet has used that fear to coerce her; I've witnessed him threatening to refer her for surgery without her consent if she didn't cooperate with an unnecessary scan. I believe he's coerced her again today, or she wouldn't be here.'

'No!' I protested miserably. 'He didn't! Charles, you . . .'

It was no use. The quorum were looking from me to Bernet with growing doubt, and I could see them thinking that he'd lied to them about me; he was probably lying about his own condition. I knew that I'd just dropped back out of the category of 'normal', new green dress and all – and that Bernet had fallen with me. My chest hurt, and I stopped, gulping.

Bernet raised a hand in a silent plea for his colleagues' full attention. 'I can see you are all very troubled by this,' he said tightly. 'You should know that Dr Spencer is a novice, on his first research posting, and his sole clinical experience has been a session as a trainee in an Oxford hospital. Naturally he wants the cases he encounters to be very dramatic – and I think, my friends, that he particularly longs for Miss Thornham's case to be dramatic, so that he can rescue the fair maiden and claim the gallant knight's reward, *nein*? *I* do not judge Miss Thornham's condition to be in any way threatening; on the contrary, I consider that any "treatment" we might give her would destroy the systems her brain has evolved to control its abnormalities, and do irreparable damage. However, I understand that Dr Spencer has also placed a question mark over my own competence and goodwill, and that you will not wish to proceed any further until that question has been resolved. Heinrich, how much longer will you be in London?'

Schellmann was startled, but replied, 'I plan to go home Friday afternoon.'

'Might you delay until Saturday morning? That would give me time to contact my doctor in Paris. I will ask him to give me another check-up, and I am willing to present the results to you, if that is what you need to set your minds at rest. Perhaps I could persuade him to look at Miss Thornham's records, as well, to provide you with a second opinion on her condition. Then, when we have cleared that up, we could hold the formal meeting to consider my proposal. Would that be satisfactory?'

They all looked relieved. 'That would be ideal,' murmured Sir Peter; and Schellmann nodded and said, 'I can change my flight. But you said before that you vere offerdue to make a submission to the Department of Health about Miss Thornham's case.'

'I can delay until the end of the week,' replied Bernet. 'So we should meet – when? Friday evening, Saturday morning?'

'I don't—' began Charles – then caught my eyes. I don't know what he saw there, hatred or desperation or despair, but it was enough to make him stop.

'Friday evening vould be better,' said Schellmann. 'But perhaps ve could holt the meeting in London instead of Greenwich, and let Peter ride the untergrount for a change? My hotel has conference facilities.'

'So does Telnet,' said Henderson jealously.

'Oh, not Telnet!' exclaimed Sir Peter. 'That place is a *tomb* after five p.m. You're at the Dorchester, Heinrich? Why not meet there? Friday at six – and then, if all goes well, we can have dinner together?'

Henderson looked offended for Telnet, but there was a general digging out of diaries and tapping in of dates. Then Sir Peter extended his hand to Bernet. 'Sorry to, um, put you to the trouble, Michel,' he murmured. 'I'm sure it's unnecessary, but we can't . . . that is, it's a serious charge, and it would be irresponsible simply to ignore it.'

'I understand,' said Bernet, through gritted teeth. He shook hands with Sir Peter, then with the others. Sir Peter came over to me and took my hand in both his.

'I am sorry,' he said, sounding sincere. 'I hope all goes well.' He glanced uncomfortably at Charles.

'Thank you,' I managed. My throat was tight.

'Until Friday, then,' said Bernet, and, with a final nod, left for the car park. I followed him in silence.

The professor strode quickly over to the BMW, then stopped, leaning over against the car's sleek side and pressing his forehead against its polished roof. I thought he might be crying, and I stopped behind him, not knowing what to do.

'Val . . .' said Charles's voice behind me, and I turned and saw that he'd followed us out.

Bernet picked his head up and turned on him with ferocious

speed. 'You *fool!*' he screamed. 'You *know* what you have done?'

'I couldn't let you hurt Val,' said Charles, expression changing instantly from anxiety to mulishness.

'So you decided to *kill* her?' yelled Bernet, bouncing up on tiptoe to glare into his eyes. 'Imbecile, imbecile! Don't you see what will happen now?'

Charles took a step backward; Bernet went after him, grabbed his shoulders, and shouted directly into his face. 'If we lose custody, she will be referred to the NHS; the NHS will take one look at her file and commit her for treatment. They will have her under the knife by this time next week!'

'They won't!' protested Charles, 'We haven't finished the assessment; we haven't made any recommen—'

'You fool, she has already had *ten times* more assessment than the health service would have given her! They will see that we have pinpointed the abnormalities in her brain; they will see that she exhibits the classic symptoms of a consciousness disorder; they will read *your* oh-so-careful reports about how she needs treatment but doesn't want it, they will speak to her parents, whom *you* have persuaded to support the idea of treatment – and they will obtain a court order allowing them to remove all the abnormal structures in her brain!'

Charles took another step back, but Bernet kept close to him. 'And then,' he hissed, no longer shouting, but low-voiced and vicious, 'and then her brain, lacking the systems of control it so carefully evolved during her infancy, will indeed *become* subject to a consciousness disorder – a far, far *worse* one than she would have had if she had merely grown up with it, because she has no habit of trying to suppress it. She will have episodes of lapsed consciousness a dozen, two dozen times a day. Her memory will fill with holes, and her personality will fragment. And the wretches, seeing this, will obtain *another* court order, and they will take out every part of her brain that was treated with Cicnip, and every part that the Cicnip-induced growth affected, and they will replace it with SGNS – and then that person who was Valeria Thornham will be *dead!*' I saw with horror that he was crying. 'She will be dead, that lovely girl, and the new person you have created in her place will be as simple as a small child. If she ever grows up, she will remember what she was before only as though it were a story she heard long ago. Oh yes, she will have a *normal* brain. She will be normal altogether, a wretched television-watching shop-girl, with no music, and no glory in her soul. You will have razed to the ground a priceless temple, and built in its place a wretched, ugly bungalow. You fool, you criminal fool!'

'You don't—' began Charles; then stopped, because I crumpled up and collapsed.

I couldn't help it. The horror Bernet was describing was the thing I had feared from the beginning, and I knew that he was right, and it was what would happen. I felt so cold and so sick that I couldn't stand; I slumped back against the side of the car, then slid down it and folded up against the front wheel, struggling to breathe. Both Bernet and Charles rushed over.

'It's not true!' Charles shouted angrily, taking my arm and trying to help me up. 'He's just trying to scare you again!'

'Ah, *ma fille*,' said Bernet, in an extraordinarily gentle voice, squatting down beside me. '*Soi tranquille! Je regrette, je devrais pas parler*. It won't happen, I will not allow it. I will not let them touch you.' I turned towards him, away from Charles, and he put his arms around me. I began to sob on to his shoulder. 'Shh,' he said, rocking back and forth on his heels. 'It will be all right. I have bought some time. I have a colleague in Paris, I will involve him. He will help you. What I said to Spencer, that would only happen if we did not fight it, but we will fight it, and it will not happen. I have bought some time.'

'He's just using you again!' said Charles, his voice thick with indignation. 'First he scares you with some baseless nightmare prediction, and then—'

'*Shut up!*' I sobbed.

'But there's no reason to think that—'

'Dr Spencer,' said Bernet coldly, 'before you say anything more, I suggest you return to the Hall, and read your messages. We made, I assure you, considerable efforts to reach you before we set out this morning, and I greatly regret that we did not succeed.' He helped me to my feet, then unlocked the car and opened the door for me. I sat down heavily in the passenger seat, still gulping sobs. The new shoes were hurting my feet. I bent over and pulled them off, tossing them into the car. I'd got dirt from the wheel on my new silk dress, and I scrubbed at it with a fingernail.

'Val!' Charles began again.

'Let her be,' commanded Bernet. 'You have done enough.'

Charles glared at him with loathing. 'I've done nothing except try to *help* her!'

'To help you need first to understand, and you do *not*! You have no idea what she is.'

'And you do?'

'More than you! You fool, has it truly never even occurred to you that the abnormal structures in her brain were controlling the episodic events? We *knew* that she should be suffering lapses of consciousness: what did you *think* was preventing them?'

Charles stared at him, sputtering. 'The trance state is dangerous,' he managed at last.

'It has never harmed her,' said Bernet coldly. 'Any statement that it *might* is pure speculation. For my part, I am becoming increasingly certain that it *will* never harm her – unlike the treatment you recommend. This is enough argument. I am going to take Miss Thornham back to the Hall; she needs to be allowed to rest. I suggest, once again, that you go there yourself and inform yourself about the situation before you say anything more.' He took hold of the car door, and I swung my legs inside so that he could close it. He went round to the driver's side of the car.

'Let me—' began Charles, taking hold of the rear passenger door.

'Let go of that!' Bernet ordered him fiercely. 'The last thing she needs just now is you.'

'Val?' Charles asked me, still holding the rear door, leaning down to look at me through the window.

I turned away from the pain on his face and huddled into the seat. 'Leave me alone,' I told him. 'You've ruined everything.'

He let go of the door. Bernet climbed into the driver's seat and started the engine. He logged on to London Traffic Control, and we purred out of the car park. I was aware that Charles was standing frozen where we'd left him, but I did not look back.

In fact, Bernet stopped only a few blocks away. He pulled over at the roadside and parked in front of a row of small shops. 'I am sorry,' he said, when he noticed me looking at him. 'I am not safe to drive, not until I am calmer.'

So we sat there for a while. Bernet was shaking and taking deep, unsteady breaths. I wasn't any better, snuffling and swallowing sobs. People going to the shops glanced at us curiously through the window.

'Would it help if I played something?' I asked at last. It would help *me*.

'Yes,' he replied at once.

I got out, got back in in the back seat, and opened my guitar case. Then I paused to find my discarded jacket and dig a tissue out of the pocket to blow my nose.

I played the Largo from the Vivaldi lute concerto, and then a theme and variations by Fernando Sor. I picked out a ripple of notes on the strings, feeling the aching sweetness of the shape they made in my heart. Eternity caged in twice six strings: this moment, these notes, were present and indestructible, whatever became of me next.

'You were lying about the check-up, weren't you?' I asked Bernet, when I'd finished. 'You have prefrontal degeneration, but the treatment's failed. You're never going to get an all-clear.' He was facing ruin and disgrace – and after that, slow death.

He nodded without looking round. 'As I said, I was buying time. If I had not, I would have been suspended at once, and you would have been referred directly to the NHS.' Then he lifted his head and looked back at me. 'You were not surprised.'

I picked out a couple more notes. 'That time in the sampler room. We all forgot the videomatic, and it caught you looking at some brain scans. I was afraid at first that they were mine, so I asked Charles about it.'

'And he suspected from my behaviour that they were mine,' Bernet said wearily. 'And guessed where I was treated, and checked what they knew . . . it is lucky that Gilles is on holiday, or I would not even have been able to buy time.'

I picked out a few more notes, then a chord.

'I am sorry,' said Bernet, turning fully in his seat to face me. 'And I am sorry that I frightened you. I was angry, and I wanted to make Spencer understand what he had done, but I should not have said such things in front of you. Truthfully, *ma petite*, you do not need to despair, not yet. I will get Gilles to take up your case, and he will tell the English court that if they try to make your brain normal they will destroy you. He is an eminent man, they will not be able to ignore him.'

'Who's Gilles?' I asked faintly.

'Gilles Debreuil, the doctor who has been treating me in Paris. He is an intelligent man, and a good friend.'

'But he's on holiday.'

'For me he will cut short his holiday. I will try to arrange it that you are referred to him, and not to the NHS.'

I let my fingers walk down the strings and back up. 'You seem to care about me,' I said tentatively. 'I thought you weren't supposed to be able to care about people.'

He shrugged. 'There are different sorts of caring. I cared that Yvette left me, even though I couldn't care when I hurt her. I do care about you, though, yes. *Eh bien*, perhaps it is because you are a lovely young woman, or perhaps it is because I know I can learn so much from you, or perhaps only because your music is so beautiful. I have wanted music more, as the degeneration proceeds. The brain is a living whole, and when a part of it dies, the balance of all the rest is disturbed. I keep wanting music, compulsively, like an itch in my mind. The last few days I have been dreaming about it.' He turned and looked out of the front of the car again. 'The other night I dreamed about you.'

I picked out the D string tune. Bernet said in a low voice, 'That was in the dream. I was trapped in a dark place under the earth, and I heard that tune coming from somewhere far above me. I followed it, at first slowly, then running, all in darkness along endless tunnels. Finally I saw you. There was light around you and you were holding the guitar and walking up a long corridor away from me. At this point, the music was the

Andante cantabile from the Mozart piece. I ran after you, and I saw that we were going to come out of the tunnels, into the light, and I was so glad, so glad.' He paused, then went on heavily, 'But just at the last moment you turned and saw me. The music stopped and I fell. When I got to my feet again everything was dark, and I knew that I would never escape.'

I shivered and stroked the guitar strings. 'I dreamed about you the other night, too,' I told him. 'My dream had tunnels in it as well. You and Charles were chasing me through them with scalpels, and then I came to a dead end, and I knew I couldn't get away.' I touched the strings again. 'But then you weren't there, and the god Apollo was, and he had a mirror. When I looked at it I saw that I was turning into a tree.'

He gave a small *huh* of recognition. 'Daphne. The nymph the god loved, but could not possess. It has a certain appropriateness. However, I think Orpheus is better still.'

'Even though it makes you Eurydice?'

'But it did not,' he said sadly. 'I knew you hadn't come to look for me. When you turned and saw me, your face was full of hatred. That was why the music stopped. Ah, well.' He started the engine. 'We should go home.'

'I don't hate you,' I told him. 'I wouldn't have stopped playing. I'd have kept on until we both escaped.'

'Thank you,' he replied, and glanced back at me with serious eyes.

It was odd, I thought, as we drove on in silence. I knew now what he'd been like before the degeneration – and I liked him. He was vain, a show-off and a snob; he'd probably always had peculiar feelings about women's brains, though I could believe he'd always been discreet about it in the past – and yet there was more to him, more intelligence, more understanding, more *depth* than Charles would ever possess. I felt . . . *kinship* was the word I wanted. We were both talented, and both doomed.

When we reached the M25, he turned west. 'I am going to leave for Paris tonight,' he informed me. 'I will drop you off at the Hall, then take a flight from Gatwick. I did consider taking you with me, but I think it is better if you remain at the Hall. There would be problems if you tried to leave the country, and

Dr Spencer would be certain to raise an alarm. When we get back to the Hall I will contact Gilles and send him your records and an explanation. I may be able to persuade him to come back to England with me for the meeting on Friday, but even in Paris he will be much better placed than I am to arrange an alternative assessment for you. He is a practising physician; I am just a researcher.'

'Oh,' I said, for want of anything more intelligent.

'For the time being, you should be safe at the Hall. I hope that Dr Spencer will appreciate that he has made a terrible mistake, and do nothing foolish. Please do not despair, *chère fille*. It is not the end. I will not let them touch you.'

It seemed to me that he was protesting too much: that he doubted either his friend's willingness or ability to help. But he hadn't given up yet, so there had to be a chance. 'Thank you,' I told him.

We arrived back at Laurel Hall at about four o'clock. Amrita Mickleson hurried into the entrance hall when the door buzzed open. 'Oh!' she exclaimed, both relieved and disappointed. 'It's you. Did Charles phone you? He hasn't been back.'

'We saw him in London,' Bernet said grimly. 'Excuse me: I must leave for Paris as soon as possible, and there are a number of things I must do first.' He stalked off upstairs, leaving me to explain to Amrita.

I didn't manage it. I got as far as telling her that Charles had confronted the professor and accused him of having a degenerative brain disease, and she exploded in sympathy and horror – sympathy for Charles, and horror that Bernet might be mentally ill. I tried to set her straight, but I was in no condition to be patient, and eventually I gave up and fled to my room.

My parents phoned a little while later to ask how it had gone. I couldn't face another confrontation: I told them only that there would be another meeting on Friday, and then hoped to God that they didn't have more luck phoning Charles than I'd had.

At about half-past five there was a knock on the door. I went to open it eagerly, hoping that it would be Bernet to say goodbye. It was Charles.

My first instinct was to slam the door in his face, but I

considered that he might have something important to tell me, and did not. I hung on the door handle, looking at him. He had not washed or combed his hair since I'd last seen him, and he looked even more haggard and exhausted than before. 'May I come in?' he asked hoarsely.

'I don't want to hear anything about how I've got to have treatment,' I told him.

'Bernet does have prefrontal degeneration,' said Charles. 'Didn't you notice that he said that that story about check-ups was just a way to buy time?'

'So he has prefrontal degeneration! He wasn't going to hurt me. You still haven't read my message, have you?'

'I've read it,' he said, flushing a little. 'Amrita gave it to me when I came in just now. But I don't know why you believed him, nor why I should trust your judgement.'

I left the door, went over to the bin, and fished out the folded court order. I handed it to Charles. 'He got that yesterday,' I informed him. 'He could have done whatever he liked – he had everything set up to sedate me and take me off to a hospital for the criminally insane. Instead he decided that he couldn't hurt me, and threw this away. He came up here to tell me that: it's what he was doing when you came in. I tried to tell you that, but you wouldn't listen.'

Charles stared at the creased paper in silence.

'He's dying, Charles, and he knows it. His wife left him because she couldn't bear what was happening to him, and he's been alone, staring into the dark. Music helps. He isn't lying about that; he's in a place where lies aren't possible.'

Charles crumpled the order and tossed it back in the bin. 'But he was applying to do more research on you! I couldn't believe it when I contacted the Foundation number in London this morning, and found out that the Board members were meeting with him *today*. And when I saw you with him, I was sure you'd been co—'

'I was not coerced,' I said wearily. 'Have you understood what the new project was *about*?'

'Something about the music played in your trance state having an effect on the listeners. I hadn't—'

'Suzy and Ahmed noticed it in their volunteers. It was a *beneficial* effect, and Professor Bernet thought it was probably something in the playing that affected the way people pay attention. He thought it had potential to help people with mental illness. He wanted to have a six-week investigation, and he meant for you to be part of it. We could've finished the assessment, too, and he said that if we told the Department of Health that there was all this research money invested in me, they would've left me alone. I insisted that you should help plan the programme and look at some of my questions as well, and Bernet agreed. I tried to phone you – but you didn't answer. When I saw you in London I *begged* you to stop, to listen – but you wouldn't. I keep trusting you, Charles; you keep saying that you're listening to me, that you're on my side, and I keep trusting you – and every time I do, you've decided that I don't know what I'm talking about, and I've ended up deeper in a hole.'

'I want to *help*!' he said miserably.

'I wanted you to help!' I replied, equally miserably. 'I wanted you to *rescue* me. And I know you were being noble, trying to save me even if I hated you for it. But the fact is, you haven't understood a single thing that's been going on or believed a word I've said about it. I believe you're honest and sincere, I believe your intentions are good, I even believe that you love me. I just also believe that you're *wrong*, and that what you want to do would destroy me – and maybe has already.'

'It's *Bernet* who's wrong,' he countered fiercely. 'No – not wrong: lying. He wants another programme of research, so he's lying, to you and perhaps to himself, and pretending that you don't need treatment when you do. You were right before, when you said he was a pervert, that he likes looking at girls' brains, and he's fixated on you. This isn't science, this is—'

'And what are you going to do about it?' I demanded wearily. 'Try to get him suspended before Friday? Let me just ask you one thing: do you think he might be *right* about what the abnormal structures in my brain are doing?'

He winced. There was a long silence. 'I don't know,' he whispered at last. 'He . . . he might be. I . . . I certainly don't want anyone to do anything to you until we've worked out what's going on; you know I've said that all along. No, of course I'm not going to try to get him suspended before Friday if that means you get . . . *hurt*. But I don't trust him. Where is he?'

'Has he left?'

'He's not at the Hall.'

I swallowed disappointment: no, of course he hadn't come to do anything so trivial as say goodbye and good luck. 'Then he's on his way to Paris. He's going to do what he said he would – see his doctor, and get a second opinion on me. He thinks he might be able to get me referred to the doctor, instead of the NHS.'

'Oh.' Charles was silent a moment, obscurely disappointed by the professor's rectitude, then said, suspiciously, 'His doctor? Gilles Debreuil?'

'That was the name. Is there something wrong with him?'

'No. He's a very eminent neurologist. But I happen to know he isn't available at the moment. I tried to reach him; he's on holiday.'

'Oh, for heaven's sake! Bernet thinks he'll cut it short. He said they were *friends*, Charles – and why shouldn't they be? You said Bernet worked on developing SGNS, didn't you? – and Debreuil uses it. They were both living in Paris. Probably they've been working together for years.'

Charles looked as though that friendship made him unhappy – but there was no reason to think Debreuil would be willing to lie to oblige Bernet, whom he must know was suffering from diminished responsibility anyway. There was no new conspiracy from which Charles could rescue me.

'Val—' he began – and stopped, looking at me. I knew, of course, what he really wanted, and why he'd come rushing up to see me the moment he got back.

His eyes were still fabulous, but they'd lost their power. I was not going to love Charles Spencer. He was honest and courteous, principled and intelligent, and he wasn't guilty of anything worse than making a mistake, but I was never going to trust his judgement again, ever – so I couldn't love him.

'I'm sorry,' I told him quietly. 'I do understand that you only want to help, and, like I said, I wanted you to, so it's partly my fault. No, a lot of it's my fault: I was with you almost all the way, I don't deny it. I . . . I wanted stability, and protection, and loyal affection, and you were offering all those good things. I said, "Yes, please!" and you got into trouble trying to deliver. I think you're a good person, and I like you, and I wish you well – vero! – and I hope your career doesn't suffer because of this. But you may have destroyed me, Charles. If the professor can't fix things up with Debreuil, or Debreuil can't fix things up with the Department of Health – if I get sent for treatment, it will be a fate worse than death. It will be. I can forgive you for that, but I can't pretend that it didn't happen, or that it doesn't matter.'

'I don't think it *would* be such a horrible fate!' he protested in anguish. 'I think Bernet's *wrong!*'

'I think he's right,' I said firmly. 'But if it ever gets put to the test, we'll see, won't we?'

There was a long silence, and I saw that he was no longer convinced that Bernet was wrong.

'I'm sorry,' he said at last, brokenly.

'I'm sorry, too,' I told him. 'I . . . wanted something to happen between us. But it isn't going to, now. I don't think it's your fault: it just isn't going to happen, and we'd better cut our losses.'

His face worked. After a long silence he said, in a low voice, 'I'll do everything I can to . . . to see that you aren't sent for treatment . . . without a whole lot more in the way of assessment.'

'Thank you.'

He nodded, opened his mouth to say something, then closed it again and shook his head. He blundered over to the door and out; I heard his feet, slow and irregular, descending the narrow stairway.

I sat down heavily on the bed. Part of me wanted to cry, but I had cried so much already that day, and the fear of the future was so overwhelming, that my main feeling was of relief. I had jettisoned some cargo in an emotional storm, and I was lighter and higher in the waves because of it.

Well, I told myself, with forced cynicism, there went another boyfriend. Then I felt ashamed of myself.

After a little while, I got out my guitar and put in some practice.

I'd forgotten about the party planned by Liz and co, but when I went downstairs for supper I found the bottles and bowls of crisps set out in the lounge, so I went back up and fetched my guitar. I didn't feel like a party, but I did feel like a drink.

In the event I drank too much, of course. I played my 'Danza' and a lot of other pieces, and danced with a boy who was doing Sociology at University College, but didn't let him take it any further than that. When I first tried to go back to my room it was about eleven, and of course the key wouldn't work, so I went back downstairs and had even more to drink. Then the drink ran out, and George Mickleson came in to tell everyone to go to bed, and I eventually fell asleep on the sofa in the lounge.

I woke up with a headache, feeling wretchedly sick. My beautiful green silk dress was stained and crumpled, and one of the little gold buttons had come off the jacket. The moment I woke, I knew that I had lost my love, that I was adrift from my friends and my family and dependent upon a man I couldn't trust. It was Thursday morning, and before me stretched an endless desert of two days, at the end of which I would learn whether I would live or be shredded into oblivion.

Thirteen

I don't know how I got through Thursday. No, I do know, of course: music. The *Miserere* of Gregorio Allegri, Fauré's Requiem; Bach's suites for solo cello, Tchaikovsky's Sixth Symphony – I sat on the bed, drinking in profound and terrible transmutations of human grief into exquisite beauty. I listened to music until I was dizzy with it, my brain fumbling and numb with melody, my own terror trapped far away behind a cage of sound. Charm is deceitful, and beauty fades, but the voice of the Lord will endure forever.

People mostly left me alone, which suited me fine. I definitely didn't want to see Charles, and the thought of trying to explain myself to the Micklesons was more than I could bear. When I went down to the dining room for supper, however – I'd skipped lunch, and definitely hadn't wanted breakfast – Liz solicitously invited me over to her table and asked me how I was feeling. 'I wondered if I should've said something about how much you were drinking last night,' she told me. 'I knew you haven't been well, and I thought it might not be a good idea – but I didn't want to preach, and this medical exam must have you worried. Did you have to have any tests today?'

I told her that Professor Bernet had gone to Paris, and would discuss my case with a colleague while he was there.

She wished me luck, then asked hopefully, 'Are we going to do any more of the musical experiments tomorrow?'

'No,' I told her. 'The one on Monday was just a trial, to see if it was worth doing more later on in the summer.'

'Oh, right!' she said. 'Well, let me know when they are, and I'll volunteer for them, if I can fit it in. It was a lot more fun than Ethical Decision Making.'

She was so kind, so cheerful, that I rebelled at deceiving her. 'Check the details first,' I told her flatly. 'Liz, I'm here because I had Cicnip-C and I have structural abnormalities in my brain. They affect the way I do music. That experiment on Monday was really to see what effect it has on people listening, and technically Bernet shouldn't have run it at all.'

Her cheerfulness vanished, and she stared at me, first in disbelief, then in disquiet. 'You – you have Cicnip-C?' she quavered.

I sighed. '*Had* Cicnip-C. It was a treatment, OK? – not a disease. I don't have episodes of lapsed consciousness; I do things with music instead. Professor Bernet thinks the abnormalities in my brain are actually there to prevent episodes. There's no reason to think that listening to what I do with music does anyone any harm – but still, you ought to know what's going on before you go volunteering for anything.'

Everyone at the table was now staring at me. I sat there, letting them look: I was past worrying about it.

'You said you were here for a medical assessment because of an accident,' said Liz reproachfully.

'Yeah, well, that's true!' I told her. 'Only the accident was when I was a baby, and the medical assessment is because everybody who had Cicnip-C *has* to be assessed, whether they've ever had any problems or not. I got arrested when I was trying to go on holiday: I'm officially in custody here, and I'm not allowed out of the house. I couldn't even get back to my room last night, because my key won't work between eight in the evening and eight a.m.' I poked angrily at my untasted supper. 'The worst thing is I'm incredibly lucky I got sent *here*.' I hadn't actually admitted that before, even to myself, but now it seemed to be something I'd known forever. 'If I'd been assessed on the NHS, they probably would have *already* taken out all the abnormal bits, and then I *would* have episodes, and I'd end up being lobotomised. They may still decide to do it, because I had Cicnip, which means I'm a cloned-brain borderline psychotic by default. Professor Bernet is trying to convince them not to, but I don't know whether he'll succeed.' I looked up at all the aghast faces. I'd never intended to say so much –

261

I'd never intended to say anything – but I found myself going on: 'It's totally crashed. I always thought I was normal. I always *wanted* to be. I wouldn't even go for the music scholarships, because they're too extreme, and I just wanted to be ordinary.' I had gone to Dartington, I realised, so that I could hide behind Alicia – bright, shining, theatrical Alicia, who loved it when she was the centre of everyone's attention. 'I suppose I wouldn't have tried so hard to be normal,' I confessed in a rush, 'if I hadn't known that I wasn't, really, but I was close enough that I could pretend. Only now everything has changed, even if I haven't, and I can't pretend any more.' I looked about at them all again, then picked up my plate and stood up. 'I think I'd better go.'

Liz cleared her throat. 'You don't have to,' she said bravely.

I considered that. I knew that if I stayed and choked down the meal, everyone would treat me with a stiff, unnatural attempt at ease, and watch me with that familiar mix of curiosity and revulsion when they thought I wasn't looking. I would be far more comfortable alone in my room. Only . . . I'd been running for so long, and now I had my back to the wall. I might as well admit and accept what I was, since I couldn't escape it. I sat down again.

'Thanks,' I told Liz.

It wasn't actually quite as bad as I'd anticipated – however interesting you are, people are always much more interested in their own affairs than they are in you. Still, it wasn't fun – and yet, when I did go back up to my room, I felt proud that I hadn't run away. I even thought about phoning Alicia. I couldn't quite bring myself to go that far, but I convinced myself that the next time she phoned me, I'd manage to be honest with her. She wouldn't turn her back on me, I knew that, and it was only my own cowardice that had kept her away.

I had trouble sleeping that night, obviously. At one point I even thought about phoning Charles and asking for a sleeping tablet. Then I wondered if Charles was still around – I hadn't seen him that day. I told myself that yes, of course he was still around, and no doubt avoiding me as earnestly as I was avoiding him. He probably wouldn't be around much longer

– he could hardly continue as Bernet's research assistant, with Bernet dismissed – but there's always employment legislation: nobody on a contract ever has it terminated immediately. Besides, he was the doctor on call at Laurel Hall: they were required to have somebody, and if he disappeared there would have been a tremendous fuss. I wondered if he would be required to hang around for another fortnight, or month, doing nothing but odd jobs. I hoped he'd be all right, that what had happened wouldn't permanently cripple his career – that he would indeed end up as Bernet had pictured him, a fat-faced hospital consultant with a big house in the country and a rose garden. Yes, and a golden retriever, and a couple of daughters who rode ponies, and a wife who wouldn't be me.

I did eventually drowse for a bit, even without the sleeping tablet, then got up at dawn, feeling completely corrupted, and performed the now-familiar ritual of killing time until my key would work.

When I finally got downstairs and had helped myself to coffee, I went back to the kitchen, found Amrita, and asked her if Charles was OK.

She shrugged, giving me a very cool look. 'I haven't seen much of him since he got back.'

'Oh.' I hesitated, then asked carefully, 'But he is around? In the house?'

'Yes. Hiding in his room, like you, and creeping out at odd hours to get food. You should go talk to him. He's not talking to anyone else.'

I shook my head. 'That wouldn't be a good idea. We . . . sort of broke up.' Odd that you can break up with somebody when you never really got together with them – but we had. 'I just . . . want to be sure he's OK. Do you happen to know what sort of contract he has? I mean, six months or a year or what?'

She banged down the pitcher of orange juice she'd been preparing. 'I don't even know whether or not he's been sacked! I thought he would be, but then the professor said he wouldn't be – and then there was some kind of blow-up in London, which I *still* haven't got to the bottom of, and it seems that *Professor Bernet* will have to step down, and instead of being pleased, you and Charles Spencer both look like you're under sentence of death. Now you say you've broken up with him. Don't ask *me* what's going on; *I* don't know!'

'Oh,' I said again, taken aback. 'I'm sorry.' It was, I realised, completely unfair to keep asking her to help and to then not tell her anything, and in her place, I'd be just as frustrated and angry as she was.

I made myself explain what had happened. I did a better job of it than on the previous occasion, largely because I forced myself to be honest, to say, 'I sometimes work myself into an extreme and abnormal brain state when I play music,' and, 'The music I play in that state has a measurable effect on people who listen to it.' Amrita was still bewildered by it – though, oddly, she seemed to understand exactly how I felt about Charles.

'Oh dear!' she said when I'd finished. 'Oh, poor Charles! No, of course you can't get involved with him now, but he must feel *dreadful*!' Then she looked at me, her eyes warm and motherly and added, 'And poor you! You mean you've been sitting in your room worrying that somebody's going to take out half your brain?'

I winced. 'Look,' I told her, 'Please don't tell me they won't do it: they might. And please don't tell me that if they do, they can replace it with SGNS good as new and everything will be OK. It won't be. My brain *isn't* normal, and if they *made* it normal they'd have to change so much that I wouldn't be the same person afterwards. I'm not the only one who thinks that: Professor Bernet agrees, and I think Charles is starting to think so as well. I don't want to argue about it: I haven't the strength.'

Amrita started to reply, then stopped, frowning. There was a long silence, with her looking at me and me, for once, looking back honestly. Then she said quietly, 'What can I do to help?'

I nearly burst into tears. I hugged her fiercely, and she patted me on the back. 'No,' she said, when I finally let go, 'I do want to help. Is there anything I can do?'

I don't know what I did to deserve that. Nothing, I suppose: she was simply that kind of person. I ended up giving her my smart silk dress to clean up, in case I needed to go up to London that afternoon.

I had at first assumed that I would be present for the formal meeting, but I'd gradually realised that I probably wouldn't. Bernet had wanted me along the first time to reassure his colleagues; I had done that, insofar as I could. To bring me along to a second meeting to which I had not been invited was pushing things, and he might well feel that my presence would be an embarrassment. Still, it seemed just as well to have something suitable to wear, just in case.

I fretted around the Hall all morning, wondering how Bernet was getting on. I wished he'd phone me. I told myself that I shouldn't *expect* him to consider how I must be feeling – after all, with his condition he was doing well to care about me at all – but I couldn't help feeling impotent and angry. Around about eleven, Amrita took pity on me and let me walk down to the village with her. I was glad to get out, but brought my phone along, in case Bernet tried to contact me. It remained obstinately silent.

The afternoon went on forever. I practised my guitar. I wrote out the D string piece, then looked at it and realised that there was practically nothing to it, and wondered why I'd bothered. Then I looked at my string quartet, and decided that it really, truly, did need another movement – a final movement, Allegro ma non troppo, that would balance and resolve the pulsing rhythms of the first Allegro molto with the slow-burning passion of the Adagio. I knew what it needed – but I was far too tense and distracted to do anything about it.

At about three, Liz and a couple of the others knocked on the door. George Mickleson was about to drive them back to London, and they'd come to say goodbye. I was very surprised that they were bothering, and very touched. They wished me luck, and I thanked them.

The house was quiet after that. I went downstairs, then upstairs, then downstairs again. I could concentrate on nothing. The music at the back of my mind kept playing in starts and broken fragments: a rattle of drums; a passionate burst of *laqueada* on the guitar; a whisper of clarinets. Once there was a woman's voice, high and sweet, singing slow falls of melody, as though she were calling someone she knew would not come. No words. There were never any words in the music I heard in my head: it came from somewhere deeper than language.

At four o'clock, Charles came into the lounge where I was trying to watch television. He looked cleaner and tidier than he had on Wednesday, but just as pale and haggard, and I could tell he hadn't had any more sleep than I had. 'Oh,' he said vaguely. 'There you are. Bernet just called.'

'What?' I cried, jumping to my feet so fast I knocked the television remote to the floor. 'Does he want to talk to me?'

Charles shook his head. 'He asked me to take you to London.'

'He called *you*? Is he still on the line? Did he say anything about—'

Charles shook his head again. 'He was calling the *Hall*. He only spoke to me because George Mickleson's busy transporting the participants. He said his flight from Paris was likely to be delayed and asked if I could I take you to London. Then he said that probably I ought to be at the meeting as well, so that everyone would know that everything was fair and above board.'

'Oh.' I wasn't sure whether I was angry or relieved to have been told nothing about the outcome of Bernet's mission. I was definitely relieved, however, that I could, after all, go to London. Travelling with Charles would be awkward, but it was still better than staying at the Hall and waiting.

'I don't have a car,' Charles said, after a moment. 'Bernet knows that, but I suppose he didn't remember.'

'How did you get in to London before?'

'Walked, bus, train, tube,' he replied promptly. 'I did most of the walking at the beginning, though, because I was so kicked up I couldn't sit still. I ended up right over in some tiny place on the other side of the Downs at five in the morning, and I had to sit on a bench for hours, waiting for things to open so I could get some coffee and use a phone. My own phone was broken. I slipped going down a hill and landed on it.'

'Oh,' I said, blinking at him and remembering the mud on his jacket. 'No wonder we couldn't get hold of you.'

'I'll ask Amrita if she can run us over to the station in her car.

266

We'll never make it otherwise.' He managed a ghost of a smile. 'Probably people who are in custody under the Mental Health Act aren't supposed to use public transport, but we'll ignore that.'

'We ought to change,' I told him. 'The meeting's at the Dorchester Hotel. You don't want to look scruffy.'

'I did before,' he said ruefully.

'Yeah, but I think you want to put that behind you.'

Amrita happily agreed to drive us to the nearest train station, and gave me my smart dress, cleaned with a damp cloth and freshly pressed. I went upstairs, changed into it, and came down again with my guitar and my computer. Charles was waiting at the foot of the stairs, more than usually pink and scrubbed in a good suit.

'Do you need those?' asked Charles, eyeing my computer and guitar doubtfully.

'I don't know,' I replied honestly. 'Probably not. But I'd feel pretty silly if I did need them, and I'd left them in Sussex.'

Amrita drove us over to the station in the Micklesons' own car, a battered red Ford. 'Will you need a lift back?' she asked, pulling up outside the small rural station.

'I don't know when we'll be back,' said Charles, frowning. 'Don't wait up for us. If we need transport, we'll get a taxi.'

The station, though small, was well within the commuter belt, and within ten minutes of arriving we had boarded a train for London. It was the time of day when the rush was all in the other direction, so the carriage was not crowded. I put my guitar and computer on an empty window seat and sat down next to them. Charles, looking uncomfortable, sat down across the aisle from me.

We travelled a few miles in silence, and then Charles said hesitantly, 'Val . . .'

I looked round at him warily.

'I just wanted you to know,' he said, nerving himself, 'that if you *are* referred for treatment by the NHS I'll send them a report supporting Professor Bernet's interpretation of your scans and strongly recommending that they discharge you with a supervision order.'

'Oh!' I said. After a moment I asked eagerly, 'Will that be enough?'

He winced. 'I don't know. Normally it would be, but Professor Bernet's views will have been discredited because of his own condition, and *my* views will be discredited because I don't have any experience, except with him. It should be enough to make them refer you for a second opinion, though. If Debreuil backs Bernet, that should settle it – unless the panel decides that he's too closely connected to Bernet, and they want the opinion of an *independent* doctor.'

'Oh,' I said again, this time less enthusiastically. I watched him closely. 'That would be bad news, wouldn't it? I mean, *you* don't entirely believe Bernet's interpretation. Another doctor, who wasn't as clever as him and might not even be a specialist, would just look at the scans and say, "Right, here's one for the chop." They won't want to discharge a Cicnip recipient with serious brain abnormalities, supervision order or no.'

He winced again. 'I think I do believe Bernet's interpretation now,' he said in a low voice. 'I've been going over the data and . . . it fits. I still think the extreme events, the trances, need watching, but I definitely agree that surgery could be disastrous.' He lowered his eyes. 'I don't know, though, that someone coming at the scans cold would see things that way, and . . . and I think I probably *have* persuaded your parents that you need surgery. I'm . . . very sorry. I'll talk to them again, but . . . if the next opinion comes down against me, they probably won't listen.'

'It wasn't your fault,' I said wearily. 'You were doing what you thought was for the best. And anyway, it's not over yet. If they want to send me for surgery, they'll have to fight.'

Surprisingly, that made him smile. 'That was the first thing I noticed about you. You came out of that cell in the police station, miserable and bedraggled, but still fighting. You looked twice as alive as anyone else in the place. I . . . Sorry.' The smile was replaced by a look of acute misery. I suspected that the misery wasn't just because he remembered that I'd ditched him, but because he suspected I was going to lose my fight. It did not make me feel any better.

We arrived at Waterloo station at about half-past five, waded through crowds of departing commuters, took the tube to Hyde Park Corner, and waded through more commuters up into Park Lane. We got to the Dorchester at five to six, which I thought was good timing, and told Reception that we were meeting Herr Schellmann on Apollo Foundation business.

'Oh, yes,' drawled the receptionist, looking askance at my guitar. 'He's booked a conference room. I'll have someone show you the way.' He summoned a flunkey and instructed her to show us to the 'Panelled Room'.

The 'Panelled Room' was mostly white, with a high ceiling and a chandelier; a few token oak panels along one wall provided the excuse for its name. Schellmann and Sir Peter Lethering were already sitting at the polished maple table, bent over the controls of the room's recording system. They both looked up in surprise when we came in.

Sir Peter got to his feet. 'Miss Thornham!' He did not sound pleased to see me, though Schellmann was smiling. 'And Dr . . . Milton, isn't it?'

'Spencer,' said Charles.

'Yes. Sorry. Yes. Did, uh . . . I, um . . . well, does Michel know you're going to be here?'

'Yes,' replied Charles, taken aback. 'He asked us to come.'

Sir Peter was so relieved to find that there wasn't going to be another shocking scene that he accepted our uninvited presence. 'Oh! That's all right then,' he declared feelingly, and drifted back to the table. 'I don't suppose either of you knows anything about videomatic systems?'

In fact, Schellmann already had the videomatic recording system running, and our help was not needed. We all sat at the table looking nervously at one another. 'Is Michel, uh, parking the car?' asked Sir Peter hesitantly.

'Um, no,' replied Charles. 'He might be a bit late. He phoned from Orly airport at about four to say that his flight might be delayed, and he asked me to accompany Miss Thornham up to London for the meeting.'

The door opened, as if on cue, but it was David Henderson. Like Schellmann and Sir Peter, he was taken aback to see us;

unlike them, he made no effort to be polite about it. 'What are you doing here?' he demanded bluntly.

'Apparently Michel told them to come,' supplied Sir Peter. 'His flight's been delayed.'

Henderson regarded Charles with suspicion and hostility. 'I'm surprised he asked *you*. Or have you changed your story?'

Charles flushed slightly. 'I'm quite certain that Professor Bernet does suffer from prefrontal degeneration, and that he should not be put in charge of any research project you may decide to set up. But I . . . I misunderstood the rest of the situation last Wednesday. Miss Thornham was not being coerced, and I've come to the conclusion that the professor is right to think that in her case surgery would actually be harmful.'

There was a moment's silence while the three took this in. 'You're admitting that your accusation was an invention?' asked Henderson.

Charles's flush darkened. 'No,' he declared firmly. 'I was genuinely concerned, and I had real grounds for it. But I didn't understand what Professor Bernet was proposing or that Miss Thornham had agreed to it. I still think that Miss Thornham's condition is more serious than the professor was pretending, but I don't think it represents a threat to anyone besides her. I think the research programme should go ahead, if with a few extra safeguards.'

The Board quorum looked at him in disbelief. '*Doctor,*' said Henderson sarcastically, 'you can't call the originator of a research proposal an irresponsible madman, and then say that the programme itself should go ahead. And you can't say that the young woman at the centre of it is seriously ill, but that she should proceed to work on the project without treatment! Even if the research councils allowed it, the insurers would stop it dead!'

Charles couldn't reply. He sat there, red in the face, and stared at the table in front of him.

'Well,' said Sir Peter hastily, 'we'll have a better grasp of the situation as soon as Michel turns up. Did he say how long he was likely to be delayed?'

'No,' muttered Charles. 'It, uh, didn't sound like he expected to be late to the meeting. It was just that he didn't think he'd have time to go by the Hall and collect Miss Thornham first.'

Sir Peter nodded sagely. There was another awkward silence.

'You haff brought your guitar,' Schellmann remarked, leaning towards me.

'I thought someone might want me to play,' I replied.

'I voult like that,' Schellmann said at once, 'although, please, I do not vant to experience this "trance state". Vill you play us something now, vile ve are vaiting?'

I got the guitar out of its case at once and checked the tuning. 'Any requests?' I asked, then added quickly, 'I don't sing!'

Schellmann shrugged and shook his head. Sir Peter cleared his throat. 'Bach? I love the lute suites.'

I had to smile. I knew those off by heart. 'Yeah, me too.' I launched into the prelude to the E major lute suite, and Sir Peter at once broke into a smile.

When I finished there was a spatter of applause. Some of it came from behind me. I turned in the chair and saw that Bernet had arrived and was standing in the doorway.

I knew at once that something had happened, but I couldn't tell if it were good or bad. The professor's face was tense, and his eyes were hot. The bruise across his nose had darkened as it faded, and stood out against his pale skin. He let go of the door handle and padded into the room like a stalking tiger. I saw then that there was another man behind him, a large bluff brown-haired man in a shabby blue suit. The stranger noticed me looking at him, and beamed.

I had no idea how to respond to this, and I just blinked stupidly.

'This is my good friend, Dr Gilles Debreuil,' Bernet announced to the room at large. 'He has been treating me in Paris, and he wished to attend this meeting in person.'

Sir Peter was on his feet again, shaking hands with Bernet, and at once extended his hand to the newcomer. 'Sir Peter Lethering,' he introduced himself. Henderson and Schellmann got up as well.

There were introductions and shaking of hands all round. I

sat and hugged my guitar, giddy with hope and fear. It occurred to me that I should put the instrument away, but I couldn't. It had comforted me in the worst of the nightmare, and I wanted, stupidly, to keep it with me.

At last everyone sat down. Henderson checked the recording equipment and formally announced the time and place of the meeting, the names of the people present, and the subject it concerned – 'an application by Professor Michel Bernet for provisional funding for a programme of neuroscientific research.'

'First, however,' he went on, 'we need to address an issue raised by Dr Spencer of Laurel Hall. He has suggested that Professor Bernet is not competent to direct research because of a degenerative illness of the brain. Professor Bernet offered to go to Paris to obtain a certificate of his fitness from Dr Debreuil, who has been treating him. Dr Debreuil has in fact been good enough to come to vouch for his mental competence in person.'

'Ah, no!' exclaimed Debreuil. 'That I cannot do. Michel, you know I cannot do that.'

Bernet shrugged. He was still very pale and tense. 'I never expected you to,' he said flatly. 'When I made the suggestion to my colleagues, I was attempting to buy a little time in which to make some arrangement that would protect Miss Thornham.'

Silence like the flicking of a switch. The looks of relief froze on the Board's faces, then ebbed slowly away. 'Michel . . .' whispered Sir Peter.

Bernet nodded curtly. 'Tell them,' he ordered Debreuil.

Debreuil gave him a curious look, but shrugged. 'Very well. I have known Michel Bernet for many years. We worked together on the development of SGNS twenty years ago – that is to say, he worked on the development, and I provided him with patients who needed his help. Eight years ago he came to me saying that people around him were complaining that his behaviour was erratic, and that he feared they might be right. We did some scans, and, tragically, discovered that he was suffering from prefrontal degeneration.'

He hesitated, then went on. 'It is a terrible condition. It alters

272

the personality first, making the sufferer callous, insensitive, impulsive – all without his being aware that he has changed. When it has done that, it proceeds to kill him slowly, destroying his motor coordination, balance, hearing . . . it ends in paralysis and death. It does not affect the intellect, however, not until very late in its course, and my friend Michel is a very brilliant man. He had recognised what was happening, even though he could not perceive it himself. That allowed us to diagnose the disorder before it did too much harm – and, as it happened, the treatment was one we had worked on together. We undertook a course of SGNS, and the illness was halted, and then reversed. Michel went back to his research, though every year he had a scan to check that the disease had not returned.

'Two years ago, to our great distress, we discovered that the degeneration had resumed. I applied another course of SGNS – but this time the new cells which were created began to die off after a few months. We tried again, with the same result. By this time, the changes in my friend's personality were very noticeable. He had always been a proud man, impatient, burning with zeal for his subject, but he had also always been a man of high principles. Now he was harsh, cold, self-indulgent, and irresponsible. I was forced to tell him that he was not competent to supervise others, and that he ought to resign his position. It made him very angry. It was very distressing, for me and for all his friends – I assure you, it is heartbreaking to watch a man you have admired gradually become a travesty of his former self.

'When we began the treatment for a third time, though, Michel told me that if this failed he would resign from the CNRS and retire to the country and continue his research only by analysing existing data. I was relieved. I knew how eager he was to finish his career with some last, truly worthwhile achievement, and I believed he was making a sacrifice.'

Debreuil glanced round the table. 'As you have realised, that was not what he did.'

Everyone looked at Bernet, who gazed unconcernedly at the panelling on the opposite wall.

'I should have suspected,' said Debreuil sadly. 'I knew he was no longer able to act responsibly. *Eh bien,* the third treatment began to fail even more quickly than the first and the second. Michel resigned from the CNRS and left Paris, though he returned at intervals so that I could monitor the disease.

'The last time he returned was in May. At that time he asked me to provide him with a fourth course of treatment. We both knew it would not halt the degeneration, but he told me that he wanted to prolong his active life. He said that he was engaged in studying data from CICNPC recipients, and he hoped to achieve some noteworthy advance in the subject by means of a novel interpretation.'

Again Debreuil hesitated, then went on, 'I don't know if you gentlemen know how SGNS works? A series of neural hormones are administered locally to precisely determined regions of the brain: these return the affected neurons to the chemical state they had in the developing embryo. Another series of chemicals, combined with neural growth factor, stimulates the cells to grow in a manner precisely determined by chemical guidelines injected into the subject's brain. Michel had had three courses of SGNS within two years. I would not normally subject a patient to a fourth course within such a short period of time, since repeated doses of these very powerful drugs can damage unaffected tissue, and cause memory loss or cognitive impairment. Michel, though, was not merely a friend, but a brilliant scientist for whose abilities I have the deepest respect. A fourth treatment would give him a few more months with his intellectual abilities intact, and I believed he might indeed achieve something in that amount of time, given the novel information we were getting from CICNPC. I also knew that he was not going to survive long, whatever I did. I provided the treatment. There did not seem to be any impairment at the time, and he went off to his retirement and his data analysis, or so I thought.

'Then, on Wednesday, while I was on holiday in the Alps, I suddenly received two telephone messages. One was from the clinic where I work, saying that a Dr Spencer' – Debreuil nodded at Charles – 'had contacted them to ask whether Michel suffered from prefrontal degeneration. I was very concerned to learn that my friend had lied about his retirement, and was in fact in charge of vulnerable patients. The other message was from Michel himself, urgently begging me to come and meet him in Paris. Well.' Debreuil shrugged. 'I came, of course, in great agitation, and when I met Michel, all he wished to speak of was some Cicnip recipient he had been working with, to whom he attributed miraculous powers.' He shrugged again. 'I thought that he was entirely deluded – that the fourth SGNS treatment had damaged his reason.'

A profound, dizzying silence. I could hear the soft whirr of the recording system, the remote gurgle of water in pipes, the beating of my own heart. Into the silence came a sound that only I heard: the plucking of a single bass string on a guitar, once, twice, a third time – and then only the silence. Bernet, I thought, had known that his friend would think that. Bernet had known that the odds were against us from the start.

'We argued about it,' Debreuil resumed at last. 'He wanted to discuss his Cicnip recipient; I wanted to run scans of his brain. Eventually he refused to cooperate with the scans unless I looked at the data he had brought. This was happening yesterday, you understand; it had taken each of us some time to arrive back in Paris and meet one another. Because it was a working day, my clinic was busy, and our scanners were all in use for our scheduled patients. I was willing to work late for my friend, of course, but I could not justifiably evict the other patients. I agreed, therefore, to look at Michel's data if he would allow me to examine him that evening, a compromise he accepted.

'So I looked at the data. It appeared to show that he had a substantial case, but I was suspicious of it. I thought perhaps Michel had tampered with it, and certainly I viewed his proposed explanations for it with doubt. Still, I was interested – though not so much as I would have been, had I not been so worried about my friend. I was in a great hurry to get him on the scanners as soon as the working day ended, so that I could see just what damage my ill-advised fourth SGNS treatment had done to his brain.'

Debreuil paused again, then looked directly at me, his eyes suddenly very bright. 'There was no damage.'

Another breathless, aching silence. The guitar sounded in my mind again, the same three notes, then a ripple of melody, sharp with hope before I had consciously begun to hope anything.

'I looked first with the fMRI scanner, and was surprised to see that when Michel completed a series of cognitive tasks, his brain function appeared entirely normal. But that was only a small surprise: the very great surprise was the prefrontal region. It was far healthier than I had expected, and it was functioning – weakly and erratically, but functioning.'

A flurry of chords; a burst of rhythmic strumming, and the massed strings of an orchestra suddenly soaring against the passionate solo voice of the guitar.

'Now, please understand. I had given Michel a course of SGNS, and the hormones and growth factors were still active in his brain, so I knew that his cortex might have recovered a little – but it had been a month, and I had expected the cells to have begun to die back again. On past experience, I would have expected them to have died back faster. I was *astonished* to see that the treatment was actually working. I said, "Michel, you have recovered some function in your prefrontal region!" He did not believe me; he took the helmet off and came and looked at the record himself. We checked it again. We checked it on the magnetoencephalograph. We checked it on the neuropharmacological sampler. It was beyond question: the prefrontal region, which had been dying, was recovering.

'Then I used the sampler to check the age of the new cells – which one can do; there are certain key hormones which are released only during cell growth, and which break down afterwards at a predictable rate. I discovered that all this growth was new, that it had occurred, not at the time of treatment, but during the last week. The SGNS *had* indeed been failing, but some powerful new stimulus had affected it and triggered it into producing the new growth. I said this to Michel, and he . . . he was overcome, and he said, "It has been four days since she played the Mozart."'

Debreuil was gazing directly into my eyes now, his face joyful and excited. 'I did not believe that, not at first. But we went back to the data Michel had sent – the scans showing the effects

276

of this new musical technique on the brains of your volunteers – and, when we had gone over them three or four times, I had to concede that it could have been so – that, in fact, the evidence that it had been so was overwhelming.'

The doctor sat back slightly, still watching me. 'By this time, it was morning – this morning – and we were both exhausted. I said to Michel, "If this is true, it has as much potential as SGNS itself." Michel said, "As much or more! But, my friend, we must impress that upon the English Department of Health, because otherwise they will decide to destroy this girl before anyone can study her technique. They are mortally afraid of CICNPC." I disputed that anyone would be so foolish, and Michel insisted that there is no limit to the foolishness of bureaucracies. Well, he has a point. He considers that the one argument bureaucracies find irresistible is money: if a thing has a value that can be enumerated, they respect it. "If we say to the Department of Health," he said, "that so much money has been invested in this, they will believe in it. I was trying to persuade the Apollo Foundation to fund the research, but my research assistant told them of my own condition, and discredited the whole idea." '

Debreuil looked around the table again. 'I do not think it is discredited now – and, gentlemen, I urge you, in the name of humanity, to do whatever is necessary to protect this discovery which has so huge a potential for good.'

I looked at Bernet, who was still watching the panelling. Then I put the guitar down and walked around the table towards him. He looked around, then stood up and caught my hands as I reached him. He looked into my face for a long moment, then bent his head and kissed my fingers. He was crying.

Fourteen

There wasn't really any doubt about what would happen after that. The only question mark was over where the research would take place and who would be in charge of it. Bernet no longer wanted to be. He wanted to be involved, yes, and he particularly wanted to participate as a patient, so that he could be sure of getting more 'therapy', but he also wanted some time off and he readily accepted that he was not fit to be in charge. Debreuil was eager to take over from him, but he wanted the research to take place in Paris, using patients from his clinic who were receiving SGNS – perhaps in partnership with another research institution or a Grande Ecole. (He also suggested that if the Apollo Foundation declined to fund the research, he could get money from the CNRS – which made the Apollo Foundation desperate to sign the cheque.) In the end it was decided to set up a 'project committee' which would resolve those issues later, but arrange preliminary funding right away.

Charles rather feebly raised the question of my health, and was slapped down. There was no evidence, said Debreuil, that I was in any imminent danger, and *of course* he would monitor the situation continuously and carefully: I was far too precious to risk. He was, he pointed out, a well-known specialist, and if the Department of Health objected to him, they were welcome to try to find somebody better. I asked him if he could speak to my parents about it, and he beamed at me again and agreed at once. (He beamed at me a lot. By the end of the meeting I'd decided that it was partly because he was grateful to me for helping his friend, partly because I represented a hope for treating some of his other patients, and partly just because he was the sort of burly energetic man who beams at people. I liked him.)

I raised the question of my music degree, and was told that oh, we could solve that later. (Bernet, however, told me I was a fool to consider staying at Dartington, that I could get into the Paris Conservatoire without difficulty, and that it was a far more appropriate place for the likes of me.)

After that the Board approved the proposal, appointed Debreuil as head of the committee with authority to nominate other members, and set aside an initial fund of a hundred thousand euros to get it set up. It was agreed that Debreuil and Bernet would jointly submit a report on me to the Department of Health, recommending that I be discharged under a super-vision order. Bernet told me apologetically that the discharge would probably have to be conditional on my cooperation with more assessment; I told him I could live with that. Debreuil told me that the project committee would draw up a contract for me as a 'research assistant', and asked me to name a salary. I said I couldn't possibly, I was too kicked up, and he laughed and said he would get back to me. Everyone shook hands. Everyone laughed and congratulated one another. Sir Peter suggested that everyone have dinner downstairs at one of the Dorchester's restaurants.

I couldn't bear the thought of eating, and felt a desperate need to be alone. I told the others that I wanted to sit down for a little while, and that I'd join them later. They all shook my hands – except Debreuil, who kissed me on both cheeks – and congratulated me, and asked if that was really what I wanted. I said it was, and, finally, they left me sitting in the quiet of the empty conference room.

After a couple of minutes, I realised that I was shaking. A part of me couldn't believe what had happened or what it meant, and expected some new cruel twist to imprison me again. A larger part was simply tired – deeply, stupidly, irresistibly tired. I knew, though, that I was far too over-wrought to rest.

So – of course – I picked up the guitar. My fingers wandered into the well-worn course of the Vivaldi piece, and the sweet cooling notes had their usual effect. When I'd finished it, I played with the strings a little, then picked out the tune on the D

279

string. There was still nothing to it, so why did it *work*? I picked it out again – and this time the back of my mind woke suddenly, and continued it, weaving it back and forth among all the twelve strings of the Segovia. I played along with it, and the music came out, simple as the opening of an eye, complex as the intricate visual systems of the brain, mysterious as vision.

When time began again, Bernet was sitting at the table opposite me, resting his chin on his hands.

'Oh,' I said.

'You called me,' he explained.

'You could hear it downstairs in the restaurant?'

He shook his head. 'I cannot eat. I am too happy. "The thirst that from the soul doth rise, doth ask a drink divine." I was sitting on the stairs.'

I looked down at the table. 'What if it stops working?' I whispered.

'Then I am no worse off than I was before. But I think it will go on working.' After a moment he went on, 'Yesterday I telephoned Yvette.'

I looked up quickly.

'I told her what had happened, that I appeared to be recovering. She cried. She was afraid to see me again, but eventually she agreed that we could meet. Just for a weekend, at first, to see.'

'Oh,' I said warmly. 'Oh, I hope – '

'I also. Thank you, *chère fille*. Thank you for bringing me out of the Underworld.'

'Professor, I . . . thank you for saving me from the knives.'

'My pleasure.'

We were both silent for a couple of minutes, and then I admitted, 'I'm still scared.'

'You are afraid that the effect will disappoint us? That something else will go wrong?'

'Yes. And besides that . . . that the thing in my head will hurt me, and hurt other people. I don't know what it is or how it works. It scares me.'

'I have a theory,' he said slowly.

'You said that once before. What?'

'It is only a theory. I think this is an effect of consciousness.'

I looked at him, and he looked back, leaning back in his seat, his eyes vivid. 'We know that consciousness involves the mechanisms of attention, combined with some mysterious process that uses the whole brain at once. It is embodied in the brain without ever being confined to any part of it. It is the soul, if you like – and I will not enter into the quibbles of the philosophers over what, then, occurs when we are unconscious; I have no patience with them. I have argued that our individual consciousness is shaped and integrated with our personality by our prefrontal systems as we grow. When the prefrontal system is damaged, consciousness persists, but its shape is unstable – if you like, we are damaged in our souls. This makes particular sense to me now, because now that I am beginning to recover, it feels to me as though my soul had become distorted, and now is returning to its proper shape.

'Your prefrontal system was injured in your infancy, and yet now it seems entirely normal. Your brain, working with the treatment it had received and with the power of music, succeeded in restoring it – but to do so it had to reshape your consciousness, and, in using music, it drew on the powerful cognitive systems that form our awareness of space and time. It left you able to alter your consciousness, to perceive time and space differently – almost to reach that state outside them which the theologians ascribe to God and the physicists to the beginning of the universe. You cannot do this all the time, but only when you reach into the altered state through the music that first shaped you.

'When you reach the music this way and bring it out, your own performance of that music reflects your perception, and that in turn alters the perceptions of your listeners. It directly affects their consciousness. Their individual consciousness then feeds this new perception back into their prefrontal systems, strengthening some links, weakening others, altering their awareness. I think that is how it was able to reach and stimulate my own prefrontal system, which was dying: it used a door which is closed to all external stimuli – the door of consciousness itself.

'This is only a theory. If I am right, though, you should have nothing to fear. This "thing" in your brain is you – your consciousness, your love of music, your own soul.' He smiled. 'It is not normal, no. You are not normal: you are extraordinary. You are so afraid of yourself, *ma petite*. Afraid of being stared at, afraid of your own genius, ready to waste yourself on a man like Spencer because he is safe and offers you protection—'

'Leave him out of it!'

He smiled again. 'I would prefer to. You do not need to be so afraid. Your soul is not going to rise up and destroy you.'

I thought about that for a while. 'I thought neuroscientists didn't believe in souls,' I said suspiciously.

'It depends how the term is defined. If you mean some immaterial homunculus sitting in the brain during life and walking away at death – no, I know of no neuroscientist who believes such a thing. But if you mean a unique individual consciousness embodied in the living patterns of a human brain – I believe in that, and many of my colleagues do as well.' He shrugged. 'I admit, I don't see how a soul could survive the death of the brain. I think we are all mortal souls.'

I walked my fingers down the guitar, then up again. 'Maybe we're like music,' I whispered. 'Like the way it exists when it comes out and time stops. Maybe we exist in time and in eternity both.'

He regarded me affectionately for a moment. 'Ah well. You understand such things better than I, no doubt.'

'But how do I know if you're right that this . . . abnormality isn't going to hurt me?' I asked, after another silence.

He shook his head. 'You cannot *know* such a thing, at this point. I have no idea how I might even check it. The operations of consciousness are, and remain, a mystery to me. You can only wait and see if this thing does you harm. All I can say is that I do not believe that it will – and I expect that after a few years when it hasn't done you harm, everyone else will believe the same.' He stretched, then stood up. '*Ma fille*, I am very tired. I had no sleep last night, and very little the night before that. I am going to book a room for myself in this inordinately expensive palace, and if you like, I will book another room, for you. I am Eurydice, returned from the Underworld: no expense is too great.'

'Thank you,' I said, meaning it. 'I didn't get much sleep either. But what about Charles?'

Bernet looked smug. 'Dr Spencer can look after himself.'

'You really are horrible to him!'

Bernet shrugged, still looking pleased with himself. 'I intend to disapprove of all your young men. I feel like a father to you, and it is a father's privilege to say that they are not good enough. Dr Spencer can take himself home or book himself a room, here or elsewhere, as he pleases. He will survive. After all, he has far better odds on it than we did.'

He picked up my computer, and we went downstairs together.